Cat Schield is an award-winning author of contemporary romances for Mills & Boon Desire. She likes her heroines spunky and her heroes swoonworthy. While her jet-setting characters live all over the globe, Cat makes her home in Minnesota with her daughter, two opinionated Burmese cats and a goofy Doberman. When she's not writing or walking dogs, she's searching for the perfect cocktail or travelling to visit friends and family. Contact her at www.catschield.com

Zuri Day is the award-winning, nationally bestselling author of a slew of novels translated into almost a dozen languages. When not writing, which is almost never, or travelling internationally, these days not so much, she can be found in the weeds, literally, engaged in her latest passion—gardening. Living in Southern California, this happens year-round. From there it's farm to table (okay, patio to table—it's an urban garden) via her creative culinary take on a variety of vegan dishes. She loves live performances (including her own), binges on popular YouTube shows and is diligently at work to make her Ragdoll cat, Namaste, the IG star he deserves to be. Say meow to him, stay in touch with her and check out her exhaustive stash of OMG reads at zuriday.com

Also by Cat Schield

Sweet Tea and Scandal
Upstairs Downstairs Baby
Substitute Seduction
Revenge with Benefits
Seductive Secrets

Dynasties: Seven Sins
Untamed Passion

Also by Zuri Day

Sin City Vows
Ready for the Rancher
Sin City Seduction

Discover more at millsandboon.co.uk

SEDUCTION, SOUTHERN STYLE

CAT SCHIELD

THE LAST LITTLE SECRET

ZURI DAY

MILLS & BOON

First Published in Great Britain 2021
by Mills & Boon, an imprint of HarperCollins*Publishers* Ltd
1 London Bridge Street, London, SE1 9GF

www.harpercollins.co.uk

HarperCollins*Publishers*
1st Floor, Watermarque Building,
Ringsend Road, Dublin 4, Ireland

Seduction, Southern Style © 2021 Catherine Schield
The Last Little Secret © 2021 Zuri Day

ISBN: 978-0-263-28290-0

0421

SEDUCTION,
SOUTHERN STYLE

CAT SCHIELD

To Ella and Bri,
who took over for a couple weeks last summer
so I could write and make my deadline.
It was so much fun getting to know you!
Best of luck with your future endeavors.

One

Sienna Burns experienced a familiar thrill as the town car, carrying her and her adopted sister, Teagan, coasted along the tree-lined avenue in downtown Charleston. As an independent art consultant, Sienna spent a great deal of time traveling and always loved the opportunity to visit a new city. And this one was breathtaking. Picket and iron fences hid lush gardens transected by hedge-lined brick walkways and dotted with palm trees and bountiful hydrangeas. The pastel buildings with overflowing window boxes imprinted her mind with explosions of vibrant colors.

"This is really beautiful," she said, as one terraced, columned mansion after another flew by.

When her sister didn't respond, Sienna shifted attention to Teagan and wasn't surprised to find her taking a selfie. Teagan knew better than to ask Sienna to join her in the picture. With her dark hair and life-long weight issues, Sienna had always felt like a plump, shabby shadow of her beautiful, trendy sister and actively avoided the limelight.

"You should try and get one of these gorgeous mansions in the background," Sienna suggested as the car stopped at an intersection. "I'll bet your followers would love that."

"Uh-huh," Teagan mumbled, pouting at the screen and showing no indication that she was paying attention to her sister.

"Why am I even here?" Exhaustion sparked Sienna's temper. She hadn't slept during her eight-hour flight from London to New York or at any point during the hectic three-hour turnaround before Teagan had dragged her aboard the private jet for their flight to Charleston. "You've been glued to your phone the entire trip."

As different as the two sisters were in appearance and temperament, one trait they shared was that they never stopped working. Teagan had spun her status as a social media influencer into several successful businesses and was constantly promoting her jewelry and accessories lines, as well as her concierge makeup service.

"I need my sister with me." Without looking up from her phone, Teagan reached over to grip Sienna's hand, the biting clamp revealing the tension hidden behind her unruffled expression. "You know I'm freaked out about meeting my birth mom's family."

Several months earlier Sienna had been shocked to hear that Teagan had submitted her DNA to a genetic testing service and discovered she was related to a prominent family in Charleston, South Carolina. The full details of how baby Teagan had come to be available to be adopted by a wealthy couple on the Upper East Side of New York might forever remain a mystery, but from what Teagan had patched together from talking with her Charleston family, it seemed that her biological mother, Ava Watts, had headed to the Big Apple in the hopes of becoming a fashion model only to become pregnant and die tragically, leaving behind her infant daughter. Apparently, Ava had cut herself off so thoroughly from her family that they hadn't discovered her death or that she'd had a daughter until many years after the fact. By then, Teagan had been adopted and the sealed court records had prevented her family from locating her.

"You shouldn't be," Sienna said, sandwiching Teagan's hand between hers and offering the comfort her sister craved. "They've been looking for you since learning you existed. I'm sure they're over the moon to have found you at last."

"Of course, but what if they don't like me?"

It never ceased to amaze Sienna that her beautiful, talented sister suffered bouts of insecurity. "What's not to love?"

"You're the best sister." Teagan leaned her head on Sienna's shoulder and absorbed all the support. "I don't know what I'd do without you."

Sienna's heart gave a painful wrench. "Luckily, you'll never have to find out."

Filled to the brim with optimism once more, Teagan turned back to her phone. Sienna released her sister's hand and returned her attention to the scenery they were passing, letting her delight in the charming view recharge the energy she'd poured into the other woman.

"You know it still amazes me how much I look like them." Teagan displayed the Instagram page belonging to her Charleston cousin, Dallas Shaw.

The image on the screen showed a smiling trio of blonde women. The twin cousins and their mother, Ava Watts's older sister, Lenora Shaw, bore an uncanny resemblance to Teagan. Sienna felt a tinge of jealousy as she imagined future pictures with her sister grinning alongside the trio, her long blond hair and riveting green eyes proof that she belonged to the Watts/Shaw clan.

"Even without the DNA test, there's little question you're related," Sienna said, overcome by a sudden blast of panic and misery at the thought of losing her sister to her new family.

"I hope they feel the same way."

"Of course they will," Sienna assured her, pushing aside her own anxiety and grief to bolster Teagan.

"I really wish you'd stay longer than a few days," Teagan said, continuing to scroll through her cousin's Instagram feed, skipping over the photos of beautifully plated dishes to focus on the images of Dallas and her identical sister, Poppy.

"This is your moment with your long-lost family," Sienna reminded her. "I don't want to overstay my welcome."

"Don't be silly. They're thrilled that you're coming with me. And... I told them you'd be here a couple weeks."

"What?" Sienna gasped, appalled. "Even if I could take that much time off, you don't know these people well enough to take advantage of their hospitality on my behalf."

"Are you kidding? You've barely taken any time off in the last three years so you're due for a vacation. And there's plenty of room at the estate. In fact, both Dallas and Poppy live on-site in the old caretaker's house. My aunt Lenora said there's an empty carriage house and bedrooms galore in the main house. Believe me, there's plenty of room."

"I'll rearrange some things and try to stay for a week."

"Ten days."

"I only packed enough for four." Yet even as she protested, her exhaustion worked against her. The idea of lingering in this charming city and behaving like a tourist was vastly appealing. The frenetic pace of her career kept her running on sheer adrenaline most of the time. What fun to just be lazy for a week.

"We can go shopping." Teagan made a face. "I mean,

do you own anything besides boring pantsuits and sensible pumps?"

"I have several dresses—"

"In a color other than black, gray or navy?"

Sienna opened her mouth to protest Teagan's criticism and recognized the futility. "Besides, did it ever occur to you that I have clients that I'm supposed to be working for?"

"You can't seriously expect me to believe that their lives will crash down around them if you don't find something boring and old for them to spend their money on."

It was a familiar argument and one that never failed to rub Sienna wrong. "I know you find what I do boring, but just like you have a passion for all things beautiful and trendy, I happen to love finding the perfect pieces of art to add to my clients' collections."

"It's not that I find it boring," Teagan said, "it's just that ever since you went out on your own, you don't make time for me anymore."

Sienna almost laughed out loud at her sister's ridiculous claim. Teagan was the busy one with a rich and active social life, centered in New York City, filled with hangers-on and acquaintances, while Sienna traveled all over the world pursuing artworks. When she went out, she preferred quiet dinners with a few close friends.

"Oh please," Sienna said. "You have plenty of people to hang out with."

"People," Teagan corrected. "Not family."

"Well, that's all about to change." Sienna indicated Dallas Shaw's social media feed. "I guarantee you'll be so happy with your new family that you won't even notice when I leave."

"But what if I don't like them?"

Teagan paused to regard a photo of three generations of Watts family members and Sienna found her gaze drawn to the single anomaly amongst the sea of blond-haired, blue-eyed Southerners. A tall man with tousled mahogany hair stood in the back, his sexy smile hinting at a devil-may-care attitude that kindled her imagination. Something compelling and a little frightening swept across her nerve endings at the strength of her interest.

She shook herself free of his spell. "Then you go back to New York and live your life."

"There's something I haven't told you." Teagan resumed scrolling.

"Like what?"

"I'm not sure I'm returning to New York."

"What?" The anxiety that had been building ever since Teagan announced she'd found her birth family exploded in her chest. "Why not?"

"I've decided I'm going to be the next CEO of Watts Shipping."

Sienna sat in stunned silence while her sister's words played through her mind. The Watts family business was a multimillion-dollar corporation with a fleet of fifty transportation vessels that moved goods all around the world. Founded in the 1920s, they were in the state's top one hundred corporations with nearly fifteen hundred employees worldwide.

While there was no question that Teagan had the Harvard education and the ambition to helm the family company, what she lacked was any knowledge of shipping and the experience needed to run a corporation with annual sales in the hundreds of millions.

"I thought your uncle was the current CEO," Sienna said, "and that one of his sons will be taking over shortly." She pictured the handsome, dark-haired charmer in the family photo, wondering how he'd feel about the competition from the newly arrived outsider.

"Ethan." Teagan scrolled back to the family photo that she'd been looking at earlier. "The thing is, he is adopted and…"

Recognizing where her sister's mind had gone, Sienna controlled a wince. Despite being their father's darling girl and the sole beneficiary of their mother's boundless attention and energy, Teagan defined herself as the adopted child. As if this somehow meant she was less of a Burns than Sienna or their brother, Aiden. The irony of this often led to Sienna wanting to rage at her sister.

As the middle sibling and biological child, Sienna was the one mostly likely to be ignored or excluded. Her brother was expected to take over the family business. Teagan had been the one their mother had adopted because Sienna hadn't been beautiful enough to dress up and show off to Anna's friends. Neither a boy nor a beauty, Sienna had slipped through the cracks of her parents' awareness.

"You think it's your birthright to run the family business," Sienna guessed, thinking how disappointed Teagan had been when despite her superior business skills and suitability to take over the Burns real estate empire, she'd been passed over in favor of Samuel and Anna's biological son, Aiden. "I'm sure you have a shot at it, but is that fair to Ethan?"

"I don't want them to give me the position," Teagan said, but her green eyes took on a frosty glint of remembered disappointment. "I fully intend to earn it. But I want the shot. And I'm going to take it."

"Sure. I guess that's…fair," Sienna said, sympathizing with Ethan now that her sister was poised to claim a position he'd grown up believing was his. "None of this explains why you need me to stay in Charleston beyond a few days. It seems like you're going to have your hands full with getting to know your family as well as Watts Shipping." She said this last with a wry smile that she hoped took the censure out of the words.

"I thought maybe we could work together."

A discordant buzzing filled Sienna's ears. Sometimes the way Teagan's mind worked terrified her. Her sister had embraced their mother's ruthless streak and honed her skills ever since her days of being Queen Bee of their Upper East Side prep school.

"Work together how?"

"You always have such good insights into people. I thought maybe you could help me get to know everyone and figure out my best way in."

"I have clients—" Sienna said, fearful of becoming embroiled in whatever scheme her sister was cooking up.

"Stop using them as an excuse," Teagan snapped, before turning the full power of her pleading expression on Sienna. "I'm sorry. I didn't mean to be such a bitch. I don't want to be all alone down here. You know I need you. Please stay and help me. I'm terrified that I won't fit in and this is when I really need my sister."

"Okay." It was easier to give in than keep resisting. "I don't have anything particularly pressing at the moment."

"Wonderful." Teagan's entire demeanor brightened as it did every time she got her way. "And you never know, you might find some new clients here. Plus, there's tons of museums and you love those."

"I do."

Yet as she gave in, what had promised to be a relaxing interlude amongst Charleston's historic charms vanished like morning mist.

Ethan Watts sat in the living room of his grandfather's elegant estate on the west end of Montague Street a few blocks from the Ashley River. On his phone screen was the email he'd received the night before. Brief and to the point, mysterious and inflammatory, the message had arrived from an anonymous source. Initially he'd dismissed the warning. The sender intended to stir up trouble and Ethan had little patience for the person's shadowy agenda. But he hadn't deleted the email. It described a threat he'd be foolish to ignore.

Teagan Burns intends to become the next CEO of Watts Shipping. She is ruthless and will use every trick in the book to get her way. Watch your back.—A friend

Even as he reread the email for the umpteenth time, Ethan wasn't sure what to make of it. He didn't believe for one second that the anonymous sender was any sort of friend. The sender obviously had an agenda and Ethan refused to trust that he and the person were on the same side.

"I think she's here." For the last twenty minutes his aunt had been watching from the living room windows, anticipating the moment that her long-lost niece would arrive from New York City.

Ethan Watts reached Lenora Shaw's side just as the uniformed driver of the luxury town car got out and circled the vehicle to open the door for his passengers. His aunt vibrated with tension as she awaited her first glimpse of Ava Watts's missing daughter.

Three decades earlier, the headstrong, spoiled youngest daughter of Grady and Delilah Watts had run off to New York against her father's wishes at eighteen. After five years of no contact, Grady had sent an investigator to see what had become of his daughter. Too late, they learned that Ava had died several years before and her infant daughter had been adopted. For twenty-five years the family had been searching for her without success. That hunt ended several months ago when both sides had connected through a genetic testing service database.

Lenora's fingers bit down on Ethan's arm as a petite brunette exited the car. "That can't be her."

"I believe that's Sienna." Based on the research his older brother, Paul, had done on Teagan Burns, Ethan knew this wasn't the missing Watts heiress. "Teagan's older sister."

The woman in question was dressed for business in a simple black pantsuit and white blouse that downplayed her hourglass figure. Neither her long, straight hair, a flat espresso brown, nor the barest of makeup she'd applied to her delicate features and soft lips commanded attention. Unlike her sister, she had a nearly nonexistent social media presence and based on what he noted of her body language and appearance, Sienna Burns obviously preferred to maintain a low profile.

"Oh," Lenora murmured, "there she is."

Ethan tore his gaze away from Sienna in time to witness a pair of long, shapely legs, clad in white high-heel boots, emerging from the town car. Moments later the highly recognizable New York City socialite appeared. A chic blonde "it" girl, who regularly appeared on Page Six and social media, she looked every inch a Manhattan fashionista in a short white romper with navy pinstripes, her gold-blond hair hanging in a silky curtain to her waist.

"She looks exactly like Ava," Lenora said, her tone tight with concern. "Let's hope she doesn't behave like her."

It was no secret that Lenora hadn't gotten along with her willful younger sibling, but Ethan was surprised that Teagan's marked resemblance to her mother had set Lenora off. The entire family had been avidly anticipating this meeting for years. He never imagined a scenario where she wouldn't be fully embraced, but something about his aunt's frown sent a trickle of uneasiness down his spine.

"Why don't we go greet her," Ethan prompted, when his aunt didn't show any signs of moving toward the front door.

Lenora shook off her somber mood and applied a social smile to her lips. "Of course."

The Shaw's housekeeper, Jillian Post, had been standing by and now opened the door to admit the new arrival. Ethan and Lenora reached the broad arch into the wide entry hall just as Teagan crossed the threshold alone. The housekeeper glanced out the door and murmured a question.

"She had something to take care of first," Teagan answered, sounding the tiniest bit peevish.

As the carved front door closed behind her, blocking the June sunshine, the socialite pulled off her enormous sunglasses and gave her surroundings a quick once over before focusing on the pair who'd stepped forward to greet her.

"Hello."

"Welcome to Charleston," Lenora said, taking the lead before things grew awkward. "I'm Lenora Shaw, your aunt, and this is your cousin Ethan."

"It's wonderful to be here." Teagan's lips curved in a picture-perfect smile, but the cool assessment in her eyes as her gaze slid over Ethan sent his thoughts back to that anonymous email. "You were so kind to invite me."

"It's your home," Ethan declared, summoning a beguiling tone to make up for Lenora's less-than-effusive welcome. "We're delighted to have you here."

"Yes, delighted," Lenora echoed while she took in her niece's sophisticated appearance. "Please, come in. Your grandfather will be down shortly."

"Grady's eager to see you," Ethan added. "He's been searching for you for a long time."

"I'm excited to meet him, as well," Teagan said as they all moved into the elegant living room.

Teagan Burns intends to become the next CEO of Watts Shipping.

Ethan scanned Teagan's expression for the duplicity the email warned him about and glimpsed happiness mixed with apprehension. Neither emotion struck him as unusual. The entire family had been buzzing with excitement and nervous energy since they'd learned about Teagan. The meeting was momentous and fraught with tension for all involved. What if they didn't like Ava's daughter or vice versa? What if they all made an immediate connection but Teagan then decided to return to New York City and her busy life there? What if she was a horror and decided to stay in Charleston? How would the family dynamic change?

"Have you been to Charleston before?" Lenora asked, gesturing toward the pale blue damask sofa Ethan had occupied moments before.

"I don't leave New York often," Teagan admitted, as she looked over the space. Was she cataloging the valuables? Trying to decide what she stood to inherit once Grady Watts died? "And when I do, I generally travel to LA or the Caribbean."

"Where's your sister?" Ethan asked, thinking about the woman who'd gotten out of the car first.

Teagan's green eyes snapped to him. "On a business call. She'll join us when she's done."

With conspiracies circling his mind like a pack of coyotes, Ethan was seized by a sharp need to clear his head. "Why don't I go check on her."

Leaving the two women to get acquainted, Ethan headed outside to see what had become of Sienna Burns. He found her sitting near the bottom of the front steps, her back to the house, an open laptop balanced on her thighs. As he descended toward her, Ethan glanced to where the driver of the town car was unloading a sizable collection of matching cream-colored luggage with champagne leather accents.

"Hello," he said as he drew within earshot of Teagan's sister.

The brunette had been so absorbed in her task that she hadn't noticed his approach. Now, she jerked in surprise, clutching the laptop as it teetered precariously. She turned to stare up at him, but bright afternoon sun splashed across her face, forcing her to squint.

"Oh, hello." She shut her computer as he passed her and slid it into the tote bag near her feet.

When he reached the driveway, he turned to face her. Ethan found his senses tingling with pleasure as he breathed in the sun-warmed scent of vanilla wafting from her. Up close he noted the pale freckles peeking through her foundation and the fact that she'd chewed off her lipstick. But what arrested him was the sharp intelligence in her blue-gray eyes.

"I'm Ethan Watts." To his chagrin, he caught himself smiling in genuine welcome instead of bombarding her with practiced charm. "Teagan's cousin."

"Sienna Burns. Teagan's…sister."

He noted the slight hesitation as she identified her connection and wondered at it. "Nice to meet you, Sienna Burns."

He held out his hand for her to shake, shocked how eager he was to touch her. Nor was he disappointed when she placed her palm against his, sending an electric charge of awareness zipping through him. From the telltale widening of her eyes and the rising color in her cheeks, he guessed she'd experienced something, as well.

"Nice to meet you," she echoed, making no attempt to take her hand back. In fact, she tilted her torso toward him while her gaze toured his face. Her lips slanted into a grin of feminine appreciation as if she liked what she saw.

This demonstration of mutual attraction set his hormones on fire. Ethan offered her a slow, wolfish smile. He wasn't a stranger to sexual chemistry and enjoyed both a stimulating chase and an easy conquest, but despite the bold appreciation in Sienna's gaze, he suspected that she wasn't going to tumble for his Southern charisma. A challenge then. He was up for that. But then the warning about Teagan popped back into his head.

She...will use every trick in the book to get her way.

Including her sister? The question stopped him cold.

"We've been looking forward to meeting you both," he said, all too aware that he should end the handshake. Instead, he was fighting the desire to slide his thumb over her knuckles. Remembering his manners, he set her free. His skin continued to tingle where it had been in contact with hers.

Sienna absorbed his words with a surprised expression. "Both of us? But I'm not anyone..."

Ethan was struck by her words. Was it false modesty or a bid for sympathy that compelled others to reassure her? "Obviously, you're someone."

"Well, of course." Sienna gave a breathy laugh. "I just mean that Teagan is the star here. I'm just along for the ride."

The way she dismissed her importance left him wondering how often she was compared to her beautiful, stylish sister and found lacking. Ethan understood sibling rivalry. Not that he'd ever gone out of his way to compete against Paul. Likewise, his brother lived in his own world and rarely engaged in such trivial pursuits, but being the second son and an adopted one as well, Ethan had always questioned his place in the family.

Sienna's case was a bit different though. She was the older daughter. The one who'd been born into the Burns family. If anyone would feel as if she belonged, it would be Sienna and not Teagan. Yet Teagan was the one who'd capitalized on the family's social status and wealth while Sienna faded into the background.

At the same time, Sienna was the more approachable of the two. The one he could let his guard down around. She seemed to lack any ulterior motives. The anonymous message had warned him to be wary. Ethan sighed in exasperation. He didn't want to ponder hidden agendas or imagine these women were scheming against him.

"Still, it's good of you to support her," Ethan said. "I'm sure it wasn't easy to take the time away from your business to accompany her on this visit."

"This is a pretty big deal for her." Sienna slid a lock of hair behind her ear, drawing Ethan's attention to her short, unpainted nails. "For your family as well, I'm sure. Teagan has been looking forward to meeting you all." Mischief flashed in her eyes. "Or should I say all y'all?"

"You speak Southern." He ramped up his drawl, relishing the flirtation.

She looked pleased by his approval. "Just a little. I have a client in New Orleans." She pronounced it New OR-lins like a local. "He's fond of inundating me with Southern colloquialisms whenever we talk."

"Such as?"

"Some of his least colorful are… Kiss my go-to-hell. If that boy had an idea, it would die of loneliness. That dog won't hunt."

"And his more colorful?" Ethan prompted, utterly captivated by the impish glint in her eyes.

"Don't piss on my leg and tell me it's raining." Her cheeks blazed with color that hadn't been there a second earlier. For all her big-city upbringing, she had a trace of shyness that enchanted him.

Could she really be in on Teagan's supposed plans for taking over Watts Shipping? Almost as soon as this notion popped into his head, he pushed it away. And then just as swiftly, he circled back. Dismissing Sienna as a nonparticipant in whatever her sister was cooking up might be the blunder that caused him to lose everything.

Watch your back.

The warning failed to dim his interest in Sienna. Worse, the potential danger in his growing fascination actually enhanced his desire. He was already plotting how to corner her in an isolated place so he could sample her soft lips and seduce her properly. If he thought he'd overcome the reckless streak that had dominated his teens and early twenties, he'd been mistaken. It hadn't been tamed, only sedated.

"Here comes Cory," Ethan said, relieved that his grandfather's caretaker was approaching. "He will take charge of all the luggage." As Sienna got to her feet, Ethan made the introductions. "Cory Post, this is Sienna Burns. She will be staying in the rose guest room. Which of these are yours?"

"That one."

Not surprisingly, she pointed to the single black bag sitting like a crow amongst doves. The hard-sided piece had seen a lot of use.

"You travel light." He shot Sienna a quick glance to confirm. "And quite a bit from the looks of your bag."

"Business trips mostly."

"What sort of business?" he asked, even though thanks to Paul's research, Ethan already knew.

"I'm an independent art consultant."

"That sounds quite interesting. I'll look forward to hearing all about it."

Her long lashes flickered. "It's really quite mundane. A lot of time spent in airplanes and dusty old houses."

"Oh, I'm sure it's not as dull as you make it sound." He leaned toward her with a smile meant to encourage her to give up all her secrets. "I'll bet you've seen some very interesting things. What's your favorite?"

She nibbled her lower lip for a second before answering. "Two years ago, a couple in Toulouse discovered an old painting in their attic after their roof leaked. One of my art world contacts gave me a heads-up so I flew to France to evaluate the painting and it turned out it was the work of the Italian artist Caravaggio."

As she spoke of her discovery, her eyes glowed with enthusiasm, turning what had been a pretty face into something quite breathtaking.

"Fascinating," he murmured, transfixed by the dimples produced by her effervescent smile.

Noting the way his heartbeat stuttered and then started to race, Ethan silently cursed. If that anonymous warning was the real deal, he needed to stay vigilant.

She...will use every trick...

Ethan gave himself a shake. He shouldn't let a stranger get into his head. For all he knew, Teagan had sent the message herself to distract him into chasing shadows. Still, whether Sienna was part of a plot or not, there was much to discover about Teagan's sister and Ethan was looking forward to finding out all about her. Until he did, the challenge would be to keep his attraction hidden from everyone, but especially Teagan. Letting her capitalize on his fascination with Sienna was a risk he couldn't afford.

Two

As Ethan escorted Sienna up the right side of the elegant stone double staircase that curved from the driveway to the front door, she couldn't help but think Teagan wouldn't find him a pushover.

"My family is probably wondering what became of us," he murmured as they slipped through the front door and entered the air-conditioned coolness of the mansion.

"Teagan is quite distracting," Sienna said. "I doubt they've noticed."

The change in temperature and drop in humidity made her conscious of her wrinkled pants and the perspiration coating her skin. In contrast, Ethan seemed impervious to the heat. She inhaled the clean scent of soap that clung to his skin and caught herself smiling. Everything about the man appealed to her.

No doubt a man as handsome and charismatic as Ethan was quite a player. To Sienna's surprise she didn't care. She wasn't planning on tossing her heart into the ring. If she was going to take some time off, she might as well have a little fun of the casual, sensual variety. Ethan might be perfect fling material.

She was floating on a cloud as Ethan guided her into the living room and introduced her to his family. Sienna thanked Teagan's grandfather Grady Watts for his invitation to stay at the house, and then settled back to survey the interaction between Teagan and her biological relatives. Despite the striking family resemblance, there were marked differences in manner.

Teagan and Sienna had been raised by a polished Manhattan socialite and her reserved husband. As approachable as Teagan appeared on social media, in person she could come off as cool or dispassionate. She rarely exhibited the strong feelings that simmered in her. To show such emotion would mar the image of effortless perfection she worked so hard to maintain.

By contrast, Poppy, Lenora and even Grady wore broad smiles and spoke animatedly about Charleston, the rest of the family and all the things they were looking forward to doing with her. Sienna noticed herself getting swept up in their enthusiasm and cheerfulness and was wondering how Teagan was fairing when her sister pulled out her smartphone and began posing with Poppy.

This seemed like a perfect opportunity for Sienna to slip out. She tugged on Ethan's sleeve and captured his attention.

"Would there be someone who could show me where I'll be staying?" A yawn snuck up on her and she covered the gaff with an embarrassed chuckle. "Sorry. I was hoping to catch a nap on the flight down from New York, but Teagan was too keyed up." Seeing the curiosity in Ethan's gaze, she elaborated. "I flew in from London this morning and didn't get any sleep on the overseas flight."

"I can take you up."

"Thank you."

They made their excuses and headed into a broad hallway that split the house down the middle. Across from the living room was a large formal dining room. While Ethan angled toward the stairs at the far end of the hallway, Sienna poked her head into the room.

"The whole family will be here for dinner tonight," Ethan explained, coming to stand beside her. "They're really excited to meet Teagan."

"How many are coming?"

"My parents, my brother, Paul, and his fiancée, Lia. Aunt Lenora and Uncle Wiley. The twins. You, me and Grady."

"Are you sure I should be there?" Sienna asked, worried that they'd view her as an interloper.

"Of course." Ethan looked surprised that she'd even ask. "You're family, too."

His response warmed her. "The house is really beautiful," Sienna said, retreating into polite chitchat as her emotional reaction caught her off guard.

"Want a quick tour?"

What she wanted was more in time his company. "That'd be great."

He led her into the kitchen and introduced her to Jillian Post, Grady's housekeeper, before showing her the library.

"The house was built in 1804 by Jacob Birch," Ethan said, as they ascended the stairs to the second floor. "Theodore Watts purchased the property in 1898 which is why it's now known as the Birch-Watts Estate. The main house's ninety-four hundred square feet have been remodeled several times, but always with an eye toward preserving and enhancing its Federal style."

"A style that dominated American architecture from 1790 to 1840," she said, aware she was showing off. "The layout is symmetrical with unadorned exteriors." She gestured toward the window where the intricate wrought iron railings that edged the upper terraces could be seen peeping above the windowsill. "Except for the porches and entries. Inside is different with elaborate molded plaster flourishes on the ceilings and borders."

"You know a lot about our architecture," he said, making no effort to cover his surprise.

The approval in Ethan's sexy brown eyes as he shot her a sideways glance sent a shiver of awareness racing over her skin. The photos of him posted on his cousins' social media had sparked her interest. Candid shots of him on a boat, buff and tanned with rippling abs and muscles galore, his hair blowing in the wind, an irrepressible grin on his sculpted lips.

In person, the man possessed the sort of easy, confident charm that women fell for in a hurry. No doubt the guy got a lot of action with the belles of Charleston. And his solicitous behavior since they met gave Sienna the impression that he'd satisfy a woman even as he took care of his own needs. Was it any wonder she was fighting a compelling urge to lick her lips and utter the first naughty double entendre that popped into her mind?

"I make a habit before I travel of reading up on the local history, the art scene, including museums and architecture, and of course the best cuisine." She smiled her thanks as he ushered her into the house. "It gives me a deeper appreciation of the places I visit."

"Do you travel a lot?"

"Generally, I'm on the road three weeks out of four." A choice that kept her from dwelling on a growing dissatisfaction with her lack of a personal life.

"Sounds lonely."

Her lips twisted into a wry grimace. "I work so much that I really don't notice."

"So there's no special someone waiting to welcome you home?"

Sienna couldn't meet Ethan's candid gaze. "Um, no one at all, actually."

She hadn't been kidding about how much she worked. Dating was both time-consuming and an energy drain. When she did venture out, she'd yet to meet a man whose companionship she craved, and if she was in the mood for sex, she had a straightforward way of scratching that itch. Unfortunately, this left her woefully ill-equipped when it came to the nuances of flirting and seduction.

On the second floor he indicated his grandfather's room and the one where Teagan would be staying.

"It was her mother's room," he added as they peeked into the sunny yellow room with green-and-white-floral draperies and comforter. "Looks like Cory delivered her luggage. Yours should be in your room, as well."

Side by side they ascended to the third floor. These stairs were narrower than the lower levels and forced Sienna into closer proximity with the Charleston charmer. She stumbled and Ethan caught her elbow to steady her. She smiled to thank him, shocked by how her heart pounded at his touch.

"This is your room." He indicated a sunny space, tucked beneath the eves with slanting walls painted an inviting rose.

The room had been furnished with a four-poster bed and a cozy love seat placed under a window with a view of roof-tops and a steeple of one of Charleston's many churches.

"This is lovely." Sienna set her laptop case down and barely restrained the urge to throw herself on the bed and groan in pleasure. "Thank you."

"I hope you'll let me show you around Charleston while

you're here," Ethan said, his alluring smile awakening an irresistible urge to grin back. "Our city has a lot to offer."

His deep voice resonated through her like a summer thunderstorm, leaving Sienna caught up in the midst of a wild and turbulent squall.

"That would be lovely," she murmured, catching herself staring at his lips and wondering if his kisses would be slow and sweet or hot and feverish.

His even white teeth flashed in a satisfied smile that was just shy of smug as he pulled out his phone. "Let me give you my number so you can call me when you get a free moment."

Sienna keyed his number into her contacts, and then at his urging she called him so he had her number, as well. The moment had come for them to part, but Sienna couldn't bring herself to make the first move.

"I'll leave you to unpack." He gave her a bone-melting smile. "And nap. We meet for cocktails before dinner. See you at seven."

"See you."

Left by herself, Sienna collapsed onto the comfortable bed and blew the air from her lungs. She glanced down at the phone in her hand, shivering as she regarded Ethan's contact information. Seconds later, she cued up her favorites list and dialed a familiar number.

"We made it to Charleston," she declared when her best friend, Gia Milani, answered. Both art history majors, the women had met as college freshmen and were often mistaken as sisters because of their similar coloring and strong bond.

"How's the family?" Gia asked.

"I've only met a few of them, but they seem nice."

Ethan's broad shoulders and mesmerizing gaze popped into her mind. What sort of hell was her ambitious sister going to put him through as Teagan made her bid to take over the running of the family's international shipping business? She sighed.

Gia must've picked up on her angst because she asked, "What's wrong?"

"I think Teagan is planning on staying in Charleston."

"For how long?"

"Maybe for good." For the first time since her sister dropped the bombshell, Sienna gave her reaction a chance to breathe. The anxiety was stronger than she would've predicted. These days she barely saw her sister. What did it matter if Teagan was here or in New York City? "She has this crazy idea that she deserves to be the next CEO of the family's shipping business."

"Is this because your dad picked Aiden over her to run Burns Properties?"

"It has a lot to do with it, but I don't think that's her only reason." Sienna thought about the comment Teagan had made about Ethan being adopted. "Long before Dad passed her over, she was hung up on this whole issue of not being a Burns by blood. And now that she's found her blood relatives, I think she believes it will all be different."

"You've met them. What do you think?"

"She might be right. I mean the family resemblance is striking. And they're thrilled that she's here."

Gia paused for a beat as she absorbed Sienna's response. "How are you feeling?"

"Me?" Sienna let loose a shaky laugh. "I'm great. Teagan asked me to stick around for longer than I'd planned so I'm going to be staying in Charleston for a week or so."

"You're finally taking time off and plan to spend it with Teagan?" Her friend sounded all kinds of surprised and disappointed.

Sienna didn't blame her. Gia hadn't understood why

Sienna had agreed to go with Teagan to meet her Charleston family in the first place. Although Gia was a wonderful sounding board for most of Sienna's problems, when it came to her relationship with Teagan, Gia had very strong opinions.

"It's a vacation. From what I've seen of it, Charleston is nice. And I could use a break."

"Okay." But Gia didn't make it sound like she was on board with Sienna's decision.

"What's wrong?"

"I just don't get why Teagan wanted you there in the first place."

Irritation flared even as Sienna recognized that she'd wondered the same thing. When Teagan had initially extended the invitation, Sienna had been too thrilled to be asked and hadn't considered her sister's motivation.

"Moral support," Sienna offered, wanting this to be true.

"I hope you're right," Gia said. "I'd hate to think she was involving you in some scheme."

"The only thing she has on her mind at the moment is making a good impression on her family."

"And taking over as CEO of Watts Shipping."

"Well, sure, but there's no way I can be of help there."

Gia hummed thoughtfully. "Maybe not. Just do me a favor and watch your back, okay?"

Ethan made sure to sit beside Sienna at dinner. He intended to get to know her a lot better and hopefully figure out her sister's plans in the process. Tonight, while Teagan wore a sequined, thigh-baring frock, with sheer sleeves, that could've graced any red-carpet event, Sienna paired black, wide-legged trousers with a modest white lace blouse. While her sister had chosen to pair chandelier earrings with her wild golden mane that framed her beautiful face, Sienna had opted for a severe, sleek look by pulling her long hair into a low ponytail and fastening small diamond studs to her earlobes.

Various family members peppered Teagan with questions about her life in New York, including her successful jewelry line and makeup concierge businesses as well as the various celebrities she'd been photographed with. Ethan noticed Sienna made no attempt to join the conversation.

"Were you able to sleep?" he asked, the images of her stretched out on the bed in the upstairs guest room sending a series of steamy pictures drifting through his mind.

"Can you still see the waffle pattern from the blanket?" She touched her cheek in a charmingly unselfconscious gesture. "I swear I was only going to close my eyes for a second and the next thing I knew two hours went by."

"Are you feeling more rested?"

"Yes, thank you." Her lips curved in a secret smile. "I think the reality of being on vacation is starting to take hold. If I'm not careful, my clients will think I've abandoned them."

Could she possibly be as uncomplicated as she appeared? Was she simply a hardworking art curator who parlayed her Upper East Side connections into a lucrative career? The dossier Paul had prepared on Teagan touched only briefly on her other family members' financial situations and public personas. In Sienna's case, the information was limited to her professional website and several references in art-related articles.

After meeting both Burns sisters, he'd understood the warning delivered by the anonymous emailer where Teagan was concerned. But did Sienna's fleeting smiles and quiet reserve hide a truly devious mind? It was hard to believe, yet didn't that make her all the more dangerous?

"I guess while you're visiting us, I'm gonna have to make

sure you rest and play." Ethan bumped his shoulder against hers in a friendly gesture.

"That's kind of you, but I can't take you away from business." Was she playing hard to get to lure him in? If so, it was working. "And what I have planned would probably bore you to tears."

Given the strength of his interest, he doubted that. "You might be surprised."

"I'm going to visit every museum in Charleston and acquaint myself with all the Southern artists represented there."

"I have to confess something." Lowering his voice, he leaned her way in a conspiratorial manner and was rewarded by the rosy flush that stained her cheeks. "I've never been in half the museums in this town. That's a shame, wouldn't you say?"

Her blue-gray eyes lost a little of their sparkle as she surveyed his face as if to gauge his motives for flirting with her. Why would she do that? Couldn't she feel the electricity between them? Without breaking eye contact, he took inventory of the women seated around the table. Sienna Burns was not the most beautiful or stylish of them, but beneath her calm exterior he sensed she sizzled with passion and determination. He just had to figure out the best way to focus that fervor on him, and the key to figuring out her sister's plans would be in his grasp.

"I wouldn't want to monopolize all your time," Sienna demurred, her elusiveness a lure he couldn't resist.

"I wasn't just being polite earlier when I offered to show you around," he said. "I wouldn't want you to leave Charleston with less than the best impression of our fair city."

"Well then, I accept."

Satisfied that he'd successfully initiated step one of his divide-and-conquer plan, Ethan glanced toward Teagan and found her watching his interaction with Sienna. He thought he noted the tiniest trace of speculation in her green gaze. Catching her eye, he smiled and inclined his head to acknowledge her interest. The corner of her mouth twitched before she turned away to respond to a question his cousin Dallas had asked.

After dinner, when the family settled into the cozy library with its red walls and comfortable seating, Ethan offered to take Sienna for a walk around the grounds. Her gaze flicked to where the twins flanked Teagan on the blue velvet sofa, the blonde trio so similar in appearance that they looked more like sisters than cousins. Sienna's expression grew pensive, and a familiar stab of angst pierced his chest. As the only dark-haired member of a family of blonds, he knew what it felt like to be an outsider.

Ethan doubted anyone noticed their departure as he guided her out the French doors that led to the side terrace, down a circular, wrought iron staircase and onto the brick walkway that ran the length of the house. They had a choice of several paths that led off through the gardens, toward the pool or the dwellings at the back of the property.

"The estate occupies a little over an acre," he narrated as they ambled past formal beds filled with boxwood and flowers. "And includes the main house, carriage and caretaker houses. The twins occupy the latter if you're ever looking for them."

"An acre is a lot of land for downtown Charleston, isn't it?"

"Over the years Grady was able to purchase some of the surrounding buildings that were original to the property and redesign the grounds."

The deep gold of fading sunshine filtered through the lush plantings as Ethan kept pace with Sienna's slow amble along the gravel path. She murmured in delight at the mix of formal and free-style design that took a landscape team several hours to maintain each week. Since his knowledge was limited to a few well-known flowering plants, he spent his time pondering the best way to approach her.

Maybe at first Ethan had expected to engage her in a rousing duel of clever questions designed to trick her into revealing her sister's plans. But watching the way her fingertips skimmed over shiny leaves and delicate flower petals, he revised his strategy. Throwing her off-balance by exploiting her latent sensuality would be way more entertaining.

He'd never had fantasies about a sexy librarian before and although he'd heard that the brain was an important sexual organ, he was usually more interested in a woman's body from the neck down. Now, however, as he drank in the soft floral scent of Sienna's perfume and noticed the way she nibbled her lip when deep in thought, he suspected he'd been missing out. Ethan was abruptly besieged by images of her in a fitted pencil skirt, her full breasts straining the buttons of a snug white blouse. The fantasy look was completed by sexy, sky-high heels and ugly black glasses that she could whip off as her long, dark hair came tumbling out of a tidy topknot.

Holy...wow!

"Did you bring a swimsuit?" he asked as they reached the open space where the pool glowed like a turquoise jewel. "Dallas and Poppy do paddleboard yoga in the mornings. Lia got them started when she first came here to help my grandfather recover from his stroke. I'm sure they'd be thrilled if you and Teagan joined them."

"I'll mention it to her." Sienna hesitated before adding, "Regarding Lia... I have a question."

Tension gripped him at her curiosity. Their easy interaction had made him relax his vigilance.

"Fire away."

"I don't want to overstep your family's warm welcome, but I have to ask…" Sienna's gaze was fixed on the open-air pool house; she seemed to be gathering her thoughts. "Before dinner when I asked Lia how she and Paul met, she told me a rather startling story."

Here was evidence of the two-pronged Burns sisters attack. Sienna dug up the dirt and passed it to Teagan to exploit. Still, it wasn't as if he was the only person with knowledge of how Lia had come to be involved with his family.

"Grady was going downhill fast after his stroke and his greatest wish was to see his granddaughter before he died. I convinced Lia to pretend to be his long-lost granddaughter, thinking this would make him happy."

Her eyes went round. "So it's true. I'm sorry, but that's an extraordinary thing to do."

"At the time it seemed like a simple plan," he admitted. "One that was supposed to ease an old man's heart." Ethan shook his head as he recalled just how complicated the situation had become. "But Lia is a miracle worker. She spent a few days with my grandfather and he rallied."

"So your brother mentioned." Sienna was eyeing him keenly.

"Paul just about killed me when he came back from a conference and found out what I'd done." Despite the strain the stunt had put on their relationship, Ethan didn't regret the scheme. Because of it, Paul was in love with a wonderful woman and happier than he'd ever been.

"But he had to be delighted at your grandfather's unexpected recovery."

"Of course, and the happy outcome is that he and Lia are getting married."

"Yet it wasn't all that simple at the time."

"I suppose it was a little uncomfortable for Paul to be falling for someone while pretending to be her first cousin."

A little uncomfortable? Ethan knew Paul had gone through hell. He just couldn't bring himself to feel bad about it. Grady was thriving. It had prompted them to try to locate their actual missing relative through a genetic testing service, and once they'd found Teagan, Ethan had decided to take a test of his own to see if his birth family was out there somewhere and looking for him.

"How did everything come out in the open?" Sienna asked, dragging Ethan's thoughts back to the conversation.

"Why are you so curious about the story?"

"I was just wondering what sort of an impact the situation would have on your family accepting Teagan. After all, they fell in love with Lia after thinking she was your cousin. Will they be more cautious when it comes to Teagan?"

It was a valid question. "I don't know. I mean, everyone was delighted to hear that we'd found Ava's real daughter. No one has mentioned any reservations to me. As far as I can tell, they have every intention of fully embracing her. Why do you ask?"

"Teagan doesn't show her emotions very often, but I know she has high hopes for becoming part of this family. I don't want her to be disappointed."

"I think you could see from how dinner went tonight that you don't need to worry about that. Teagan is a Watts through and through."

Sienna looked somewhat mollified. "You've been so kind to show me the grounds, but I should probably be getting back."

"It's been my pleasure," Ethan declared, surprised how reluctant he was to part ways. "And I meant what I said earlier about showing you around Charleston. Let's start by having dinner tomorrow night."

"Okay."

"Wonderful."

Pleasure flared at her quick acceptance. "I'll pick you up at six."

They returned to the house in the fading light. At the bottom of the stairs that spiraled up to the side terrace, he bid her good-night.

"Thank you for making me feel welcome." Her hand rested on his sleeve for too brief a second.

Lightning flashed along his nerve endings at the barely-there contact. "Of course."

"Good night."

Given his body's agitation, Ms. Sienna Burns appeared to have won this round. Teeth grinding, he let his gaze linger on her departing form a heartbeat too long before heading for his car.

Watch your back.

Wise words, but Ethan wasn't sure his back was the part of him in danger.

Three

Sienna was seated with her laptop on the comfy love seat by the window when Teagan entered her room without knocking. She'd been reviewing an art collection that was being auctioned off in Salzburg in two weeks and making a list of the pieces that might interest her clients.

"We need to go shopping," Teagan announced, homing in on Sienna's closet like a fashion-seeking missile. Paying no attention to her sister's objections, Teagan threw open the door, gave the contents a disgusted glance before turning to face Sienna. "Everything that we brought from New York is all wrong."

Knowing it was fruitless to argue, Sienna looked up from her laptop and sighed. "You may have packed the wrong things, but everything I brought is perfectly fine." Ignoring her sister's disparaging snort, Sienna continued. "And for that matter, so is everything you brought. You're just looking for an excuse to go shopping."

Teagan's expression spoke volumes. "I never have to

look for an excuse to buy clothes. And you know I'm right."
Teagan was wearing a loose-fitting white crop top, floral
midi skirt and black-and-white colorblock pumps. With
red lipstick, blond hair sleeked back into a low ponytail
and chunky earrings, she looked ready to lunch at La Gre-
nouille. "Everything that I brought looks too New York. I
stand out and that's the last thing I'm trying to do."

"For once," Sienna muttered, too low and too fast for
Teagan to catch.

"I don't want my family to think, there's the girl from
New York City, every time they look at me. I want to fit
in. I want them to think, hey, she belongs in Charleston."

A brand-new email popped into Sienna's inbox, taking her attention away from her sister. She'd sent several
images from the upcoming Salzburg auction to one of her
bigger clients and he'd gotten back to her.

"Could you please stop working for five minutes and
talk to me?" Teagan demanded.

"Is this still about you taking over at Watts Shipping?"
Sienna asked, scanning the message before typing a quick
reply.

"Of course. How can I convince them to consider me for
the position if I don't look as if I'm planning on staying in
Charleston? I need to look like I'm assimilating."

As uncomfortable as Sienna was with her sister's plan,
she couldn't argue with the logic. Appearances counted.
A fact that had been thrown in her face starting when she
was old enough to dress herself.

First it had been her mother's despair that no matter
how much she spent on Sienna's clothes, the high-end designer fashions look frumpy on her. Then came high school
where even though they wore uniforms, the truly fashion-
able stood out. Whether it was a trendy haircut, the way

they styled their jewelry or the shoes they wore, something about the influencers set them apart.

Needless to say, Teagan was one of the trendsetters while Sienna, who'd never been confident about her looks, had faded into the background.

"Well, you're right about fitting in," Sienna said. "You'd better go shopping. Have fun."

Expecting that this would send Teagan on her way, Sienna was caught off guard when her sister planted her palm on the cover of the laptop and snapped it shut. Sienna yanked her hands back just in time to avoid a solid rap on her knuckles.

"Hey!" she complained. "What's the big idea?"

"You're coming with us."

"When you say us…?" Sienna asked, reluctantly setting aside her laptop. "Who else is coming?"

"Dallas and Poppy, of course," she said, naming the twins. "And Paul's fiancée, Lia."

Sienna had watched her sister operate before. Every time she found herself in a new situation, she gathered people to her cause, charming, bribing or blackmailing them into assisting, whichever worked best. In this case, she needed to avoid making enemies, so charm and bribery it was.

"Sounds like you'll have plenty of people offering opinions." And of course, bestowing compliments. "You don't really need me."

"Of course I need you." Teagan reached down and clamped her hand on Sienna's arm, tugging her to her feet. "I know you'll give me your honest opinion."

Sienna snorted. "You want my opinion about fashion?" She crossed her arms and leveled a hard stare at her sister. "What's your real reason for wanting me along?"

"Okay, fine. I knew you wouldn't come if I told you that I want to go shopping to buy you some new clothes. I know what you're gonna say," she rushed on, holding up her hand to forestall Sienna's protests. "But honestly, there's not a flattering outfit in there. You need some clothes that accentuate your curves instead of hiding them, and a whole lot more color."

Sienna glanced down at her serviceable navy pants and white shirt. It wasn't that Sienna didn't care how she looked; it was more that she'd hated being compared to her glamorous, fashion-influencer sister and had stopped trying to keep up with Teagan a long time ago.

"I don't see the point in spending a bunch of money on things I won't wear to work."

Teagan waved her sister's objections away. "It wouldn't kill you to add some stylish pieces to your work wardrobe." Looping her arm through Sienna's, Teagan snagged her sister's purse and drew her out of the room. "Besides, you need a few things to wear while you're down here. Honestly, no one will give you a second look if you don't make an effort."

"Why do I care if anyone gives me a second look?" Sienna asked.

Yet although it pained her to admit it, Sienna was delighted to be included. In New York, Teagan had a hundred distractions. Between her hectic social life and three flourishing businesses, no one received Teagan's full attention.

"You need it because I saw the way you were looking at Ethan," Teagan said with a sly smile. "You're attracted to him and if you want him to notice you, you need to put on a pretty dress, fix your hair and apply a little makeup."

Sienna's face went hot. "I am not interested in Ethan."

"Oh, don't even," Teagan interrupted with zeal. "You were looking at him like he was a chocolate cake and you wanted to devour every bite."

Remembering his smile, the electric zing of attraction when he'd taken her hand, Sienna opened her mouth to deny it again, but they'd reached the second floor and she was afraid the exchange would be overheard.

"If it motivates you," Teagan said, "I think he's interested in you, too. You'd make a cute couple."

"I don't think I'm his type," Sienna protested, hoping Teagan wouldn't give the matter another thought.

Her sister was so accustomed to being the center of attention that when someone showed an interest in Sienna, Teagan turned on the charm. She didn't do it on purpose, but with her looks and vivacious personality she was the sun that the rest of them revolved around.

"You don't think you're any man's type," her sister countered. "But you and I know that's not true."

In truth, several men had found her attractive. Unfortunately, once they met Teagan, they'd found her far more appealing.

"And I think he's into you, as well," Teagan confided, as they reached the door that led to the back terrace and the stairs to the extensive gardens between the back of the house and the garage.

While they were visiting, Teagan and Sienna had been offered the use of one of several vehicles gathering dust in Grady's garage since his stroke many months ago.

"Where are we headed?" Sienna asked, sliding into the passenger seat. She would've preferred to be the one behind the wheel—Teagan rarely got out of New York City to practice her driving skills—but her sister liked being in control.

"Poppy is working so I thought we'd swing by her salon and pick her up."

Sienna should've realized something was up, but until she was herded into a stylist chair, she hadn't realized the reason they stopped at Poppy's salon was so that she could be bullied into having her hair cut and highlighted. While Teagan and her cousin discussed Sienna as if she was a shabby doll rather than a living, breathing woman, Sienna sipped white wine and surrendered to the transformation. An hour and a half later, she stared at her reflection, marveling at the caramel highlights and wavy layers that added volume and dimension to her hair.

"You have gorgeous hair," Poppy said, obviously pleased with herself. "Your cut just needed to be freshened up a little bit."

A little bit was an understatement. Finishing up her second glass of wine, Sienna stared at her reflection and barely recognized herself. Had she really avoided competing with Teagan to the extent that she'd stopped trying to look her best? Apparently so, because the smiling woman reflected back at her appeared not just beautiful but also happy about it.

Feeling a little off-balance, Sienna got up from the chair and tried to pay Poppy.

The hairdresser laughed and waved her off. "You're family. And family doesn't pay."

Determined to find a way to repay Poppy's kindness, Sienna exited the salon and followed the other women down the street to begin their shopping. What followed was a blur of wine, women and far too much fashion for Sienna to keep it all straight. Not long after she was halfway through her third glass of wine that afternoon, Dallas and Lia showed up to offer their opinions. The quartet kept putting more outfits in the dressing room for Sienna to try on, barely giving her space to notice that she modeled five outfits to one of theirs.

In the end, after repeating the routine in several more stores, she exited the final one having spent more money on clothes in a single afternoon than in the whole of last year. They swung by the car to drop off her purchases and then headed to the twins' favorite watering hole with rooftop seating. Dallas had worked in several award-winning kitchens around Charleston and was well-known in the restaurant scene. When the bartender spied her leading their group in, he sent over a specialty cocktail for them all to try. As Sienna sipped the delicious fruity martini, she surveyed the view and savored being one of Teagan's posse. Of course, she reflected, it wouldn't last. Her sister did nothing out of the goodness of her heart. If she dragged Sienna shopping, there would be a motive behind her actions. It was only a matter of time before the purpose was revealed.

"To Sienna's new look," Teagan began, lifting her glass in a festive gesture. "Here's hoping a certain someone will notice."

While the other three echoed the toast, Teagan locked eyes with Sienna and smirked. Even though she'd been expecting it, Sienna shivered in dread at her sister's Machiavellian manipulation. Obviously, Teagan intended to throw Sienna at Ethan, but to what purpose? Nor could she demand an answer from her sister. Teagan was a slippery eel when it came to admitting she was up to anything. Sienna would just have to keep her eyes open and hope when the ax fell that she saw it coming soon enough to get out of its way.

Ethan bounded up the front steps of his grandfather's home, eager to spend the evening with Sienna Burns, and find out what she knew about her sister's plans. He found her seated at the dining room table, her laptop open, her fingers flying over the keys. His initial thought was that she hadn't been kidding about being a workaholic. His second impression took longer to coalesce. As his gaze skimmed over her, his senses came online, so that his body—not his mind—dominated his reaction to her transformation.

Someone—he guessed his cousin Poppy—had transformed Sienna's long hair to better enhance the creamy perfection of her skin. Gone was the low ponytail of forgettable brown. Instead, wavy strands of rich chocolate, threaded with caramel, framed her oval face and drew attention to her blue-gray eyes and plump lips.

And the changes didn't end there. Her utilitarian uniform of dark pants and white top had been replaced by a floral organza dress in peach-and-coral tones that enhanced her abundant curves. Ruffles fluttered along the V of her neckline, drawing attention to the swell of her breasts and offering eye-popping glimpses of her ample cleavage. She looked feminine, approachable, absurdly kissable. He wanted to wrap his fingers around her small waist and pull her tight against his body. To savor the lavish delights of her pillowy breasts squashed against his chest.

Holy hell! He was getting aroused just looking at her.

Ethan caught hold of himself and wrestled his expression into easy congeniality. It would not serve his plans to scare the girl right off the bat by leering at her like a man who was only after her body. He'd save that for later in the evening.

"Hey," he said, his voice sounding rusty. He swallowed and tried again. "Are you ready to go?"

"Just about," she said without looking up from the laptop screen. "I have a client who wants a piece that's going up for auction in a couple of weeks and I'm trying to gage the level of interest out there so I can give him an idea how much it might go for."

"Take your time," he murmured, content to trail his gaze over her for a few more unguarded minutes. "I like your dress."

"Thank you." She made a face, but whether it was about what she was typing or his compliment, he couldn't tell.

"Is it new?"

"Yes." Her gaze finally slid his direction. "Why do you ask?"

The look in her eyes as she surveyed him in turn was a gut punch he didn't see coming. Appreciation made her lips curve just the tiniest bit. As his heart beat harder, he wasn't sure if he should resist his attraction or channel it into his plot to use seduction to uncover her sister's plans. If not for that damned email, he could see himself having fun with Sienna. Her blend of intelligence and artlessness was a fascinating combination he was eager to explore.

With Teagan, every facial expression and word she spoke seemed practiced and prepared. Behind her beautiful green eyes he'd spied a shrewd brain that plotted and planned. That was why after meeting her, he'd had no trouble believing the anonymous emailer's claim that she intended to battle him for control of Watts Shipping.

Sienna was much harder to figure out. One moment she was blushing at something that had passed between them. The next she looked like she'd enjoy a lusty romp in the bedroom. And just when he thought he'd figured her out, she threw her intelligence at him and retreated behind a wall of facts and candid observation. Had he ever met a woman this complex? Which facets represented the real Sienna Burns and how did he exploit them to his advantage?

"Because," Ethan said, realizing he'd taken too long to answer, "I can see the price tag."

"Oh." She began a frantic search that was equal parts comical and charming.

Ethan cursed to himself even as his lips curved into a grin. If his intention was to seduce her, he should've slid his fingers up her side to indicate where the tag was. His touch that close to the swell of her breast would no doubt have a predictable effect on them both. Instead, he stayed rooted to the spot and enjoyed the show as she twisted and turned, offering him an eyeful of cleavage that lay previously hidden beneath the floral ruffles.

There was no way he'd make it through the night without getting his hands on her.

While she retreated to the kitchen to find scissors, he glanced at her open laptop. A quick perusal of her email exposed no damning messages between her and Teagan or anyone else for that matter. Not that he expected there to be. Surely they were clever enough to cover their tracks.

In minutes Sienna returned to the dining room, the hem of her floral dress fluttering about her knees, drawing Ethan's attention to her shapely calves. She was barefoot, having abandoned her coral-colored sandals beneath the table. They were beyond easy reach and she would have to crawl under the table to fetch them.

"Let me get those," he said, dropping to his knee before she could. Snagging the straps, he pulled them out and arranged the shoes before her feet, glancing at her smooth, pale legs as he did so.

"Thanks," she murmured huskily, biting her lip as if unsure what to do about his apparent interest.

"My pleasure." He'd never spoken more truthfully.

As if disconcerted by the fact that he didn't immediately rise, she plopped down on the chair where she'd been sitting before. His current position at her feet was too close to enable her to fasten the straps so they stared at each other for an awkward beat before he stood and stepped back.

Proximity to her made his stomach pitch oddly. The sensation was magnified when she glanced up at him from beneath her lashes. Her expression, an intriguing mixture of curiosity, concern and confusion, rocked him back on his heels. Either this was a big act or she was unlike any woman he'd ever been attracted to.

When it came to sex, he liked his partners experienced

and willing. He didn't want to worry about awkwardness or hurt feelings in the aftermath. Usually that wasn't a problem for him. He had a reputation around Charleston for being an impossible catch.

He'd already decided to exert all his charm on Sienna and hope she trusted him enough to relax her guard and talk about her sister's plans. What remained open-ended was how far to take things. Sleeping with her might be the highlight of his busy social schedule, but he wasn't sure he could trust himself to remain indifferent.

"Are you ready to go?" he asked.

"Let me run my laptop back to my room and grab my purse."

While he waited, Ethan pulled out his phone and reflected on the latest message from the anonymous sender.

Sienna is very adept at reading people. Be careful how much you tell her.—A friend

The reason this particular warning bothered him had little to do with the content of the message and more that his anonymous "friend" seemed to have an inside track on Ethan's activities. Who could be behind it? He doubted it was someone close to him. Anyone in his life who had his best interest at heart would know to come to him directly rather than go all clandestine with sinister warnings.

Nor was this particular advice earth-shattering. Ethan rarely trotted out his thoughts and feelings to those he trusted. He wasn't about to give away the store to someone he'd just met.

By the time Sienna returned, Ethan had settled on his strategy. They would head to a romantic restaurant where he would order wine and ply her with delicious seafood and a decadent dessert. Then, with her lulled by great food and scintillating conversation, they would stroll under the moonlight where, with the table no longer a barrier between them, he would offer tantalizing hints of the sexual pleasures that awaited her. All leading to the eventual spilling of her secrets in the sweaty daze of postlovemaking bliss.

Four

They passed through a wrought iron gate and navigated a meandering brick pathway bordered by densely planted landscaping to get to the restaurant Ethan had chosen. To Sienna, it felt like stepping into a hidden garden. Inside, a mix of old and new offered a cozy ambiance. Large contemporary chandeliers warmed the oyster-toned, velvet-lined walls hung with hundred-year-old portraits. The effect was inviting and Sienna couldn't wait to see the menu.

The hostess escorted them to a quiet table for two in the back corner. As Sienna settled onto the banquette seat that ran the length of the restaurant's back wall, she realized that while she had a view of the entire restaurant, Ethan's only scenery was her. This proved immediately disconcerting as he set aside his menu and brought the full power of his attention to bear.

"Is this place okay?" Ethan was behaving like a perfect gentleman, a swoon-worthy date, bringing her to a romantic restaurant, checking in to make sure she was happy.

"It's perfect." *You're perfect.* Too perfect. Yet, she was hopelessly ignoring the red flag flapping in her face.

"Wonderful." His alluring smile sent butterflies whisking over her nerve endings. "I want your first dinner out to be memorable."

"Oh, I'm sure it will be that," she murmured, mentally removing his linen jacket and slipping the buttons of his white shirt loose one by one.

Charleston's sultry heat left her craving endless hours of sweaty, energetic, creative sex with a man who made her feel like the most beautiful woman on the planet.

Ethan Watts fit the bill.

"Good." He drawled the word, the vowels lingering decadently on his lips and tongue.

Sienna sipped water and resisted the urge to fan herself. She wasn't accustomed to being wooed. Or maybe it was better to say that she wasn't comfortable being romanced. The only way she'd found to keep her heart from being broken was to remain in charge of whom she dated and when she slept with someone. For the most part she chose unsophisticated men with no connections to her career who were wildly romantic. It was hard to take men like that seriously and she was able to enjoy their bodies without ever engaging her mind or heart.

That's what made Ethan so dangerous.

The last of her restraint was fraying beneath his outrageous flirting and come-hither gazes. Not only was she dying to get her hands on his gorgeous body, but she was also keenly aware of the sharp mind beneath his flagrant charm. Hot and smart was a combination destined to inspire a whole host of needs. And there were so many.

"To the first of many visits you'll make to Charleston," Ethan said, extending his wineglass toward her. Since they'd both decided on the blue crab ravioli, he'd suggested a bottle of Châteauneuf-du-Pape Blanc.

"To firsts." She breathed in the wine's peach and floral scents before taking a sip. Fruity and fresh with notes of honey, the white wine slipped along her tongue, making her smile. "Oh, this is delicious."

"I'm glad you like it." His deep, rich voice had a rumbling sort of purr that wove pictures in her mind of long, slow kisses and his hands skimming over her heated naked flesh. "Would you like to start with the muscles?"

"Um." Sienna blinked. "Sure." Having no idea what she'd just agreed to, she lifted her wineglass again and set it to her lips.

"It's my favorite appetizer on the menu."

Oh. Mussels. Not muscles. Amused and all too aware she was blushing, she shifted uncomfortably in her seat. It didn't help that Ethan watched her with narrowed eyes as if he could read every nuance of her expression.

"Sounds great."

To her relief, the waiter approached and took their dinner orders. This brief respite gave her enough breathing space to regain her composure. After he left, she took control of the conversation.

"What was it like growing up in Charleston?"

"I have to think it was like growing up anywhere." His throwaway answer was telling. He didn't want to talk about himself. "School, friends and family. I think you've already figured out we're a close-knit group."

"I have, and it seems as if you all have embraced Teagan as one of you own." Sienna paused to consider her next words. She didn't want to be disloyal to her sister, but at some point, Teagan's true nature was going to show. "She isn't quite as laid-back as you all are so I hope you're ready for her to bring her New York energy to your Southern city."

"I think she'll be a good influence on my cousins. She's very driven and they could use a little of that."

"Oh she's driven," Sienna said, trying to keep the irony out of her voice. "And so it seems are you and Paul."

"Paul is in a league of his own." The pride in Ethan's voice was at odds with his sardonic smile, suggesting that the brothers had a complicated relationship. "He's always been obsessed with computers and of course no one in our family has any idea what it is that he does, except that he does it very well."

"The two of you are the only ones who live outside downtown Charleston, right?" Sienna found it interesting that the siblings had chosen to distance themselves from the rest of the family. "And both of you are on the water."

"Paul's Isle of Palms house is on the beach, but I like to spend as much time on the water as I can drinking beer and fishing with my buddies. My house has access to the river where I step out my back door and onto my boat."

Her phone buzzed in her purse and she made an involuntary move to pull it out before remembering that she deserved this night off.

"I guess that enjoying boating makes sense for a man whose family runs an international shipping company," she said, determined to keep her attention focused on Ethan.

"I got my love of the water from Grady. He keeps a cruiser at the yacht club. Anyone in the family can use it, but I'm the only one who does."

When her phone sounded again, Sienna ground her teeth and wished she'd turned the damned thing off before leaving for the restaurant.

"Do you need to get that?" Ethan asked, showing no annoyance at the interruption.

"I really don't."

"But you want to?"

Sienna shook her head. "It's more that I suffer from a Pavlovian reaction to any noise my phone makes. Since I deal with clients and art dealers both here and abroad, it isn't unusual for them to reach out to me at all times of the day and night. Usually, I jump on every communication. But tonight, I'm totally focused on you."

His delighted grin let her know she'd said the perfect thing. Sienna found herself wishing she was seated on his lap, running her fingers through his thick, dark hair.

"You are really dedicated to what you do." He cocked his head. "Do you love it that much?"

"I love the treasure-hunting aspect of it. Seeing the thrill on my client's face when I secure something beautiful for them makes the long hours worthwhile."

"You're lucky to do something that makes you happy."

"I am, although sometimes I dread the idea of getting on another airplane."

"Have you considered staying in one place and curating for a museum?"

"Sometimes. Or I think about finishing my art history PhD and teaching somewhere."

"What's stopping you?"

Sienna grimaced. "The idea of standing up in front of a room full of college students and watching their eyes glaze over as I lecture."

"I can see where that might not be ideal, but surely you could use your credentials in some other fashion."

"I could," she hedged, uncomfortable with the idea of change, "but the fact is I haven't yet found a reason to slow down."

Ethan's curiosity sharpened. "What would it take?"

"I don't know." But that wasn't completely true. Since meeting Ethan she'd started imagining lazy Sunday mornings in bed and endless hours of conversation and great sex. "Maybe the right guy to come along?"

"You don't sound convinced."

Sienna regretted her impulsive answer. "Obviously, it's all just speculation and I won't know how I feel until I find him." For some reason, talking with Ethan about a potential relationship with a nonexistent man was making her anxious. "And that's not likely to happen anytime soon."

"You never know. He might be closer than you think."

Sienna shook her head. "It's a chicken-and-egg thing. I don't have a man in my life encouraging me to slow down and I can't invest time in a relationship unless I slow down."

"Sounds like there are a lot of unhappy men in Manhattan who haven't had the pleasure of your company," he stated, brown eyes dancing with sensual intent. "So if you're not dating, how do you spend your downtime?"

"In bed." When he raised his eyebrows, she clarified. "Sleeping." His disappointment made her insides do funny things. "Or hanging out with my friends."

"What about your family? Do you see much of them?"

"Tegan and I text a lot, but she's busy and my parents…" The way she trailed off was telling and from Ethan's expression, he wanted to ask her more about it. "Let's just say I'm a middle child and that my parents are both more preoccupied with my siblings."

"You make it sound like you feel left out."

Was she imagining things or had he leaned forward as if her answer bore some significance for him? She pondered the family photos on his cousin's Instagram feed. How his dark hair and brown eyes made him stand out among his blond relatives. Did he also feel like an outsider? Yet were their situations at all the same? His family so obviously adored him.

"It's more like I'm different than either of my siblings,"

Sienna explained. "Aiden is just like my dad. He's super outgoing and knows everybody in town. He's also a bit lazy and can be frustratingly scatterbrained at times. But he's the only boy and firstborn. As far as my parents are concerned, he is the golden one."

"And Teagan?"

"My mother's pride and joy. Beautiful, blonde and built like a model with impeccable fashion sense." *Everything I'm not.* "Around the time Teagan turned thirteen, my mother got the idea to start her own fashion line. Since I love to draw, I contributed some sketches and a couple of them were developed for the first collection. But somehow my mother forgot to give me any credit and when it came time to choose the face of the company, my mother picked Teagan. They've been a wildly successful fashion team ever since and nobody has any idea that I was once involved."

"So you draw?"

"I do." She paused to adjust to the change of topic, relieved to move on from her difficult childhood. With an impish grin, she added, "When I'm inspired."

"What inspires you?"

You do. "Mostly the human form." She'd already mentally undressed him earlier. It couldn't be much naughtier to imagine sketching him in all his naked glory. "My senior thesis was devoted to the human body in all its forms."

"I'd be happy to pose for you." His eyes danced with wicked allure. Could he read her mind? If so, sex with him would be beyond amazing. "If you're feeling inspired, that is."

"Well." She took a sip of wine to ease her suddenly dry mouth. "Point me to the nearest art supply store."

After dinner, Ethan and Sienna strolled historic streets south of Broad through the shadows created by streetlamps and lush landscaping. A light breeze, perfumed by jasmine and roses, offered intermittent relief from the weight of the humid air. Beyond the iron fences and tall brick walls, light spilled through the windows of hundred-year-old mansions, the warm glow guiding their path.

Ethan savored watching Sienna absorb the beauty of the historic district the same way he'd relished each bite of his dinner. He enjoyed the sensual pleasure of hearing her inarticulate delight as some sculpture or architectural feature caught her eye. The brush of her arm against his as her balance shifted while she negotiated a transition in the pavement from concrete to brick.

"You're probably bored to tears," she said as they reached a corner and had to decide whether to keep going straight or turn. "I'm used to the noise and bustle of New York. It's so peaceful here."

"I'm fine to keep going if you are," he answered. "White Point Garden and the Battery are a few more blocks down. The sun has already set so you won't be able to see much, but at least you'll know where it is in case you want to come back during the day."

"I think to save my feet for all the sightseeing to come we should head back." But what she did next surprised him.

A formidable brick wall bordered the sidewalk where they stood. Sienna took a backward step toward it, gliding into the shadows cast by a nearby crepe myrtle. Her fingers caught the sleeve of his linen jacket, the tug so delicate he might have missed it if not for the way her invitation lit up his body. Did she hope he'd press her against the wall, slide his lips over hers and make her moan? Because that's what he wanted to do. Yet, instead of following through on his impulses, he stared at the pattern of her bright dress against the dull red-gray bricks, all the while wondering what the hell was stopping him.

"I wouldn't want you to end up with blisters from too much walking," he said, trying to sort out if she needed a moment to rest or if her mind had swerved down the path his had gone.

If he closed the gap between them, would she wrap her arms around his neck and draw him into her space?

"Oh," she breathed, with just the right amount of self-deprecating amusement in her voice to make him smile. "I'm sure you can tell by looking at me that I'm not that fragile."

Ethan moved forward while she was lifting the heavy curtain of hair off her shoulders and neck. Her exposed skin glowed in the contrasting shadows and his mouth went dry.

"I will say, though," she continued as he took another step toward her and placed his palm on the bricks beside her head. "Next to you I feel positively delicate."

"You are. You have a delicate nose and chin." He traced each with the tip of his finger. "Delicate bone structure. Delicate hands and delicate feet." He lifted his free hand and placed his palm against hers, demonstrating their different sizes.

She rasped her nails along the light stubble just below his jawline and his breath hitched. A lightning bolt of hunger shot through him. Dismay followed. This was supposed to be his game. His pursuit. She wasn't supposed to arouse him with a single touch. He was in charge of the seduction, of enticing her into surrendering her secrets and her gorgeous body.

Yet Ethan found himself threading his finger into her luxuriant waves and savoring the silky slide of the soft strands against his skin. He half closed his eyes and watched her expression transform from bold curiosity to wary anticipation. The war between her uncertainty and longing confused him. What could make her afraid to want him? And which emotion would rule the day?

He had a solid plan to find out.

Or he did until she ran playful fingers through his hair.

"Thanks for the fun night." Her soft breath puffed against his cheek before she kissed him there, a warm peck that gave him a quick sample of her soft, full breasts pressed against his chest and left him aching for more.

It was a friendship buss, he realized, barely holding back a tormented groan. Worse, he no longer knew if she was playing him or if her sweetness was honest and legitimate. He searched her eyes for the flicker he'd seen over dinner, the one that matched the fire building beneath his skin. For one breathtaking second he saw what he'd been looking for. That moment was all he needed to take her hand in his and lift the inside of her wrist to his lips.

"It was my pleasure," he responded, thrilling to the gasp that escaped her.

The irregular rise and fall of her chest was creating chaos inside him. He was dying to have those soft breasts squashed against him. To peel off her clothes and expose their perfect contours to his eyes, hands and mouth.

"No, really," she murmured, "the pleasure was all mine."

He dove into her gaze, saw her eagerness and her vulnerability. She wanted him. The discovery didn't fill him with triumph so much as wonder. All his suspicions and scheming fell away. When it came to this woman, this moment, he wanted nothing to get between them.

"There's more than enough pleasure for us both."

Taking her chin, he tipped her face to the perfect angle. Anticipation was eating him alive, but he would only get one shot at a first kiss with her. He intended to make it memorable.

Her startled eyes slid shut as he grazed his lips over

hers. The kiss reminded him of jazz. A call and response exchange with bright notes of trumpet, intricate piano improvisation and beneath it all a heartbeat thrum of bass.

Ethan wrapped his arm around her waist and slowly brought her snug against him. This was everything he'd craved, but so much more. The world slowed, compressed, faded. Images of the future flashed in his mind. Bare skin. Soft moans. Greedy hands. Feverish lips. The sharp nip of her teeth. The hot, snug grip of her around his erection.

Sienna melted in his arms, her lush curves pliant against him. Releasing her chin, he feathered the tips of his fingers down her neck and over her collarbone. His mind fogged as she shivered. In that moment, he knew there was nowhere else he wanted to be. They fit together. Belonged together. It was as if his entire life he'd been moving toward this exact instant. A perfect first kiss with a woman who brought every cell in his body to full awareness.

His skin tingled where her fingertips explored. Along his cheekbone, around the rim of his ear, down his neck and around to his nape. Letting the embrace slowly build was both torment and pleasure. He trailed his tongue along the seam of her lips, knowing she'd open for him. Satisfaction exploded when she did. Their breath mingled. She tasted of the raspberry-and-dark-chocolate dessert they'd shared.

The blare of a car alarm hit them both like an ice bath after a muscle-loosening sensual massage. Sienna responded by jerking free of the kiss. Silently cursing the untimely interruption, Ethan tightened his fingers for the briefest of seconds until he registered the tensing of her muscles and let go.

Her gaze darted about as if searching their surroundings for a place to hide. When the empty street offered no protection, she fluffed her hair, gave a nervous laugh and retreated a step. Ethan ground his teeth and acknowledged that the sexy mood was shattered.

"I guess I should take you back to my grandfather's house." While it was the courteous offer to make, he was counting on her to suggest a different destination entirely. In fact, he was on the verge of inviting her back to his place when she nodded.

"It's getting late," she agreed, "and I have a 6:00 a.m. call with an art dealer in Paris."

"Aren't you supposed to be on vacation?" He offered his arm to her before turning back the way they'd come."

Sienna's fingers closed around his biceps. "I have a hard time doing nothing."

He felt a wolfish smile form, thinking of all the ways he could keep her entertained. "If you like to keep busy then I'm the guy for you."

"You don't say." She sounded slightly breathless. "What did you have in mind?"

"Have dinner with me again tomorrow," he suggested, shooting a friendly leer her way. "And I'll show you."

Five

The morning after her dinner with Ethan, Sienna headed to the Gibbes Museum of Art on Meeting Street in Charleston's historic district. Housed in a beaux arts building since 1905, the museum had a collection of ten thousand works of fine art with many connected to Charleston or the South. She'd been particularly eager to study the depiction of the city's complicated past, from the highs of wealth and culture to the lows of slavery and war.

When she'd announced her plans the day before, several of Teagan's family members had offered to accompany her to the museum. Knowing that her measured pace viewing the exhibits would frustrate any companion, she'd turned them all down. For Sienna, art wasn't just a commodity that her clients invested in, but an opportunity to see inside someone's heart, mind and soul and experience what they were feeling. She loved that moment when she gazed at a painting and found her mind opening to another's point of view.

With so much to absorb, Sienna planned to spend the entire day at the museum. Her last stop before breaking for lunch was the observation windows that allowed visitors a behind-the-scenes look of the work of curators and conservators. Her best friend, Gia, was a conservator for the Guggenheim back in New York and Sienna found the work fascinating.

After picking up a salad at the museum's coffee shop, Sienna wandered through the classically landscaped Lenhardt Garden. Then it was back inside to view the exhibition of twentieth-century American regionalism and the Charleston Renaissance that spanned thirty years beginning in 1915.

She was admiring the innovative display of three hundred miniature portraits when her senses were assailed by a familiar masculine scent. Glancing to the side, she spied Ethan an instant before he wrapped a strong arm around her waist and brushed his firm lips over her temple. Although the casual display of affection jangled her nerves, she relaxed against his side and savored the latent power of his hard body. In her world people greeted each other with fake smiles and air kisses. The demonstrative familiarity from Ethan and his cousins was slowly dissolving her usual reserve.

"You look fantastic," he said, the compliment slipping easily from his lips.

Today, she was wearing another outfit purchased during her shopping expedition with Teagan and her cousins. Sienna felt feminine and comfortable in the loose-fitting maxi dress, though with a print of pink watercolor poppies on a black background, it was a bold choice for her.

"Thanks." She found herself blushing for no good reason except that his hungry gaze hit the accelerator on her sexual drive. "You do, too."

He was casually dressed in khakis and a blue-and-white-striped button-down open at the neck and with the sleeves rolled up to expose his muscular forearms. Honestly, the man could wear a parka and a ski mask and his massive amounts of sex appeal would still be overwhelming.

"Have you enjoyed the museum?" Ethan asked.

"Yes," Sienna replied in a breathless rush, delighted by his unscheduled appearance. "It's quite wonderful." She glanced at her watch and saw that it was nearly three o'clock. "What are you doing here?"

"I thought it might be fun to see the museum through your eyes so I canceled my afternoon meetings and skipped out early."

"I'm so glad you did, but are you sure it's okay to do that?" She imagined Teagan's glee at finding out that Ethan was shirking his duties.

"If you don't want me here…" Disappointment shadowed his eyes as he trailed off, misinterpreting her question.

"Oh, no!" she exclaimed, reaching for his arm, eager to reassure him that his company was welcome. "It's not that. I was thinking this might not be the most exciting afternoon for you. I've been known to lose track of time while staring at a painting."

"If I get bored, I'll just stare at you." He took her hand and brushed a kiss over her knuckles.

At the touch of his lips, she let loose a disconcerted chuckle. She scanned his expression, searching for mockery. "I definitely won't be able to concentrate if you do that."

A smug smile came and went as he turned to the display case before them. "What are you looking at here?"

"These are miniatures. Before photography, people had tiny portraits painted of their loved ones. They were tokens of affection they could keep close to their hearts. Some of them were worn as jewelry." She pointed to a two-inch-high oval frame of pearls and rubies that encased an enamel-on-porcelain painting of a gentleman. "Some of them were exchanged between courting couples." She indicated two miniatures that had been painted in 1801. "These would've been worn on a chain and might've included some ornamental hairwork or a romantic inscription."

When she glanced over to see if she'd succeeded in boring Ethan to tears, she caught him eyeing her in bemusement. She hid her relief behind a wry smile.

"Now you see why I usually come alone to a museum. I find all this stuff far too fascinating for the average person."

"You really are passionate about all this, aren't you?"

"You sound surprised."

A fond glow lit his brown eyes. "I guess it's because you keep surprising me."

His response struck all the right notes. Sienna slipped her hand around his biceps and almost purred at the power surging beneath her fingers. Her stomach fluttered as her mind recalled the kiss the night before. Would there be a repeat today? She was feeling needy enough to make sure it did.

"I feel the same way," she admitted, and then experiencing that same click of connection she'd noticed the night before, Sienna beamed at him. "In fact every moment in your company is wonderful."

When he didn't respond right away, she worried that she'd freaked out the elusive bachelor. She was scrambling for a way to gracefully backpedal when he stopped walking and before she knew what hit her, he'd wrapped his arm around her waist and spun her into a romantic dip.

There, in the middle of the museum, Ethan tangled his fingers in her hair and dropped a lingering kiss on her lips. She threw herself into the embrace, as deliriously happy as any heroine in a rom-com, letting herself be swept up in the sizzle of his kisses and the excitement of being so sweetly manhandled. By the time he broke the kiss, she was breathless, light-headed and tingling all over.

"I think it goes without saying," he murmured, his gaze sliding over her bright cheeks and parted lips, "that I find your company pretty wonderful, as well."

"You do have a knack for saying the perfect thing to get a girl's heart fluttering," she bantered back, uncharacteristically giddy as he maintained his snug hold on her for several seconds before whirling her back to a full upright position.

Swaying on her feet, Sienna commanded her foolish heart to settle down as he made a show of reluctance before releasing her. She blew out a quiet breath as they moved arm in arm toward the next exhibit. Thank goodness she wasn't going to remain in Charleston much longer. Knowing this interlude had an expiration date allowed her to experience something she'd never felt before without fear that she'd end up brokenhearted.

An hour later, they exited the museum and emerged onto Meeting Street. Squinting at the bright sunlight, Sienna paused on the checkerboard walkway that led from the entrance to the street and dipped into her purse for her sunglasses.

Thus armored, she glanced Ethan's direction. "Where to?"

"I'd planned for us to go out on my family's boat and then have a quiet dinner."

She picked up the past tense. "If something came up, I understand. We can try another time."

His eyebrows lifted at her quick response. "Are you trying to get rid of me?"

"Oh, no. Of course not."

"Good. Remember when I said that I'm generally the only one who uses the family boat? Well, Poppy sent me a text and invited us to go out on it with her friends."

Ethan appeared displeased at the turn of events and Sienna wondered how many of his past conquests could be counted amongst his cousin's friends. Was he worried if she met them that the stories she might hear would scare her off? If so, it was rather charming that he cared about her opinion of him.

"So," he continued, "we can either go with them or skip the harbor tour and find something else to do before dinner."

Her skin flushed as she imagined all the things they could do to kill the time. "I'm okay with whatever you want to do."

Sliding his gaze over her hot cheeks, he smiled. "Let's head over to the boat. Poppy indicated they won't arrive for a while yet. We can have it all to ourselves for the time being."

Knowing exactly what was on his mind, Sienna found herself tongue-tied and dry mouthed as they headed to the marina on the Ashley River, not far from his grandfather's estate. The boat was an immaculately maintained forty-five-foot cruiser complete with a kitchen above and two staterooms with adjoining heads below, and an indoor/outdoor lounge area. Sienna recalled the way Ethan had lit up when discussing being on the water and noticed how he grew instantly relaxed as soon as they stepped aboard.

"This is quite a party boat," Sienna exclaimed, noting the swim platform off the back, seating for six inside the cockpit and room for another eight on the back deck.

"It's seen its share of good times," Ethan murmured cryptically, indicating the stairs that led below.

"I imagine."

Ethan peeled off his coat and shoes before depositing them in a closet located in the large aft cabin. While he rolled up his sleeves, Sienna kicked off her sandals and tucked them and her purse into the same cabinet. Then, they faced each other in the snug space and their eyes met.

A delicious thrill rushed though Sienna. "When did you say your cousin and her friends were coming by?" Her gaze flicked to the bed a few short feet away.

"Sometime around five." He stepped closer and caressed her arm.

Tiny hairs lifted as his touch passed over them and she shivered. When his hand neared hers, she spread her fingers and he slid his between them. A zap of sensation flashed through her body and she gasped.

"That's almost an hour away." As anticipation zoomed through her, Sienna struggled to breathe. "What are we going to do to fill the time?"

He slid his hand beneath her hair, playing with a loose curl before cupping her nape. "We could start with a cocktail?"

"We could…" The slow buildup of hunger was both torment and pleasure. The ache between her thighs needed relief, but she was loving the hazy rise of passion too much to rush.

His thumb brushed her cheek. "Or…"

"Yes?" She set her hand over his, ready to guide him to where she burned.

"I have a couple other ideas."

Suspecting they would be far more intoxicating than alcohol, she purred, "Do tell."

"How about I show you instead?"

He took her by the shoulders and turned her until she faced away from him. Her nerve endings prickled with delight as he shifted the heavy drape of her hair aside and trailed his hot breath along her neck.

"You smell so good," he murmured, dipping his nose into the sensitive skin beneath her ear.

"Oh," she blurted out in a breathless moan, moisture breaking out on her skin as his tongue flicked the underside of her ear.

"Oh?" he echoed, his wicked laugh making her nipples tighten and her stomach muscles clench.

"Oh."

A throaty half chuckle, half cry tore free from her as he caged her body against his with a palm over her ribs just below her breasts. Although she couldn't have summoned the strength to escape his embrace even if she'd been inclined, she could only quiver and pant as he drove her crazy. He nuzzled and nipped down her neck and along her shoulders. The combination of soft lips and rough stubble caused her intimate muscles to contract.

"Sienna." He whispered her name and she melted, her bones liquifying as he skimmed his fingertips over her abdomen and hesitated just below her belly button.

"Yes, Ethan?"

He traced the top edge of her panties through the fabric of her dress. "Can I touch you?"

"Yes." Her voice, stripped bare and raw, broke as his fingers slid toward her mound. "Please."

A whimper built in her throat when he shifted direction and coasted his hand over her hip and down her leg. At the rate he was moving, it would take forever before he located the hem of her dress. To aid him, she grabbed handfuls of the silky material, lifting the long skirt and baring her thighs to his questing touch. She sucked in one wildly erratic breath after another as she waited for him to reach the impatient throbbing between her thighs.

"Ethan." Reaching back, she gripped his thigh and rotated her hips, rocking against the bulge hardening below his belt.

"Sweet mercy, woman," he growled.

"Touch me," she rumbled back between clenched teeth, the depth of her lust fueling her desperation.

"Easy."

But chaotic cravings tormented her. For a second she thought he might be inclined to tease her further and she was about to go into more detail where she so badly wanted his hands, but then the pads of his fingers drifted past the raised hem and stroked the front of her panties, grazing her clit through the fragile barrier. Pleasure detonated in her belly, ripping a startled cry from her, followed by a long moan. She quaked and shuddered as he touched her in the exact same spot again before venturing lower.

"Holy sh…" he hissed as he feathered the panel above her core. "You are so wet."

"Do that again. Only more." She was unconcerned that she was begging. "Please."

Ethan dipped beneath the elastic of her waistband and slipped over her folds. "How's this?"

"Good."

"Good?" His husky tone caressed her senses even as his long fingers slanted into her wetness, spreading the moisture over her clit over and over, circling it in relentless, intoxicating strokes. "Let's see if we can't do better."

Craving his invasion, she widened her stance, opening herself up. He teased her entrance, before gently easing a finger inside. Her breath stopped as he touched a particular spot inside her. Her vision went black for a second as pleasure rocked her.

"Oh…"

"You like that?" The husky question brought her back to

the cabin and the wonderful play of his finger as it moved in and out of her.

Dizzy with pleasure, she rocked her hips and he increased the pace to match. Her legs trembled as her skin burned. Too hot. Too reckless. She needed…to…come…

Sweat broke out on her forehead as her climax began building. She strained toward the goal, barely aware that she'd thrown her head back against Ethan's shoulder and there were wild sounds erupting from her throat.

"Come for me," he crooned, fingering her faster, deeper, driving her toward a powerful orgasm. "Let it go."

And then she became unhinged. As she gasped for a breath that would never come, her hips bucked and twitched. She ground herself against Ethan's hand and felt the pleasure tearing loose inside her. She was poised on the edge.

"Sienna."

It was her name on his lips and the tortured breath he sucked in that pushed her into an electric orgasm. Twisting her face toward him, she closed her eyes and focused on the fire burning up through her core and spreading to every cell in her body. Lightning flashed behind her eyelids as Ethan's mouth closed over hers, his tongue plunging deep inside as she climaxed like never before.

Aftershocks continued to rock Sienna as her consciousness resettled into her body. Grounded once more, she realized Ethan's arm around her waist was the only thing keeping her on her feet. A lusty chuckle gusted out of her.

"Wow." She turned in the circle of his arms and slid her arms around his neck. "That was amazing."

She was just about to plant her lips against his and begin round two when the muffled thumps of footsteps sounded above her head.

"Damn." Ethan settled his forehead against hers with an

unhappy groan that echoed the frustration raging in Sienna. As lively voices filtered down from the deck, he gave her a brief kiss that was filled with promise before he stepped back and raked his fingers through his hair. Shooting her a sidelong glance, he murmured, "To be continued."

Ethan gestured for Sienna to precede him from the cabin, giving him a much-needed couple of seconds to recover from the explosive moment he'd just shared with her. As far as revelations went, the most obvious one was that despite her appearance of reserve when it came to sex, she turned it on faster than any woman he'd ever known. He was all the more eager to get her into bed. In fact, the urge to blow off this impromptu party with his cousin and her friends and take Sienna back to his house immediately was strong as he reached the top step and stopped just behind Sienna, reluctant to join the chaos of six chattering women all trying to fix drinks and organize the food they'd brought.

He curved his hand over Sienna's waist, noticing a slight buzz of energy at the contact as he leaned down to murmur, "If you don't want to stay, we could make some excuse and get out of here."

Relief flashed on her face. "Could we?" She smiled uncertainly as she gazed toward the animated women. "It wouldn't be rude to just take off?"

"I'm not sure they'd notice," he murmured, grazing his fingertips up her bare arm and along her shoulder blades to the nape of her neck, smiling when she shivered. Damn, the woman was sensitive. "And I'd really like to continue what we started earlier."

"So would I," she purred.

He hadn't pegged her as a woman who would sleep with a guy on the second date. Date? Is that what they were doing? Damn. He'd sure been behaving more like he had a romantic interest in Sienna than he was spending time with her to ferret out whatever information he could about her sister's plans for his family.

"We need some sort of an excuse for why we have to go," he said, reaching for his phone.

Several new emails had come in since he'd last looked and his blood froze as it had often since the first message about Teagan from his anonymous friend. Relief swept through him as cued up his email and saw nothing that immediately worried him, but near the bottom was one from a sender he hadn't been expecting.

Ethan had to give the address a hard look before he realized what he was seeing. A preternatural calm came over him as his attention shifted from the email address of the genetic testing service they'd used to find Teagan to the subject of the message. A match had been found. Worry drove a cold spike into his gut. Had the service made a mistake or was it possible they'd found another child of Ava Watts?

He cursed.

Sienna glanced over her shoulder at him. "Is something wrong?" She covered his hand where it rested on her waist and the warm pressure grounded him.

Ethan shook his head to clear it. "I'm not sure," he muttered, keeping his voice low to avoid being overheard. And then for good measure, he brought his lips close to her ear and added, "I got an email from the genetic testing service."

The women's voices fell away as Sienna turned around and fixed him with her gaze. Their lips were so close, the tiniest movement would put her mouth in contact with his. He could lose himself in the lush softness of her lips and forget about the damn email for at least a little while.

"Something having to do with Teagan?"

"I don't know. Let me check."

Ethan opened the email and read the message. His heart stopped. He reread the words. A curse slipped from his lips as their implication washed over him.

"Ethan?" Sienna's hand curved over his thigh, sending his nerve endings into overdrive. "Is something wrong?"

Her voice sounded as if it came from a long way off. Blood roared in his ears. He read the message again as if doing so might change the words and alter the meaning.

"Are you okay?"

"No." He had no idea what question he was answering. "I mean, yes, I'm okay. Everything's fine."

He looked up and found Sienna's blue-gray eyes fastened on him. The concern he read there caught him off guard. She didn't know him. How could she possibly be concerned about him? And yet there it was.

"It's just… I really need to get out of here," he said. "I'll go get our stuff and meet you on the dock."

To his relief, she merely nodded and began moving toward the women. Ethan's heart was pumping madly as he grabbed their shoes and walked through the group, adding his excuses to Sienna's as he went.

"Where are you going?" Poppy demanded as he bid her goodbye and kissed her cheek.

"This party is a little too rowdy." Ethan lacked the wits to come up with a better excuse.

Poppy regarded him dubiously. "You usually like being the only guy surrounded by a pack of beautiful women." Poppy's gaze went past him to where Sienna waited. "Or maybe it's just one beautiful woman you're interested in these days."

"Ah…" Damn, what did he say?

Poppy leaned in and murmured, "We all think she's great."

Ethan forced a smile. He lacked the time or the inclination to explain that his interest in Sienna was in part to keep an eye on what she and Teagan were up to regarding the CEO position at Watts Shipping. That was his problem and for now, he didn't want it to influence how any of the other members of his family viewed Teagan.

He gave a short nod. "That she is."

Arriving beside Sienna on the dock, he handed over her sandals and purse. While she slipped into her shoes, he took a few seconds to clamp down his expression and gather his scattered emotions.

"Okay, what's going on?" Sienna demanded when he took her hand and began to move along the dock. "You seem really freaked out."

"The service found a match." He exhaled, surprised how shaky he felt. "For me. A family member wants to make contact. If I agree, the testing service will make our email addresses available to each other."

Through his daze, Ethan noticed Sienna scrutinizing his expression and immediately wondered if he'd just made a huge mistake. No doubt she was already dying to run to Teagan with the information so they could plot how best to use it to oust him from Watts Shipping.

"That's good news, right?" she said, nothing but concern in her voice.

"I guess." He met her gaze, fearing his stark confusion was on full display. "I didn't see this coming."

"But you took a test. Didn't you think you'd make a connection?"

"It's been months. I didn't imagine that I'd connect with anyone." He paused, letting that sink in for a moment, before finishing, "After all this time."

"I get it." And no doubt she did, having experienced her sister's recent discovery about her connection to the Watts family. "Teagan had been in the database for almost two years before she found you guys."

Sienna squeezed Ethan's hand. Her show of solicitude appeared genuine and part of him welcomed her comfort. But a stronger impulse warned him to reject her reassurance. He couldn't appear weak. When he stiffened, Sienna frowned, but maintained her firm hold. Her solace pained him. How could he accept her help when he didn't trust her?

"Sorry," he murmured. "It's a lot to take in."

And he wasn't accustomed to sharing his true self with anyone. Much less exposing his innermost fears to someone he shouldn't trust.

"Of course it is." Her gaze softened. "I imagine your head is spinning right now."

He forced his lips into a smile, resenting her compassion even as it warmed him. "It is."

"If you need a sympathetic ear to hear you out, I have some idea what you're going through."

They'd only just met, yet she obviously hoped he'd bare his soul to her. That was brazen of her. Why didn't she assume he'd save his confidences for his family? Yet when he considered how upset his mother and father would be when they discovered he'd been searching for his blood relatives, Ethan realized that having a neutral person to talk to might be helpful. Not that Sienna was a disinterested party. He needed to worry what she'd share with Teagan.

"Maybe tomorrow," he heard himself saying, troubled by the temptation to confide in her. "I need some time to wrap my head around things."

"Whenever you're ready, I'll be there for you."

Ethan blew out his breath as emotions buffeted him. "You know," he began slowly, measuring his words. "I never thought about how this must've been for Teagan. Or maybe I didn't want to think about it."

Sienna paused before answering, as if carefully preparing her response. "It's been a roller coaster of a few months," she admitted. "I think it's the fear of the unknown that worried her so much in the beginning."

"That was a concern for our family, as well. You know about Lia's and my role in that." Guilt flashed through him. He rubbed his eyes. "It caused a lot of confusion and no small amount of heartache when the truth came out. And then we found out about Teagan." He heaved a sigh. "Once the initial proof determined she was Ava's daughter, our family was excited that we'd found her at last, but wary, as well."

"Your mother said you'd been searching for her for a long time."

"Years and years. I don't know why it hadn't occurred to us to try a genetic testing service sooner."

"Maybe you didn't expect that Teagan would be looking for you in return."

"Why was she looking?"

"After our father made it clear that he wanted our brother to run Burns Properties, Teagan became determined to find her biological family. I think it was the first time she got a taste of what it felt to be snubbed." She covered her mouth, eyes widening as if regretting the disloyal remark. "It was a stressful journey for her, but I know she's really happy to find you all."

"It's been good for us." Beneath his lighthearted response was a deep well of melancholy he'd kept hidden. "Being able to bring her back to the family has given my grandfather a great deal of peace."

"It's none of my business and you don't have to tell me if you don't want to, but what prompted you to look for your biological family?"

"You mean after all this time? Why now?"

Sienna nodded. "Was it because your family was so determined to find your missing cousin?"

"I guess seeing the happy ending that we got with Teagan made me think my own could be just as good."

"But now you're not sure?"

"It's definitely a step into the unknown." He was shocked by the acute fear twisting in his gut. It was clear that he'd assumed the genetic testing service was a long shot and hadn't prepared for the potential heartache of learning the reasons he'd been rejected by his birth mother.

And was he afraid of who she might be? In Teagan's case, she'd been adopted by one of Manhattan's wealthiest and most influential families and found out her birth family was equally powerful in Charleston. How would she have felt if she'd been the daughter of a couple of nobodies who could cause her embarrassment? Teagan's businesses thrived because of her public image. Negative publicity from some deadbeat relatives could become problematic.

Ethan might not have those same concerns, but he did have a lot of money. If his birth family wasn't well off, meeting Ethan might be akin to finding out they had a relative who'd won the lottery. They might all descend on him with their hands out.

"As for why I started looking," he continued, "it's like I'm out of sync with the rest of my family. Nothing concrete has happened and I can't point to what prompted me to feel as if I don't belong."

This time when Sienna attempted to soothe him, he didn't resist. In fact, he was thinking the best way to escape the heavy emotions weighing him down would be to re-create the moment earlier when she'd come hard and fast beneath his touch.

"I would never claim to understand the emotions an adopted child or adult might experience," she said, her blue-gray eyes the quiet sea after a storm. "But I'm not a stranger to feeling like an ugly duckling among a family of swans."

"Something else that's been bothering me since submitting the test," Ethan said, "is what if they weren't looking for me? What if it was just some random test that they took because they were curious about their genealogy? What if they had no idea that they were going to connect with someone?"

"You won't know until you contact them," Sienna said. "But I'm sure no matter what caused them to be in the database, they can't be anything but thrilled to welcome you into their family."

In any case, the genie was well and truly out of the bottle. And instead of clamping down on his inner turmoil and presenting a confident facade to Sienna, he'd given her a significant glimpse of his fear.

"I hope you're right."

Six

Sienna was a little surprised when Ethan insisted on taking her to dinner in the aftermath of learning he was on the verge of connecting with his birth relatives. He took her to the Peninsula Grill where they sat across from each other in a cozy booth beside a hand-painted mural of a low-country rice harvest, sipped coconut cake martinis and ate oyster stew with mushrooms and grits.

Although he seemed mostly present as they chatted about southern cooking, Charleston's history and Sienna's plans to visit the Old Slave Mart Museum the following day, Sienna could tell his attention wavered numerous times during the meal. So, after vacillating between the restaurant's famous coconut cake and key lime pie, finally settling on the latter, Sienna decided to address the elephant in the room.

"I know earlier we talked about continuing our evening in a more private setting," she began, heat flooding her cheeks as she replayed their sexy encounter on the boat.

"But I think you've got a lot on your mind and I should probably head back to the estate."

"I do and you deserve nothing less than my full attention."

Despite her disappointment with how the evening was ending, Sienna's lips twitched into a half smile when he took her hand as they exited the restaurant. After their companionable conversation over dinner, both Ethan and Sienna were silent during the short drive back to his grandfather's home.

For her part, Sienna was keenly aware of his strength and temptingly masculine scent. As they neared the estate, she was on the verge of saying to hell with her earlier decision and begging him to find them a quiet spot to make out when they reached the driveway and the chance slipped away.

Gallant as always, Ethan walked her up the stairs to the front door and punched in the code that unlocked it. Sienna hesitated before entering, her nerves popping and zinging as she wondered if he'd kiss her good-night.

"I'm really glad you came to Charleston," he said, his heartfelt tone surprising her.

Her stomach fluttered. "You are such a charmer," she said, retreating into flirty banter.

"I mean it."

She gave an awkward chuckle. "I'd better go in before I say something foolish and awkward." She'd hoped her teasing would summon one of his heart-stopping smiles, and there it was.

"Like what?"

A breeze caught her hair, blowing strands across her face. With her expression concealed, she summoned the courage to speak her heart. "I like you."

"I like you, too." Ethan swept her hair behind her ears, and then cupped her face. "A whole lot."

Sienna counseled herself not to overthink it as his lips claimed hers in a kiss of such directness and determined passion that her whole body came to life. She moaned as her muscles melted, but before things escalated too far, he broke off the kiss.

"Thanks for dinner," she murmured, setting her hand on the door handle. "And if you want to talk about what came up today...let me know."

"About that," Ethan began, a frown appearing. "Can you not mention that I might've found my birth family?"

"Of course." She was a little shocked that he believed she'd share such an intimate and personal revelation. On the other hand, given his close-knit family, no doubt they had trouble keeping things from each other. "I wouldn't dream of telling anyone."

Sienna was in a thoughtful mood as she trudged up the stairs to her room on the third floor. As she replayed all that had happened in the last few hours, her mind and body tugged her attention in opposite directions. She couldn't settle on what to process first. Although Ethan's discovery about his birth family was by far the safer topic for her to ponder, that incredible kiss on the boat continued to reverberate through her body, filling her with anxiety and eagerness.

The strong attraction between them promised the sex would be fantastic, but with everything he now had going on, she was left to wonder if they'd go out again. And when that happened, how she could make sure next time they'd end up at his house alone?

Suddenly, she was imagining her hands sliding over Ethan's broad chest, her lips gliding down the strong column of his throat. Would he groan when she played with his nipples? Lose his mind when she wrapped her lips around his erection?

"You're home early."

Caught up in her lusty thoughts, Sienna yelped when she entered her room, not realizing Teagan had come up behind her. Her sister crossed to the love seat beneath the window and sprawled on it. Disappointment flooded Sienna. She'd been looking forward to some time alone to relax and fantasize about Ethan. With her sister curiously regarding her, Sienna slammed the door on her emotions lest Teagan figure out a way to use them to her advantage.

"What are you doing up here?" Sienna asked, dropping her clutch onto the bed and kicking off her heels.

"Looking for you." Teagan swung her feet off the love seat and patted the empty space beside her. "Come tell me all about your dates with Ethan."

Sienna's blood froze. "They weren't dates."

"So we did all this for nothing?" Teagan said skeptically, pointing her finger at Sienna and tracing random squiggles in the air to indicate the makeover. "Tell me, does he like your new look?"

"I guess." Her heartbeat sped up as she recalled his long, slow perusal of her new dress and the way his attention had lingered over her legs, cleavage and lips.

"You guess." Teagan's drawl said she wasn't fooled by her sister's stab at indifference. "Is that why you're turning red? Because you only guess he liked your new look?" When Sienna just stared at her, Teagan gave a throaty laugh. "As for it not being a date, let's talk about that, shall we? You went out for dinner."

"Yes, but he was just being friendly since you were going out with the twins."

Teagan arched an eyebrow. "It's nearly eleven. I'm sure you haven't been eating all this time. So, what did you do after dinner?"

"We talked a bit. He took me for a walk down to the

waterfront. The city is just as beautiful at night as it is during the day."

"And did he kiss you?"

Sienna rolled her eyes as if this was a ridiculous question, but saw from her sister's broadening grin that Teagan wasn't fooled.

"From your blush I'd say he did kiss you. Did it curl your toes? Or did you do one of those rom-com foot lifts?"

When Siena stared blankly at her sister, Teagan leaped to her feet and pantomimed lifting one foot off the ground while her arms were wrapped around an invisible lover.

Had she? To be fair it was possible. Her whole body stopped behaving rationally the instant his lips touched hers. As for curling her toes… There was no question in her mind that his kisses had done many disquieting things to her anatomy.

"Don't be ridiculous."

"You like him." Part glee, part taunt, Teagan's declaration plowed into Sienna like a runaway train.

"He's very nice. And so different from the men I meet in Manhattan." Or anywhere else for that matter. Even before Teagan and the twins had taken her shopping or Poppy had cut and highlighted her hair, Ethan had treated her like a woman he was interested in getting to know better.

"Is it that smooth Southern drawl of his? I'll bet it's persuaded more than a few women to do naughty things." Teagan looked like she was enjoying herself a little too much at her sister's expense. "Or his charming manners that hide the fact that he's a wolf in sheep's clothing?"

These reminders of Ethan's player reputation seemed at odds with Teagan's earlier matchmaking. Did her sister want Sienna and Ethan to get together or not?

"I think it's the fact that he doesn't rush me about anything," Sienna said. "The way he takes his time allows me to relax. But I think the best thing is that he never tries to compete with me. He just let me talk and talk. Nobody does that."

"*You* talked?" Teagan made no effort to hide her surprise. "That's not like you."

It irritated Sienna that her sister assumed her reserve was part of her nature instead of a reaction to their dynamic. From the moment Teagan had arrived in the Burns household, Sienna had been relegated to the background. Teagan commanded everyone's attention and had no qualms about overshadowing anyone who tried to be noticed.

"Maybe you don't know me as well as you think," Sienna murmured.

"Don't be ridiculous," Teagan declared, all frivolity fading from her manner. "You are an open book to me."

"Really?" Sienna made no effort to hide her scorn. Teagan was far too consumed with her own issues to bother with her sister's complex inner world. "So you know what I've been going through these last few months since you found out you were related to the Wattses?"

"You were happy for me."

Something strong and dark rose up in Sienna, a wave of anger and sadness that shocked her with its intensity. "That was only part of it."

"What else?" Teagan asked, looking completely baffled.

Sienna sucked in a steadying breath and let it out slowly. "I was worried about losing you."

"Why?"

"You'd been obsessed with finding your birth family for so long, and then you found them." Sienna was conflicted about opening up and telling her sister how much she loved her. What if Teagan brushed aside the confession as if it didn't matter? "You wouldn't need me anymore."

"That would never happen," Teagan assured her, flopping back onto the love seat. "You are my sister. That will never change."

"I know that." But deep in her heart lurked that niggling bit of envy at how quickly Teagan had bonded with her Shaw cousins. The three women didn't just look alike, they were outgoing, shared a love of fashion and enjoyed being social.

"So let's get back to you and Ethan. Are you going to sleep with him?"

"Teagan!" Sienna felt her cheeks heat. Confiding in her sister about Ethan would be extremely foolish. "I like him, but that's as far as it goes."

"Well, if you decide to take it further, know that I am wholeheartedly on your side. You are so serious and I think he'd be good for you." Teagan sounded completely genuine. "And since I'm planning on staying in Charleston, it would be nice to have someone besides me to visit whenever you come back to town."

This reminder that her sister intended on taking Watts Shipping away from Ethan dimmed Sienna's good mood. "Anything between Ethan and me won't survive if you succeed in becoming the CEO at his company."

"One has nothing to do with the other," Teagan said, her dismissal coming fast and hard.

"Don't be so sure. I'm your sister. He'll know I'm on your side." And afterward, win or lose, Sienna doubted he'd want to have anything more to do with her.

Teagan narrowed her eyes as she regarded her sister. "You don't expect me to give up my interest in Watts Shipping because you want to hook up with Ethan?"

"No." Sienna dreaded what Teagan would do if she thought Sienna was standing in the way of her plan. "I'm just being realistic. With what you are trying to do, there will come a time where I can't be loyal to both you and him. And when that day comes, you are my sister. You know where I stand."

The morning after Ethan received the notification from the genetic testing service, he swung by Paul's cybersecurity company on his way to Watts Shipping. After dropping Sienna off at his grandfather's house, he'd sent an affirmative response about connecting to his blood relative through the testing service and learned the person looking for him was his birth mother.

After receiving her name and email address, he'd composed a brief, cautious email and sent it, shocked at how his heart had pounded. While waiting for her response, he'd been unable to sleep. Thoughts swirled and bumped in his mind like koi in an overstocked pond. He'd considered how his mother and father would react. Paul was the only member of his family who knew Ethan was looking for his biological family. He hadn't wanted to upset his parents with the search, knowing that they'd both take it hard. It wasn't that they hadn't been great or that he didn't love them deeply, but lately he'd been hounded by this feeling that a piece of himself was missing.

Maybe it was because in the last ten years his grandfather had grown more and more agitated about his missing granddaughter, spurring Ethan to wonder if someone in his birth family was desperately searching for him. He hadn't anticipated the turmoil of dread and eagerness that would erupt when he discovered they were.

"Sorry to drop by without calling," Ethan said, taking a seat on the couch in Paul's office. He accepted a cup of coffee and scrutinized his brother's face. "Damn. You look really good."

"You say that like it's a bad thing."

"I guess I'm still trying to get used to you looking so relaxed and…happy."

Paul smirked. "Quite a change, isn't it?"

Before Lia had come into his life, Paul had been completely absorbed in his business. Since falling for the free spirit, he'd shifted more responsibility to his staff so he could spend more time with his fiancée. Accustomed as Ethan was to his older brother's serious nature, the way Paul smiled all the time these days, and knowing that Lia was the reason, gave Ethan a great deal of satisfaction. After all, she wouldn't be in Paul's life if Ethan hadn't persuaded her to pretend to be their cousin in the first place.

"Honestly, it's a shock that you're in a good mood all the time."

"It's love. You should give it a try."

Ethan shook his head. "You can't expect me to settle down with one girl when there are so many out there looking for a good time."

"I might've bought your too-many-fish-in-the-sea argument before I met Lia. But from the moment she entered my life, I knew that committing fully to the woman I love is the only way to go."

"I'll take your word for it," Ethan said dryly, concealing a flash of envy at what his brother had found with Lia. "But I didn't come here to talk to you about your love life. There are a couple of things on my mind right now. First off, did you have any luck figuring out who sent the emails about Teagan?"

"No. Whoever it is covered their tracks very well."

"Almost as if they knew that a cybersecurity specialist might be hunting them down," Ethan put in.

"Do you think if we dig deeper into her background, we'll find a lot of people who have it in for her?"

"Probably." Ethan didn't find it strange that a successful New York businesswoman had picked up an enemy or two. But was that all it was? Someone out to make trouble for Teagan?

"So, can we check into some of those people?"

"Already on it." Paul gave his brother a searching look. "But all this is something we could've talked about over the phone. What's your real reason for stopping by?"

"I got a different sort of email yesterday."

"Another warning? Or some kind of threat?"

"Neither." Ethan leaned forward, his forearms resting on his thighs, his fingers intertwined. "I submitted my own genetic material for testing."

Paul sat back, understanding dawning. "You got a hit."

"I got a hit," Ethan echoed. "Last night while I was out to dinner with Sienna. She gave me some things to think about."

"Such as?"

"How my reaching out to my birth family will impact the people who raised me and the brother I love."

"If you're worried that Mom and Dad will feel betrayed that you were curious about where you came from, don't be. The minute we found Teagan we all understood what it's like to fill the hole that's been in our lives." Paul paused and considered his brother's expression. "Plus, it's not as if you're going to find anyone better than us."

Paul's unexpected humor made Ethan grin. "The best thing I ever did was invite Lia into our family. She's had an enormously positive effect on you."

"Typical Ethan," Paul said. "Always taking credit for other people's hard work."

"So, you think Mom and Dad will be okay that I've done this?"

"I think they'll support you in whatever you have to do. You know that."

Ethan nodded. "I'll tell them after my trip to Savannah."

"What's in Savannah?"

"My birth mother."

"What?" Paul breathed, looked uncharacteristically staggered. "You found…"

"Her name is Carolina Gates." His voice faltered on her name. "I'm heading down there Wednesday night to meet her."

Paul was recovering his equilibrium. "I think you should tell Mom and Dad before you go."

"What if it doesn't go well with Carolina? Why upset our parents before I figure out if I intend to have a relationship with her?"

"You always keep a wall up between you and those of us who love you. One of these days you're going to find out what a mistake that is."

"Maybe." Ethan bristled. Paul couldn't stop himself from playing all-knowing older brother. "In the meantime, I was hoping you could do a little research on my birth relatives so I know what I'm getting into."

"Of course." Paul pulled out his phone and quickly typed something into it. "I'm glad you're taking steps to protect yourself."

"You know I'm always careful," Ethan said while in the back of his mind crazed laughter erupted.

Who was he kidding? His behavior had grown more destructive over the last year. From lying to everyone about Lia being Ava's daughter to keeping this enormous secret about his search for his birth relatives from his adoptive family and isolating himself in the process. And of course he was letting himself get far too involved with Sienna when he knew she didn't have his best interest at heart.

"I can clear my schedule if you want company on your trip to Savannah."

"I wouldn't want to take you away from Lia."

"Given the situation, I'm sure she wouldn't mind if I was gone for a few days."

While Ethan didn't want to involve his family, Paul's offer made Ethan realize that it would be nice to have company, someone he could talk to if things got a little too intense. Last night Sienna had demonstrated she understood what he was going through, having recently experienced a similar situation with her sister.

"Thanks," Ethan said. "But I think I'll ask Sienna to come with me to Savannah."

"Sienna?" Paul's eyes narrowed. "But you barely know her."

"True, but she's already been through this with her sister and it'll be easier to be with someone who isn't emotionally involved."

"I thought you didn't trust her."

How did Ethan explain his increasingly conflicted feelings about Sienna? "Not when it comes to helping her sister take over Watts Shipping, but I think in this instance, she'll be helpful."

And with the two of them alone in Savannah, they could more fully explore the attraction between them. Ethan was looking forward to that as much as meeting his birth mother.

"I guess you know what you're doing," Paul said, sounding like a skeptical older brother.

"If I don't," Ethan began with a dry smile, "it wouldn't be the first time I ended up in over my head." But until things blew up, he intended to have the time of his life.

Seven

Sienna sat on the back terrace, laptop open on the table before her, gaze riveted on the charismatic man heading in her direction along the garden pathway. If her sudden breathlessness was anything to go by, her attraction to him had only grown since last night.

"There you are," he declared, a warm smile drawing her attention to the sensual curve of his lips. "I was looking for you."

She closed her laptop and gestured to the chair beside her. He shook his head and held out his hand.

"Walk with me instead."

Sienna couldn't help the delight that spread through her as she took his hand. When he led her away from the house to the relative privacy of the pool house, she had a pretty good idea of what this was about.

"You got an email from your birth family."

"My birth mother." He pulled a folder out of his briefcase. "This was what Paul was able to find on her."

Sienna stared at the thick file, wondering if the cyber-security specialist had created similar dossiers on her and Teagan. As soon as the question popped into her mind, she knew the answer. Of course he had. And no doubt Ethan had read both. So, with all his questions about what she did, he'd already known the answers. Sienna felt the tiniest bit betrayed, but pushed the feeling inside. Given the Wattses' wealth, they would've been crazy not to investigate Teagan and her adoptive family.

"Who is she?" she prompted, curiosity getting the better of her.

"Carolina Gates from Savannah, Georgia. Her family owns Gates Multimedia. My mother…" He swallowed hard, Adam's apple bobbing as he grappled with his feelings. "She submitted the DNA test after finding out I was alive."

Sienna gasped. "What? She thought you were dead? How?"

"She didn't go into the details, but it sounds like she was seventeen when she got pregnant with me and it was a complicated birth. Long story short, she thought I died."

Hearing the anguish in Ethan's voice, Sienna gripped his arm. Part of her wanted to lend him support, but mostly she craved a connection with him in this emotionally charged moment.

"How could she not know?"

From his somber expression and the crease between his eyebrows, he was bothered by this same question. "She said she'd explain when we met."

"How did she find out you were alive?"

"There was a nurse who knew that I'd survived. She died recently and left a letter with her lawyer for my mother, explaining what had happened."

The whole situation sounded mysterious and Sienna

worried that Ethan might be heading into trouble. "When are you heading to Savannah?"

"I thought I would go down there Wednesday evening and return Sunday. Would you like to come?" This last he said so casually that she thought she'd misheard him.

"I'm not sure I should. This is your first meeting with your biological family."

"It would help if you were there."

His husky-voiced admission made her ache to support him. But it wasn't her place. They barely knew each other. Yet each moment in his company deepened the connection between them. At least on her end. She'd never been in love, but surely this is what it felt like to fall for someone.

"I know it's a lot to ask," Ethan persisted when she didn't give him an immediate answer. "But you've been through this with your sister and since you have so much experience dealing with the whole meeting-the-birth-family thing, I thought maybe you'd understand what I'd be going through."

Although Sienna would never claim to know everything about Ethan after such a short acquaintance, she recognized that asking others for help wasn't something he did easily or at all. Obviously, meeting his birth mother entailed more emotional upheaval than he wanted to go through alone.

"Wouldn't you be better off bringing one of your own family?"

"Honestly, I like the idea of having a neutral party along. I'd be afraid if I asked anyone from my family that they would make it all about them." He caught her gaze and held it. "You haven't done that with Teagan. I could really use your company."

Sienna didn't think he would've asked her without feeling an actual need. She told herself not to be flattered. She was a logical choice given everything he just explained.

But the trip might be a good opportunity to see where their connection might lead.

"If you think it would be helpful then I'd be happy to go with you." Sienna paused. "Let me run it past Teagan first. After all, she's the reason I'm here in the first place."

"Of course. I wouldn't want to take you away from your sister. But if you could not mention anything about my birth mother. I haven't figured out what I'm going to tell my parents yet."

"I understand perfectly." Sienna recalled their mother's devastation when Teagan announced that she'd been searching for her blood relatives. "I'll get back to you as soon as I can."

Since Teagan had made plans to go out with the Shaw twins after work, Sienna knew she wouldn't run into her sister at the house and reached out by phone.

"Ethan invited me to go with him to Savannah for a long weekend," she announced when Teagan answered, aware that her voice reflected how excited she was by the prospect. "I thought it sounded like fun."

She expected Teagan to grill her about the trip. But even if Ethan hadn't specifically asked her to keep the reason for the visit secret, Sienna wouldn't have mentioned anything about going to meet his birth mother. This was something Teagan would love to use to stir up turmoil between Ethan and his family.

"He wants to take you out of town," Teagan said, her voice filled with glee. "That's perfect."

Sienna's radar went on full alert. "What do you mean perfect?"

"Just that I know you really like him," Teagan replied, her breezy tone giving nothing away. "And it seems as if he's into you, as well."

"I don't know if that's true," Sienna hastened to assure

Teagan. "He invited me along because he thought I might
be interested in seeing a little bit more of the South."

The excuse sounded incredibly lame to her own ears,
but what did it matter if her sister thought Sienna and Ethan
were running away for a romantic few days? Except that
Teagan was obsessed with the top position at Watts Shipping and would use any means to sabotage Ethan's chance.
Including her sister.

"I think he's interested in seeing a little bit more of you."
Teagan's sly glee tainted what could've been a supportive
declaration. "And if you can keep him there longer, please
feel free. The less time he's around, the more time I have
to convince everyone I'm the best one to run the company."

There it was.

Suddenly, Sienna's eagerness to go away with Ethan
dimmed. She hated being caught between her sister, whom
she loved, and the man she was eager to get to know better.

"You know I hate being a part of your schemes," she said
as if stating the obvious would influence her sister's plans.

"What scheme?" Teagan countered. "All I'm looking
for is an opportunity to show everyone at the company
what I can do without Ethan's years of experience overshadowing me."

Sienna rubbed her temple where a painful hammering
kept time with her heartbeat. "Have you been up-front with
Ethan about your interest in being the CEO?"

"Why?" Teagan scoffed. "So he can block me at every
turn? The direct approach isn't going to work and you know
it."

Teagan's determined words warned Sienna that any argument she might make would fall on deaf ears. Her sister had decided on a course of action and she would see it
through to its bitter end.

"I still think you should say something to him," Sienna grumbled, aware that she was wasting her breath.

"I'll think about it," Teagan said, her tone saying she'd do no such thing. "Meanwhile, keep him nice and distracted in Savannah for me. And be careful. If he finds out how you feel about him, he'll use that to turn you against me."

"Ethan isn't like that." But even as the hot denial left her lips, she wondered if that was true. How far would he go to secure the CEO position? Was he as ruthless as Teagan? Willing to use any means—anyone—to achieve his goals?

"I've talked to people," Teagan countered. "He's exactly like that."

Knowing it was fruitless to dig for information about her sister's supposed sources, Sienna murmured something noncommittal before ending the call. She sent Ethan a quick text indicating she was free to go, and then turned her attention to what she might take with her. She'd replaced her battered suitcase with a brand-new set of luggage that would accommodate her recently expanded wardrobe.

Sienna opened the armoire and regarded her newly purchased clothes, wondering what she should take. Teagan and the twins had encouraged her to buy things that were perfectly suited for the climate and highlighted her curves. Yet she still felt a little bit like an imposter when she wore them. Teagan believed that fashion made the woman and had been badgering Sienna for years to adopt whatever look was trending.

It wasn't that Sienna couldn't be bothered to shop or spend time becoming a more glamorous version of herself; it was more that she hated being compared to her thinner, beautiful, fashion-forward sister. But was this even an issue anymore? They were no longer in school where every second of every day their peers offered brutal critiques and doled out humiliation.

Buying clothes that flattered her figure and made her feel feminine and happy, followed by seeing Ethan's re-action to her appearance, Sienna knew she'd undergone a fashion revolution. But although she couldn't imagine reverting back to her conservative, well-made suits and monochromatic color palette, she couldn't abandon them altogether.

She selected a couple outfits suitable for meeting Ethan's family and dinners out as well as some more casual things for daytime. After their first moonlight kiss, she'd indulged in some truly luxurious lingerie, and carefully packed every silky item in her new suitcase. She intended to be prepared in case being all alone with Ethan for several days led to something happening between them.

Immediately her body was awash in anticipation, but Sienna took herself in hand. Ethan would be totally focused on meeting his birth mother. The last thing he would be thinking about would be sex with her. Still, she couldn't stop herself from hoping that he'd turn to her if the week-end became emotionally overwhelming. And she planned to welcome him with open arms.

Ethan picked Sienna up at his grandfather's house a lit-tle after five. During the two-hour drive from Charleston to Savannah, Sienna watched the landscape flow by and didn't once complain about Ethan's silence. Now, as they neared Savannah, his sense of urgency was transforming into anxiety. Since discovering his birth mother wanted to find him, he'd been focused on meeting her as soon as possible. Now he felt the first inklings of doubt holding him back.

When the sign for the Georgia state line flashed by, Ethan realized he had a death grip on the steering wheel. He flexed his fingers and blew out a long, slow breath.

"Are you okay?"

"For years I thought my mother gave me up, and now I find out she had no idea I was even alive. I didn't acknowledge how angry I was about not being wanted by her until I was notified about the match and now…" He clamped his lips together, recoiling from the wild churn of emotion that swept over him.

The wide expanse of Little Black River appeared ahead of them, its wind-ruffled surface sparkling with early evening sunlight. Bright shards lanced into his eyes, making them water. He blinked rapidly and cleared his vision.

"Now?" she prompted.

"I'm still mad," he went on, "but also relieved. And anxious. There's something troubling in why she thought I was dead and I'm not sure what sort of a situation I'm walking into."

Recognizing his distress, Sienna squeezed his arm in a friendly manner. Her touch galvanized him and without thinking, Ethan reached out and wrapped his fingers around hers. The contact immediately soothed his unease.

"I'm sure she has a lot of story to tell."

He was grateful for her knack for reading his moods and going with the flow. Just one of several things about her he appreciated. He wondered if she had any idea that during the drive, when he wasn't brooding, he'd been eye-balling the impressive amount of silky leg and cleavage bared by her flirty red-and-white polka-dot wrap dress and pondering how quickly he could get her out of it once they arrived.

"Do you want to stop for dinner before we get to where we're staying?" he asked, a hefty dose of lust lightening his mood. "Or settle in, and then go out?"

"There's a third option," she said, pausing for emphasis. "We could order room service."

He cleared his throat. "Actually, I had my assistant rent us a house, so I'm afraid we're fending for ourselves." He'd been eager to have Sienna all to himself without the awkwardness of public hallways and electronic door locks. "I thought you'd enjoy being in the historic district and as it happens, my birth mother's home is within walking distance."

"I can't wait to explore." Her warm tone gave no hint of reluctance or concern. "Since we'll have a kitchen, why don't we pick up groceries so I can fix us something."

He liked the idea that she wanted to cook for him. The domesticity felt oddly intimate. "That sounds good."

Ethan gave her the address of the house where they were staying and Sienna used her phone to search for the nearest place to buy what they needed. She located a grocery store and began navigating. Her initiative intrigued him. The women he dated expected him to plan and execute everything. In contrast, Sienna demonstrated she was accustomed to doing things on her own. Being with her felt more like a partnership and he enjoyed sharing responsibility with her.

After the grocery stop, they drove through the historic district toward Forsyth Park and their accommodations.

"Did you ever consider coming here for college?" He indicated a sign for Savannah College of Art and Design.

"New York's School of Visual Arts was my first pick, but I actually applied to SCAD as well as several other art schools around the country. SCAD is a great school and what they've done to revitalize Savannah is really impressive, but I am a New York City girl at heart."

Ethan was still pondering her remark as he escorted Sienna up the front walk of the home his assistant had rented for them. He'd been so caught up in the anxiety of meeting his birth mother that he hadn't considered that Sienna would be heading back to New York after their time in Savannah was done. Her leaving meant Teagan would no longer have the advantage of a spy at her disposal. He should've felt relief. Instead, the thought of not seeing Sienna every day filled him with dismay.

Had she told her sister about the reason for their trip to Savannah despite his specific request to keep the matter quiet? It had been a test. If Sienna spilled his secret, he would know exactly what she was made of and that she couldn't be trusted. He had yet to consider what he'd do if she kept his confidence.

"This is a lot of space for just the two of us," she remarked as they entered the expansive foyer, carrying the groceries and their bags.

The rental was a three-thousand-square-foot historic house across from Forsyth Park, a block down from the landmark fountain, one of the most famous sights in Savannah. Given Sienna's love of all things that gave a city its character, he was looking forward to viewing Savannah through her eyes.

"I wanted to make sure you were in the middle of everything."

They found a chef's kitchen at the back of the house and while Sienna put the groceries away, Ethan took their luggage upstairs. Not knowing which of the four bedrooms she'd choose, he left their bags on the landing at the top of the stairs before heading back down. He found Sienna in the living room, perusing one of the guidebooks on Savannah left by the property owner for visitors.

"I did a little reading up before we came." She flashed him a wry smile when he snorted. "And while you're with your family, I will have plenty to keep me occupied."

"About that. I thought maybe you'd come with me to meet my mother. And afterward we can go play tourist." Seeing her surprise at his invitation, he rushed on. "There are a couple graveyards if you're into that as well as several historic buildings and lots to see near the river."

"You didn't come here to sightsee," she reminded him.

"No, but I do so enjoy showing you around."

"Have you spent much time in Savannah?"

Her question awakened him to the fact that he had family here. Family he hadn't known existed until now. Realizing that he had been so close several times in his life to the mother who gave birth to him sent a chill over his skin.

"I've been here a couple times. Once for a wedding and once to apply for an internship during college."

She looked at him in surprise. "An internship? I would've thought that you only worked at Watts Shipping."

"That's basically true. When my older brother followed his passion for computers and started his cybersecurity company it naturally fell to me to step into the family business."

She studied him for a long moment. "Was there something else you wanted to do?"

Was she searching for insight to pass along to her sister? Ethan shoved aside his suspicions for the moment.

"Honestly, I never had the chance to consider if I was passionate about pursuing something different."

"Because no one else in your family showed any interest in Watts Shipping?"

"Something like that."

While it was true that he'd toyed with the idea of not working for the family business, in the end, he knew that others were depending on him. The burden of that had sat heavily on his shoulders for most of his twenties. He pondered his fury over Teagan's plans to take Watts Shipping away from him. How ironic that once he'd stopped resisting the future that had been prescribed for him, a challenger would come along and threaten to usurp a job that he wasn't completely sure he wanted.

And now he'd learned that his blood relatives owned a family business of their own. Maybe there was a place for him there. If so, Ethan could stop worrying about Teagan and explore whatever was happening between him and Sienna.

"Shall we go upstairs and figure out where we're going to sleep?"

He hadn't meant for the question to electrify the atmosphere between them, but suddenly he was imagining her beneath him on the bed, naked and eager. The look she shot at him sent blood pounding through his body.

"Ethan."

It was just his name, yet the sound of her voice, half worried, half entreaty, went through him like an electric charge. He slid his arm around her waist, drawing her against him.

"What are we going to do about this?" he asked, dipping his head to nuzzle the sensitive flesh behind her ear.

She shivered as his lips coasted over her skin. "What do you want to do?"

"I'd like to take you upstairs and spend the rest of the night making you come." He cupped her breast, savoring the full curve. "What do you say?"

"I say…let's go."

Her hesitation, slight as it was, caused him to lift his head and stare down at her expression. "If you're not sure, I understand."

"It isn't that I don't want you or this." She pressed her hand over his where it rested on her breast and offered up a slow smile.

"But?" he prompted.

"I just want…" The vulnerability shining in her blue-gray eyes looked entirely genuine. "To be more than a… distraction."

He snorted. "You've been a distraction from the moment you stepped out of the car on that first day." Something her sister had recognized and was probably trying to capitalize on. Ethan tamped down his suspicions and focused on the heat building in his body. "In the best way possible."

"Oh."

Her dazed expression was so enchanting that for a second Ethan wondered if he was wrong to be suspicious. She'd have to be one hell of an actress to affect guilelessness this long without a single slip.

Well, there was one way he could figure her out. Scooping her into his arms, he headed toward the stairs.

Eight

With her stomach in free fall, Sienna wrapped her arms around Ethan's neck and let herself get swept up. They'd been moving toward this moment since he sat down beside her on the front steps of his grandfather's house. Her chest tightened, limiting the amount of air she could pull into her lungs. She knew it was foolish to feel as if she'd known him forever when in fact, they had met less than a week ago. Yet she found herself reading his mind and noticing every shift of emotion that crossed his expression.

He set her down beside the bed and gave the bow of her wrap dress a gentle tug. The garment fell open as the belt came undone, exposing the satin and lace she wore beneath it. He eased the fabric off her shoulders and sent the dress arcing across the room toward the chair in the corner.

Dipping his head, he grazed his lips over her earlobe, and rumbled, "You are so damn gorgeous."

Men had called her beautiful before, but she took their words with a grain of salt. Ethan's compliment sent vivid emotions blazing through her. Her desperate need to believe him made her surrender her power. She could only hope he'd handle her with care.

She began to unbutton his shirt, eager to explore all the muscle rippling beneath his warm skin. While she worked, he popped the buttons on his cuffs so that by the time she slipped the last one free, his shirt just slid off his shoulders and landed on the floor. With both of them breathing a little hard, they stared at each other for several seconds.

"This is happening," she murmured, her heart climbing into her throat.

His eyebrows rose. "If that's what you want."

Was he seriously giving her an out? Sienna had never been more obsessed about having sex with anyone. When it occurred to her he probably didn't feel the same way, she took a half step back. Was she making too much of this moment?

"Of course it is." Suddenly, she was shivering in the air-conditioned space, awash in discomfort as she stood before him in the silk lingerie she'd purchased with him in mind. "Unless you don't want to."

With a husky laugh he eased his palms along the delicate fabric, riding the curve of her hip and indent of her waist. Up and up to the outer curve of her breasts. She'd forgone a bra and his thumbs whisked over her hard nipples, eliciting a low cry.

"I'll always want to."

Always struck her as a definitive word, suggesting something more complicated than scratching a sexual itch. Panic fluttered in the back of her mind like a trapped bird. This was just supposed to be an easy and fun romp before she went back to New York City.

Shutting down her mind, she lifted one hand to his sun-bronzed biceps and flattened her other palm over his heart. "Make love to me, Ethan."

He stroked the thin straps of her slip off her shoulder. The silky fabric caught on her full breasts so she shimmied and wiggled until it reached her hips, baring her torso to his greedy gaze. He ducked his head and grazed his lips over her nipple. Her back arched as he ran his tongue in a circle around the tight bud.

Sienna spread her fingers and sifted them into his thick hair, using the grip to keep her balance as he kissed his way along the slope of one breast and into the valley of her cleavage before making the ascent on the other side. This time, instead of lightly teasing her nipple, he drew it into his mouth, teeth scraping gently against the sensitive flesh, tongue swirling. The suction made her groan with pleasure. The sound transformed into a whimper as he stroked his fingers into the dampness between her thighs, parting her folds so he could tease her entrance.

"You okay?" he murmured, his drawl thick with pleasure as his lips coasted along her neck.

"Good. Great." She gasped, rocking against his hand, feverish to feel him inside her. "More."

"Like this?"

His fingers plunged inside her, catapulting her back to those moments on the boat when he made her come. She arched her back and welcomed his invasion. Tonight there would be no one to interrupt them.

His strokes became a pattern, a slow thrust of his fingers, a sweep around her clit, followed by another deep penetration. Each circuit drove her desire higher, stole all rational thought, made her wild. She clung to his shoulders, writhing against his hand, a shrill keening breaking from her throat as the torture became unrelenting pleasure.

And then the dam burst and the climax hit her. She

quaked as wave after wave of ecstasy pummeled her. Electrical charges short-circuited her muscles. Her knees gave way and only Ethan's strong arm around her waist kept her upright. Brushing sexy kisses over her lips, he eased them both toward the bed. As the backs of her legs touched the solid surface, she sat down with an awkward "oof" and released a wild chuckle.

"Are you all right?" he asked, peering down at her.

"I'm better than okay." She set her heels on the mattress and lifted her hips to move her slip from beneath her, snagging her silk panties with her thumb as she did so and sliding everything down her thighs, leaving herself utterly, wantonly naked. "Or I will be when you come here."

Ethan hadn't spent the entire time ogling Sienna as she'd stripped. After his own pants had hit the floor, he'd stooped to fish out the condom he'd stashed in his pocket. When he straightened and lifted his gaze to find Sienna reclining like some exotic goddess waiting for her human subject to pleasure her, he could do little more than gape.

"Ethan?" She blinked in concern as she looked at him. "Are you okay?"

With the condom clutched between his fingers, he dropped to his knees beside the bed, settled his shoulders between her parted legs and stared at the glorious untamed bush at the apex of her thighs. The women he knew trimmed and waxed to such an extreme that he'd forgotten how glorious their natural beauty could be.

"You are gorgeous," he murmured, trailing his fingers over her. "This is a total turn-on."

"Oh."

"I'm going to make you come again."

With a surprised bark of laughter, which turned into a sharp cry as he ran his tongue through her hot, damp core,

Sienna gave herself over to his mastery. Quicker than he imagined possible, she came a second time, harder than the first. As she lay like a rag doll, limp except for the agitated rise and fall of her chest, Ethan shifted onto the bed and covered her with his body. With a smile, he brushed a stray lock of hair away from her face.

"I think making you come is the highlight of my day."

In the grasp of a powerful climax, she'd been absolutely breathtaking. And nothing compared to knowing that he'd been the one to give her pleasure. To drive her into that white-hot orgasm. And she trusted him enough to let go completely.

"How about we see if that's true for me, too?"

She trailed her soft lips along his neck, fanning the fire raging in his veins. Her tongue flicked against the racing pulse in his throat as she slid her fingers over his hip and grazed his erection. The woman was killing him. Half-dizzy from the sensation, he ground his teeth together and fought to keep from erupting like some newbie with his first girlfriend.

Breathing hard, he swooped down and captured her lips, letting lust consume him as he held her round rear end tight in his palms. The throbbing in his shaft grew worse as he slid down to pay homage to her spectacular breasts, enjoying the frantic sounds emanating from her throat.

"No more," she moaned, suddenly levering herself up on her elbows and grabbing the condom he'd left on the mattress beside her. "Put this on. I want you inside me." Her urgent, sexy words made him smile.

"If you're sure…"

"So sure."

His hands weren't all together steady as he sheathed himself. She watched his every move and the light scrape of her fingernails along his thigh drove him to distraction.

As soon as he finished, she wrapped her fingers around his erection and the sensation of her strong grip sliding over him made him grit his teeth.

Ethan settled between her thighs. His lips grazed hers. She plunged her tongue forward, stroking deep inside his mouth. A series of deep, drugging kisses followed. Ethan lost himself in their connection, restraining the lust pounding through his veins, wanting to build her pleasure once more to make their joining perfect.

But her frantic gyrations slowly ate away at his willpower. He settled his forearms on either side of her head, raising himself to a plank position over her. He needed to see her face, to reassure himself she was all in. Their eyes met and he saw the desire flickering in her blue-gray depths. With nothing more holding him back, he guided his shaft forward. Positioning himself against her entrance, he nudged the blunt head of his erection against her tight heat.

"Now, Ethan," she gasped, flexing her hips in hungry supplication.

Muscles straining, he eased inside her, feeling her tightness expand to accommodate him. Inch by inch he moved, sliding deeper into heaven.

"This is so good." He needed her to know how amazing she felt.

"Oh, hell yes," she exclaimed, her lashes lifting, fingers digging into his skin.

Finally seated deep inside her, he grazed her lips with his. "I've never needed this more."

"Me neither."

Need roared to life, demanding he move. He pulled back, feeling her inner muscles tighten on him, resisting his withdrawal. Just as smoothly, he thrust into her once more, memorizing her impassioned gasp, knowing it would belong to him forever.

"You like this?" he asked, leaning down to nip at her earlobe.

Her body quaked, muscles clamping down on him once again as he drove into her with more vigorous movements.

"Oh, yes."

"You like how it feels to have me inside you?"

"So much," she panted as he continued to drive into her. "I like it... So, so much."

The sounds she made as he withdrew and pushed forward again made his chest ache. Why did it have to be Sienna he felt this way about? She was everything he'd ever wanted and the timing couldn't be worse. Yet as they strained together toward their fulfilment and Sienna's focus never shifted from his face, Ethan was sure his expression exposed everything he was feeling. But instead of retreating, he let her have it all, showing every emotion from worry to joy to deepest appreciation.

"Oh."

Sienna tensed, her muscles quaking as she squeezed him with fiery, demanding strength. Her gaze snagged his in a soul-stealing connection that turned his world inside out. Her longing ripped him open and made him whole.

Ethan drank in her gasps as she began to come, her body bucking and straining beneath him. As his own pleasure surged, he held on for a brief moment of triumph before she dragged him straight into an explosive, intoxicating orgasm that plunged him into a deep pool of satisfaction.

In the aftermath, he rolled them to their sides and gathered her against him. With their legs tangled, Sienna limp and sated in his arms, her breath a contented purr against his neck, the most astonishing peace claimed him. Ethan nuzzled against her hair and listened to their wild heartbeats sync and slow.

"I think I died and went to heaven," she murmured,

lifting her chin so she could peer at him from beneath her long lashes.

A bright bolt of energy lit him up like the midday sun when she smiled. All too aware that her power over him was something that should be freaking him out, Ethan pushed it to the back—way back—of his mind.

"And to think we have the whole weekend ahead of us."

"Not the whole weekend." She placed her palm against his cheek and stroked her fingertips against his forehead and nose. "You are here to meet your mother and spend time with her."

"But we'll be together at night. Here. In this bed."

"Just this bed?" Sienna's gaze flickered toward the window that overlooked the courtyard. "Didn't you say you love the water? There's a secluded courtyard with a pool behind the house."

Amused at where her thoughts had gone, Ethan dipped his head and kissed her with tender passion. "And a bathtub big enough for two up here."

"How's the shower? I've always had a fantasy…" She trailed off and shot him a wicked grin. "I guess I'll have to show you."

"I guess you will."

As the morning sun filtered through the bedroom windows, Ethan awoke to an empty bed and a flare of panic. Sienna was gone. Anxiety sharpened, waking him more fully. Thrusting up onto one elbow, he rubbed sleep from his eyes and gazed about the room, finding it empty except for Sienna's dress and his pants. His shirt was missing. Above the rapid thump of his heart, the clack of crockery filtered up the stairs and Ethan collapsed back onto the pillows.

His disconcerting response to finding himself alone this

morning left Ethan questioning how far his perspective had shifted where Sienna was concerned.

Covering a jaw-cracking yawn with the back of his hand, Ethan slipped from bed and stretched. His stomach growled as the scent of bacon and coffee drifted upstairs. Before seeking out Sienna in the kitchen he fished out his phone and scanned the emails that had appeared in his inbox overnight. Seeing no message from his anonymous source, he breathed a sigh of relief.

Immediately he was disgusted by the level of trust he'd put in some unnamed meddler as opposed to trusting his own instincts. Surely with all the time he'd spent with Sienna, something would've triggered his suspicions by now. And it wasn't as if he'd turned a blind eye because he was attracted to her. For the last week he'd actively been watching for any slip up.

Well, there hadn't been any last night. Not a single qualm had marred their hours of soul sharing and blissful lovemaking. In the aftermath of connecting physically with her, he'd felt safe sharing his darker thoughts and insecurities with her. In so many ways they were kindred spirits. Both of them held back pieces of themselves from those around them.

Most people perceived him as uncomplicated and fun to hang with. He worked hard, enjoyed weekends on his boat and Charleston's nightlife. But with Sienna he'd let her glimpse what lay beneath his casual exterior. Not only had he admitted how being adopted left him feeling like an outsider, but also revealed his yearning to discover where he came from.

Would he have opened up to her if she hadn't revealed her pain at her parents' indifference? As if being a middle child wasn't hard enough, she'd been sandwiched between an older brother poised to take over the family business and a younger sister adopted because she was beautiful. Was it any wonder Sienna had retreated into intellectual pursuits that only reinforced her isolation?

What she'd disclosed about her childhood had aroused an urge to defend her against further mistreatment. Starting with the way his nameless "friend" had maligned her. For the first time since the messages began, Ethan decided to respond. He opened the most recent message he'd received from the anonymous sender and shot back a terse reply. Pouring out his frustration about all the secrecy, Ethan rebuked the sender for the vagueness of the warnings and lack of specific detail about the threat the Burns sisters represented.

Message sent, Ethan slipped on his boxer briefs and headed downstairs. He paused in the kitchen doorway to admire Sienna's sleep-mussed hair, passion-bruised lips and the appealing way her high, firm breasts filled out his shirt. Noticing his arrival, she poured a cup of coffee and came around the center island toward him. The sight of her bare legs recalled how she'd wrapped her thighs around his hips and begged him to slide deeper inside her. His erection stirred at the memory and as she neared, he wrapped his arm around her waist and eased her lower half into contact with his.

"All my favorite smells," he murmured, accepting the cup of coffee she offered, before nuzzling her neck. "Coffee, bacon and you."

He slid his lips over the spot that made her shiver. Mission accomplished, he gave her butt cheek a firm squeeze as she slid her palms over his bare chest and offered him a smoky smile.

"I thought we could use a big breakfast," she murmured, "since we missed dinner last night."

Despite having only known each other for a week, they

moved in orchestrated rhythm around the kitchen, casting heated, appreciative glances at each other while they sipped coffee, poured orange juice, whipped eggs for omelets and engaged in a ritual of morning-after-great-sex kisses and casual-not-casual touches and caresses. Although they'd indulged their appetite for each other several times the previous night, his hunger for her was starting to take precedence over the emptiness of his belly. The urge to sweep the breakfast fixings off the center island so he could take her hard and fast on the granite countertop distracted him to the point where he cut his finger while slicing strawberries.

Sienna grabbed his hand and ran the cut under cold water. His chest tightened at her adorable fussing as she found a bandage to cover the minor injury. After she pronounced that he would live, he slid his fingers into her disheveled locks and dipped his head for a kiss. He'd only meant to show his appreciation for her concern, but things quickly escalated. In the end, they made good use of the space between the kitchen island and the refrigerator.

Afterward, Sienna braced her hands on Ethan's shoulders and blew out a weak chuckle. He slid his palms along her thighs and up over the curves of her butt, marveling at the peace wafting through him. This woman surprised him over and over. And it wasn't just their sexual chemistry. He noticed himself craving nothing more than to snuggle her in his arms and spend hours listening to her breathe. What was happening to him? Before a satisfactory answer came to him, Ethan's stomach growled. Sienna regarded him with a wry smile.

"Sounds like someone's worked up an appetite," she teased, easing away.

As the cooler air struck his overheated flesh, he shivered. "I can't believe we've only known each other a week," he admitted, watching her slide back into his shirt.

"I know what you mean," she admitted, gazing at him from beneath her long lashes. A shadow of smudged mascara beneath her eyes gave her a sultry look. "I don't usually connect with people, especially men, very fast."

"So I'm special?" Ethan asked sincerely.

She looked surprised that he had to ask. "Of course you are."

"Because this feels special."

"For me, too." She expelled a shaky sigh. "To be honest I've never had such amazing sex in my life and there has to be a reason for that, right?"

"I'm new to this," Ethan admitted, hiding his conflicted feelings in vagueness.

Sienna offered him a hand up and a shy smile. "Me, too."

How was it possible that his appetite for her was so strong even as he questioned whether he could trust her? Was it the game they were engaged in that heightened his desire? He was struggling to reconcile the woman who was scheming with her sister to rob him of the future CEO position with the seemingly guileless woman who'd given herself over to their lovemaking without reservation last night and this morning. Was she that good at acting? Or was she an unwitting pawn? Either way she was dangerous. He just needed to understand if it was the risk that made her irresistible.

"What time are you meeting your mother today?" she asked, oblivious to his churning thoughts.

"She's expecting us at ten this morning."

Sienna's gaze flicked to the clock on the microwave. "Are you sure you don't want to meet with her by yourself?"

"Absolutely."

Of all the decisions that Ethan was second-guessing, following his instinct to bring Sienna along on this trip was not one of them. Despite his suspicions about what she and her sister were up to, he couldn't ignore that Sienna's presence had a steadying effect on him. And he really needed someone in his corner for this meeting.

"Are you nervous?"

"I have a lot of questions." Starting with who his father was and why his mother had believed Ethan was dead all these years.

"I imagine your mother has a lot for you, as well."

"What if I don't like her?" The words slipped out before he considered the implication. What if she didn't like him? Would they have an immediate mother/son connection or would they remain strangers torn apart by fate and unable to overcome the years of estrangement?

"I think you'll have to give yourselves a chance to get to know each other," Sienna said. "Don't expect anything and you won't be disappointed."

Ethan considered that although the advice was directed at him, it could be a reminder to herself, as well.

Nine

Sienna studied her reflection in the bathroom mirror as she put on simple pearl earrings, her mother's gift for her sixteenth birthday. She'd put a lot of thought into how she should dress for her first meeting with Ethan's mother. At first, she'd reasoned that since Carolina Gates was a businesswoman, Sienna should go with one of the expensive suits she'd brought from New York. It would broadcast that she was a career woman who could be taken seriously. On the other hand, she wasn't there to impress Carolina as much as to support Ethan, and he'd articulated his appreciation for her new style of dressing in soft fabrics that fluttered and flowed, revealing flashes of skin and highlighting her curves.

In the end she settled on a romantic dress with open lacework details that contrasted with the demure neckline and below-the-knee skirt. When Ethan's eyes widened in admiration she twirled for him before exiting their rental, thrilled that her choice had met with his approval.

He tucked her hand into his arm in a gallant gesture as they crossed the street and entered Forsyth Park. Although the moss-draped branches of the live oaks filtered the strong morning sunlight, enough got through to make Sienna glad she was wearing a wide-brimmed hat. Tourists and residents alike flocked to the park to see the fountain or stroll the shady sidewalks that bisected the wide green expanses. Ethan and Sienna passed families with strollers, couples with cameras and numerous dog owners exercising their pets.

A ten-minute walk brought them to the wrought iron fence that surrounded the historic home where Ethan's mother lived. With her own heart pounding madly as anticipation overtook her, Sienna glanced toward Ethan to see how he was doing. His features were set in grim lines as if he was working hard to keep calm.

As they approached the gate, she could feel his tension rising. Long before their intimacy of the previous night she'd been growing ever more tuned in to his moods. She peered at his profile, noting the tightness of his mouth and the rigid set of his jaw muscles. Everything in her screamed to comfort him, to reassure him, but she hesitated to reach out.

The fear of rejection continued to plague her. Despite what had happened between them last night or how well they'd been hitting it off since she'd arrived in Charleston, they were virtual strangers. She didn't know if he'd appreciate or reject her sympathy. Yet unable to repress her concern, she bumped her shoulder against his in a spirit of comradery. The eyes he turned toward her smoldered with anxiety and excitement. Touched that he'd let her glimpse his true emotions, she gave him a reassuring smile.

"Thank you for being here." Ethan surprised her by reaching out and taking her hand in his. Squeezing her fingers gently, he added, "It means a lot to me that you were willing to come with me to do this."

"Of course." Her heart soared at his words. She'd been right to accompany him to Savannah. He was obviously more distressed than he let on. And she was honored that he would share this momentous meeting with her.

The first thing that struck Sienna as they entered the Greek Revival mansion were the modern updates to its architectural elegance. The walls, trim and original hand-carved plaster molding had been painted bright white while the honey tones of glossy heart pine flooring warmed the stark palette.

Ethan and Sienna followed the maid who answered the door into a formal parlor, with a traditional white sofa and modern chairs upholstered in navy velvet with brass frames. Between the chairs sat a bronze elephant table. Contemporary metal sculptures sat atop antique tables, and throw pillows bore an abstract watercolor design. Monochromatic curtains in a graphic pattern flanked a live-edge writing desk that sat before the window overlooking Forsyth Park.

As they settled side by side on the sofa, Sienna noticed Ethan was also studying the home as if searching for a clue to the woman who lived here. Fortunately, they didn't have long to wait before she swept into the room. Carolina Gates was a stylish woman in her early fifties who looked ten years younger. In an expensive power suit of cobalt blue, she was five feet eight inches of female empowerment. The matriarch of the Gates family wore her chocolate-brown hair brushed back from her forehead in a sleek bob that grazed her shoulders. Her keen brown eyes peered out from an unlined face.

As Carolina drew near, Ethan's grip tightened on Sienna's fingers. She answered with a squeeze of her own for reassurance. Then they were both getting to their feet and he was setting her free so he could take Carolina's outstretched hands. Mother and son stood staring at each other. Shock, grief and joy radiated from both of them. Sienna stepped to the side to give them a little space.

"You're here," Carolina announced unnecessarily, her throat working convulsively as she surveyed her son. "It's so wonderful to have you here."

"I've been looking forward to meeting you for a long time," Ethan answered, his deep voice husky, but in control.

"You're tall just like your father." Tears brightened Carolina's gaze to dazzling sharpness. "And handsome like him as well, but I think you have my nose and eyes."

Sienna's own eyes began to tear up as she observed the poignant scene. She gave her cheek a surreptitious swipe as Carolina's gaze shifted her way.

"I'm sorry," Carolina said, nodding her greeting, obviously unwilling to let go of her son now that she'd finally gotten ahold of him. "I should've introduced myself. Carolina Gates."

"Sienna Burns."

"Her sister, Teagan, is my long-lost cousin," Ethan explained. "Finding her through the genetic testing service is what prompted me to submit my own sample."

"And I'm so glad you did," Carolina said.

"It's really nice to meet you." Sienna offered Ethan's mother a warm smile. "I hope you don't mind that I came along with Ethan."

"It's wonderful that you're here." Carolina's enchanting smile was a mirror image of her son's charming grin, while her warm brown eyes remained similarly guarded. "Sit down, both of you."

Carolina pulled Ethan toward the sofa he and Sienna had vacated, leaving Sienna to settle across from them. As if Carolina's staff had been waiting for the trio to sit down, the maid appeared with a tray containing a silver coffee service and three bone-china cups. The ritual of pouring and distributing cups of coffee gave all three a little time to assess each other and let the charged emotions ease.

"Forgive me for staring," Carolina declared with a husky laugh. "It's just that I can't believe my son is alive and sitting beside me."

"You said over the phone that you'd explain what happened."

"Straight to the point," Carolina murmured wryly. "You're definitely my son."

From the clean lines and muted tones of her decorating style, Sienna had gathered that Ethan's mother was direct and exacting. This was also reflected in her sleek hairstyle, understated makeup and the expensive sapphire-and-diamond earrings that were her only jewelry.

"Your father was the only man I ever loved. We met when I was a freshman in high school—he was two years older—and we dated for three years. When he graduated, he joined the navy and was killed in a training exercise my junior year. I didn't know until after his death that I was pregnant or we would've gotten married. My father was furious when he found out about the baby. I was an only child and he expected me to take over Gates Multimedia one day, but of course that meant attending college and getting a degree in business. How was I going to manage a rigorous class schedule at a top university while caring for an infant?"

"You said you didn't give me up, so what happened?"

"My father bribed a nurse to steal you and fake a death certificate."

An angry flush stained Ethan's cheekbones. "I was his grandchild. Why would he do that?"

"He never approved of Tony." Carolina went over to a

cabinet and pulled out a scrapbook. "Antonio Bianchi," she murmured, smoothing her palm over the cover. Her features softened into an expression of such fond devotion that Sienna's heart contracted. "My father wasn't happy that I was dating someone below my social standing. Tony's family moved here from Boston. His father was a production worker for Gulfstream Aerospace."

What would it be like to love a man so deeply that three decades of separation couldn't dim her affection? Sienna wasn't one for throwing open the doors to her heart. What had she missed because she'd played it too safe? Heartbreak obviously. But what about the highs of being in love? Observing Carolina, Sienna doubted Ethan's mother would trade in three years of loving Tony Bianchi to avoid three decades of grieving his death.

Carolina returned to her place on the sofa and opened the photo album across her knees. Pointing to one picture after another, she told the story of two young and happy lovers. Sienna's muscles relaxed as she watched Ethan, tracking his journey from wariness to bemusement and finally anguish as he realized he'd never know this man whom his mother had adored.

Slowly the overwhelming surge of emotion eased from the room and by the time lunch was announced, Ethan had recovered his equilibrium. Once again he took Sienna's hand as they went into the dining room and her heart sang at the contact even as she recognized that he sought comfort rather than romance.

"I'd love for you to come to Gates Multimedia tomorrow," Carolina began as plates of crab-stuffed artichoke bottoms were placed before them. "I can give you a tour and you can meet George, Montgomery and Byron." The husband and children of Carolina's cousin Vera who worked for the media company.

When Ethan hesitated, glancing Sienna's way before replying, she quickly piped up, "That sounds like a great idea. I really wanted to visit the Telfair Museums and worried that Ethan would be bored to tears. Sounds like this will work out best for everyone."

"Then it's settled." Carolina covered Sienna's hand with hers and gave her a grateful smile.

Warmth flooded Sienna at the older woman's friendly gesture. She found Carolina delightful and approachable. Definitely someone she'd like to spend time with and get to know better. It wasn't until Sienna's gaze shifted to Ethan that she sensed he wasn't quite as enthusiastic about his mother.

While his lips were curved into an indulgent smile, his eyes were watchful. He clearly wasn't ready to throw open the doors to his heart and invite Carolina in.

Ethan showed no inclination to linger after lunch and Sienna followed his lead, though she would've happily chatted about Carolina's collection of modern paintings for a good hour. After the older woman gave her a surprisingly demonstrative hug, Sienna allowed Ethan to lead her out the door.

After shutting the gate behind them, Ethan took her hand and whisked across the street, his long strides forcing Sienna to trot in order to keep up. Only when they'd reached the sidewalk that ran north and south through Forsyth Park did he slow his pace. Instead of heading straight back to the rental house, he detoured north past the famous fountain. As always, Sienna had scoured the internet and had dozens of facts at her disposal.

"The fountain was built in 1858 and modeled after the Place de la Concorde in Paris. Did you know it was ordered from a catalog?"

When Ethan didn't respond, Sienna glanced his way. Although their hands were linked, he was miles away. Not wanting to push him to open up to her before he was ready, she turned her attention to enjoying the play of sunlight in the water arching from the two-tiered fountain as well as the smaller sculptures around it. Yet as they resumed walking, she couldn't help but do a little deep thinking of her own about fate and the sort of difference it would've made in both Teagan's and Ethan's lives if they'd grown up surrounded by their biological families.

Sienna suspected if Teagan had grown up as a Watts, she would've found acceptance and belonging rather than criticism and judgment. Would being praised by her adoptive parents for her beauty rather than her intelligence have blunted her sister's need to win at all costs?

In Ethan's case, Sienna had learned enough about him to recognize that he used his charm as both a weapon and defense. His darker coloring isolated him in a family of blonds with blue and green eyes. No doubt he'd looked at every family photo and wondered where he truly belonged. He used his charisma and easy confidence to win every heart while never sharing his with anyone. If he'd grown up a Gates, would his grandfather's negativity have turned him pessimistic and volatile? Would he indulge in bitterness and lash out?

By the time they entered the house where they were staying, Sienna was dying to hear Ethan's thoughts on all he'd learned, but she could see that she needed to reconnect with him before that happened. Which was why she pulled him toward the stairs. She'd stripped him out of his suit coat and removed his tie before he awakened to what she was up to.

"Don't you want to go sightseeing?" He worked at the buttons of his shirt, his gaze devouring her while she slid out of her dress.

"Later," she murmured, tossing her clothes aside and

stepping out of her heeled sandals. Naked, she framed his face between her palms and snared his gaze. "Right now, all I want is to make love with you."

Late Friday afternoon, Ethan returned from spending the day with his mother at Gates Multimedia. Their conversation had left him in turmoil and he was eager to share his thoughts with Sienna. Unfortunately, she hadn't returned from her tour of the historic district, so Ethan headed out to the pool with a bottle of beer and settled into a lounge chair. Usually, being around water brought clarity to his thoughts and offered him a measure of peace. Not today.

All his life he'd kept his own counsel, sharing little of his troubles with those around him, even his own family. He didn't like feeling pain so why would he want to dwell on the cause of it? But ignoring his melancholy hadn't helped. The sense of being an outsider in his own family had not diminished because he'd kept it to himself.

The last twenty-four hours had been a series of dramatic firsts. From the earthquake of making love to Sienna to meeting his birth mother and learning the truth about his past, Ethan had been hit by an unrelenting wave of charged emotions.

Sharing with Sienna his deep anguish about his grandfather's rejection had helped him process what he'd learned. His mistrust of her should've kept him from opening up fully. Especially, when he suspected she'd give Teagan ammunition against him. Yet, he couldn't stop himself from revealing the pain he'd felt over discovering that his Gates grandfather had given him away like an unwanted puppy.

"Hey." He felt Sienna's gentle touch on his shoulder, suffusing his body in warmth. "How'd it go with your mom today?"

"She offered me the CEO position with Gates Multimedia."

"Wow." Sienna perched beside him and scrutinized his expression. "That's huge."

"It totally caught me off guard."

"Not that I don't agree with her choice, but did she say why she wanted to step down?"

"She took over after her father's death with the intention of finding someone who could eventually run the company." Ethan had been surprised by Carolina's reluctance to hand over the helm to her brother-in-law or either nephew—all of whom worked for the media company.

"And now she has you."

"And now she has me." Except he wasn't convinced Gates Multimedia was where he saw himself in the future.

While Sienna headed into the kitchen to grab him another beer and fix some snacks to tide them over until dinner, Ethan grabbed his phone, intent on shooting Paul a quick message regarding Carolina's offer. When his brother had decided to start his own company instead of joining Watts Shipping, Ethan had felt obligated to step up. Now, with Teagan demonstrating an interest in the family business, Ethan was free to explore other options.

Before he began an email to Paul, Ethan scanned his inbox. Spying a familiar address, his heart began to thud.

Before you defend Sienna, you should ask her why she was blackballed from the art gallery circuit in New York.— A friend

Although Ethan was sick of the anonymous emailer's cryptic warnings, he nonetheless forwarded the message to Paul and asked his brother to check if this was true.

After that, he set aside the phone and rubbed his dry eyes

as exhaustion swept over him. Why, when she seemed like the perfect lover, confidante and friend, was he constantly besieged by doubts that suggested she wasn't?

"Here you go."

At the sound of Sienna's voice, Ethan looked up to find her placing a plate loaded with crackers, cheese and fruit on the table beside him. In her other hand she held two beers.

"What are you wearing?" he asked, his gaze coasting over her bare shoulders as he accepted one of the beers.

"Don't you mean, what aren't I wearing?" With a wicked smile she whipped off the towel and dropped it on the lounge beside his.

Before Ethan gathered his scattered wits, she'd executed a flawless dive into the water. He had his shoes and shirt off before her head breached the surface.

"Aren't you coming in?" She set her feet on the pool bottom and rose out of the water like some gorgeous water nymph. His breath hitched as more and more of her pale skin appeared above the surface. A millimeter before she exposed her dusky nipples to the air, she raised her eyebrows. "The water's fine."

Ethan tossed his pants over a nearby chair, wishing it was as easy to cast aside his doubts. But when he plunged into the water and gathered Sienna's naked body into his arms, the need to protect his heart mattered less than his couldn't-stop-if-he-tried hunger to lose himself in her kisses.

Before coming to Charleston, Sienna was accustomed to choosing her wardrobe based on function rather than fun. That had changed since meeting Ethan. She continued to marvel how his eyes lit up when she entered a room.

Awakened to the power of how the right outfit made her feel sexy and beautiful, when it came time to dress for the dinner with his family, she once again stepped outside her fashion comfort zone. She paired a full skirt of white tulle with an off-the-shoulder black lace top. Leaving her long hair flowing about her shoulders in luxurious waves, she slipped her feet into black stilettos with ankle bows and chose a black satin clutch to complete the outfit. Sienna felt confident that she'd captured a look that was partly New York and a little bit Southern.

Ethan was handsome in a lightweight gray suit and white shirt opened at the neck. As she descended the stairs, she noticed that although he appeared relaxed and smiling, his eyes remained watchful.

"I'd love for you to do me a favor tonight," he began, as he closed the front door behind them. "You can say no if it's too much to ask."

"I'm here for you. Whatever you need."

"Keep your eyes and ears open. From the way my mother spoke about everyone today, I'm wary about what I'm walking into with this family and it would really help to get your impressions of everyone."

"Of course. I'll do my best to get a sense of what they're all like."

"Thank you."

Tonight they were dining at Olde Pink House restaurant on Reynolds Square in downtown Savannah. The landmark home had been built in 1771 and went from a residence for James Habersham Jr. to a bank in 1811 and after years of neglect became a restaurant in 1992. When they arrived, Ethan and Sienna followed the hostess to the second floor where a large square table had been set before the fireplace in what had originally been the home's study. Open French doors led out to a cozy balcony where a bartender was serving cocktails.

Carolina spotted Ethan and strolled over, accompanied

by a distinguished younger man who hovered possessively at her side. Carolina exuded strength and charm. She looked none the worse for the emotional encounter with her son earlier that day as she introduced her companion as Rufus Knox.

Keeping to her promise to act as Ethan's eyes and ears among his family, Sienna strolled alongside him, politely smiling as she was introduced to Carolina's cousin Vera Pruitt, her husband, George, and a trio of young women who turned out to be the girlfriend, fiancée and pregnant wife of the couple's three sons.

Met with cordial smiles that weren't exactly friendly, and from the whispering that followed in Ethan and Sienna's wake, she got the sense that Carolina's relatives weren't all that happy that they had a new family member. While Ethan fell into conversation with Carolina and Rufus, Sienna decided the best way to gather more information was to make a solo circuit of the room. Excusing herself, she headed out to the balcony to chat with Ethan's second cousins.

"Hello," she said, "I'm Sienna Burns."

The three men introduced themselves as Montgomery, Aaron and Byron. Each had their father's dirty blond hair and mother's cool hazel eyes. They were a couple inches under six feet and dressed in dapper summer-weight suits that flattered their lean, toned bodies. Surly expressions marred their classically handsome features.

"How are you enjoying Savannah?" Byron asked. His was the warmest greeting.

"Very much."

"What can you tell us about our new cousin?" Montgomery's gaze swept over her body, his interest blatant and sexual.

"What do you want to know?" Sienna asked lightly, her stomach muscles knotting in discomfort.

"Y'all are from Charleston?" Aaron drawled, swirling the bourbon in the crystal tumbler he held.

"Ethan is," she explained. "I'm from New York."

"How do you make the relationship work being so far apart from each other?" Byron asked.

"Oh, we only just met a week ago," Sienna explained. "My sister is Ethan's cousin. She just recently found out that she's related to the Wattses. She found them the same way Ethan found you all, through a genetic testing service."

Sienna went on to answer their questions about Teagan's adoption, leaving out how their mother had preferred her beautiful adopted daughter over the plain child she'd given birth to.

"Congratulations on your recent engagement," Sienna said to Montgomery, pushing her ineffectual frustration aside for the time being. "Have you set a date for your wedding?"

Aaron gave a rough laugh and clapped his brother on the shoulder. "If Hy's smart she'll tie the knot with this one before he wanders off to greener pastures."

Montgomery shot his younger brother a quelling look. "Hyacinth wants to be a June bride and needs a year to plan the wedding."

"At least," Byron muttered in amusement.

Sienna turned her gaze on Aaron. "And congratulations to you, as well. Your wife said she's due next month and that you're having a girl. Are you looking forward to being a father?"

"Is anyone?" Aaron gave another hearty laugh.

Sienna was disconcerted by his thoughtless comment and Montgomery's inappropriate regard. Was their boorish behavior a symptom of rot within their family or just a case of overcompensation because of their insecurities? She couldn't help but mark the contrast between their rudeness and the way Teagan had been welcomed with open arms by the Wattses.

"I understand your grandfather started Gates Multimedia in the late sixties," she said, to no brother in particular. "Do all of you work for the company?"

"I do," Montgomery said. "I'm the president of Gates Technology." He stated this with a pompous air, then tipped his glass to indicate the youngest brother. "Byron is the regional manager for our broadcast network on the West Coast and our father is CFO."

"Carolina is lucky to have so many family members that she can count on." No one seemed to hear the irony in her voice so she turned to Aaron and asked, "What is it you do?"

Montgomery spoke up before his brother could. "Aaron has dabbled in quite a few ventures, but hasn't found anything that suits him."

Deep resentment filled the gaze Aaron directed at his brother. "I'm between projects at the moment."

After making both his brothers uncomfortable, a satisfied smile twisted Montgomery's lips. "And what is it you do?"

Sienna explained her business, and then went a step further and shared her sister's early business successes, all the while wondering if she imagined the surprise on both their faces. There was no question in her mind that their mother and romantic partners were not interested in pursuing careers. They came from wealthy families and while they might have dabbled in some sort of work, once they settled on a husband, they intended on dedicating all their energies to being the perfect wife and mother.

Did it bother them that the person in charge at Gates Multimedia was a woman?

At dinner, Sienna found herself seated between Byron

and Montgomery. As everyone sat down, Sienna noticed that while she and Ethan had been expertly separated, the rest of the assembled couples had remained paired up. Divide and conquer? She caught Ethan's eye and noted that he too had recognized the ploy. A thrill went through her at their silent communication. It seemed implausible that they'd only met a week ago and yet their minds were already operating along similar lines. Or maybe it was just wishful thinking on her part.

The last person with whom she'd developed a quick and powerful connection had been her best friend, Gia. The two had immediately clicked freshman year and supported each other through four years of college and beyond. Sienna couldn't imagine her life without Gia in it. If that was the same attachment she was developing with Ethan, what changes did her future hold? What if their relationship was a one-sided affair? She'd heard enough stories of Ethan's romantic escapades to recognize that he wasn't the sort to commit. Was she on the verge of putting too much of herself into their affair only to end up disappointed and hurt?

Montgomery raised his eyebrows. "So you and our cousin aren't dating?"

Caught off guard by the blunt question, Sienna's cheeks heated beneath Montgomery's scrutiny. What label did she apply to their romance when she wasn't sure where things were headed? "We're…friends."

"Seems like there's a little bit more to it." Montgomery's gaze dropped to her lips and then lowered to her breasts. "Or maybe he doesn't know a good thing when it's right under his nose."

Sienna's cheeks heated even as outrage surged through her. Surely the man couldn't be hitting on her with his fiancée sitting beside him. She glanced to where Hyacinth was deep in conversation with her future father-in-law before glancing across the table and noticing Ethan's stony gaze fixed on Montgomery. Had he seen the interaction and wondered what was going on? His displeasure worried her. The last thing she wanted to do was cause trouble between Ethan and his new relatives.

"We understand Ethan and his father work for Watts Shipping," Byron began as soon as the waiter had taken their drink orders.

Sienna saw past the younger man's polite curiosity to the concern that Carolina's newfound son might be interested in joining Gates Multimedia and the detrimental consequences that could have on their futures.

"At the moment," she said. "His grandfather was chairman of the board until his stroke a few months back. He's been steadily improving and has taken back some of his duties."

"But he has a brother and several cousins," Byron continued. "They don't have any interest in the family business?"

As long as she stuck to public information, Sienna saw no harm in answering these questions. "His brother, Paul, owns a cybersecurity company. Ethan also has twin cousins. One is a chef, the other a hairdresser."

"It sounds as if Ethan is the one most likely to run his family's company in the future," Montgomery piped up, exchanging a satisfied glance with his brother.

"I wouldn't know." Sienna thought about the panic that would set in with her dinner companions if she mentioned Teagan's ambition regarding Watts Shipping. "But it seems as if that would make sense."

The waiter brought their drinks, and Sienna took the opportunity to change the subject. The rest of the dinner was an ordeal as she parried questions about Ethan, declaring that they'd only known each other a short time and his cousins would be better off asking him directly. She continuously redirected the conversation to generic topics like the city of Savannah and got them to discuss their own lives.

She discovered Byron and his girlfriend, Melinda, had gone to the same high school, but hadn't begun dating until after college. The pretty redhead was the most down-to-earth of all the women involved with the Pruitt boys. Montgomery deferred to his fiancée about their upcoming wedding and Hyacinth's plans carried them through the dessert course.

When no one seemed eager to linger over coffee, Sienna was thrilled to bid her dinner companions goodbye, assure Carolina how nice it had been to meet her and escape to the powder room. By the time she reached the sidewalk outside the restaurant, Ethan was standing alone and frowning at his cell phone. He was so absorbed that he didn't notice her approach until she spoke.

"Is something wrong?"

His head whipped up and he shoved the phone into his pocket. "Not a thing."

"Are you sure? You look upset."

At first the smile he offered her seemed a little strained around the edges, but after he wrapped his arm around her waist and deposited a sizzling kiss on her lips, she lost track of her concern.

"Let's get out of here," he murmured against her ear. "It's our last night in Savannah and I want it to be memorable."

Sienna tunneled her fingers into his thick hair and let her kiss communicate her total agreement to that plan.

Ten

Sunday morning, Ethan left Sienna slumbering and crossed Forsyth Park to have breakfast with his mother. He was no more eager to have a conversation about her offer to join Gates Multimedia than he was to deal with the ongoing battle between his ever-increasing emotional attachment to Sienna and the events—pointed to by the anonymous caller and confirmed last night by Paul—that depicted her as a liar and a cheat. If she'd been any other woman, Ethan would've immediately ended their association. But the thought of never seeing Sienna again aroused an ache that couldn't be wished or willed away.

Entering his mother's house, Ethan pushed Sienna to the back of his mind and followed the maid into the dining room where Carolina sat in a voluminous caftan, sipping coffee. He greeted her and sat down, smiling absently as she poured him a cup from the coffeepot beside her and handed it over.

"Thank you for last night's dinner," she began, a warm

expression in her brown eyes. "I think everyone enjoyed themselves."

"I'm glad to hear that." On the way over Ethan had debated whether to continue the fiction that all was well, or to come clean about his thoughts. "Although I suspect not everyone was happy to welcome a new family member." If he hadn't kept a close eye on his mother's reaction, he might've missed her microgrimace. "They already suspect you've invited me to join the company."

"You're my son. The company should be yours."

Ethan resisted a grimace of his own. He didn't want to shut any doors, but what she was offering him could change everything. And not necessarily for the better. "I appreciate where you're coming from, but you barely know me. And there's my position at Watts Shipping to consider. I can't just walk away and leave them hanging."

Yet wasn't that exactly what he could do? With Teagan actively working to take away what all along had been his, it would be the perfect solution for everyone. Nor could he ignore how long he'd been pondering an opportunity like what his mother was offering. So what accounted for his resistance?

"I understand that this is all very sudden," Carolina said. "All I'm asking is for you to give it some thought. Maybe come down and spend some time with me getting to know the business. See if you like it."

Her request was completely reasonable and despite the disquiet roiling in his gut, Ethan found himself agreeing to do just that. The conversation shifted to a discussion of his cousins. Carolina had a lot to say about Montgomery's upcoming wedding and Aaron's pending fatherhood. Despite her attempts to sound positive, Ethan could tell she wasn't fully sold on any of the Pruitt siblings, although she seemed most optimistic about Byron.

They lingered over breakfast longer than Ethan intended and he suddenly realized the time to head back to Charleston was fast approaching. His mother escorted him to the front door and bid him goodbye with a sad smile. Her forlorn expression made him regret that he couldn't stay a few more days. Before heading out, Ethan impulsively bent to kiss her cheek, the first show of affection he'd initiated. Eyes bright with unshed tears, Carolina set her fingertips over the spot and watched from the doorway as he headed down the walk.

Light-headed, with heart thumping madly in his chest, he crossed the street. His emotional response to leaving Carolina plagued him as he strode across the park. The gush of fondness felt like a betrayal of the woman who'd raised him. He barely knew Carolina and it was certainly too soon for him to claim he loved her, but some emotion had him solidly in its grip.

After entering the house, Ethan completed a quick circuit of both floors and found no sign of Sienna. No doubt she was taking one final stroll around the historic district. He shook off the niggling disappointment at her absence. When had he become a man who craved the company of one particular woman? The answer followed him into the bedroom they'd shared.

Sienna's voice reached his ears as he collected his charger from the nightstand. She was in the courtyard behind the house. Opening the door that led to the back terrace, Ethan was about to let her know he was back when he realized who was on the other end of the call.

"Honestly, Teagan," Sienna said, "this is a huge deal and you absolutely can't tell anyone in the family about it."

Even though he wasn't surprised Sienna had betrayed him to her sister, he was astonished how much it hurt.

Counting on her to have his back had been a risk, especially with what he'd been warned to expect from Teagan.

"Because no one knows." Sienna's reply was everything Ethan had been dreading. "He hasn't said anything to his family yet."

In a weak attempt to change the topic, Sienna started going on about all that she'd seen around town.

"Savannah's a bit different from Charleston. The historic district contains more than twenty squares and several churches. The house we're staying at is across from Forsyth Park and I've visited a couple really nice museums."

Obviously, Teagan wasn't to be distracted because after a momentary pause to listen, Sienna dropped all talk of Savannah.

"I think it's a little premature to talk about whether or not Ethan's going to inherit," Sienna responded in a quelling tone.

Silence filled the courtyard for several seconds before Sienna spoke again.

"If Ethan became CEO of Gates Multimedia, that would make things a lot easier for you, wouldn't it? Then the way would be clear for you to be the CEO of Watts Shipping."

Ethan hadn't really needed the warning emails. Teagan hadn't exactly been subtle about learning all about Watts Shipping's operations, and then demonstrating her business savvy in lengthy conversations with the current CEO. His dad had taken several of her suggestions under advisement and Grady, current chairman of the board, was singing her praises.

Still, it wasn't Teagan's machinations that bothered him at the moment, but the information she was receiving from Sienna. Caught up in meeting his birth family, he'd forgotten to be wary.

"Sure," Sienna said bitterly. "It's a win-win for every-body."

In the silence following her statement, Ethan's thoughts whirled. While Teagan's eagerness to poach his position at Watts Shipping annoyed him to no end, he couldn't deny the simplicity of her suggestion.

"And if he doesn't want to work for Gates Multimedia?" Sienna asked, letting her annoyance come through loud and clear. "I should convince him?"

Lost in the passion of their strong sexual connection, he'd lost track of her role in her sister's schemes.

"You're crazy if you believe that he's into me that much."

Ethan pondered Teagan's opinion and considered how he'd been feeling these last few days. His gut clenched when he remembered Sienna's hands roaming hungrily over him. Her passionate kisses. The sexy sounds she made. The thought of all that incredible sex being a vehicle for Teagan's ambition made him sick.

"He's not falling in love with me," Sienna protested, sounding oddly withdrawn. "I don't care what his family says."

Ethan's hands balled into fists. That his family had been speculating about his feelings for Sienna didn't surprise him. Nor was he shocked that Teagan had encouraged her sister to capitalize on how smitten he appeared to be about her.

But Sienna confiding his private business to her sister after he requested she not reveal the information until he could share it with his parents was a betrayal he couldn't stomach. Especially not when he was poised on the brink of falling for her.

Ethan had heard enough. He eased the French door closed and retreated. In so many ways, it was almost a relief to have his suspicions confirmed. Now he could stop worrying about fighting whatever emotions had begun to develop. Proof of her deception meant that he wouldn't give her a second thought when she returned to New York. Even before she'd shown her true colors, the possibility that anything between them could survive beyond these couple weeks had been crazy. Their interlude had been a means to an end. A way to keep tabs on what Teagan was up to.

Today's overheard conversation demonstrated why he'd developed a relationship with Sienna. Now that he was in possession of valuable insight about how Teagan intended to use her sister, he was free to do whatever it took to mislead his rival.

The weekend in Savannah was fast becoming a precious memory as the city vanished in the distance behind them. Sienna sat in the passenger seat beside Ethan and fought back melancholy. The intense connection that had developed during their time together these past few days had surpassed anything she'd ever experienced. Being with him as he'd navigated the emotional storm of meeting his birth mother and his blood relatives had connected them at a spiritual level she hadn't expected. The glimpse of his fears and insecurities had allowed Sienna to drop her guard. With their true selves exposed, they'd come together in bed with feverish urgency and the sex had blown her mind.

And now they were heading back to Charleston and she had to face the fact it was almost over. Already, she'd lingered beyond the original few days she'd planned to stay. All too soon she would be heading back to New York City. Back to isolation and the grind of long days spent flying around the world, brutally awakened to the realization that filling her hours with work wasn't the solution to loneliness.

She glanced at Ethan's profile. Maybe that could change. He hadn't come out and declared that he wanted to see more of her, and she might be kidding herself that he had felt anything for her beyond desire, but the fact that he'd invited her to Savannah said something. But now, with Ethan being so uncharacteristically silent, Sienna wondered if she was on his mind at all.

Before they'd left, he'd gone alone to have breakfast with his mother and said little since returning. No doubt leaving Carolina was difficult after having just found her. Or had he made a decision about her offer to join Gates Multimedia? He'd shut her down when she'd asked, claiming he had a lot of thinking to do.

Despite her spinning thoughts, Sienna must've dozed because the next thing she knew the car wasn't moving. Blinking to clear the fog from her brain, she lifted her head off the passenger window and spied the curved double steps leading to the front door of Grady's estate.

Covering a yawn, she turned her head toward Ethan. "Sorry." The word died on her lips as she noticed his expression. "What's wrong?"

"What's wrong?" he snarled, gaze slashing her way. He gripped the steering wheel with one hand and pointed his phone at her with the other. "Your sister. That's what."

Sienna's heart sank. Had Teagan succeeded in accomplishing her goal? Was she going to be the next CEO of Watts Shipping?

"What did she do?" Sienna whispered.

"As if you don't know."

"It's Teagan," she muttered. "There are any number of things she could get up to."

"She told my parents that I went to Savannah to meet with Carolina."

"Oh, no."

"Don't act so shocked," he said in disgust. "You knew she knew."

"I—"

Breath hissing through her teeth in dismay, Sienna closed her eyes and tried to think. What could she say to defuse the situation without lying to him? She'd suspected that Teagan wouldn't keep the information to herself. Why hadn't she warned Ethan that her sister knew all about Carolina and Gates Multimedia? Because she loved her sister and was falling for Ethan. Trying to keep both of them happy when they were competing for the same job was doomed to fail.

"I heard you on the phone with her," Ethan continued. "You were telling her all about my birth mother and Gates Multimedia."

"I didn't tell her anything." Her lungs worked as if she was running full out. She couldn't seem to gather enough breath to make her case. "She already knew."

"You expect me to believe that?" His sarcastic tone lashed at her. "Only you and Paul knew and he didn't blab to her."

The fact that Teagan had known the real reason for their trip to Savannah demonstrated her sister had found others besides Sienna to do her bidding. Who besides her and Paul could've spilled the beans?

"I swear she knew." This was her chance to set him straight, to declare herself a victim of Teagan's actions, to fight for...what? Every kiss. Every touch. Every murmured endearment between them. It had all been amazing, but what was between them was destined to end even before this conversation. "I'd never do that to you."

I care about...you.

More than any other man she'd ever known. The reality of it struck her hard.

"And I'm just supposed to believe you?" He scoffed.

"It's true."

"You don't seriously think I'm going to take your word for it." His icy manner was a shock to her system. "Especially not after your sister asked you to convince me to leave Watts Shipping and go to work for Gates Multimedia."

Sienna appreciated that he had every right to be irritated with Teagan's scheming. And by keeping quiet about her sister's plans, Sienna had in effect sided with Teagan. The secret had become harder and harder to maintain as her feelings for Ethan had developed. How long before she would've confessed the truth? And at what cost to both her relationship with Teagan and her budding romance with Ethan?

"Would that be so terrible?" Sienna hated that he was right to doubt her. "It's a fantastic opportunity."

"And it benefits your sister."

"It benefits you both. You told me how you'd been feeling like an outsider lately. That you weren't sure how or if you fit with the Wattses anymore. I thought that meeting Carolina and seeing how happy she was to have you in her life was exactly what you'd been missing. Her suggestion that you take over the company is just icing on the cake."

For a long time he stared at her in silence. "I turned down my mother's offer to run Gates Multimedia."

His declaration set off a bomb of anxiety inside her. "Being welcomed by your family. Becoming CEO of Gates Multimedia. Isn't this exactly what you hoped for? Or am I wrong?"

"That's what I let you think."

With the revelation that he'd overheard her talking to Teagan, a dramatic shift had occurred in the way he was behaving toward her. Or had it? *That's what I let you think.* Had he been lying to her all this time? Disarming her with his irresistible smiles and seducing her to keep her off-balance? Sienna flushed with humiliation. Had she really been duped so easily? Had he been laughing at her this whole time? Flattering the unattractive sister until she believed he could truly want her?

"What you let me think?" she echoed, wishing that she'd heard him wrong. "Why?"

"I knew what Teagan was up to from the start."

Sienna's stomach dropped to her toes.

She decided to play dumb for the moment. "What Teagan is up to?"

"Your sister wants to run Watts Shipping."

Since lying would only get her into more trouble, Sienna gave a reluctant nod. "Teagan is one of the most ambitious people I know. And once she gets something into her head—"

"Never mind that I have ten years of experience and she knows nothing about shipping."

Sienna made a helpless gesture. "Her determination to take over Watts Shipping has nothing to do with your qualifications."

"Then what is it exactly?" Ethan demanded.

"You have to understand where she's coming from. She thinks that she deserves to run the company because…" Sienna gulped, horrified at having to explain her sister's reasoning. "Because she's related by blood and you're—"

"Adopted." Beneath Ethan's bleak tone lurked more pain than he'd ever let her see before and Sienna's stomach wrenched.

Overcome by regret at the misery she was causing him, Sienna sank her nails into her palms and soldiered on. "She has her reasons for thinking that way."

"I'm sure."

Sienna found herself in the exact position she'd been

dreading, caught between her familial loyalty to Teagan and her new and shockingly fierce feelings for Ethan. Now, faced with his anger and criticism, she stumbled and fell into the familiar habit of making excuses for Teagan.

"Our father refused to let her run the family company and she believes it's because she's adopted." Sienna rushed through the explanation, hoping that Ethan's own experiences would allow him to understand what Teagan was going through. Of all the things she had shared with Ethan, she'd avoided discussing her sister's insecurities with him. "That's not the reason though. Aiden might not be the best choice to take over, but he's firstborn and a son. My father is quite traditional that way. He wouldn't have let me run the company if I wanted to either."

Ethan looked utterly unmoved by her explanation. "You always stick up for her, don't you?"

"She's my sister."

"Yes," he mused, his disapproval plain. "So what's your plan now that you know that I'm not going to leave Watts Shipping?"

"I don't think Teagan will succeed in taking Watts Shipping away from you."

"Are you willing to help make sure that's the case?"

Sienna shifted her gaze and stared miserably out the windshield. For the last three days she'd been the happiest woman alive. While it seemed unfair that her relationship with Ethan had to implode like this, she should've expected that standing with one foot on the boat and the other on the dock would be treacherous.

"Please don't ask me to get in the middle of this."

"But you're already there. Whose side are you on, Sienna? Will you keep quiet that I know what she's up to? Or are you going to continue doing her bidding?"

"Her bidding?" Sienna echoed, bile rising in her throat.

Suddenly, she was thrown back to high school and all the times her sister had used her in some meticulously plotted scheme. Those days, she hadn't been strong enough to resist or outthink her sister. "What exactly is it you think I've done?"

"It's pretty obvious."

"Not to me." She scanned his expression while her thoughts raced frantically. "I'll admit that I knew that she was determined to be the next CEO, but I never said or did anything to you or any of your family to help her."

Ethan looked completely unmoved. "Of course you'd deny it—"

"It's the truth," Sienna interrupted, frustration boiling up in her. Seeing his doubt, she continued, "Okay, fine. Maybe I had very selfish motives for encouraging you to accept your mother's offer. I'd hoped if you became the CEO of Gates Multimedia and Teagan ran Watts Shipping then both of you could be happy." And her heart wouldn't be torn in two. "But now I'm starting to see that neither of you gives a damn about being happy. You both just want to win."

"*We* want to win?" Ethan snorted derisively. "That's hilarious coming from someone who has done the things you have."

"What things?"

"I know that you've overinflated the value of a painting to increase your commission and that you've hired someone to bid on something at auction to drive up the price your client will receive."

Sienna recoiled from the accusation, her insides turning to ice. Was someone deliberately feeding him lies or had he twisted events from her past to substantiate that he was right to mistrust her? Fumbling with the handle, Sienna managed to open the door, but before she could exit the car, Ethan's long fingers wrapped around her wrist. His grip was firm, a hair's breadth from painful.

"If you believe all these terrible things about me," she panted, desperate to escape him before the tears blurring her vision turned into full-on sobbing, "then why didn't you confront me about this sooner?"

"Because I didn't want you to know I was onto you and your sister."

She thought about the long hours she'd spent in his arms. The sex had been fierce and hungry. With their time together shrinking, she believed he'd been equally distressed that they'd soon be parting. Instead, the whole time they'd been intimate, he'd viewed her with such contempt.

Before despair immobilized her, she pushed away such thoughts. "You found out how?"

"That's not important."

"It is important because if you had Paul investigate me then you'd know that's not who I am."

Ethan's expression hardened to granite. "It was someone anonymous."

"So, some unnamed source spews vile lies about me and you just believe it?" Her voice grew screechy as her throat closed up. "After everything… I just… I can't…"

What the hell was happening? Frantic to escape, she yanked against his grip. Her despair was reaching a fever pitch when he set her free so suddenly that she practically tumbled out of the car. Without a backward glance, she raced up the entry stairs, not caring that she'd left her laptop and her suitcase behind.

Eleven

Ethan entered the two-story, L-shaped house where he and Paul had grown up. Passing beneath the elegant arch that led into the formal parlor, he stepped straight into hell.

Usually walking into the home was like being enveloped in a comforting hug. Not today. His parents' penetrating stares sent a bone-deep chill through him before he'd taken more than three steps into the room.

They must've known he was on his way because his mother sat in a straight-back chair rather than her favorite spot on the sofa, her spine ramrod straight. His father stood just behind her, his hand resting on her shoulder. Their position was a clear warning that they'd allied against him.

"I'm sorry," Ethan began, rushing forward with an apology even as his feet stopped moving.

"We're very disappointed that you didn't think you could come to us," Miles Watts intoned, the deep throb in his voice broadcasting his sadness.

"I was going to tell you." Ethan clenched his teeth

against the frustration rising in him. The absolute last thing he wanted was to be in his current mess.

"When exactly?" his father asked.

"As soon as I got back from Savannah."

"Did you give any thought to how difficult it was going to be for your mother and me to hear about this from someone other than you?"

"Of course. This is the last thing I wanted." That it had been Teagan who'd spilled the beans thanks to the information provided by Sienna made it all the worse. "Teagan had no business saying anything."

"She didn't appear to realize we hadn't been told."

Ethan gathered breath to dispute that. He knew perfectly well that only this morning Sienna had asked her sister not to say anything. That an hour later Teagan had spilled the beans over brunch to his entire family was one more reason she would never be in charge of Watts Shipping. They didn't need someone with such poor character at the helm.

"I wasn't the one who told Teagan," Ethan said. "It was Sienna."

"Why are you surprised? You brought her sister with you to Savannah," Miles pointed out. "Surely the two of them discussed why."

"I asked her not to say anything to anyone."

"So you trusted her with your news," his mother said, speaking up for the first time. *But you didn't trust us.* The implication sliced into Ethan.

What could he say? His reasons for confiding in Sienna seemed the height of stupidity now that she'd betrayed him. Leaning on her support hadn't felt risky while they were in Savannah. Their closeness during the trip had even led to him defending her to the anonymous emailer. What an idiotic thing to do.

"We've spent a lot of time together this last week."

Something about this seemed to take his mother aback. "I see."

"None of this changes the fact that you told a virtual stranger before you shared it with us," his father added.

His father labeling Sienna a stranger bothered Ethan more than it should. Granted, strong sexual chemistry didn't necessarily translate into a relationship, but there'd been moments when he felt they'd made a true connection.

Too bad it had been one great big lie.

"Searching for your birth mother was a huge decision," his mother said. "I don't understand why you didn't feel like you could come to us."

"I know I should've said something…"

"Did you think we wouldn't approve?" his father demanded, eyebrows lowering.

"No." Ethan rubbed the back of his neck. "Of course not."

Lies. Even now, confronted by his parents' despair, he couldn't be honest. What was he afraid of? That they'd reject him? Tell him that he was no longer part of their family? The pain that blasted through him indicated that's exactly what he feared.

How was that even possible? They'd done nothing except make him feel loved and included. The problem was his. The insecurity fabricated by his mind.

"Then what?" Miles thundered.

Constance gripped her husband's hand as if to rein him in. "What your father is trying to say is that we're struggling with this big secret you kept from us."

"I didn't want to upset you for no reason if nothing came of the testing."

Miles sighed. "It would've been nice to know what you were going through."

"Maybe we could've helped." Constance was trying to

look brave, but her lips quivered with suppressed emotion. "Why don't you start at the beginning and explain the best you can," his mother said, loving concern resonating in her voice. "When did you decide to look for your birth mom?"

"It happened when Lia was pretending to be Ava's daughter," Ethan began. "When Grady decided to try the genetic testing service, I started thinking about submitting my DNA, as well. I don't know that I actually expected to be matched with anyone."

Miles grunted. "If that was the case then I'd like to think you could've come to us."

"I wanted to." Ethan grimaced. Why hadn't he taken Paul's advice and told them right away? "I should've."

"But you didn't," his father pointed out. "And I'm sure you can see how much that worries us."

The stark disappointment in his father's eyes made Ethan feel like a child who'd misbehaved. His parents had never yelled or punished. They'd always explained what he'd done wrong and calmly discussed the consequences for his actions.

"I never set out to hurt you."

"We know that," his mother said, blinking rapidly.

"I just needed some time to meet my birth mother and sort out how I was feeling." Ethan badly wanted to go to his mother and feel her fingers stroke his hair like when he was little and Paul had gone out to play with his friends, leaving Ethan behind. The memory startled him. Ethan hadn't thought about how it felt to be abandoned by his brother in a long time.

"How were you feeling?" his mother asked, her voice so low he almost missed it. "What was going on that you couldn't come to us?"

Ethan swallowed. He'd been trying to avoid telling his parents the truth. Would they understand that his feelings of being an outsider had nothing to do with them or how they'd raised him?

"I was restless. Out of sorts." How could he make them understand? Especially when he wasn't so sure what was going on himself. "I kept thinking that I didn't fit in. I don't look like any of you."

"Why does that matter?" his father asked.

"You are one of us though. A Watts through and through," his mother put in. "You know that, right?"

When Ethan remained silent, grappling with how to clarify things, his mother spoke up again.

"You can't possibly think that because you are adopted, you aren't part of this family."

"Everything is about legacy in Charleston. Who your blood family is matters more than what you've done or how rich you are. It isn't a place that welcomes outsiders. No one can buy their way in. Being adopted makes me feel like I don't truly belong. I didn't mean for you to think you aren't the two most amazing parents a guy could have."

He added this last as his mother had gone quite pale.

"We understand." Miles took his wife's hands and offered her support. "But realize when you choose not to trust us with what you're going through that it seems as if we've failed you in some way."

"You haven't failed me." This was the exact scenario Ethan had hoped to avoid. He'd known his parents wouldn't understand his motivation when he was having such a difficult time wrapping his own head around it. "If anyone has messed up it's me."

"Don't say that."

The agony in his mother's eyes shredded Ethan's heart. Helpless to stop his mother's misery, Ethan focused all his frustration on the woman who'd caused this problem. This was all Sienna's fault. If she had just kept her mouth shut, he could've been the one to tell his parents. Instead they'd been blindsided.

"You know my birth mom will never be more important to me then you and Dad."

Only he could see neither one believed him. No matter how vigorous his assurances, the words came too late. The damage was done. His parents felt betrayed and there was no undoing it. Ethan could only hope that with time they might forgive him.

"Of course we know that," Miles said, his words belying the lines of stress bracketing his mouth and the death grip on his wife's hand. "And we hope you know that if we're upset it's only because we're worried about you."

"What is she like?" his mother asked.

"Carolina?" Ethan swallowed hard. How did he explain the feeling of homecoming when he met her? Or the closure he received finding out why she hadn't raised him? "She runs Gates Multimedia. Never married and never had any more children. The man she loved—my father—died in a training accident. He was in the navy."

Although Ethan knew he was coming at his mother's question sideways, he hadn't yet taken the time to process his feelings.

"Oh, Ethan." His mother looked stricken. "I'm so sorry to hear that your father died."

"What prompted your…birth mother to try to find you after all this time?" Miles asked.

Ethan explained the circumstances surrounding his birth and what his grandfather had done. His mother clapped her hand over her mouth and regarded him with horrified eyes.

"We had no idea," his father said. "It was a closed adoption and we trusted the lawyer that everything was done in a legal manner."

With this reassurance, something unraveled inside

Ethan. He didn't realize until now that since discovering the circumstances surrounding his adoption, he'd been afraid his parents had been in on the scheme. Some of this must've shown in his face because his father scowled.

His mother got to her feet and came over to wrap her arms around him. "We're happy you found your birth mother," she whispered, her voice urgent. "She is lucky to have you back in her life."

Ethan hugged her tight and realized for the first time in a long time that he felt at peace. How ironic to discover that he had to figure out where he'd come from in order to know who he was and where he wanted to be.

Heartbroken following her fight with Ethan and angry with herself for giving up when she should've fought harder to defend herself and get to the bottom of the anonymous accusations, Sienna sobbed herself to exhaustion, fell asleep and woke after dark with a headache and an empty stomach. Feeling like an intruder, she snuck down to the kitchen, quickly made herself a sandwich and then fled back to the guest room. To her relief, she met no one coming or going. Still, she wondered how long she could stay before someone decided she was the root of all evil and kicked her out.

Before that happened, she would pack and make arrangements to fly back to New York. First thing tomorrow, if at all possible. It was imperative that she get the hell out of Charleston. Not just for her sanity, but because once again she'd done what she'd sworn she wouldn't. She'd neglected her business and given Teagan her full support. Which once again resulted in her getting kicked in the head and feeling as if her whole body was one big raw nerve.

It wasn't until she got back to her room and threw open the armoire that she remembered the last time she'd seen her luggage: it was in the trunk of Ethan's car. With a heavy sigh, she headed back downstairs. To her relief, she found her suitcase and laptop just inside the front door. Grabbing everything, she headed back upstairs. As she reached the second floor, bumping her heavy suitcase up the steps made enough noise to draw Teagan from her room.

"Are you just getting back?" her sister asked, eyeing the luggage.

"No. I just hadn't brought my bag upstairs." Sienna didn't pause as she spoke, but headed for the next flight of steps.

"So…" Teagan trailed after her. "Is Ethan going to take the position with his mother's company?"

It was on the tip of Sienna's tongue to tell Teagan what Ethan had shared with her, but wasn't that exactly the sort of thing he'd accused her of doing? Helping Teagan in her bid to become the next CEO of Watts Shipping? Well, she would eventually find out what Ethan had decided.

"I think you should ask him that question."

"He didn't tell you?"

Sienna's irritation spiked, but she waited until they reached her room before venting her frustration. Swinging her suitcase onto the bed, she whirled to face her sister. "Why did you tell Ethan's family about meeting his birth mother after I specifically told you not to?"

"They deserved to know."

"That wasn't your call."

Teagan waved her hand as if Sienna's irritation was a cloud of smoke that offended her. "Why are you acting all huffy? You knew from the beginning that I intended to beat him out for the CEO position. Whatever it took."

"He accused me of telling you." Sienna narrowed her gaze. "You never did explain how you found out."

"It's not important."

"It is to me." Sienna found herself on the verge of tears and ground her teeth in frustration. "He thinks I betrayed him."

"I can't reveal my source," Teagan said. "If I do, they won't be useful to me anymore."

"Like I've been useful? This whole time you didn't give a damn what it meant to me that Ethan and I were hitting it off. You deliberately let me think he was interested so you could get the inside track to Ethan." Sienna paused to glare at her sister, hoping that Teagan would deny it. When her sister gave an offhanded shrug, Sienna growled. "You are the worst."

Driven by a burning need to get as far away from Charleston and her sister as possible, Sienna crossed to the armoire and began unloading its contents onto the bed.

"Did you seriously think I would ignore the opportunity presented when Ethan found you attractive?"

"I guess not." She'd known better than to trust her sister's motives, yet she'd allowed herself to be sucked in. Despair filled her. "But for once I guess I hoped you'd be happy for me because a man I was attracted to liked me in return."

"And you had fun, didn't you?" Teagan shoved Sienna's suitcase aside, disrupting her neat piles of clothes in the process, and plopped onto the bed. "I mean, come on, the guy is gorgeous and charming and I'll bet he's great in—"

"I really care about him," Sienna interrupted, shocking herself at the admission.

Teagan's eyes went wide. "You've known him a little over a week."

Had she really believed her sister would give a damn? Why did it have to be stupid and foolish to wish Teagan would support her for a change?

Opening the second suitcase, she began to fill it, packing as if her life depended on being done in the next ten minutes.

"What are you doing?" Teagan demanded, her gaze flying from the armoire to the suitcases and finally to Sienna.

"Packing."

"I can see that. But why?"

"I have work waiting for me in New York."

"You can't leave. I need you here."

That summed up Sienna's reality. When it came to her sister, their relationship was a one-way street with all lanes flowing toward Teagan.

"Did you miss the part where Ethan blames me for what you did?" To her dismay, Sienna found herself choking up and forced down her misery. She would absolutely, positively not cry after becoming her sister's victim once more. She would return to Manhattan and throw herself back into her career, putting Charleston and Ethan Watts in her rearview mirror. "It's over between us and I'm devastated. For the first time in your life, why don't you try thinking about someone beside yourself?"

"I am. These people have been looking for me for decades."

"These people? They're your family." Sienna stopped throwing clothes willy-nilly into her suitcase and stared at her sister. "Why did you come here? You obviously don't give a damn about any of them."

"It's not that I don't care about them." To Teagan's credit, she looked visibly upset. "I don't know them."

Sienna's heart melted. "So get to know them. After all, you've been searching for them for years. Appreciate that you have relatives who love you. Aunts and uncles and cousins who don't want anything from you. They're just happy to have you in their lives. Can't you feel the same way?"

"Ugh. You just don't get it." Teagan spoke brusquely as if she hadn't listened to anything Sienna had just said. "If you don't want to help me then just go back to New York. I'll figure out something else."

Sienna didn't realize how much she hoped her words would get through to her sister until that bubble burst. An ache started in her heart and spread throughout her body. Was it possible that Teagan's obsession with controlling and dominating everything in her life had rendered her blind to the risk of losing everyone who loved her?

"Come with me," Sienna tried again. Reaching for her sister's hand, she squeezed her fingers in a fierce grip.

"You just don't get it," Teagan complained, wrenching away from her. "I don't belong in New York anymore."

Following her sister's drama-filled exit, Sienna puzzled over Teagan's impassioned declaration. What had Teagan meant? She was way more suited to New York City than Charleston. Between her social life and her wildly successful businesses, the Big Apple was Teagan's oyster. In contrast, Charleston's pace and old-school style were at odds with Teagan's trendsetting ways.

Was this about her being passed over for Burns Properties? The lengths to which Teagan was going to become the next CEO of Watts Shipping seemed to point to her needing a confidence boost. That being said, manipulating situations to her advantage was the exact sort of thing that her sister thrived on. Even before she could speak, Teagan had deployed her big green eyes and sweet smile to win the hearts of everyone she met. And if charm didn't work, she wielded her clever mind like an assassin, taking out her opponents by clandestine means.

Sienna knew better than to trust her sister and had spent

her entire life avoiding her sister's machinations. Why had she picked now to turn a blind eye to the potential fallout of her sister's scheming?

Because she'd fallen in love.

Logic went out the window when the heart was involved. As things had heated up between them, she'd fallen prey to the fantasy of a future with a man who turned her on and made her happy. Naturally, she believed Teagan's assurances that Ethan was developing feelings for her. Sienna had been desperate for that to be true.

With her new suitcases crammed to the point of bursting, Sienna booked herself on the earliest flight back to New York the following day and got ready for bed.

Twelve

"I hear congratulations are in order," Teagan said, strolling into Ethan's office.

Ethan flipped a glance toward his cousin. With her signature confidence, she strode toward his desk as if she had already been named CEO. Today Teagan wore her version of a New-York-City-meets-Charleston power suit: a hot pink blazer with matching shorts that bared her legs and a blush-colored blouse with an enormous bow tied with a flourish at her throat. On her feet were black ankle boots. No doubt she thought this look let her stand out while fitting in. If so, she'd missed the mark.

"I'm not sure what you're referring to," he replied, returning his attention to his computer monitor.

"You've been offered the CEO position at Gates Multimedia."

He noted she hadn't bragged about where the information had come from, but just knowing it was a subtle reminder that she'd outsmarted him.

"I have."

Instead of taking a seat in one of his guest chairs, she settled her palms on his desk and leaned forward. "They must be very excited to have someone of your caliber taking over."

Was Teagan playing games? Hadn't she spoken to Sienna? Ethan struggled to keep the surprise off his face as he processed this. Did Teagan not yet realize her entire scheme had blown up in her face or was she unaware that he'd turned down his mother's offer? There was only one way to find out.

"I turned them down."

Teagan's eyelashes flickered as she absorbed his declaration, the only sign that she was stunned by his news. Whoever coined the phrase, "Never let them see you sweat," must've taken a page from Teagan Burns's playbook.

"But why? I would think you'd jump at the chance to run your family's multimillion-dollar corporation." As she would surely jump at the chance to run Watts Shipping once he was out of the way.

"Except my place is here." He paused for a beat, letting his stare crystallize into something hard and cutting, before adding, "*At my* family's multimillion-dollar corporation."

Only the most subtle tightening of her lips betrayed that she was annoyed at the emphasis he'd put on *my*.

"But surely you won't be taking over here for many, many years whereas you could step right into the top position at Gates Multimedia."

She straightened, showing less confidence than she had when she'd first arrived.

"Yes, but Watts Shipping is where I belong."

"Of course," Teagan soothed, "but I'll bet your real mother would love it if you joined your birth family's company instead. After all, if she hadn't given you up, all this time you would've been her obvious successor."

"She didn't give me up," he explained, unsure why it was important for her to know that he'd been wanted all along. "My grandfather thought seventeen was too young for her to be a mother and arranged to have me adopted. She thought I'd died."

"Oh, that's terrible. She must've been devastated to lose you."

For the first time since he'd met her, Ethan heard something in Teagan's voice that resonated with him. They'd both been adopted as infants. And in both cases their mothers hadn't given them up. Teagan's mother had died. Ethan's had been tricked. Until he'd heard the true story about what happened to him, he hadn't understood how much pain he'd been in at the thought of being abandoned by the woman who'd given birth to him.

Suddenly, Ethan was weary of all the verbal fencing. "Cut the crap."

"I'm sorry?" She blinked at him in poorly feigned confusion.

"I know what you've been up to…" Ethan cued up the first anonymous email he'd been sent and showed it to her. "…all along."

Teagan read the message and stiffened in surprise. A second later she glanced at him, a small smile playing on her lips.

"Someone you don't know sends you an inflammatory email lying about me and you take it as a fact?" She paused to let her dismissive tone sink in. "Is that how you plan to operate Watts Shipping if you're chosen to lead this business? You're going to chase rumors and lies? If that's true then maybe you're not the person who should be in charge."

Ethan had paid careful attention to her reaction and suspected she knew who was behind the message. Although she tried to mask her thoughts, she was obviously shaken. Time to capitalize on this moment of weakness.

"Are you denying that you came to Charleston intending to take over Watts Shipping?"

"Are you criticizing me for thinking I deserve a shot at running my family's company?" she responded, acting surprised and offended.

He wasn't fooled by her innocent act. "Deserve a shot…" he murmured ironically. "More like staging a coup."

"Are you seriously afraid of a little competition?" A taunting smile played over her lips.

"Not if it's fair and aboveboard."

"What else could it be?"

"You convincing Sienna to distract me while you schemed to undermine my position here was hardly honest."

"It didn't take any convincing." Teagan arched her eyebrows. "So, you've known all along what I was up to and turned my sister's attraction to you to your own advantage. Well played."

Teagan's calculated assessment recalled the argument between him and Sienna. She'd seemed genuinely distraught at being caught participating in her sister's scheme. Not coolly disappointed to be bested as Teagan was at the moment, but cognizant of the repercussions for him.

"Played," he repeated, keeping a firm grip on his fury. "So, you admit you've been treating this as a big game."

"Don't use my words against me. I saw an opportunity and I took it. There's nothing wrong with that."

"You twisted your sister's emotions for your own ends. In my book that's not what family members do to each other."

"She likes you. I thought you liked her. It seemed as if she could use a little fun. That's all I was thinking about."

For an instant he recalled Sienna's face as she realized that he'd slept with her after finding out that she'd been blackballed from the primary art market for her sketchy activities. No doubt she'd felt betrayed. Well, that was nothing compared to how he'd felt as he'd stood before his parents yesterday.

"Well, just so you know, you will never be the CEO of this company." As much satisfaction as he took saying those words, the sense that he had made the right choice was more important.

"That's not really up to you to decide," Teagan countered.

"You're right. It's up to the current chairman of the board—my grandfather—and the current CEO and president—my father. And after I shared with them that you deliberately spilled the story about my trip to Savannah when Sienna asked you not to—"

He actually hadn't said anything, but Teagan wasn't the only one who could use lies and misinformation to throw his opponent off track.

"Did Sienna tell you that?" Teagan interrupted, rolling her eyes. "Of course you believe her."

"She didn't tell me anything. I overheard her asking you to keep quiet yesterday morning."

He paused and waited as her poker face slipped before continuing. "You had no qualms about hurting me or my family to get what you wanted and when they heard that, they were pretty clear that you're not the sort of person they want running the company they spent their lives building."

He watched the lie sink in for several seconds, feeling no guilt whatsoever at the horror and grief she displayed.

She rallied faster than he could've believed possible. "I'm surprised that you went to them with no proof."

"Do you seriously think I need to prove anything to them?" Ethan offered a flat smile. "They know me. They trust me." And then, because he knew from his conversations with Sienna exactly how to push Teagan's buttons, he added, "And I'm not the outsider in this little scenario. You are. I might not be a Watts by blood, but I am family."

The point being that she couldn't come in with her New York City tricks and expect to shatter a lifetime of love. Love. As if the woman had any clue what the word meant. She certainly hadn't shown that she cared for her sister. If she had, she would've known that what she was doing to Sienna would rip her apart.

Sienna was on her way to the front hall with the first of her suitcases when she met her sister storming up the stairs in her direction. Seeing the angry flush coloring Teagan's cheeks, Sienna braced for another confrontation.

"Hey," she began as they met on the landing between the first and second floors. "How come you're home?"

"Declan Scott is the devil!" Teagan declared, her eyes narrowed with murderous intent.

"Well, yes," Sienna agreed, thinking about how many times since they'd first met in high school that Teagan had clashed with the handsome real estate tycoon. "So?"

"So?" Teagan echoed in outrage.

"He's back in New York," Sienna reminded her sister, resisting the urge to roll her eyes at Teagan's melodrama.

"No. He's here. In Charleston. I just ran into him. I don't know when exactly he showed up, but I suspect not long after we arrived."

"What is he doing here?" Sienna clutched the handle of her suitcase to her suddenly churning stomach. When Teagan and Declan were in the same space, their battles had a tendency to damage everyone around them.

Over the years the two strong personalities had struck at each other in a private war that began when Teagan had gone after his sister, who'd been a classmate of Sienna's. She'd never understood what had motivated Teagan, but the incident had caused Declan to notice her and they'd been enemies ever since.

"Ruining everything." Teagan flipped her long hair, eyes becoming arctic jade as she continued, "He tipped Ethan off from the start."

"From the start?" Sienna grabbed for the railing as her knees wobbled. Ethan had known all along that Teagan was out to steal the CEO position from him? "What do you mean? Tipped him off how?"

"He sent Ethan an anonymous email the day we arrived, warning him that I intended on taking over Watts Shipping. He's been playing with me this whole time."

Click. The pieces snapped into place. Was Declan responsible for Ethan learning about her troubles with the New York City galleries? She thought of Ethan's pursuit of her and cringed. The charm that had swept Sienna off her feet took on a sinister quality now that she recognized the manipulation behind it. Every time he'd taken her into his arms, it had been a sham. Every smile he'd bestowed on her. All of it had been a lie. Sienna flushed hot with shame. A second later she shivered as humiliation and despair moved through her like a biting wind off the ocean.

"Why would he do that?" Sienna asked, her fury blazing to life. Declan Scott was one area where the Burns sisters agreed.

"Because it's Declan," Teagan said, tossing her head. "He takes any opportunity to ruin my life."

"And mine, as well," Sienna muttered, recalling all the

times the war between the two had spilled over. "Was he the one who told you about why Ethan went to Savannah?"

"No."

Despite Teagan's closed expression, Sienna believed Declan wasn't the source of that information. But her short-term relief ended with her sister's next words.

"Don't worry. I have a plan to get rid of him."

This only reaffirmed Sienna's decision to leave Charleston. "Good luck with that."

As she began moving past her sister, Teagan blocked Sienna's path.

"You can't leave me here alone. Ethan told his entire family that I'm only here to take over the family company."

Good! Yet Sienna couldn't crow about her sister's scheme falling apart. The setback would only cause Teagan to dig in and try harder.

"Isn't it better for you to be up front about your intentions?"

"Are you kidding? Thanks to him they're all going to hate me."

"I'm sure that's not true," Sienna soothed. "But there is an alternative. You could return to New York and give up this crazy idea of running Watts Shipping." The instant that suggestion left her lips, Sienna realized she'd made a mistake.

"Give up?" Teagan looked appalled. "And let Ethan and Declan win?"

"Win?" Sienna couldn't believe what she was hearing. "This isn't a game. These are real people with real feelings."

"You don't understand. You never have."

"I do understand. Better than you realize. All my life I've been in your shadow. I watched you fight and scheme to be on top. So that everyone would love you." Sienna gulped in air and rushed on. "Why don't you stop relying on your beauty and success and let people love you for who you are?"

Speaking her mind for the first time left her heart pounding so hard she thought she might stroke out. No matter how many times Teagan had hurt her in the past, Sienna loved her and only wished for her to be happy. It just seemed that Teagan was always going about it the wrong way.

"Really?" Teagan sneered. "What would you know about being loved? Our parents adopted me because you weren't good enough."

Compared to what she'd been through with Ethan, this declaration landed like the punch of a downy feather. Sienna's mind went oddly calm. Her relationship with Teagan had always been a complex scramble of love and pain and understanding and exasperation.

"You don't think I know that?" Sienna began. "Mother placed more value on appearance than anyone I know except perhaps you. I'm not beautiful. And I don't share your aggressive ambition to rule everyone and everything in my orbit. But I am smart and loyal. I have a career I love and friends I trust who support me. Those things might not be important to you, but they matter to me." Rehearsed hundreds of times in her mind, the words poured out of her in a jagged rush. "And the best part of all is that I can look myself in the mirror every day and not be ashamed of who I hurt or the harm I've caused. Can you say the same?"

Sienna was gasping for breath by the time she finished her impassioned speech. Yet in the aftermath of the fervent soliloquy, she wasn't suffused with triumph or vindicated. One look at Teagan's scornful expression left Sienna hollow and empty.

"I don't need you," Teagan declared, her voice low and biting as she headed toward the door. "I never have and I never will."

Fighting tears of helpless frustration, Sienna resumed manhandling her heavy luggage down the endless flights of stairs. She was hot, angry and miserable by the time she exited the house with the second suitcase only to discover that the car pulling into the driveway wasn't her ride to the airport, but was driven by the last person she wanted to see.

"You're leaving?" Ethan asked unnecessarily, eyeing her suitcases.

What did he expect? Even if things between them hadn't exploded into a million shards of anger, resentment and pain, she'd planned to head back to New York in a day or two. Neither one of them had spoken about her staying longer or him visiting her between business trips. The revelations over the last twenty-four hours didn't change the reality that they'd had a fling and now it was over.

"There's an auction in Salzburg coming up next week." She would be bidding on pieces for four clients. "I need to head back to New York to prepare."

"I thought you'd planned to stay a little longer."

"That was before."

Had he already forgotten his brutal indictment of her as Teagan's feckless pawn in the battle for control of Watts Shipping? He couldn't possibly expect that she'd stick around for more abuse?

"And you weren't going to say goodbye?"

Sienna gaped at him. "I thought we already had."

The ride she'd been waiting for pulled into the front driveway and came to a stop behind Ethan's car. She began rolling her luggage toward it as the driver got out and went toward the trunk.

"I spoke with my parents," Ethan began from behind her, his deep voice heavy with anguish and rage. "They are devastated."

She winced as her heart clenched. The impulse to comfort him rose in her, but she gritted her teeth and resisted. He wasn't interested in being consoled by her. He wanted to punish. Handing off her suitcases to the driver, Sienna turned to Ethan.

"Do you feel at all guilty about what you and your sister have done?" he continued, speaking each word with deliberate care, letting his distaste show.

"The only thing I did was not tell you that Teagan wanted to be the next CEO of Watts Shipping," Sienna reiterated, wishing he'd just let her leave. "Besides that, I haven't done anything to you or your family."

"No regrets then?"

"Just one. I regret coming here." Because if she hadn't, she never would've met Ethan or had her heart torn apart in the battle between him and her sister. Sienna sighed. "No, that's not true. I'm glad I met you. I just wish that you weren't like Teagan." Misery shredded her voice. "You knew all along what she was up to and used me to get to her."

She hadn't realized how much it would hurt to face him, knowing that he'd been misleading her about his feelings this whole time. He'd accused her of sleeping with him as part of a scheme, but obviously that was what had motivated his actions. He'd lied to her. Used her desire against her. And he'd manipulated her as if she was nothing but a pawn in his chess match with her sister.

She searched Ethan's expression for remorse or grief, but saw only righteous obstinacy. How had she missed such devious calculation on Ethan's part?

"Stop playing the wronged innocent," he retorted, his tone roughening with irritation. "You could've warned me what Teagan was up to, but you didn't."

"You're right, but to be fair, she's my sister and you're—"

"Just some guy you had sex with?"

"Sure…that." She held strong against the bitterness in

his voice and met his eyes without flinching. Maybe she'd been a fool to fall for him in the first place, but she didn't have to keep making the same mistake. "So tell me, if you haven't trusted me from the start, why did you bring me with you to Savannah to meet your family?"

Why make her feel like her company mattered to him? That he appreciated her support and craved her affection?

"Maybe because I was curious to see how far you would go for her." He leaned toward her, pinning her with his dark stare. "I guess this weekend I found out."

Sienna recoiled from the implication that she'd seduced him to gain his trust. "I didn't sleep with you to help my sister."

"No?"

"No. I care about you and I thought you felt the same way about me." Sienna put her hand on his forearm. When his forbidding expression remained unchanged, she let it fall back to her side. "Until today I had no idea how wrong I was."

"I had to know what you were up to."

How had she been so blind? She should've recognized that it was beyond crazy that Ethan could be falling for her.

Sienna offered him a tight smile. "I guess that means we can both stop pretending that last weekend meant something."

"It meant something to me," he said in a shocking turn-around, his expression like granite, his gaze steady and sincere.

"Damn you, Ethan Watts," she cried, confused and terrified by the way her heart reached for him. "I'm done being manipulated by you. Now, if you'll kindly move." Desperation gave her the strength to wedge her laptop case into the space between him and the car and shift him aside. "I have a plane to catch. And I really can't afford to miss it."

Thirteen

The two days following Sienna's departure from Charleston didn't go as Ethan expected they would. He assumed that with her gone and Teagan rethinking her strategy, his emotions would calm and his focus would shift back to work, socializing and family time. Instead, he caught himself snapping at his employees, brooding alone at his house and turning down invitations from everyone. In fact, his antisocial behavior had gotten so bad that he'd stopped answering calls altogether.

Which was why he wasn't all that surprised when Paul appeared in his office with no warning, a thick file in his hand. "So, I finally got a line on your anonymous friend," his brother said, skipping the lecture about how the family was worried about him.

Ethan stuck out his hand and accepted the file. "I thought you said the email address was impossible to track."

"Did I say that?" Paul smirked. "Maybe what I should've

said was that it was impossible to track through normal channels."

"Do I want to ask?" Ethan began, knowing when his brother started talking about the dark web it was like watching a foreign language film without subtitles. "Nope, I don't wanna know. Who is he or she?"

Paul slouched in one of Ethan's guest chairs and propped his cheek on his hand. "A guy by the name of Declan Scott."

Ethan scanned the file without registering much of the data. His thoughts churned as he imagined what he'd like to do to the guy whose misinformation had made Ethan doubt Sienna.

"Aside from the fact that he's from New York, how is he connected to Teagan?" he asked.

"They attended the same high school, although they were three years apart. Since then they've appeared at the same events, but never together. They have friends in common, but from what I can gather they can't stand each other."

Having been on the receiving end of Teagan's scheming, it made sense that she would've made enemies. "Okay, so that explains why the guy warned me against her, but what's with all the cloak-and-dagger business?" Ethan spread several photos across his desk, of Declan Scott. He looked like an aloof Ralph Lauren model, with classic *Town & Country* stuffiness. "But what does he get out of involving himself in our business here in Charleston?"

"Why don't you ask him?" Paul got to his feet. "He has a suite at Hotel Bennett."

"He's here?" The news propelled Ethan to his feet. He snatched up his car keys. It was the most alive he'd felt in two days. "I don't suppose you got a room number."

Ten minutes later Ethan was heading for the boutique hotel. He had attended several parties there, including one wedding, and been to Gabrielle, their signature restaurant, on several occasions. In fact, if he and Sienna hadn't gone to Savannah, he would've taken her there.

He'd lost count of the number of times over the last two days when he'd imaged how Sienna would've reacted to a place or an experience. Thoughts of her consumed him. As did the melancholy he couldn't seem to shake since she'd left. And as many times as he'd reminded himself what she'd done and that he couldn't possibly care about someone who'd been working against him, nothing seemed to ease the constant ache in his chest.

He missed her. All the damned time. No matter how angry he was with her for what she'd done. No matter how many times he called himself a stubborn fool for allowing himself to trust her with his secrets and fears. Despite all that had happened, Ethan couldn't shake the certainty that he'd been wrong to let her go back to New York.

The lack of closure was making him crazy. That was the only thing that could account for his sleepless nights and manic restlessness.

At the hotel, Ethan pounded on the door to Declan Scott's suite, letting his frustration out. The man who answered was tall, lean and dressed in a crisp navy suit, but not Declan Scott.

"I'm here to speak to your boss," Ethan said, comfortable with his assumption that the busy real estate mogul wouldn't stop working even while away from New York.

"He's—"

"Let him in," a voice called from inside the suite, the laconic tones rich with amusement.

Ethan found his quarry idling on the sofa, a tumbler of amber liquid dangling from his long fingers. The New Yorker made no move to rise and greet his guest, prompting Ethan to set aside his southern politeness and charm.

"So you're my anonymous friend?" Ethan twisted the

last word into an insult as he surveyed the tall man. "Declan Scott, is it?"

The other man inclined his head. "Sorry we're meeting under such difficult circumstances."

"Difficult circumstances?" Ethan fumed at Scott's utter lack of sincerity. He so obviously didn't give a damn that his meddling had ripped apart Ethan's world. "You caused this mess."

"I didn't." Scott's calm fanned Ethan's temper, making it flare even hotter. "All I did was warn you about Teagan. You chose how to use the information."

Was this the sort of reckless game they played in New York? If that was the case then maybe he was glad that Sienna was gone.

A dagger-thrust of pain in his chest said otherwise.

"What exactly was your purpose in contacting me?" Ethan demanded, making no attempt to disguise his disgust.

"I didn't think you were up to the challenge of dealing with Teagan on your own. She can be quite a handful." Scott assessed him with a pointed look. "Was I wrong?"

Ethan ignored the question. "So what's your interest in all of this?"

"Teagan refuses to let me have something I want." Scott tugged at his shirt cuff. "I decided to show her how that feels."

Whoa. Ethan mentally reviewed the additional information Paul had uncovered about Teagan and her connection to Declan Scott. The pair had been sworn enemies since the beginning. Although the reason why escaped him. Had they rubbed each other wrong from the start? Had they once been close and had a falling out? Or had they loved each other at first sight?

Ethan recalled his own reaction when he'd glimpsed

Sienna on the driveway outside his grandfather's home. And the hurt in her eyes the day she left. Pain he'd caused.

Rather than face his guilt, Ethan attacked the man before him. "But it wasn't just Teagan you harmed with your games."

"My games?" Lazy amusement curved Scott's lips. "You're one to talk You've been playing games of your own with Sienna."

The accusation hit home, but Ethan countered hotly, "You fed me misleading information."

"Seems to me," Scott began, his level of detachment impossibly high, "that you are blaming me for your failure to trust the woman you love."

Love.

"I don't know what you're talking about. I'm not in love."

What did Ethan know about that emotion? He knew how he felt about the parents who'd raised him and the grandfather who believed in him. He would do anything for the Shaw twins and his brother, Paul. Yet he'd been holding back his heart for a long time. Not believing they could possibly love him because he wasn't one of them, he'd gone through the motions of being a good son, brother, friend and ally. He'd spread his charm around, but hadn't truly given of himself.

With Sienna it had been different.

He'd opened up to her about his feelings of isolation and let her glimpse his fear of not being loved. She in turn shared what it was like to grow up feeling unworthy and unloved. He felt closer to her than anyone he'd ever known. So, of course, he'd messed it up.

Unable to believe that her friendship and affection had come without strings, he'd asked her to choose him over her sister. She'd refused and he'd used that as proof that she was against him. He hadn't trusted that her feelings for him could possibly be real. The sting of betrayal had been a loud screech in his brain, drowning out all rational thought.

"So you're perfectly fine since Sienna returned to New York?"

"How did you—?"

Ethan never finished the question. It didn't matter how Declan knew so much. What consumed him was Sienna's absence. He was definitely not fine. Being without her these last few days was proof that the joy she'd brought into his life was addictive and made everything brighter and clear.

"You don't wish things had turned out differently?" Declan Scott continued. "Like perhaps if you'd given her the benefit of the doubt that you might still be together?"

The way the man asked the question—as if he already knew the answer—irritated Ethan. The level of the New Yorker's insight into Ethan's private thoughts spooked him. It was almost as if Scott had an inside track to the hell Ethan had been going through. A hell the other man had been partially responsible for creating with his misleading emails about Sienna.

"Look," Ethan said, realizing that his initial reason for confronting Scott no longer mattered. Sienna had been the victim in the feud between her sister and this man. Criticizing her for being loyal to her sister hadn't been fair. "I don't give a damn what sort of twisted games you and Teagan play, but going forward, leave Sienna alone."

"Or?"

"You'll find out, if you ever bother Sienna again." Without waiting for Scott's comeback, Ethan turned and strode from the suite.

The confrontation with Scott had given Ethan's perceptions a much-needed reset. Before leaving Charleston, Sienna had confessed to caring for him, but he'd been too angry and stubborn to believe her. Now, with the New

Yorker's words compelling Ethan to confront his feelings for Sienna, memories of their time together ran on a loop in his brain. Too late, he was grasping that the reason he'd been so drawn to her was that they both felt like outsiders around the people they loved. Yet with her, he'd known a sense of belonging that made everything better.

And instead of sharing his heart with her, he'd let her board a plane and fly away.

Could he fix it? Would she give him the chance? One thing was certain: he couldn't win her heart from here in Charleston. He needed a boots-on-the-ground approach and that meant flying to New York City.

And if in his absence Teagan got the toehold she was after at Watts Shipping?

Ethan brushed aside the question. No career was more important than being with the woman of his dreams.

Following the art auction in Salzburg, Sienna took a few extra days in Europe to reach out to some of her contacts and pursue leads on new clients. Throwing herself into work offered a temporary reprieve from heartache, but she couldn't run herself ragged indefinitely and after ten days, she returned to New York.

While the plane taxied to the terminal, Sienna checked her messages and spotted a text from Gia. Worn out by endless, sleepless nights trying not to think about Ethan[, Sienna had neglected to organize a car to pick her up. To her delight, Gia had taken matters into her own hands and a driver would be waiting in the baggage claim area to drive her into Manhattan.

But when Sienna stepped off the escalator, the man holding a sign with her name on it was the last person she expected to see. With her heart in her throat and her mind struggling to adjust to seeing Ethan in New York, she shuffled toward him.

"What are you doing here?" she demanded, wishing she wasn't quite so overjoyed.

"I came to see you."

How dare he spring this surprise visit on her and embroil her friend in the scheme. Sienna would have to have a stern chat with Gia. "I really wish you hadn't."

"I don't believe you mean that."

"Believe it." With a rude snort, she turned her back on him and marched toward the carousel, hoping to spot her luggage and get the hell away from Ethan. She wasn't surprised when he followed her.

"I'm sorry how I handled things with you about the whole Teagan-wanting-to-be-CEO thing."

She shot him a sidelong glance. "Neither one of us deserves stellar marks for what we did."

"I shouldn't have gotten angry because you wanted to help your sister."

Sienna held firm against her longing to have everything be all right between them. He'd hurt her and she wasn't going to let a few pretty words lead her astray again.

Conscious that they were in a crowded airport, she lowered her voice. "But you do realize that I didn't help her by sleeping with you to get information?"

"Yes." He dropped his volume to match hers. "Deep down I knew better than to believe something like that."

A familiar piece of luggage was gliding in their direction and Sienna began moving to intercept it. Ethan was there before her, his strong arm reaching past her to snag the handle and lift it off the silver belt as if it weighed significantly less than its forty-six pounds. If she'd hoped to secure her suitcase and escape Ethan in a taxi, she was doomed to be frustrated. Instead, she ended up chasing after him as he moved purposefully toward the exit that would take them to the helicopter shuttle leaving for Manhattan.

Sienna withdrew into herself and maintained radio silence as they switched from shuttle to helicopter to taxi. She grappled with the conflict between her instincts and her brain. One wanted to believe that everything would be okay now that he recognized he'd been wrong. The other insisted that misunderstanding hadn't created the problems between them, but Ethan's lack of trust and her failure to be up-front with him had.

When it became obvious outside her building that she wasn't going to shake Ethan until they cleared the air, Sienna invited him up. As the elevator ascended, she turned to face him.

"Look, if you want to be friendly because my sister is your cousin, then I can do that." She noticed his whole manner brighten and didn't know what to make of it. "But really, this could've been resolved over the phone. You didn't have to come all the way to New York."

"But if I called, you might've avoided answering and I wanted to make sure you knew just how serious I am about making things right between us."

While she wasn't immune to his enticing half smile and earnest puppy-dog eyes, her weeks apart from him had sharpened her need for self-preservation.

Making herself sound as prickly and forbidding as possible, she said, "We could've video chatted."

"We could've," he murmured, his voice whiskey smooth. "But don't they say make-up sex is the best?"

Sienna would give anything to stop the way her body electrified at the thought of being in his arms once more. Heat flooded her cheeks despite her best effort to remain aloof and immune. She shoved her hands into her pockets to avoid snatching his lapels and yanking him toward her.

As much as she wanted to give in to her longing, she didn't know if she was strong enough to have sex with him one last time, and then say goodbye.

"I think what happened in Savannah should stay in Savannah, don't you?"

This didn't crush him the way she hoped. Fortunately, the elevator doors opened and she was able to make a break for it. Once again, she realized escaping Ethan was impossible.

"Not at all." His long stride eliminated her brief lead, and he matched her pace as they drew near her apartment door. "I refuse to believe that we're done."

Pausing outside her apartment, she gaped at him. After they'd spent their time together lying to each other about what was going on with Teagan and the CEO position at Watts Shipping, how could he possibly think they had any chance in hell of making something work? Yet her skin prickled as joy rushed through her. Did he want to put the past behind them and start fresh?

No. Impossible.

"Done?" She drew in a shaky breath before continuing. "I don't think we ever got started."

"I disagree."

"You were so busy suspecting me of conspiring against you that we never had a chance to develop real feelings for each other." She paused and smiled through her pain. "Besides, from the moment we met, I knew that it was only a matter of time before you'd move onto someone new."

"So, I was just a fling for you?"

Was that actual disappointment in his dark brown eyes? Sienna badly wanted to believe that she'd meant something to him.

"It started that way," she admitted, biting her lip to

keep from confessing more. "Whatever. Look, none of this matters now."

"It matters to me."

"Why?" She wished he'd stop tormenting her with possibilities. "Can you honestly say that after what happened we can put the past behind us?"

"I can and I will." Ethan took her hands in his and squeezed until she met his gaze. "Asking you to come with me to meet my family had nothing to do with your sister or her schemes. I wanted you with me. I didn't understand at the time why I valued your companionship and your support, but now I do."

Although Sienna dropped her gaze from his beguiling expression, she was already too susceptible to hope. Could she trust that he'd had a change of heart?

"I've had a lot of time to put things in perspective these last few weeks," Sienna began, tears stinging her eyes as she forced herself to be rational. "What stands out to me is that you and Teagan both want everyone to admire you. It's all showmanship and sparkle. And I fall for it every time."

"You fell for me?" A wicked smile kicked up one corner of his lips.

"This isn't a good thing." Sienna scowled at him, edging ever closer to despair. "I realize that I have a type and that type is charming and manipulative."

Tears blurred her vision as she shoved her key into the lock. She got it in on the first try, stunned that her shaking hands hadn't made this impossible. Twisting the doorknob, she then threw the door open.

"But you did fall." When she refused to repeat her confession, he seized her by the shoulders and gave her a little shake. "I fell for you, as well."

"I'm over it now." She broke free of his grip and shoved her suitcase ahead of her into the apartment.

"Well, I'm not," Ethan called after her. "I fell hard. Harder than I imagined possible."

Five half-stumbling steps later, she burst into the living room and gaped at the extravagant bouquets that filled the space with scent and color. Multiple surfaces held gigantic flower arrangements but the centerpiece was a massive display of red roses.

"I love you, Sienna."

She whipped around and spotted him standing four feet away. Everything seemed to freeze. Her heart. Her lungs. Ethan's earnest expression. It was as if his words had hit the pause button on her life, allowing her thoughts and feelings to process every moment they'd spent together and make sense of the rush of data.

"You love me?" she repeated, experimenting with the words. "You can't."

"I can and I do." His teeth flashed, amusement brightening his whole appearance. He came toward her with his hands outstretched, but even though her whole body ached for his embrace, she backed away.

"But how? I mean, after everything with Teagan… You hate me." This last came out as a ragged whisper.

"Never." He seized her hands and raised them to his lips. "I was angry and scared, but never, ever did I hate you." Ethan wrapped one arm around her waist and brought her tight against him. "For a long time I felt like I was on the outside looking in. And then you came along and that feeling stopped. Being with you makes me feel like I'm a part of something. The whole thing about being adopted wasn't what was eating at me. It was that I'd closed myself off to everyone I loved. You changed that."

"I love you," Sienna blurted out, the words exploding from her in a gush of relief. "I thought I was crazy to feel such a strong connection to you so fast, but every moment with you makes me so happy."

"And I want you to continue to feel that way. Whatever it takes. If it means I give up Watts Shipping so there's peace between us and Teagan…"

"I can't ask you to do that for me." While Sienna appreciated that he was ready to make sacrifices for her, their relationship would only work if both of them were happy. "You asked me to side with you against Teagan and I'm willing to do that. You are my family now. My loyalty is yours no matter what."

Sienna wrapped her arms around Ethan's neck and brought her lips into contact with his. The kiss held both passion and promise. Loving him made her world better and she was beyond blissful that they'd found a way past their mistakes.

"You're the most fascinating and genuine woman I know," Ethan said, his eyes soft with affection and joy. "I love that you're brilliant and funny, not to mention obsessed with learning interesting facts about everywhere you go. You knew exactly what to say when I grappled with finding my birth mother and how to give me the space to process my feelings. Your curves go on for days and sex with you is the best I've ever had." He grew serious. "I've never been comfortable being myself around anyone the way I can be with you. It's peaceful and feels like home."

"That's how I feel when I'm with you."

"Then I hope that means you see us having a future."

"Of course. In fact, I'd already given some thought to moving to Charleston."

"You don't say," he teased, dropping a kiss on her nose. "Well, I'm glad to hear that, because I want to marry you, Sienna Burns."

Sienna smiled as she realized the future she'd dreamed

about while in Savannah with Ethan was about to become a reality. "I love you and want to spend the rest of my life with you as Mrs. Ethan Watts."

They sealed the moment with a long, hungry kiss that left them out of breath and grinning.

"Now, I'll be wanting to put this on your finger." Ethan produced a gorgeous solitaire diamond ring. "So you can't take back your promise to be with me always."

As stunning as the ring was, Sienna only had eyes for the man who slid it over her knuckle and into place on her left hand. "Always and forever."

* * * * *

THE LAST LITTLE SECRET

ZURI DAY

For we hopeful romantics
who know love always wins

No matter the challenges
when the journey begins

Love exposes our secrets,
a new world to unfold.

While nourishing our bodies
and filling our souls.

One

"Mr. Breedlove, your two o'clock is here."

"Thanks. Send her in."

"Will do."

"Hold my calls, Anita. I don't want to be interrupted."

"Got it, boss."

Nick shut off the intercom and second-guessed his decision for the fifth or sixth time. For a decisive man like Nick Breedlove, that didn't happen often. Hands down, Samantha Price was one of the best interior designers in the business, the only one he'd put complete confidence in to get him and the company out of an impossible jam. That she had become available was nothing short of a miracle. Hiring her was no doubt a sound business decision but personally, was it wise? He heard a soft knock and braced himself. If seeing her again caused the same reaction as last time, he might lose control of the meeting before it began. It had been more than four years but the memories from that night flooded his mind as though they'd happened just yesterday. The door opened. There she was. In the flesh. More beautiful than he remembered.

He stood, with hand outstretched. "Hello, Sam. It's been a long time."

"Hey, Nick," Sam replied, her smile tight yet polite as she clasped his hand ever so briefly while maintaining a good distance between them.

Was she remembering, too? Was the attraction that threatened to tighten his groin and quicken his breathing a mutual situation?

"I appreciate you coming on such short notice," he managed, a 007 coolness hiding a set of hormones suddenly raging as if he were fifteen instead of the twenty-seven he'd turned just a few short months ago. He willed his body to relax, behave and not embarrass them both. *Get it together, bro!*

"CANN International is one of the largest, most successful hotel developers in the world. Plus, with the urgency given to meeting as quickly as possible, I was curious and couldn't resist."

"Thank you for coming."

Once again Nick willed away the untimely musings and forced his thoughts more fully into the present. He motioned for Sam to have a seat in one of two chairs facing his desk, while he returned to his executive chair. A wide, paper-strewn desk created a physical barrier between them. Nick was appreciative of being reminded about this meeting's intent—all business, nothing personal. His body would do well to get the message, too.

He watched Sam place her briefcase on the floor, then sit back with squared shoulders. Professionalism oozed from her pores. Of course she wasn't daydreaming about that night long ago. She'd made time for the company and a possible job, not for him. Nick mentally chastised himself for the moment of weakness that had taken him down memory lane, and the discipline it took to rein in his body now. No matter that her hands were softer than he remembered, the designer suit failed to hide those dangerous curves, and the subtle scent that tickled his nose when he'd neared her for that handshake had made him want to pull her into an embrace. If the interview went well and Sam joined his team, they'd be working very closely together. Too close for a casual sexual dalliance. He'd do well to stay focused and remember that.

"Can I get you anything before we begin?"

"No, thank you," Sam replied. "I'm more than a little curious about what your assistant called an urgent matter but was unable to provide details."

"As I'd instructed," Nick said, leaning back in his chair. "I was equally intrigued with the news about you—that you were not only back in the States but here in Vegas and looking for clients."

Sam crossed her legs in one graceful, fluid motion with no idea, Nick assumed, of how utterly sexy a move it was.

"How did you hear? Probably someone from the function I recently attended," she continued before he could answer. "I did a great deal of networking to get the word out about the rebirth of Priceless Designs."

"Possibly." Nick shrugged. "It's a small town. News travels fast. Especially when your mother is Victoria Breed-love."

Sam smiled, this one genuine and relaxed. Her shoulders, tense and squared since entering his office, softened along with her face.

"How is your mother?"

"Still as nosy as she is wonderful."

"I don't know her personally, of course, but from everything I've read or heard about her she appears to have a great heart. That was evidenced at the luncheon, and the generous check presented to the Women in Business organization. I didn't see her, though. Someone else presented the check."

"Mom wasn't there. She and Dad have fallen in love with Scandinavia and since he's assured Mom his retirement is permanent, Dad has cloaked hotel location scouting missions under the guise of Nordic vacations. The girls stepped in to fill the gap left in her increasingly frequent absences."

"The girls?"

"Lauren, Ryan and Dee, my sisters-in-law, or in-love, as Mom always corrects me."

"Oh. Right."

"Their marriages were the wedding bells heard round the world. Surely you read about them."

Sam gave a slight shake of the head. "I'd heard about Christian's wedding but only learned that two more brothers had tied the knot upon returning to the States. How many brothers besides you does that leave standing single?"

"I stand alone," Nick dramatically intoned. "We have several business partners on the continent who said their nuptials made a big splash even there."

"While in Africa, I lived in a rather insular world."

"Since word on the street is you married a prince, a luxurious one, no doubt."

"Yes."

A physical wall couldn't have made Sam's intentions clearer. Whatever had happened while abroad, she didn't want to talk about it. But Nick couldn't resist.

"Yet you're back here and working. What does your husband think about that?"

"It doesn't matter. We're no longer together."

"Separated?"

"Divorced."

The tone beneath that one word closed the door on the subject of Sam's personal life better than King Tut's sealed tomb. It only made Nick even more curious, about both her failed marriage and her current love life. Now was obviously not the time to talk about it, but one day... Patience was not a virtue Nick knew well, but one he could employ when necessary. Now was definitely one of those times.

His body language remained relaxed but he adopted a businesslike tone. "Whatever brings you back to Las Vegas, your timing couldn't be better. I need the best and fastest-working designer that money can buy. Before running off to become an African princess, that was you."

A grin accompanied Sam's twinkling eyes. "I'd like to think it still is. What's going on?"

"A project that has to stay on schedule and a designer who isn't delivering on the promises she made."

"How many rooms are we talking about?"

"Not rooms...homes." Nick noted Sam's surprised expression. "This isn't a hotel design. It's a series of private island homes being advertised for vacation rental among the world's most elite."

"Wow. I had no idea you guys had expanded beyond the original hotel framework. Considering how the hospitality industry is changing, though, it sounds like a smart move."

"It's proven to be right on time with industry trends."

"Does that smirk confirm the obvious, that this was your idea?"

"Still a smart-ass, I see."

"Takes one to know one."

"Ha!"

"So I'm right."

"All of the brothers are involved but yes, it's more or less my baby. Which means failure is not an option. You feel me?"

"Tell me more."

Sam leaned forward, unconsciously revealing the slightest peek of a creamy quarter-moon of her breast. When his attention returned to her face, Sam was frowning. *Damn.* To her professional credit, however, she didn't comment on eyes determined to rove on their own. She simply adjusted her blouse and sat back, waiting, to learn why Nick had brought her here.

Nick leaned back as well, determined to take control of a meeting he'd called, ensconced in the comfort of discussing an industry he knew better than he knew himself. Business now, pleasure later, he thought as he began discussing his baby, CANN Isles. There was no way around it, even pushed to the back of his mind. The attraction for one Ms. Samantha "Sam" Price was real, intense and not going away.

Before it was mere speculation. Now she was sure. It shouldn't have mattered how much she wanted to see her old lover. Not only should Sam have not returned Anita's phone call, she shouldn't have made this appointment. She shouldn't be here with Nick. Her body was clear about it even if her mind wasn't sure. Every cell of her body had lit up, awakened by the irrefutable attraction that hadn't dimmed in all this time away. An attraction that given the sticky situation that even thinking of working with Nick presented, and the increasingly troublesome email and text exchanges with her ex, had no chance of being acted upon.

Being this close to him in proximity was TROUBLE, all caps. Just seeing him relax made her heart skip. She watched the lines on his forehead fade away as he broke into a spiel he'd probably recited a hundred times. Clearly, speaking about the company was his forte, his stomping grounds, his zone. But that brief look of desire she'd glimpsed before Nick realized he'd been caught staring at her cleavage suggested something impossible. That he still felt the attraction, too. Surely after all this time it was something she must have imagined. While the night she shared with Nick was seared into her conscience, and intimacy with her husband had been fleeting at best, she imagined there'd been a constant stream of women in and out of Nick's bedroom to make him forget all about it.

She wasn't quite sure when her attention went from what Nick was saying to the lips forming the words that came out of his mouth. But somewhere within his glib delivery about CANN International's latest expansion beyond casino hotels and spas into the lucrative and growing industry of offering private rental vacation homes, she was struck by the perfectly formed Cupid lips enunciating goals and intentions and reminding her of how skillfully they'd brought her to and over the orgasmic edge and changed her life forever. If her body was a violin, Nick's tongue was the bow that had played a melody etched in her soul, stamped into her mind and burned inside her heart. That night just over four years and nine short months ago when her world was rocked and shifted on its axis, was one she had no idea would be the catalyst for an adventure that took her from America to Africa and from fairy tale to nightmare, in less than five years.

"…Djibouti. Have you been there?"

Uh-oh. The uptick of his voice suggested to Sam that she'd just been asked a question. She had no idea what about.

"Um, not sure."

Wrong answer. Nick's frown told it all.

"Djibouti isn't the most popular of tourist destinations, but it is certainly memorable. Yet you're not sure?"

"No, I'm sure. I've never been there. Sorry, I got distracted. I silenced my phone but it's still vibrating." Sam reached into her purse. "I'll shut it off."

"Back less than a month and already in demand?"

"Something like that."

She quickly checked her text messages. It wasn't a slew of potential clients trying to reach her, but the very reason why she shouldn't be sitting there. Why as much as she wanted to, needed to, was desperate to, even, she couldn't take this job. No matter the pay, which she knew would be top-shelf.

Shooting off a quick reply, she then turned off the vibrating notifier and dropped the phone in the tote on the floor. "Sorry."

"No worries."

"You mentioned Djibouti. One of the islands CANN International owns is located there?"

Nick nodded. "Just off the coast on the Gulf of Aden. The first property built there is one of our smaller hotels, only eighty-nine rooms. All suites, though, with living and dining spaces, and spectacular ocean or mountain views. The casino is the building's jewel, of course, boasting a Michelin-star restaurant and world-class spa."

"I believe you guys are onto something. From all I've seen and understand, Africa's the next great economic frontier."

"That's what we believe, with Djibouti becoming the next Dubai. It's why we're building more hotels all over the continent and have either purchased or designed a number of islands to house our luxury home rentals."

"So…you contacted me because you need someone based in Africa?"

"No. The projects needing immediate attention are mostly here in the US, along the eastern seaboard. But there are a couple in Hawaii and one in the Bahamas as well."

"All of this sounds amazing, Nick, but I don't yet understand the urgency or why I'm here."

"Because the designer we hired walked out. Last week. Couldn't keep pace with CANN's lofty vision, or take the pressures of a somewhat demanding boss—" Nick paused, Sam smiled "—and an increasingly tight deadline."

"What's happened to shrink the timeline?"

"Demand. The PR and marketing have been minimal but extremely targeted. Christian's wife, Lauren, designed the brochures and the job she did was outstanding. We knew they'd attract interest, but the response was far beyond what we'd planned. Instead of a slow rollout with an expected thirty to forty-five percent vacancy, almost eighty percent of the properties have already been booked. Including the ones that are not yet finished."

"That's impressive."

"And with the abrupt departure of our designer, problematic as well."

"So what you're saying is…the work she started on these homes needs to be finished?"

"Her work wasn't entirely up to our standards. You may be able to work your magic and salvage a few of the properties. Others will most likely need to be stripped and totally redone. Still more you'll have the pleasure of designing from the ground up. The homes were completed to the point of being an interior designer's blank canvas."

"Sounds major. How many homes are we talking?"

"Counting the properties in Hawaii and the Bahamas, twenty-three total."

Sam took a deep breath. That was a lot of designing, even for her. "And what's the desired completion date?"

Nick looked at his watch. "As of this morning…less than twelve weeks."

"Whoa!"

"Exactly. That's the urgency and why I called you."

"And why you didn't want your assistant to get into it."

"I didn't want you to get scared off before the entire scenario could be laid out. Because we know what a massive undertaking this is, and the immense pressure that will come from pulling it off, we're willing to compensate the designer who can handle the impossible with an equally unique offer."

Nick then laid out the compensation package, one so lucrative that not to accept would be stupid, insane, not even an option.

Still, she hesitated. "Can I think about it?"

"The employment package I've designed has never been offered to anyone," Nick responded. "Anywhere. Ever." Barely veiled frustration crept into his voice.

"No question the opportunity is amazing, but…"

A raised brow was Nick's only response.

"There are personal matters I'd need to consider, logistics that would have to be thought out."

"It's a phenomenal offer," Nick said, a slight frown marring his handsome face as he eyed her intently. "What's there to think about?"

"I have a son."

Crap! Did I say that out loud?

Nick's expression, subdued as it was, suggested that she had. The one thing she hadn't planned to share with Nick had just tumbled out before she could stop it.

"You have a child yet divorced the father? It's none of my business, but that had to be tough."

Sam nodded. It's all she could do.

"How old is he?"

"He's four," Sam replied, wishing the floor beneath her would turn to quicksand and swallow her whole.

"A boy, huh? I had no idea. Given all of the travel that's required, that adds a bit of a wrinkle that I didn't expect."

His eyes narrowed as he thoughtfully rubbed his chin. Sam could almost see his mind turning.

"We can add a childcare allowance to the package, work out an acceptable live-in arrangement so that your son's life isn't disrupted."

"That's an expensive suggestion and only a partial solution. Trey's life has already been upended with the move from Africa to America. I'm not sure how comfortable I'd be either leaving him with a virtual stranger or dragging him all over the States. I'd planned to put him in preschool for a bit of routine, stability. I don't know, Nick…"

"Given what I've just learned, I agree, Sam. It's a big ask. But I can't think of anyone who can do what needs to be done in the time that's required. Someone I trust. An award-winning, formerly sought-after designer whose skills I've seen firsthand.

"Listen, a large part of the charity my mom runs is geared toward helping children. Her network is filled with the best au pairs, teachers, tutors, childcare professionals, you name it. If you'd like, I can give you her number or have her call you. She can help you work something out, something beneficial for both you and… Trey, is it?" Sam nodded. "She can help with an arrangement in the best interest of both you and Trey. Don't let single motherhood be the reason you don't take the job."

Sam asked for a day to think about it, then left—translated, "escaped"—Nick's office. Accepting this meeting was a very bad idea, even worse than she imagined. Nick thought her having a child was the biggest challenge to working with him? No, the gargantuan one was that Nick was Trey's father…and didn't know it.

Two

"I didn't know Sam had a kid."

That was Nick's greeting later that day after walking into his twin brother Noah's house unannounced.

"Good afternoon to you, too, bro."

"You knew and didn't tell me?" Nick eyed Noah as he crossed the living room and plopped on the couch.

Noah shook his head. "No idea. How'd you find out?"

"During her interview for the design job."

"So you called her, huh? How'd that go?"

"Not as I'd planned. Because we need her like last week, I offered an employee package too generous for anyone to refuse. She asked for a day to think about it."

Nick laid out the package details.

Noah sat back, his look one of amazement. "What's there to think about?"

A lazy grin crept onto Nick's face. "That was my question exactly. And how I found out she'd become a mom."

Noah's phone pinged. He picked it up, tapped the face, then returned a quick text. He looked over at Nick. His expression changed. "How'd she look?"

"Sam? Better than the last time I saw her."

"The costume party, right?"

"Catwoman," Nick replied with a slow nod, allowing his mind for the briefest of moments to return to that night. Him, as a *GQ* Superman in a tight-fitting royal blue tux, red muscle shirt, and black-and-red mask. He'd been at the party for about an hour when he felt an energetic shift in the room. Samantha Price. The award-winning interior designer who'd flitted on the outskirts of his social circle for years. He flirted. She teased. As they'd always done. This time, though, he asked her to dance. After three minutes of slow dancing they left for CANN Casino Hotel and Spa, North America's only seven-star hotel and the jewel of Las Vegas. For the next twelve hours they stirred up enough electricity to light up the Strip. It was an unforgettable, mind-blowing night, when one sexy Catwoman became that Superman's kryptonite.

His twin, with whom he shared everything, was the only one he'd told.

Noah reached for his phone, viewed the lit-up screen. "You never saw her after that, right?"

"We were supposed to get together. But she left town, remember?"

"Vaguely."

"She met a prince and obviously started a family. Her body still looks amazing. I couldn't believe it when she told me she'd had a child."

"So the royal family is moving to America?"

Nick shook his head. "They're divorced."

"Sorry to hear that."

Nick nodded. That was an institution the Breedloves didn't believe in. He probably should have felt sorry, too. But he didn't.

"How old is the kid?"

"Four."

"Boy or girl?"

"Boy. His name's Trey."

"What type of father would let his kid, especially a son, move to the other side of the world, divorce or no?"

"I thought the same thing. She clearly didn't want to talk about her personal life so I dropped the subject." Nick thoughtfully rubbed his five o'clock shadow, remembering the encounter. "She was different though, no doubt. Distant. Guarded. Not at all the carefree woman I remember."

"Having had to deal with whatever was bad enough to end her marriage, that can be understood. Maybe she was hoping they could have worked it out. Stayed together for the child's sake at least."

Noah's words reverberated. *Worked it out. Stayed together for the child's sake.* Nick didn't know how he felt about that.

"That design job is a beast with a time schedule from hell. I don't see her being able to do it. Not with a child."

"That definitely complicated the situation. Where there's a will, there's a way."

The room fell silent. Nick looked up to see Noah's speculative gaze.

"What?"

"Are you sure this is about getting the homes completed before summer?"

"Absolutely."

"It has nothing to do with Sam and the fact that she's single again?"

"Nothing."

"Liar."

They both laughed. "I'm focused on work, bro."

"I can understand that," Noah replied. "Plus, those Anderson twins are probably giving you all that you can handle."

"A gentleman never kisses and tells." Nick stood and headed toward the door.

Noah got up and walked toward him. "Where are you going?"

"I have a meeting."

"With whom?"

"The only person who can help me with the childcare dilemma." The brothers looked at each other and both said, "Mom."

Nick climbed into his flashy McLaren, sped down the road and spun into the circular driveway of his parents' estate in nothing flat.

"Mom!"

Helen, the housekeeper who after all of the decades she'd been employed there was more like an aunt, greeted him in the hallway. "Hello, Nick." The two shared a hug. "She's in her new favorite place."

"The solarium. Thanks, love."

Nick walked to the back of the home toward the newly added indoor/outdoor paradise that spanned a great length of the home. He walked over to where Victoria was engrossed in weeding a bed of vibrant plants. He sneaked up behind her and kissed her cheek.

"Oh!" Victoria swatted him. "You scared me!"

"Good thing I wasn't a burglar," he teased. "Did you have a chance to work on what I asked you or have you been here all morning, communing with nature?"

Victoria pulled off her gloves and set them on the rim of the wooden box before crossing over to a canvas-covered divan. "Your multitasking mother managed to do both." She poured a glass of lemon water and held up the pitcher.

"Please." She filled a glass for Nick and handed it to him. "Thanks."

"I ran across a picture of Sam online."

By "run across" Nick knew Victoria had scoured the internet to the edges of the earth to find out what she could about her.

"She's gorgeous, son. Those deep brown eyes. That flawless skin. Stunning."

"Yes, she's attractive."

"And married to a prince. Why is she back here and working, with a child to care for?"

"Those details aren't our business, Mom."

"I was just curious. I'd imagine her child is equally beautiful. Does he look like her?"

"How would I know?"

"She didn't show you a picture?"

"It was an interview, Mom, not a social visit."

"Still, son, it's a rare mother who doesn't offer up pictures of her children at the slightest opportunity."

It would be even rarer if one such mother didn't begin another round of internet sleuthing to find one.

"Any success on finding contacts I can pass on to Sam?"

"I've asked Hazel to pull together a list of possibilities."

"Your new assistant?" Victoria nodded. "How is she working out?"

"No one will ever top Lauren's skills, but Hazel is a close second. She'll compile a list of names and agencies and forward them to you by end of day."

"You're amazing."

"I try."

Nick stood. Victoria followed suit.

"I've got more work to do." He kissed her forehead and pulled her in for a hug. "You're a lifesaver, Mom. Thanks."

"Keep me posted on how it all goes."

"I will. Love you, Mom."

"Love you more."

Nick returned to his car and immediately called Sam. It would have made more sense to wait until he'd received the list, but he wanted to hear her voice now.

"Hello?" Sam sounded breathless, liked she'd rushed to the phone. A thought flashed about another time when heavy breathing occurred, but he immediately shut it down.

"Sam. Nick."

"Hey, Nick."

"Good news. I'm about to solve all your problems."

"You know them all?"

Nick laughed. "You have that many?"

"A few." No laughter. "Is this about the job? You said I had until tomorrow, right? I still haven't made up my mind."

"If part of the indecision is about childcare, a solution is on the way."

"It is?"

"Yep."

"So…let me guess. In addition to being a vice president in a multibillion-dollar corporation, you own a childcare center?"

"No, but I know…hey. What are you doing?"

"Right now?"

"Yes, right now."

"On the computer, research stuff. There's a lot to do to get settled."

"I bet. Where are you staying?"

"South Vegas, temporarily."

"I'm headed that way. Let's discuss the childcare solution I've come up with over dinner."

"I can't do that. I need to get dinner for…for my son."

"That's no problem. Bring the little guy, too. I know a kid-friendly spot not far from our hotel. You and Trey can meet me there." Silence fell as Noah exited the freeway and headed toward CANN Casino Hotel and Spa, a towering landmark anchoring one end of the Las Vegas Strip. "Sam, you there?"

"Yeah, um, I'm here. Thanks, but no. I'm going to run us through a drive-through and get right back online. What's the name of the daycare center? I'll check out their website."

"All of your options are being compiled. I'll have them later today. With the long hours and frequent travel, the list will most likely include au pairs or child assistants with degrees in child education. That way if Trey travels with you, he'll still stay on course with his preschool studies. I think the best candidate would be someone who can look after Trey and whatever temporary households you establish wherever you're at."

"Sounds awesome, Nick, but even with your company's amazing offer, I'm not sure I could afford an arrangement like that. Her salary, airfare, extra lodging, food. It would be a huge expense."

"You're right. I thought about that, which is why her employment would be a part of your package. She'll be employed by the company and, like you, would be given a company card for travel and other expenses."

"Wow. This is… I'm speechless. Where would you find such a person? How…"

"Mom. Plain and simple. She's a better problem-solver and negotiator than a top corporate exec, including my father. Including me. The people on the list have been pre-vetted and most likely were recommended by someone Mom personally knows."

"I… I don't know what to say."

"That's easy. Say you'll be by my office tomorrow to complete the paperwork. You can meet the au pair, sit with our real estate executive to help you with housing and get ready for a trip to New York next week."

"Whoa, Nick, slow down. You're throwing a lot at me. It's almost too much."

"You can handle it."

"I appreciate your confidence but with all of the amazing designers out there, why are you doing all of this to get me?"

"That's simple, Sam. Because you're the best."

"How can I argue with that?"

"You can't."

Why did Sam's laughter make Nick feel like beating his chest and unable to wipe the grin off his face?

"I don't know, Nick. This is a lot to think about."

"You still have a few hours. Why don't you stop by the office tomorrow, say three o'clock?"

"Okay."

"See you then. And Sam?"

"Yes?"

"Just so you know. When I see you tomorrow, the only acceptable answer to my job offer is yes."

Three

Sam reached the hall at one end of the living room, turned and retraced her steps back to the fireplace on the opposite wall. She'd paced this way for the past fifteen minutes. Talking with her cousin, the one who'd graciously taken in her and Trey after their abrupt stateside return. Making her case.

"I can't take this job, Danni. There's no way!"

"There's no way you cannot take it. That job is everything you need right now. With childcare included? Girl, please."

"This isn't about the money. It's about…" Sam looked toward the hallway where her son shared a room with his cousin. She went to sit by Danielle and lowered her voice. "This is about Trey. I can't imagine what would happen if Nick ever found out."

"He's Trey's father, Sam." Danni's voice was a whisper as well. "He shouldn't have to find out. He should be told. The sooner the better."

Sam understood what was behind that last statement. Her ex, Oba, what he knew and how he could use the information if things turned ugly.

Danielle reached out and placed a hand on Sam's arm. "As much as you wanted to deny it, cousin, you knew this day would come. I told you it would."

Sam stared at the fireplace, feeling tears threaten. She watched flames dance and felt a personal inferno.

"It all happened so fast. I was so scared back then. Your friend Joi called. We talked. She gave her brother my number. Oba reached out, then flew over. The next thing I knew I was saying I do. An admittedly hasty arrangement that at the time seemed to solve both his and my problems. I thought leaving without telling Nick was best for everyone. I planned to keep the secret for the rest of my life."

"I know. I'm not blaming or judging you for your choices. If anything, I feel partly responsible. I hate that I shared what Joi told me about her brother looking for a marriage of convenience to beat their egotistical brother to the throne."

"Don't blame yourself. I jumped at the chance. Knowing how Nick felt about marriage, let alone children, made Oba's proposal seem like a magical solution. That I was pregnant gave me an advantage over the other possible candidates. At the time it seemed like a win-win for everyone."

Sam thought back to the morning after she and Nick had been together. How he'd questioned her about birth control, asked if she was protected. She told him yes because she'd been absolutely sure at that time that she could not get pregnant. A problem with fibroids that she'd had for years. He'd worn condoms from then on, two more rounds before leaving the suite that afternoon. All except for that wild, hedonistic, incredible first romp when Trey was created.

"You did the best that you could at the time. But when we know better, we do better."

Now it was Danielle who stood and began walking a hole in the rug. "This is all my fault, really."

Sam looked up. "Did you not hear a word of what I just said?"

"I heard you, Sam. If I'd never heard about the prince or told Joi you were pregnant…"

"As a wise person just told me, you did what you thought was best at the time. When we know better, we do better."

Danielle returned to the sofa. "What's the best decision now? Not just for you but for Trey, even Nick? It doesn't seem right that your ex-husband knows he's not Trey's father but Nick doesn't know that he is. I know that's advice you didn't ask for but…"

"No, you're right. I can't keep the secret forever. Nick deserves to know that he is a father and Trey needs to grow up with his dad."

"Does Trey ask about Oba?"

Sam shook her head. "Trey was always a means to an end for him. He wasn't harsh or anything—they had playful interactions. But Oba isn't overly affectionate and was never hands-on. He also felt child-rearing was 'the woman's job.'" Sam used air quotes, and made a face. "Plus, he was always gone, handling royal business, or jet-setting all over the world."

"From everything you've told me about Nick's offer, sounds like you'll be the one jet-setting now."

"For sure. Designing luxury homes on beautiful islands with an unlimited budget would be a job beyond my wildest dreams." Sam sighed, rested her head on the back of the couch. "But how can I work with Nick and not tell him about Trey? And once that happens, how could he hire me or, if I've taken the job, keep me on?"

"All good questions," Danielle said, as she stood to leave the room. "And only one way to find out."

Sam had just gone to bed when her phone pinged. She checked the text. Oba. Again. Danielle was right. She needed to tell Nick about Trey. But with her mother's cancer battle draining Sam's savings, and the rest used to flee Africa for the safety of home, she also desperately needed the job.

Sam got little sleep that night. She was grateful that Danielle had made arrangements for Trey to join his cousins at day care again. Her husband, Scott, left just before Danielle and the kids. Sam found a yoga video online, one that focused on specific postures and deep breathing. For an hour she worked to think about nothing at all and was mostly successful. As soon as the last chime on the video sounded, however, it was like all of the thoughts and questions she'd held at bay during the workout rushed in at once.

Would Nick be angry?

Would he consider giving a job to someone who lied by omission, one he'd almost surely not trust?

Would the powerful Breedloves fight to take her child?
Could she support her son financially without them?

Sam took a shower, then walked to her closet to dress for success. From the time she was young her mother told her, "When you look good, you feel good." It was a lesson Sam never forgot. She flipped through the meager wardrobe she'd packed and considered a well-fitting yet respectable red dress with long sleeves and a scoop neck. She remembered yesterday's meeting, and how Nick's eyes had slid to her legs when she crossed them, his surreptitious glance when she'd shifted in the chair and her blouse played peek-aboo. It had taken everything to act as though she hadn't noticed. Or that muscle memory from their single rendezvous hadn't kicked in, and caused her to clench and harden in places that should he become her boss would be totally off-limits. His charm drove her crazy and he was still as fine as forbidden fruit. But the only thing more out of the question than whether or not she should work with Nick was whether to sleep with him. That answer was a big fat irrefutable *no.*

When she pulled into CANN Casino Hotel and Spa's valet parking, Sam still hadn't made up her mind. Time had run out before the right answer revealed itself. She entered the building, retraced her steps from the day before and decided to go with the flow. While walking through the opulent lobby, with its contemporary motif of marble, stainless steel and crystal chandeliers, her phone rang. She almost didn't answer it. But it could be about Trey.

"Sam Price."

"Hey, it's Nick."

"Am I late? I'm in the lobby and—"

"No, you're not late. I'm hungry. I hope you don't mind that I've moved our meeting to Zest, one of our restaurants. Just get on one of the upper-floor elevators. It's got its own button."

"Oh, okay. I'm on my way." Before having time to process this change of events, the sleek, fast elevator had whisked her far above the bustling metropolis below and landed her into the kind of luxury she came to enjoy as the princess of Kabata, the province her ex-husband Oba and his family had ruled for several generations. Her heartbeat quickened in anticipation.

"Good afternoon. Welcome to Zest."

"Hi, I'm Sam. Samantha Price. I'm here to meet—"

"We've been expecting you, Ms. Price," the hostess said, with sparkling blue eyes and a genuine smile. "Please, come right this way."

Sam took in the floor-to-ceiling paneless glass that blended the clear blue sky with the room's similarly painted ceilings and expected to be escorted into the dining area. Instead, they went along the outer hall of the smartly appointed main dining room to a series of doors along the dimly lit corridor. The hostess stopped in front of the first door on the left, tapped lightly and opened it.

"Mr. Breedlove, Ms. Price has arrived." She stepped back to allow Sam to enter the room. "Enjoy your meal."

Sam thought she'd do better at seeing Nick this time, since she'd just seen him hours before. But his handsomeness still unnerved her. His gentlemanly action of standing as she entered warmed her insides. What guy did that these days? The way his eyes swept her body touched her to the core, brought back feelings from that one single night as though it had just happened. Which was why in that moment she knew their one-night stand was the first thing they needed to discuss.

"Hello, Nick," she said, holding out a stiff arm. A firm handshake was all of this man's touch she could handle.

"Sam, good to see you." He motioned to a chair. "Please, have a seat. I hope you don't mind that I moved our meeting. I've been here working since before seven this morning. It wasn't until Anita reminded me of our meeting that I realized I hadn't eaten all day."

"It's no problem at all."

"Are you sure?"

Sam knew why he asked. She was acting strangely, not like herself. If she was going to work with him, a possibility that was not yet decided, she'd have to pull it together.

"Positive," she managed, trying to relax as she spoke.

"Are you hungry?"

"I'm fine."

"I know that," Nick said with a mischievous grin. "You're still as beautiful as ever. But would you like something to eat?"

Sam refused to be distracted by Nick's limitless charisma. "I'm not hungry, thanks."

"I hope that wasn't offensive."

Sam looked away from his unflinching gaze, deep chocolate orbs framed by curly black lashes. That's how the dance that started at the party all those years ago had ended up in a luxury suite. She'd gotten lost in those eyes.

Nick continued. "In this post-#MeToo world, we male execs have to be extra careful. But given our past friendship, well, I hope complimenting you wasn't uncomfortable. I meant no disrespect."

"No worries."

A second later, there was a knock at the door. A white-haired server entered with a rolling tray containing glasses and a pitcher filled with pomegranate iced tea.

"May I recommend the chateaubriand today, sir? It is exceptional."

Nick looked across the table. "Sam?"

"Nothing for me, thanks."

The server looked at Nick. "I'll take the chateau, Fredrich," he said, resting against the high-backed leather chair.

"Excellent choice," Fredrich replied as he poured two

glasses of tea. "The tenderloin comes from an award-win-ning ranch not far from here." Fredrich winked at Nick, then looked at Sam.

"If I may," Fredrich began with a benevolent smile. "May I have the pleasure of choosing something for you, some-thing light, or a smaller dish if you prefer?"

"The beef is from my brother Adam's ranch," Nick added. "It's some of the best in the country. Plus, I'm buy-ing, and this place has a Michelin star."

When Sam hesitated, Nick continued. "Come on, woman. It's not wise to turn down a fancy free meal."

The server looked so hopeful Sam couldn't refuse. "Sure," she said, blessing him with a smile. "Thanks."

Fredrich gave a short bow and left.

"Good choice. You won't be sorry." Nick raised a glass. "To a productive meeting."

Sam wasn't so sure about how productive it would be. But she raised a delicately chiseled crystal goblet, clinked it against Nick's and said, "Cheers."

"I know twenty-four hours wasn't a long time to make this decision, but I hope you've had time to think about the benefits of accepting our offer."

"It's all I've thought about," Sam honestly responded. "But before we talk about the job offer, there's something else we need to address."

Nick reached for his glass and sat back. "Oh?"

"That night the last time we saw each other. I don't know about you but for me, it's the elephant in the room."

"If memory serves me correctly, I believe it was a cat." Nick smiled. Sam didn't.

"I need to make sure that what happened years ago has no bearing on our potential relationship now. If I decide to work for CANN International, the interaction between you and me must be strictly professional. Nothing else."

Nick gave her a look. "Of course."

It was the exact answer Sam wanted, but did he have to reply so quickly? As if the thought of a rekindled affair, even briefly, had not even crossed his mind?

Four

Nick was taken aback by Sam's statement but like the great amateur poker player he was, he didn't let that fact show on his face. Sam had just laid out in no uncertain terms the boundaries of their relationship. Hers was a wise choice, the only one really, especially given the time crunch they'd be under. What else was there to say?

"I didn't mean to imply that you… I just didn't want to assume anything. I wanted to be very clear that this is a business relationship."

"A business relationship? Does that mean you're giving serious consideration to the job offer?"

"I'd be crazy not to," Sam admitted. "Especially since you offered to assist with childcare, which was a major concern, and probably the number one challenge to me accepting the offer."

Number two, she inwardly corrected herself. Her secret about Trey was numero uno.

"If that issue is resolved, you'll take the job?"

"You've made it a very difficult offer to turn down. If it was just me to consider, the decision would be easier. But I have to think of my son. As I said yesterday, he's had what was a very stable world turned upside down. He's been relocated across continents and removed from almost all of the people he knows."

"I can't imagine." Nick's eyes conveyed the compassion he felt. "You a newly single mom. His dad now so far away."

Or not, Sam thought, but said nothing.

"Listen, Sam. CANN International, this project, means a great deal to me, but family is everything. I wouldn't want to do anything to compromise the well-being of your son.

It's why throwing in the benefits of an au pair plus was a no-brainer. Both Christian and Adam swear that their assistants are invaluable, like part of the family."

"That's who helped compile the list of childcare options you sent over, your brothers?"

"I talked to them, but Mom and her assistant Hazel made the list. She thinks live-in help who can also provide tutoring would be the best type of aide for your situation. Isabella and Kirtu, the young women who work for my brothers, are very important components in the smooth running of their households. Given what you've just told me about Trey, I know that familiarity and routine are extremely important right now."

Sam nodded. Was it her imagination or did a softness enter Nick's voice when he said his son's name?

"I think Trey having another constant in his life, someone who'd be there no matter where you're working or what the hours, would be a good thing."

"What happens when the job is over?"

"Good question, though one you might not have to confront right away. CANN International is a huge corporation. Lots of properties to decorate and stage. I could see you being a part of it for the long haul."

"That's what I thought about my marriage," Sam mumbled.

Nick rarely squirmed. At this comment, however, he shifted in his seat. "I'm sorry."

"No, it's not you. It's me. There's a lot going on. I would like to explore working with CANN but honestly, Nick, I'm in no shape to make long-term decisions right now."

"Fair enough. We could bring you on as a contractor and if it works out, look at something more permanent later on. Would that work?"

Sam hesitated before nodding her head. "It sounds like a great opportunity. I'd love to take you up on it."

Nick felt his shoulders relax. Until that moment of relief,

he hadn't realized how badly he wanted to hear some type of yes in her response.

"Good answer." The door opened. Nick looked up as Fredrich entered behind a rolling tray. "And perfect timing."

Fredrich placed a bread basket in the center of the table, along with a carousel of butters and jams. Nick reached for the butter knife with one hand and a biscuit with the other.

"These are legendary," he began, spreading a lavish amount of herbed butter on the still-warm bun. "Made fresh daily, as are all of the bakery items. Come on, you've got to try one."

"I have to admit that the smell coming from beneath that cloth is amazing." She lifted the linen, perused the assortment of mini-treats and picked up a roll. She sniffed. "Parmesan."

Nick paused to watch her. She closed her eyes and took a bite. Despite his determination to keep their relationship professional, the look of pure bliss on her face reminded him of a different type of nibbling they'd enjoyed one other time.

"These should be illegal," she said after finishing the roll.

"I told you," Nick said, with a laugh. "Bon appétit."

They spent the next several minutes discussing specifics of the contract. Fredrich returned with a medium-rare delight for Nick and an exquisite chopped salad topped with velvety slices of chateaubriand for Sam. Conversation was momentarily paused as Nick dug into his roasted vegetables and Sam poured a tangy vinaigrette over her fare.

After a few bites, she put down her fork and picked up her napkin. "I had some amazing meals while living in the palace. But I never knew a simple salad could taste like this."

"I wouldn't use that word in front of the chef. He'd probably say there's nothing simple about it."

Sam took another bite of the delectable combination of brussels sprouts, kale, sweet onion and beef, drizzled with the sweet tangy dressing and sprinkled with a finely grated cheese. She closed her eyes, chewed slowly and moaned.

Nick's dick jumped. *Down, boy.* Memories best forgotten threatened to derail his thought process again.

Sam opened her eyes. "You're right. It looks that way. So few ingredients. But the depth of flavor…"

"Sounds like you know your way around a kitchen."

"Not at all. My cousin does, though. Cooking shows are her obsession."

"The cousin you were with at the party that night?"

"Yes. Wow. I'm surprised you remembered."

It was a memorable night. "What's her name?"

"Danielle. We call her Danni."

Nick nodded, thinking back to the pillow talk they'd enjoyed in between sexual romps. Sam and Danni. Boy names for the bad-boy toys. Those had been her words that night. He kept that memory to himself. When Sam quickly changed the subject, he followed her lead.

"How did your family get into the vacation home rental business?"

Nick finished a bite of food. "By accident."

"And now you've got houses all over the world? Some accident."

"It's the truth." Nick shrugged. "At least the short version."

"What's the longer one?"

Nick finished his plate and sat back with his drink. "It started with my oldest brother, Christian, who built the hotel off the coast in Djibouti. Around that same time, I had business on an island off the coast of New York."

"The property you now own?"

"Yes. It is close to the city yet completely private and already had what we needed in place—utilities, roads. It's small, not large enough for a hotel but perfect for smaller homes. After securing that property, and as research continued, we purchased islands off the coasts of North and South Carolina, Georgia, California and Maine. All of this information will be in your sign-on packet and goes into deeper detail. Next week, you'll see it firsthand."

"Hotels, homes and islands, too? CANN International is bigger than I thought."

"Which is why coming on board to work with us is the best decision you could have ever made."

"With your biased opinion I think it best that I be the judge of that."

"Ha! Touché."

The conversation continued, becoming lighter and more organic as Sam continued to loosen up. By the time Fredrich removed the dessert dishes and poured the black coffee he'd suggested as their digestif, the easy camaraderie from that past casual encounter had returned. Nick felt even better about his decision to reach out to Sam. Not only was she the best woman for a job of this magnitude, she could be a lot of fun.

"Thanks for talking me into eating," Sam said as they stood. "I didn't think I was hungry until I took the first bite."

"Breedloves take food seriously," Nick joked. "We put as much thought into hiring chefs as we do floor designs."

They stepped out of the private dining room and continued down the hall that ran alongside the main dining area. Workers scurried from table to table, making each a perfect presentation for the dinner crowd. Nick acknowledged a few of them as they passed by, left the restaurant and headed toward the elevator.

Nick pressed the button and stepped back. "I'll have paperwork drawn up and faxed over ASAP. You have a passport, obviously, so we don't have to worry about that."

"Passport? Aren't all of the builds for this project happening stateside?"

"The last home we'll renovate is in the Bahamas. Other than that, international travel will most likely not be required. We make sure everyone working for us has the paperwork required to travel to any number of our CANN properties, just in case."

The elevator arrived. They stepped inside, both quiet during the ride down one hundred floors.

Once in the lobby, Nick held out his hand. "Welcome aboard, Ms. Price."

"Those papers aren't signed yet, Mr. Breedlove." Sam teased. "But I don't foresee any problems."

She accepted his handshake. Her skin was warm, velvety soft to the touch. Their eyes met. Something happened between them. Faint, but perceptible. A current of erotic energy sparkled in their midst. Sam pulled her hand from Nick's grasp. The spell was broken. But Nick had definitely felt it and was 99.9 percent sure that Sam had felt it, too.

They said goodbye and went their separate ways. Yet long after their meeting and into the night, Nick wondered about the elephant that Sam had brought up. It wasn't that lone, torrid night of the past that he was worried about. It was the undeniable chemistry still sizzling between them, and how long it could be successfully ignored.

Five

There were a few showers when April arrived, but for most Nevadians the warmer breezes were a welcome change from the previous month's unseasonably cold temperatures. Sam barely noticed. After signing the project-specific contract and faxing it back to CANN International, the next eight days passed in a whirlwind—a flurry of house hunting and childcare interviews. She ignored Nick's suggestion to move to Breedlove, an unincorporated area not far from Las Vegas, but accepted the born-and-bred native's advice on the best areas in Las Vegas to rent. She also politely declined the company's offer to assist with her search for a nanny. Telling Nick the truth about Trey was inevitable. But until she was ready and the time was right, Sam planned to keep the Breedloves and CANN International far away from her child. After last night's conversation with Oba, she was thankful that an ocean separated them, too. She couldn't believe he'd had the nerve to call.

"Oba?"

"You forget my voice already, baby?"

Sam didn't have to work to give her ex the silent treatment. She literally had nothing to say.

"How is life in America?"

Really? He was treating this as a social call? After how their relationship ended, and all that had happened since then?

"Oba, I'm busy, on my way to begin a very important project. I can't talk now."

"A working woman? Oh, no, *masoyina*! That is not the life for you."

"I am no longer your love, your wife or your responsibility. I thought we agreed a clean, complete break was best. Why are you calling me?"

"I miss you, baby. I miss my son."

The endearment was spoken with a low and heartfelt intonation, an emphasis on the second syllable, as was his way. The same voice she at one time appreciated now brought knots to her stomach. Oba had given Trey only a passing interest. What was this really about? That the marriage was one of convenience had been something they'd both willingly entered and ended. He needed to let it go.

"Last week, my father delivered very bad news, baby. He is still very angry at our deception."

Our deception?

"That he welcomed Trey into the family with a ceremonial tribute reserved for only those with tribal blood."

And this is my business because...

"I'm sorry that your father is unhappy, Oba. But his learning about Trey not being your son isn't my fault. That was your brother's doing. We've both suffered because of the decision Isaac made. I lost a lot, including the little money I'd been able to save while living there. I'm doing what I have to do to rebuild my life and am not sure how what is happening within your family involves me."

"My father has severely limited my royal responsibilities and by extension, my allowance."

"At least you have one."

"It is not how I am accustomed to living. He has banished me to the apartment in Lagos, a place I've only stayed in sporadically and not for several years!"

Sam visited that apartment once. It was a two-story unit with four bedrooms, five bathrooms, a tennis court and a pool. Poor baby.

"Oba, what do you want from me?"

"I need to make some moves, Sam. Maybe come to America."

"You've got Joi here. Ask her for help."

"She doesn't have any money."

"I don't either," Sam quickly retorted.

"But you can get it." Oba's tone changed, became firmer and a little less friendly. "Ask Nick to give it to you."

"What?" Sam's voice rose several octaves. That after several shocked seconds before she could actually speak, the nerve and unmitigated gall of his suggestion rendering her paralyzed and dang near mute.

She sat straight up in bed. "Are you freaking kidding me? Are you out of your mind? I don't have any money to give you and asking Nick or anyone else for help is out of the question."

"Does he know about Trey?"

"Keep Trey out of this."

"That sounds like a no."

"I don't give a damn how it sounds or what you think you know about Trey's relationship with his biological father."

Sam hoped that sentence was enough of a dam to stop the potential flood of truth hinted at by Oba's veiled threat.

"Trey is the innocent party in all of this and totally off-limits. As for what's happened because of your brother, well, we've both suffered from his actions. If anyone can and should help you it's Isaac, not me. And definitely not Nick."

"You know I'm the last person with whom Isaac would share his wealth. I helped you out when you were in trouble. Now you need to return the favor."

"How many ways do I have to say it? I don't have any money."

"According to my sister, that's about to change. She sent me a link to a press release. You're working with CANN International."

Sam hadn't given a thought to making news, would not have believed the hiring of a contractor warranted a public announcement. Damn the company and their PR efficiency, and damn Joi for not minding her business.

"It's a temporary contract," she replied, then quickly searched the web for the announcement, and hoped the verbiage didn't go into detail.

It didn't, thank God. But Oba already knew too much.

"My getting work doesn't change the answer. There is nothing I can do to help you."

"Listen, Sam—"

"No, you listen. I'm done talking." Sam stopped, took a breath, removed the crease from between her brows and calmed down. Offending Oba right now would do her no good. "I wish you the best, Oba, and hold nothing against you. But because of Isaac, we are out of each other's lives. Let's continue to move on, going separate ways. We're both doing our best under the circumstances. Please don't call me again."

Sam arrived at the airport in Las Vegas for a flight to New York. She reached the gate and looked for Nick. He wasn't there. The boarding announcement sounded over the speakers. Still, no Nick. She pulled out her cell to call him but changed her mind. He wasn't her responsibility. Maybe he'd decided not to accompany her. No big deal. She was an accomplished designer who didn't require hand-holding. That he'd planned to come at all had been a surprise in the first place. Sam had a first-class ticket but waited until several had boarded before getting on the plane. After accepting an orange juice from the attendant, she settled in for the flight, convinced she'd hear from Nick after landing in New York. Instead, just before the doors closed, he rushed in and took the aisle seat beside her.

"Hey," he said, passing off his briefcase and buckling his seat belt in a rush.

"Cutting it a bit close, aren't we?"

"Didn't mean to. Saw a buddy of mine in the lounge and got to talking. Lost track of time."

"It's all good. You made it. Considering the success of

the company you work for I'm surprised you fly commercial at all."

"I don't often," Nick admitted.

"I hope you didn't lower your standards on my account." Sam smiled to show she was joking. She was. In a way.

"I'd hardly call spending time with you in any way lowering my standards," Nick easily replied, his voice lower than usual and sexier than Sam would have liked. "Plus, with it being so long since we've seen each other I thought the long nonstop flight would be a perfect chance to catch up.

"So…" he continued, after casually chatting while the plane reached its cruising altitude. "Tell me about living the life of a princess."

It was a fair question, one Sam might have asked were the situation reversed. She shifted in her seat. "Well, as Meghan Markle would probably attest, it's not always all it's cracked up to be. But it wasn't all bad."

"How'd you meet Oba Usman, the grand prince of Kabata and rumored heir to the throne?"

"Someone's been busy online, I see." Said as Sam prided the exterior she managed, one that masked the angst she felt just beneath the surface. Given what had happened that caused Oba to lose his right to the throne, the less Nick knew about her ex, the better.

"A little background research on our latest corporate partner. This would have normally been all done beforehand had I not been under the gun to hire someone so quickly."

Sam couldn't fault him for researching her via web. She'd done the same to him after meeting that night at the party. It's where she first learned he was a successful confirmed bachelor who didn't want kids.

"Danni, who you remember from the party, was friends with his sister. Shortly after meeting me she talked to him. Thought we might make a good match. We were introduced via a video chat and it went from there."

"Interesting. Things must have moved fast. I mean, one

minute we're hanging out at a costume party and the next you're married and living on the other side of the world."

"Yes, everything happened quickly." For reasons that remained unsaid. "I admit to moving forward with stars in my eyes. Every little girl dreams of being a princess, and fantasizes about knights in shining armor once we reach our teens."

"And Oba seemed to be that?"

"I thought so, in the beginning."

"What changed?"

Sam took a deep breath and spoke thoughtfully. "I've come to realize that even under the most normal of circumstances, marriage is hard. That mine was high-profile and involved a royal family added to the challenge."

Nick whistled. "Going through that had to be tough. One of the main reasons I'm in no hurry to do it."

"Smart move."

"Why'd you marry so quickly?"

"Oba was under pressure to find a wife. Being married and producing an heir was a requirement for him to be considered as a successor to the throne, something his younger brother who'd become engaged the year prior was in a race to do. When… I became pregnant…we married right away."

"Was it what you wanted?"

Sam avoided looking into Nick's penetrating gaze. "It's what I felt best for Trey."

"And for you?"

"At the time I thought the decision best for the both of us."

"Hmm. How is the little guy? Did you find a suitable nanny?"

"I think so. For now, Danni is graciously handling everything between Gloria, the nanny, and Trey. I'll fly them up later, probably next week."

As the flight attendant began the first-class meal service, Sam and Nick retreated to their individual thoughts.

Sam was relieved for the reprieve, a time to recover from the stress felt during that conversation. She replayed and mentally tucked away what had been said, in order to make sure that the story she told now, in this moment, was one she'd remember if ever asked again.

"What about you? I know you're in no hurry but with all of your brothers married, you're not feeling the slightest pressure to walk down the aisle, have a kid or two, and contribute to the Breedlove legacy?"

Nick stretched his long, lean legs in front of him. "Not at all."

Sam couldn't help but laugh at the hasty response, even as Nick not being ready to have children made her heart skitter around in her chest.

Nick positioned his chair to lean back. "For now, these island homes are my only babies. It's the biggest company project I've taken on to date, and while the family hasn't applied any pressure, I have my own point to prove.

"In the past few years," he continued, counting on his fingers, "Christian's build in Djibouti opened up the entire African continent. Adam's Wagyu beef is the best in America, and with his land research and development gem finds he's contributed greatly to the company's bottom line. Last year Noah did the impossible by opening up a casino in what is arguably the country's most conservative state. While paralyzed."

Sam gasped. "Oh no! What happened?"

"Horrific ski accident. You didn't hear?" Sam shook her head. "Wow, you really were isolated."

"Mostly by choice. Before, my phone and the internet were like an extension of my physical self. It was nice to step away from all that and live in the real world, such as it was."

"I can't imagine, but I hear you."

"How is Noah now?"

"Much better, thanks for asking."

"Sounds like the past few years have been very productive for the family. Now it's your turn?"

"Yes."

"Do they have kids, your brothers?"

Nick nodded. "Christian has a daughter, Christina, and a son, Larenz. Both Adam's and Noah's wives, Ryan and Dee, are expecting. They conceived three months apart."

"Wow! Sounds like Uncle Nick is going to be busy."

"Yeah, being the uncle is great. I can be the fun adult, spoil them and then send them home."

They laughed, and the conversation paused as the flight attendant returned with menus. She'd been flirting with Nick since he sat on the plane and now was no exception.

"Mr. Breedlove, may I recommend the salmon." She paused, batting long lashes and flashing flawless pearly whites as she refreshed his drink. "It's really good and healthy, too. You seem the type who likes to stay in shape."

"You're right about that." He handed back the menu. "I'll have that with asparagus and rice."

"Great choice." She looked at Sam. "And for you?" Asked with no sparkling eyes, a mere hint of a smile and no move to freshen her drink.

Sam almost laughed out loud. "I'll have the Cajun chicken salad, please. And a glass of cabernet."

Both of them watched the attendant walk away.

Sam nodded in her direction. "Looks like you have an admirer."

"She's just doing her job."

"Seriously, Nick, you can't be that naive. Your modesty, though, is appreciated."

He took a sip of water. "Tell me about your family. Do you have siblings?"

"A brother from my mom's first marriage. He's seven years older than me, a techie who lives in Seattle. My dad lives in LA."

"Is that where you grew up?"

"Born and raised."

"And your mom?"

Sam quieted, swallowed past the sudden lump in her throat. "She passed away right before I moved to Africa. Breast cancer."

"I'm sorry."

"Thank you. I miss her every day."

"How is it that you were at the costume party?"

Sam knew exactly which party he was talking about, the one where they slept together and her life was forever changed.

"Danni moved here years ago, a professional dancer with stars in her eyes. Got hired for a few shows. Then she met Scott, got married and started a family. Her mom, my aunt, was my mom's sister. They were very close, always together, which led to Danni and I being more like sisters than cousins."

"What did she think about your quick wedding?"

Back to that again? Sam wondered why Nick was so fixated on a marriage that was over. She chose to answer rather than ask the question; figured the more open she was about that part of her life the less he'd feel the need to pry further.

"She's always wanted what was best for me. Since I was happy, she was happy."

"And now that you're divorced?"

Sam tried not to let her chagrin show but she had tired of this line of questioning. "Again, she supports whatever is best for me, and is happy I'm back stateside."

"Please forgive my insensitivity for asking. I imagine that ending a marriage is never easy, no matter the reason, and that talking about it could be painful."

"You're right. It's not easy. But in the end, it was for the best. Enough about me. Let's talk about your love life."

"I already told you. The only love affair I'm having right now is with the CANN Isles project."

"If that's your story you can stick to it. But an architect's art renderings can't keep you warm at night."

"Ha! True that. I go out here and there but mostly I've been too busy to date."

Sam found that hard to believe but didn't push. The conversation wound its way back to business and the cluster of island homes in New York, the first that Sam would be stamping with her designs. Were circumstances different she'd definitely date Nick. Smart and confident with a wicked sense of humor, he wasn't hard to like. That he was easy on the eyes didn't hurt, either. Being far and away the best lover she'd ever experienced would be the cherry on top of the sundae. If things were different. But they weren't. Sam needed to keep that in mind and stay focused on doing her job.

The flight attendant returned. The flirting continued. Sam put on a brave smile and hid the anguish in her heart. The best thing that could happen was for Nick to fall madly in love, thereby erasing any perceived chance of a future between them. She, Trey and Nick would not ride off into the sunset as one big happy family. Whatever feelings that were trying to resurface were best quashed before having a chance to blossom.

No doubt someone as good-looking as Nick had scores of women, one in every town. Except for the time-sensitive project and the secret she kept, Sam wouldn't have minded being one of them.

Six

Clients staying at a CANN Isles property were ferried from a port or marina in each city to the island by private yachts either purchased or leased by the company. Less than an hour after arriving in New York City, Nick and Sam had been driven by limo to the marina in Brooklyn where the boat was docked and waiting.

"Impressive," Sam said, as the two settled at the end of circular seating that could double as a sunbathing pad on the right type of day. "CANN International most definitely does everything first class."

"Nothing you're not used to, right? The life of a princess had to have been at least this upscale. Given Nigeria is Africa's richest nation, even more so, I'd imagine."

"It was very opulent living," Sam admitted, looking out over the water.

She offered nothing more, but Nick pressed the issue. The more he interacted with Sam, the more he realized how little he knew about her. Being hesitant about getting into her personal life was understandable, but Nick was determined to get past the superficial or work conversations they had mostly had to this point.

He sat against the couch, stretched his arms across its back. "I've been to several countries in Africa, but never Nigeria. We hear so many stories. How was it living there?"

"Not like most residents, I'd suppose. Most of my life happened on the grounds of the palace, which were massive. Almost everything one could imagine for living was on the premises—pools, tennis courts, parks and spas. If something wasn't readily available, it was obtained by the staff. If it was something that I or other household members needed to personally approve, wardrobe, furniture, stuff like that, it was either handled online or personally brought in."

"That sounds super restrictive. Was it because of security concerns?"

Sam didn't answer immediately. Nick wondered if he'd overstepped.

"My ex-husband's family were very protective of not only family members but also their brand." Again, she paused, as if choosing her words carefully. "They went to great lengths to protect their privacy. However, I don't believe their actions or attention to safety went beyond that of other royals. As I said, their land holdings are massive, about an hour from Lagos, a sprawling complex that's completely secure. Life was somewhat scripted but not as rigid as it sounds."

"You loved a good party back in the day. I know you were a married woman with a child but there were no fun times on the beach or wild nights at the club?"

Sam sighed, frowned slightly. "The homes of the wealthy are gated playgrounds. There wasn't really a need to go other places."

Nick quickly and keenly felt her mental retreat. He changed course. "Did you visit other countries?"

"Several."

"Do you have a favorite?"

"Each had its own beauty. I could live on the island of Madagascar."

"Madagascar's a sweet spot for sure. What about Maasai Mara?"

Sam shook her head. "Never heard of it. What's there?"

"Lions, cheetahs, zebras."

"A safari?"

"The best country to go on one, or so we were told. I have to admit they were right, based on the experience I had."

"What about the country where the CANN hotel is built?"

"Djibouti? Beautiful."

"How'd your brother find it?"

"You know what? Good question. You need to ask him the next time we meet."

Both slipped into silence as the boat skimmed the dark blue waters, taking them farther from the city into the deep part of the sea. Sam excused herself to call Danni and check in on Trey. Nick used the time to call the office, read his emails and return a call to his mom. Thirty minutes later, he stood and stretched as land came into view.

He walked over, opened the cabin door and yelled below. "Sam!"

"Yes?"

"We're here."

"Okay. Coming right up."

The boat docked. Within minutes, Nick and Sam were in an ATV, their luggage behind them, traveling over the bumpy terrain at a high rate of speed.

"Slow down!" Sam yelled.

Nick laughed. "Hang on. I've got this!"

As the vehicle rounded a curve and the house came into view, Sam's jaw dropped. An architectural masterpiece of glass-fiber-reinforced concrete, gleaming steel and pane-less windows was far and away the most beautiful home she'd ever seen.

"This place is amazing." She spoke in a hushed, awe-inspired tone, just barely above a whisper.

"That's exactly the type of reaction we want from our guests."

Adam leaped out of the ATV, then went on the other side to let Sam out. A house employee appeared as if by magic to handle their luggage and fulfill any requests from the boss.

"The inside isn't as finished as the outside," Nick warned. "But don't let that scare you as it did the designer before you."

"Thanks for the warning," Sam replied, her heartbeat slightly quickening as they walked through an atrium filled with lush tropical plants, angel statues and an impressive waterfall. "For the inside to come anywhere close to this home's exterior is a very tall order."

Adam reached the door, then stepped back for Sam to enter. "I believe in you."

Sam stopped just inside the door. "Oh. My. Goodness." She turned to Nick. "When you said the interiors needed designing, I didn't think that meant from the studs up."

"This is one of the least finished models. Others aren't quite this bad."

"This job is way bigger than I imagined. Large crews will be needed if there's any hope of finishing these homes in eight to twelve weeks. Have workers been lined up and contracted?"

Nick shook his head.

"No carpenters, painters, installers, nothing?"

"Again, some of the other homes are a bit further along than this but basically, many of the jobs are from the ground up."

Nick watched as Sam reached into her tote, pulled out a tablet and began jotting down notes as she walked room to room.

"I'd be lying to not admit that this feels overwhelming. Where was my luggage taken? It contains some of what I'll need to get this ball rolling. I need to get started right away."

Nick made quick work of finishing the tour, ending on the third floor of the massive mix of contemporary and bungalow styles.

"Here are the two remaining master suites," Nick pointed out, having shown her five in all. I had the maids prepare these two for our stay."

"You're staying?"

Nick worked to hide a smile. That Sam seemed concerned about the close proximity of their bedrooms pleased him more than he could let on. "Don't sound so alarmed.

It's just for the night. I have an appointment in New York tomorrow morning."

"Oh, okay."

"I've got work to catch up on while you do your thing, but what say we take a break around seven for dinner to-night?"

"Thanks, but that's not really necessary. I'd rather grab something quick and continue working."

"No problem. A panel similar to the one I showed you just beyond the foyer is also in your room and can be used to summon the chef or any of the other employees to help you. If there is anything at all that you need done, don't hesitate to ask."

"Okay, thanks, Nick. I'll see you later."

Nick retired to his room but with Sam consuming his thoughts, there was no work getting done. After basically doodling and checking social media accounts for over an hour, he donned a pair of swim trunks to douse his heated bod in the Atlantic's cold waves. Knowing Sam was down the hall would make it a challenge, but he purposely wore himself out swimming in hopes of a good night's sleep. Back at the house, he took a hot shower. Noah called just as he finished drying off. Having passed Sam downstairs hard at work on her tablet, he strode naked from his suite to the hall linen closet, looking for a particular robe he was told had been placed there, a simple terry number to replace the heavier one left in the room.

"Are you flying up or no?" he asked his twin, entering the walk-in hall closet and bypassing several robe choices before finding the one he preferred and slinging it over his shoulder. "Cool. Then let's meet at the restaurant in the of-fice tower lobby and go over the plans before sitting down with their group."

Nick stepped out of the closet just as Sam rounded the corner.

"Oh!" she yelped, her eyes appearing to take him in like

a tall glass of water in an arid desert before remembering to be professional.

"Sorry." Nick kept his eyes squarely focused on Sam as he casually slipped on the robe. "Your room is on the other side."

Sam said nothing, just wheeled around and headed in the opposite direction.

"Call you back, twin." Nick hurriedly ended the call. "Sam!"

The only response he heard was the sound of her door closing, and the lock being firmly latched behind her.

Seven

Shit! Sam reached her room, closed the door and repeated the expletive. About a dozen times. Why hadn't she paid more attention to her surroundings before leaving the room? She'd commented on the matching masters and what a good selling point that would be for potential renters. Why hadn't she focused on where she was going? And why the hello fantasy island did he have to be naked when she entered? At the thought, his image sprang into her mind. Hot. Hard. The appendage that had brought her both instant and lasting pleasure still amazingly impressive, even in its languid state. Only now did Sam think about how long it had been since she'd had sex. Too long to be on an island alone with a gorgeous man. *Shit!*

Sam jumped as her phone pinged. She picked it up. Nick.

Sorry that happened. U ok?

In her mind, sarcastic responses stumbled over each other. But her response was short and sweet.

I'm ok. ☺.

Liar. What happened wasn't okay at all. So much so that a short time later she sent Nick a second text feigning exhaustion and asked if they could meet first thing the next day. Cross-country trips and changing time zones could be tiresome, but fighting the attraction to Nick is what zapped Sam's energy. After making contact with a few of her old suppliers and surfing CANN International's website to study hotel room pics, she took a shower and slid between designer Egyptian cotton sheets. The material felt soft and seductive against her skin. The memory-foam mattress caressed her body. The pillows smelled faintly of lavender, a scent known to relax the body and quiet the mind. The combination worked wonders. Soon, Sam was fast asleep.

It seemed only moments later when the door to her room opened. Sam looked up. Nick, once again in all of his practically naked glory. He seemed ethereal, almost otherworldly, his partially clad body backlit by subdued hallway lighting. His steps were slow, measured, as he boldly approached her. He reached the foot of her bed and silently waited for an invitation to join her. Sam sat up, letting the sheet fall to reveal her bareness. Her exposed nipples pebbled quickly. Goose bumps broke out all over her ebony skin, and not just from the cool breeze through the open balcony doors. He shook the robe he wore from his shoulders, let it puddle at his feet, then crawled onto the bed like a panther, stalking its prey.

He stared deep into her eyes. Not a word had been spoken.

Sam watched as though mesmerized as Nick pulled down the sheet and exposed every inch of her body. He took a finger and slid it lazily from the heel of her foot to the insides of her thighs, flicking it along the folds of her paradise before branding her with his touch on the way back down, then sexily licking his finger. Without warning, he bent over and sucked a toe in his mouth. So delicious was his touch, so amazing, so forceful, that Sam almost had an orgasm right there!

But she didn't.

Instead, she lay back against the fluffy pillows, writhing as Nick's tongue bath continued over her ankles and shin. He kissed a sensitive spot behind her knee before trailing kisses up the insides of her thighs, gently parting her legs wider until she was fully exposed. Only seconds passed before she felt his lips touch her nether ones, before his tongue swiped the dew from between her folds, until he feasted on her feminine flower. Sam felt short of breath and tried to get away lest she die from pleasure. But Nick wasn't having it. He held her firmly by her thighs—licking, sucking, biting, kissing—until an orgasm that began at the core of her being burst forth on the waves of a scream that reverberated around the room. She lay back spent, finished.

Nick was just getting started.

He positioned himself just beyond her shoulders, his thick, stiff manhood dangling precariously close to her face. Obviously, he figured that turnabout was fair play. Who was Sam to argue? She wrapped her hands around his massive sex weapon, kissed the tip and then sucked him into her mouth. His gasp of breath let her know that she was onto something. She continued the assault, breathing him in, pulling him out, setting up a rhythm to match the pace of his hips as she ran a hand over his hard cheeks and outlined his mushroom tip with her tongue. One last thrust to her face and apparently Nick couldn't take it any longer. He pulled her up, turned her over and in one long, glorious plunge, entered her from behind.

Ah!

Sam relaxed to take in all of him before rocking back and forth in their dance of love. She moaned when he massaged her breasts and twiddled her nipples, never missing a beat as he drove himself deeper and deeper inside her, until he touched the very core. She came once, twice, but still Nick wasn't finished. He climbed off the bed, took her into his arms and walked through the open balcony doors. There, under the light of a full springtime moon, he sat on one of the lounge chairs that dotted the large balcony and directed her to sit on his still-engorged shaft. She felt like a sex goddess, watching his eyes flutter closed, feeling the wind on her sensitive buds, throwing back her hair and enjoying the ride. She rose up until only his tip was inside her, then slid down his pole like a trained firewoman. Back and forth. In and out. They made love for minutes. Or was it for hours? Or days? Finally, she felt Nick's pace quicken, heard him mumble unintelligibly until he, too, let himself go and went over the edge. The orgasm was so climactic it made her ears buzz. The sound began as if in the distance, then got louder and louder until…

She woke up.

Sam looked around the room, disoriented to find herself back in bed and not on the lounge outside. The bedsheets had been tousled and were now wrapped around her. Nick wasn't in her room. Unfortunately, she was very alone.

That had been a dream?

The buzzing she'd heard earlier sounded again. She looked to see a light coming from the phone on the table beside her. Taking a deep breath, she picked up the receiver.

"Hello?"

"Good morning, beautiful."

"Hey, Nick."

Sam fell back against the headboard. On one hand she was glad that their making love had not happened in real time. On the other, she was sorely disappointed.

"Meeting in Manhattan got changed from lunch to break-fast but I wanted to touch base with you before leaving the island."

"You're leaving right now?"

"In about five or ten minutes. In addition to the meeting change there's a storm coming in. The captain suggested we get an early start. It sounds like I may have awakened you, though, so go ahead and finish your sleep. I imagine you have a long day ahead. We can catch up next week, when you're back home."

"Sure. I'll plan and sketch today and will forward the 3-D renderings. Perhaps we can chat by phone before I schedule contractors from the names you sent over. Thanks for those."

"No worries at all. I look forward to the sketches."

Sam heard a beep.

"Ah, I have to take this. Call me if you need me."

"Will do."

"Bye, Sam."

Just as she was about to put down her phone, a text came in. She tapped the screen. Oba. Well, wasn't that just the wake-up she needed. It was a warning to not get caught up in the feelings of her exotic dream. Because in her waking world, unless she was very careful, life could turn into a nightmare—snap—just like that.

Eight

For the next couple weeks, Nick and Sam didn't see each other but were in almost constant communication. In the mornings he'd receive detailed 3-D images of each room's design plan, sometimes updates from plans sent before. Nick appreciated that unlike the previous designer, Sam kept him apprised of the progress without being prompted. He wasn't usually a micromanager, but with the challenging timeline and the millions of dollars at stake, rest came easier knowing of any potential challenges with contractors or material deliveries and having an overview of what was happening overall. At night they'd communicate by phone, text or email, and not always about work. Nick encouraged Sam to get off the island and take advantage of being in the city that never sleeps. Sam teased at Nick that she'd do that as soon as a certain taskmaster stopped cracking the whip. While working in New York, Sam was also viewing the floor plans of the homes off the coast of Georgia and the Carolinas, which were next on the schedule. Every idea was well-thought-out and top-notch, homes to fulfill every whim of the wealthy, just as he'd envisioned.

On the professional front, all seemed to run smoothly. Yet his thought often returned to the day after he arrived in New York, and the conversation he'd had with Sam just before leaving. Nick wondered if it was his imagination, or had he heard a bit of trepidation in Sam's voice? Had she tossed and turned half the night, had trouble sleeping as had been the case with him? There was a lot on his corporate plate but Nick didn't try to fool himself. Sam being just down the hall was the reason he'd found it hard to rest that night. That more than anything is why he'd left early.

The stress of another night in the same house but different beds with that woman would have taken years off his life.

Nick clicked on the 3-D image that showcased Sam's plans from an aerial perspective. He projected it from the computer to the eighty-inch wall-mounted screen, then walked over to take a more in-depth look.

A soft tap sounded behind him. Nick turned around.

It was Noah. "Got a minute?"

"For you, I do. Come over and take a look at this."

Noah stopped a few feet away to fully examine the life-like rendering, before stepping up for a closer look. He pointed to an area near the screen's left side. "Is all of this part of the atrium?"

Nick nodded. "It's already finished. And absolutely gorgeous, bro. It definitely makes an immediate statement to our guests. Sam suggested putting at least a modified version on as many homes as possible. What do you think about that?"

"What does the team think?"

"I'll find out in the meeting on Friday. Didn't you get the memo?"

"Probably. I've been tied up with Bionics all week. I'm sure Essie placed it on my calendar."

Noah's attention returned to the screen. "Do you have real photos of that?"

"I sure do. Hang on." Nick walked to his desk and reached for the mouse. His cell phone rang. A frown accompanied his greeting. "Breedlove."

"Hello?" A few seconds and then, "Who is this?" Nick sighed as he ended the call and slid the phone back to the desk.

"What was that about?" Noah asked.

"I don't know. It's been happening for a couple days now."

"Someone probably has the wrong number and keeps

calling hoping that whoever they're trying to reach will answer the phone."

"You're probably right." He clicked a remote to begin the slide presentation. "Check this out."

Nick showed Noah the New York renderings and what he had so far on the other homes.

"What about Hawaii and the Bahamas?"

"Navigating the world of contractors in both locations is a bit tricky. If necessary, I'm hoping to be able to fly in the manpower we need while employing as many of the townsfolk as possible. Doing that often makes it easier for the officials to be more agreeable in other areas."

"If Sam can duplicate what's happened in New York everywhere else, she'll indeed be a miracle worker. But I don't know, man. We're into April, about ten weeks away from the first reservations. It's going to be tight."

"It's going to be amazing."

Anita interrupted via intercom. "Gentlemen, your mom is on line two."

"Who does she want to speak to?" Noah asked.

Nick picked up the phone. "Who did she call?" He pushed the blinking extension and placed the call on speakerphone. "Hey, Mom."

"Hi, Mother." Noah gave a wave as he turned and walked out the door.

"Is that Noah?"

"It was. He just left."

"Oh, dear. I hope I didn't interrupt anything."

"Just discussing trying to finish a project valued in the hundreds of millions is all."

"Oh, good. Then of course you've got time to talk with me about next month's carnival."

Nick suppressed a groan as he sat and swirled his executive chair. He knew where this conversation was heading. "All the time in the world, Mother. What's up?"

"We're finalizing the carnival's special guest list. Have you spoken with Samantha about bringing her son?"

"First of all, why are you talking about her as though she's someone you know? No one calls her Samantha, Mom. She goes by Sam."

"Duly noted. Have you asked her?"

"Honestly all I've talked about with her are the island homes."

"How are those coming along, son?"

"I'm happy to report that so far, so good. I just showed Noah the slides from what was just completed in New York, and the 3-D pictures of the next focus, which are our islands in the Southeast. Her plans look amazing."

"So did the other designer's, as I recall."

"The difference is that Sam has the reputation and with what we've seen in New York, the experience to back up that vision."

"Sounds like this Sam is quite a woman."

"Quite the interior designer," Nick gently corrected. "That's the part of her that plays a part in my life."

Victoria chided right back. "Oh, come now, Nick. Those working alongside us have never been mere employees. Every time someone joins the corporation, our family expands."

Nick's lips went into a straight line. His grandma Jewel taught him that when one didn't have something good to say, they need say nothing at all.

"Is it possible to get Sam's email address so that I can send her a proper invitation?"

"She's really busy, Mom. I don't think—"

"Good. You don't have to. Just send over the address so that our amazing interior designer can decide for herself whether she'd want her child to attend the carnival of any child's dream."

"Send over the invitation to my cell phone, Mom. I'll forward it."

"Excellent! As soon as possible, sweetie. Have a beautiful rest of day, now. Bye-bye!"

Classic Victoria. Light a bomb, then scatter before the flame reaches the end of the wick. Being around Sam in a playful atmosphere was probably not the wisest move, but he'd do as requested and forward the invite to her. To further balk or outright refuse would only serve to make his mom that much more curious and determined. Given the pace she'd kept up for almost two weeks, Sam would probably want to spend the weekend doing something much more productive than petting animals or watching her kid's face get painted. Like sleeping.

I wouldn't mind spending the weekend sleeping in, too... with her.

The thought popped into his head before he could stop it. He was mostly successful at keeping it at bay, especially since Sam had made it clear that she didn't want to mix business with pleasure. Now with his mom's interest pricked, he definitely wanted to keep things platonic. If Victoria connected with Sam, felt she was a possible Breedlove bride and got the slightest whiff of romance, she'd start searching for suitable wedding venues and order the cake.

His phone dinged. The invite from Victoria. He clicked on it and downloaded the attachment but finished viewing Sam's latest renderings and making notes before placing the call. By then he'd mentally placed her back in the work safe zone and convinced himself that he was making too big a deal of the carnival invite. She and Trey would be two of over a thousand people his mother expected to descend on the estate next weekend.

Noah texted the invite to Sam, then got up to take in the all-encompassing Las Vegas view from his high-rise corner office. "Sam, good morning."

"Almost afternoon on the East Coast. You're calling about the Southeast island designs?"

"Yes, and something else. I just texted you an invite."

"An invite? For what?"

"Did you get it?"

"Hold on." Nick watched a plane descend toward the nearby airport. "A CANN Kind of Carnival?"

"Yes, that's it, forwarded at the specific request of my mother."

"Please join us for…" Sam's voice diminished as he imagined her quickly scanning the invitation.

"Um, yeah, this is very kind of Victoria, but I'm going to have to decline."

"About that feeling like you have an option? You don't. It's why I called."

"Let me make sure I've got this straight. My first weekend off and I'm required to attend a carnival?"

"One hosted by the CANN Foundation, which my mother heads up? Yes. It's going to be an amazing event with the proceeds benefiting children in hospitals, foster care and at-risk situations. My mom has dreamed up a ton of creative efforts over the years, but this literal fair on the grounds of the estate is a first."

"And you're saying this is mandatory?"

"I'm saying it would be in your best interest."

"Why? I don't remember attending CANN charity events being in my agreement."

"Mom knows you're new to town and a single mother. She feels an outing like this would be a great way for you and Trey to meet other moms and young kids in the community."

"That's very thoughtful of her, but honestly, I was looking forward to a simple weekend, a movies-and-pizza kind of affair. Especially with the Carolinas on the schedule next week and a few potential material availability fires already cropping up. Since you're such an ace business negotiator, why don't you decline the RSVP on my behalf."

"Because Victoria is a partner possessing debate skills that make winning arguments darn near impossible. I believe the invitation allows you to include a friend or two. Perhaps your cousin or another mother would like to join you? As much as I appreciate your focus, a short break from the stress might do you good. You'll enjoy yourself and your son will love it."

After a pause, Sam responded. "I'm sure he'd have fun. I could probably find an hour or two to hang out there."

"Good."

She chuckled. "Is that relief I hear in your voice?"

"Ha! Picked up on that, did you? If you knew Mom, you'd be relieved, too."

"I don't understand."

"Victoria Breedlove lives life on a chessboard. She never makes one move without having thought three or four moves ahead. I've played on this board all my life and know for sure that it would be better to say yes to this invitation and have whatever conversation she obviously wants to have with you, than to decline and make her even more determined to make a connection."

"Does she know about us, I mean, our one-night stand?"

"No."

"Does she usually meet with or invite all new employees to charitable functions?"

"I can't say that she does. Look, I don't want to frighten you. But you might as well know that you'll be under the V-radar. Mom looked you up online. She saw your picture, thinks you're gorgeous, is familiar with your work and is an incurable matchmaker. She'll more than likely want to get all up in your business and has the uncanny knack to be halfway through your personal secrets chest before you realize the lid has been opened. Be cordial, but know that you are under no obligation whatsoever to share anything outside of casual pleasantries. I'll introduce you to the girls, who between the three of them can share a bevy of appropriate diversionary comebacks."

"The girls...your in-laws."

"My in-loves—Lauren, Ryan and Dee."

"Ah, right."

Nick heard the sound of a beep and a whispered expletive on the other end of the line.

"Nick, I've got to go."

"Everything all right?"

"It will be."

The line went dead.

In the world of construction, delays, snags, errors and snafus came with the territory. The angst heard in Sam's voice was not uncommon, especially given the scope and scale of what they were building. Yet it bothered him to hear it, to think that something was dimming the light in those gorgeous brown eyes.

A few minutes later, his cell phone rang. Unknown caller. Again.

"Breedlove." A slight rustling was heard on the otherwise silent line. "Hello? Who is this? Look, whoever you're looking for is not at this number. Do not call it again."

Nick ended the call more than a bit chagrined. The calls were increasing to the point of becoming a nuisance. An unknown number could not be blocked. Much like the errant erotic thoughts that kept springing up about Sam.

He couldn't block them. That bothered him, too.

Nine

Every part of Sam's mind was exhausted. With the unexpected delays and back-ordered materials, her stay on the idyllic island was by no means a vacation. But she'd gotten the job done. Except for the furnishings that had been ordered but not yet delivered, CANN Isle-New York was finished, enough so that Sam felt confident moving on to the Carolinas next week. After speaking with Danni about the woman she'd hired to look after Trey, and watching the nanny's interaction with her son, she also felt very good about hiring Gloria Monroe.

"Come on, little man. I've got him, Gloria, thanks."

Sam reached into the car seat and pulled the sleeping tyke from the car seat, then followed an equally tired live-in nanny into the condo. The driver pulled their luggage from the trunk and deposited it at the entrance.

"Would you like me to take these inside, ma'am?"

"No, that's okay. We can get it from here." She reached inside her purse and pulled out a bill. "Thank you."

"I appreciate it, ma'am. Have a good night."

While Gloria handled the luggage, Sam continued on to Trey's room. She set down her purse and undressed her son. She'd just pushed his last extremity into his favorite Black Panther superhero pajamas when her phone rang.

She fished it out of her bag, placed it on Trey's bed and pushed the speaker button. "Hey, cuz, can I call you right back? I just got home and am putting Trey to bed."

"Okay. Call ASAP."

Sam's brow creased. Danielle didn't sound happy. Sam tucked Trey into bed, proceeded to her room and even though she wanted nothing more than a quick hot shower and her soft, warm bed, she had a brief chat with Gloria, giving her the weekend off, then retreated to the master.

She hit Redial. "I've got a date with a pillow, cousin, so make it quick. What's up?"

"I'm not sure you want to know, but you need to."

The cryptic answer pushed a bit of Sam's exhaustion away. She sat straighter on the bed. "You don't sound good, Danni. What's going on?"

Sam heard a deep sigh on the other end of the line.

"I recently met up with a few girlfriends. One of them had heard talk." A beat and then, "About you."

"Me? I barely even live here. Who can say what about me?"

"Not as much you as Trey."

Sam's blood cooled. When she spoke her tone was low, deadly. "What is being said about my son?"

"The word is out that Oba is not Trey's biological dad, and a few nosy Nancys are speculating on the father."

"Why don't they speculate on minding their business?"

"You working with one of the town's most eligible bachelors makes you their business. Especially Joi, who's obviously been running her big mouth."

"Dammit."

"I know, girl. I almost called you the night I found out but I know how busy this job has got you—figured tonight would be soon enough."

"You know what? I'm not totally surprised. Oba's been calling."

"No way. For how long?"

"Off and on since I've been here. But they really ramped up a few weeks ago when his dad kicked him out of the palace. Said he needed help maintaining his lifestyle."

"And he thought you, a single, working mother, was the one to give it to him?"

"When I told him I didn't have any money, he suggested I ask Nick. There was a barely veiled threat with the request but honestly I thought he was bluffing. Now, with what you're telling me, and especially at the mention of his sister, the recent conversations make even more sense."

"There always was something about that girl. Don't get me wrong, she has a kind side. We've always been cool and used to hang out all the time before the kids came along. It's how she gossiped and talked about others that used to bug me, and the way she treated those she considered subpar. I guess because her messiness was never directed toward me, I ignored it. I shouldn't have. Asking Nick for the money may have even been her idea."

"Probably. She's how he found out we were working together."

"And the only other person who knew that Oba wasn't Trey's father."

"Until Isaac sneaked a piece of Trey's hair, had a DNA test done and ensured their whole family knew the truth."

"I think it was Joi. Like I said, she's got a messy side."

Sam flopped back on her bed. "I've got to tell Nick, now, at the worst possible time."

"While the two of you are working so closely together."

"That's not all." Sam told Danielle about the carnival happening that weekend. "I can invite a guest. Will you go? Please?"

"Absolutely, I'll go. Jaylen and Trey will have a ball. You'll be fine, too. It may feel like the end of the world, Sam. But it's not."

The next morning, Sam slept in and enjoyed a light breakfast with just her and Trey before getting them dressed for their outing.

Once in the car, Trey asked, "Where are we going, Mama?"

"First, to pick up Danni and Jaylen and then to a town called Breedlove."

"What's in Bead Love?"

"It's BREED-love, honey, and it's a surprise."

Less than forty-five minutes later, Sam bypassed the stately wrought iron privacy gates to the Breedlove Estate and continued via the texted instructions to a tree-lined side road about a half a mile down from the family mansion. Signs had been erected welcoming guests to the CANN CARNIVAL, with directions to parking lots and the main entrance. Rounding the corner, Sam couldn't believe her eyes. A fairground rivaling any town, big or small, had been erected on Breedlove land. The boys squealed, their heads pressed to the glass as they chatted excitedly.

"A carnival!"

"With rides and everything!"

Upon reaching the entrance and receiving a map to the grounds and armbands allowing free rides and other niceties for special guests, Sam sent Nick a text.

I'm here, FYI. Wow. Amazing!

The women had their hands full with two wide-eyed boys and put them on the first available ride simply to catch their breath.

The ride finished. Nick texted back. Where are you?

Near entrance. Boys on the first ride they saw.

☺ There will be a raffle in the casino in an hour. Meet me there.

Sam referenced the map as the group made their way around the carefully planned scene. There was a Ferris wheel, merry-go-rounds, carnival games and a petting zoo. There were bumper cars and a video arcade, along with more adventuresome rides for teens. The adults hadn't been left out, either. Towering zip lines and soaring rock-climbing walls had been erected aside more traditional rides like the

Kamikaze and Tilt-A-Whirl. A large tent housed the mini-CANN casino described on the back of the map, complete with slot machines and poker, blackjack and roulette tables. Music and other sounds filled the air. Dotted throughout were food trucks and sweets stands. In short, Nick's mom had organized a child's best dream. The meticulously manicured lawns had been carefully turned into a Memorial Day wonderland for both the young and the young at heart.

An hour later and Sam still wasn't ready to face Nick. She was sure that meant meeting his mom and possibly other members of his family.

"Why don't I take the boys to the petting zoo?" Danielle offered.

Sam could have kissed her. "That's a perfect idea. Keep your phone handy. I'll text you when I'm done."

She watched her cousin and the boys walk away, then crossed over to and stepped inside the casino. After pausing for her eyes to adjust to the dimmed lighting, she looked around and spotted Nick almost immediately. He looked up to catch her staring, smiled and waved her over. Sam gave herself a pep talk, remembering Danielle's parting words before she left with the boys. *They don't know anything until you tell them. Remember that.*

"Hey, Nick."

"There she is. The miracle worker!" Nick pulled Sam into an enthusiastic hug. "Congrats on a bang-up job out there. Our New York guests are in for a treat."

Sam was embarrassed at the show of affection but appreciative of the praise. She was also über-aware of other eyes on her. "One down, twenty-plus to go. Let's not pop the cork yet."

"Just a matter of time," Nick responded, full of confidence. "I picked the one person in the world who could get the job done."

At this, an older woman standing near him, who even

in casual slacks and an oversize top oozed refinement and class, smiled and held out her hand.

"You must be Samantha. I'm Victoria, Nick's mom."

"It's a pleasure to meet you, Victoria. Please, call me Sam. Thank you so much for the special invitation to attend this spectacular event. My son is already over the moon. He won't want to leave."

Victoria looked to both sides of Sam. "Where is your son?"

"With his cousin visiting the petting zoo."

"Always a child favorite. I'm glad he's having a good time."

A young woman walked up. "Excuse me, Victoria, but it's time for the raffle."

"Of course. We'll talk more later, Sam, all right?"

No, it was not all right. "Sure."

During the raffle, Sam met Noah, Adam and Christian. Their wives and several others assisted Victoria on stage. The guys were fun and easygoing. Sam was happy to know she'd overreacted. What could go wrong at a carnival, where folk walked around with big smiles on their faces? Even after the raffle, when Nick insisted on walking with her to meet back up with Danielle, Sam only felt the slightest of flutters. Nick didn't yet know what she hadn't told him. There's no way he'd have an inkling that Trey was his. Nick had a light complexion. Trey had inherited his mom's richly melanated skin. Trey was tall for his age but he was still only four, bearing hardly a hint of resemblance to the six-feet-plus of deliciousness his father carried around.

"Danni, you remember Nick?" she said, once she and Danielle reunited.

Danielle smiled. "Of course. Nice to see you again."

"Likewise." Nick shook her hand.

"Trey, Jaylen, this is Nick. I work with him building houses."

Nick knelt to their level and held out his hand. "Hello, Trey. Hello, Jaylen. Are you boys having a good time?"

"Yes!" They sang in duet.

"Uncle Nick!" A high-pitched yell rose over the din of noises before a little girl wearing pink overalls and a straw hat burst through the crowd.

As soon as she reached him, he scooped her up. "Hey, Angel!"

"My name's not Angel, it's Christina!"

"But you look like an angel."

Curls bounced as the four-year old shook her head from side to side. "I don't look like an angel. I don't have wings!"

Christian strolled up to them. "Another debate within seconds? You two never see the world the same."

"Which is what makes life so exciting," Nick said, easing Christina to the ground. "The world opens up wider when viewed through the eyes of a child."

Christian turned to Sam. "Do you believe that?"

"Sometimes."

Nick put an arm around Sam. "Good answer. Where's Lar?"

Nick looked around for Christina's little brother, Larenz, and saw Christian's wife Lauren pushing a stroller. Sam quietly watched the family's interactions. The adults, thoroughly enjoying each other, the kids clearly loved. This was the life her secret kept from Trey. It wasn't fair and considering the rumblings, it wasn't wise, either.

"You know what, Nick. I need to speak with you about something."

"Okay."

"Uncle Nick!" Christina interrupted. "Can you take me to ride the horses?"

"We can ride them?" Trey asked wide-eyed.

Danielle looked toward the large white tent where she'd taken the boys. "I didn't see horses at the petting zoo."

"They're not a part of the carnival. They're on Adam's ranch."

"Horses," Trey cried. "I want to ride horses!"

Sam took the arm of a child on his way out of control. "Trey! Come on, honey. The horses aren't here. Let's go ride the merry-go-round or Ferris wheel."

"Those horses are fake," he announced, spitting out the last word as if it were vile, before doing something he rarely did. Began to throw a fit. "Horses! I want to ride the horses!" Screaming and crying, with Sam looking at him as she would a stranger.

Whose child is this?

"Hey, hey, hey." Nick knelt until they were face-to-face. "Trey, look at me. Only big boys can ride the horses. With you crying like that, and screaming and stomping, you'll scare them away. Trey, do you hear me?"

Somewhere in his wall of hollers Nick's words sank through. The crying stopped as quickly as it started.

"Yes," he answered, throwing in a sniffle for good measure.

Sam watched, amazed and more than a little touched. Their first father-son interaction and neither of them knew it.

"Mom, can I go ride the horses? I'm not crying now."

Sam looked at Nick, who only now realized his error.

"You said it."

"I did, didn't I." He lifted Trey into the crook of his arm. "Tell you what. The horse I have in mind for you to ride doesn't like crowds. But if you act like the little man that I believe you can be for the rest of the day, I'll ask Mommy to bring you back in the morning, and we'll go riding then. But you have to be good. Your mom will tell me if you're not. Deal?"

Trey nodded in reluctant agreement.

"Is that okay with you?" Nick asked Sam.

"Well, since you've just made a huge promise to a four-year-old," she said under her voice before announcing, "I guess…yes."

"Sorry." Nick talked softly as well so that only Sam could hear. "I guess I shouldn't have done that. In my effort to come off as the savior, I've committed you to another day at the fair, or back here to ride horses at least."

"Worse could happen."

"Indeed."

The group split up soon after the convo ended. Sam and Danielle ended up staying much longer than they'd planned and enjoyed the goings-on possibly more than adults should. For Sam, it was the first time since accepting the contract that she allowed herself to unwind, to forget about materials and drawings and deadlines and simply have a good time. By the time moms and sons left the fairgrounds, both Sam and Danielle were glad they'd brought strollers. The kids were knocked out.

"How did it feel to see—" Danielle tilted her head toward the back seat "—with his father."

"It's hard to describe." Sam caught a mental image of Nick picking up Trey. "I didn't know there was that much love in my heart."

"For the son...or the daddy?"

"I can't help but love Nick. He's the father of my child. But that and my temporary boss is all that he is."

Danielle let it go and changed the subject. Sam was glad that she did. The truth of the matter was that she wanted Trey to get to know Nick better and looked forward to tomorrow. Hopefully the more Nick felt an affinity with Trey, the easier it would be to accept that he was his son, too.

That night she lay in bed thinking. *It's coming together. I may be able to rebuild my life after all.* The good feeling lasted a full fifteen minutes, until her phone buzzed and she read the text that had just come in from overseas. Without checking the name, she knew who it was.

No more asking. No more waiting. Wire 500K to my bank account before the end of the month. Or I tell Nick everything.

Ten

Nick took a seat at the long patio table on his parents' back porch, then waved away his twin, who'd prepared to sit beside him.

Noah's brow raised. "Are we expecting someone?"

"I invited Sam over. Yesterday Christina mentioned riding horses in front of her son and suddenly the Merry-Go-Round became a poor second choice."

Noah walked around to sit across from Nick. "So Sam's bringing him over to go riding?"

"Yep. You're welcome to join us."

"Thanks, bro, but I'm going to stay close to sweet lady. She's had a couple premature contractions and chose to stay home."

"Makes sense. Then why are you here?"

"To pick up the cinnamon rolls she craves. And now that I know Sam is joining us…to stick around a little while for the show."

Nick knew Noah was talking about the creative ways their mother tended to question any female she deemed clan-suitable. While his mother had only spoken casually with Sam yesterday, that she'd done online research was enough for him to know his designer was on her radar.

Brunch was in full swing when one of the housekeepers brought Sam, Trey and another woman around to the back. Nick took in her unsure expression and met her at the patio's edge to make her welcome.

"There they are! Hey guys." He noticed a dip in conversation as the duo approached.

Nick knelt down. "How are you, little man?"

"Fine."

"Ready to ride horses?"

"Yes!"

He turned to Sam. "Hello."

"Hi." She looked at the woman beside her. "I hope you don't mind that I brought my nanny, Gloria. She was so excited by what I shared yesterday that I felt bad at not inviting her."

"No worries. She can join Chris's au pair Kirtu in the other room with Christina and Lars."

He looked beyond her. "No Danni today?"

"Like me, she's never ridden a horse. Unlike me, she'd like to keep it that way." After brief instructions to Trey on how to behave, he and Gloria headed toward the kids' room.

"You've never taken a ride before?" Nick asked, leading them toward the buffet line. He noticed Sam's eyes flicker just enough to confirm she'd caught the double entendre. "No, I've never before ridden a horse, though I once caravanned on a camel."

"I thought you'd never gone on a safari?"

"I haven't. That ride occurred during a tour of the Egyptian pyramids."

"There you go! You'll be fine."

After walking through the buffet line and loading up their plates, they took their seats at the table.

"Everybody, you remember Sam from yesterday? Those who weren't there, this is Sam Price, the extraordinary interior designer who's ensuring our island guests are properly blown away by their surroundings."

A variety of greetings rang out from the dozen or so gathered around the table. Small talk ensued, mostly about the success of the CANN Carnival, raising millions of dollars for children needing assistance in Nevada and beyond.

During a lull in the conversation, Victoria spoke. "Samantha, I understand you recently moved back from being an expat in Africa. Do you miss that beautiful continent or were you happy to return home?"

"You're right, Victoria, there are areas of Africa that are absolutely stunning, some of the most beautiful scenery I've seen. But I'm very glad to be back in the States."

"Well, I can tell you that Nick for one is glad you're back as well. He sings your praises as a designer."

Sam smiled at Nick. "Thank you." Then to Victoria, "CANN is an excellent company. I am thankful to have gotten such a wonderful opportunity so soon after arriving."

"You two seem to get along very well. Did you know each other prior to coming on board for the island project?"

"Aren't these crepes delicious?" Noah asked, a question so unlike what he'd normally ask that everyone knew its purpose and laughed at the blatant subject change to bail out his twin.

Nick stuffed a bite in his mouth and talked while chewing. "Ah, bro, they're delish!"

"For sure," Adam added. "With these sweet potato crepes Gabe has outdone himself!"

The conversation was successfully diverted long enough for Nick and Sam to finish their dishes and make a graceful exit. They stopped next door where the kids were playing board games. With Gloria and a very excited Trey in tow, they headed toward Adam's ranch and the stable of horses he kept there.

Nick introduced Sam to the ranch manager, Rusty, who walked them over to where Adam's growing collection of prized horses was housed. He picked an apple from a barrel near the barn's entrance and gave it to Nick.

"For when the little one meets Queen."

"Ah, good choice," Nick said, about the gentle mare. "Little man and I will be riding together." Rusty nodded. "We'll want someone equally gentle for Sam here. It's her first time riding."

"No worries, pretty lady," Rusty said. "We'll get you fixed right up." He gave them apples, too.

Sam turned to Gloria. "Am I the only one on a maiden voyage, or have you not ridden before either?"

"It's been a long time ago, back in Oklahoma on my grandpa's farm."

"It's like riding a bike," Rusty assured her. "Sit the saddle properly and it's all downhill from there."

When they reached Queen, Nick handed Trey the apple. "One of these always helps to make a proper introduction."

Trey took the apple and was properly awed as Nick guided his hand for the horse to softly remove it, then picked him up to pet Queen's mane.

Nick winked at Sam. "He's a natural, same as Noah and I were when we were his age."

The four got saddled up—Nick and Trey on Poker, Gloria on an Appaloosa named Lucy, and Sam on Queen. Gloria's was an easy mount, but Sam needed help. Nick was happy to oblige. Any excuse to caress her glorious backside would do. Queen began to prance. Sam tensed up right away.

"Just relax," Nick said, his tone low and soothing. "Animals can smell fear. Hold the reins with confidence. She needs to know you're in control."

"That's still up for debate."

Nick helped Sam until she felt more comfortable, walking them around in a circle near the gate.

"You ready?"

Sam nodded. "I think so."

With that, they took off across the glorious countryside at a comfortable pace. Even after spending his entire life on the land, Nick was still moved by its beauty. After about ten minutes, when he felt Sam had a handle on Queen, Nick gave his horse his head and sped up a bit. Trey squealed with delight. Nick focused on Trey, even as he himself enjoyed the chance to get out in nature and feel the wind on his face. All the brothers had grown up in the saddle, but he and Christian rode far less often than Noah and Adam. Today reminded Nick he needed to change that.

"Let's go fast again, Nick!"

"Okay, buddy." Nick secured Trey in his grip, then lightly touched the horse's flank.

"Nick!"

"Don't worry, Sam! I've got him."

"It's Sam, Nick!"

Nick turned toward the sound of Gloria's voice in time to observe Queen's trot increasing to a gallop at a quick pace. Sam must have unknowingly directed the horse to run. Without thought, he wheeled Poker around and headed toward Sam.

"Relax, Sam! Don't pull so hard on the reins!"

Nick quickly eased alongside Sam and grabbed the horse's reins. Within seconds, the horse slowed down. Nick made a few sounds and talked to Queen until the horse came to a stop.

"You all right?" He'd been so busy getting the horse under control that only now did he see the tears in Sam's eyes, or that an ashy sheen to her deep chocolate skin alluded to how frightened she was, as did the shaky hand that had grabbed him once he was close with nails now almost piercing his cotton shirt.

Nick didn't need to hear her answer. She was not okay.

By the time the horse stopped, Gloria had rounded back to where they all were. "Can you ride with Trey?" he asked her.

She nodded. "I think so."

"Good. Because Sam's going to ride with me." Nick glanced at his watch. "The carnival opens in an hour. We'd planned to go to the house to freshen up anyway. We'll just do that now."

Nick helped Sam into the saddle, then mounted behind her. Immediately, he knew he was in trouble. Sam's body, warm, curvaceous and shaking, folded into his embrace. For the woman he'd always seen as strong and confident, the vulnerability was foreign. The need to protect her sprang up with force in his chest. He felt capable and needed, feelings that opened up a space for Sam in his heart. Instinctively, a protective arm went around her. He tilted his hips back in an effort to hide an oncoming arousal, but Sam followed his body with her own, as if his touch alone reassured her. It made him powerful; his testosterone surged. He grew heady from the scent of her cologne, the feel of her soft locs brushing against his neck and chest and her body folded into his own. By the time they reached his home, he was on fire with desire, felt almost drunk with need. He helped her down, then took the horse around back and dismounted in private, until his own privates were under control.

She was standing by the window when he entered, seemingly still as shaken in his living room as she'd been outside.

Gloria stood near her, a concerned look on her face. Trey hid behind Gloria's legs. "Is there anything I can do for you?"

"I'll be okay."

Nick watched Sam attempt a reassuring smile for her observant son. He guessed she was trying to assure herself as well.

Nick's doorbell rang. He frowned slightly at the unexpected intrusion. "Who could that be?" he murmured.

"It's probably Kirtu," Gloria offered. "We talked about meeting up so that the children could continue playing together. I'll tell her we'll meet later on."

Sam shook her head. "No, please, you guys go on to the carnival and text your location. I'll be along shortly."

Nick opened the door. Indeed it was Christina's nanny. She spoke to everyone.

"Where's Christina?" Gloria asked.

"With Lauren. They're spending a bit of time together before she goes off with Christian. We're supposed to meet them at the food court."

Gloria turned to Sam once again. "Are you sure?"

"Absolutely, Gloria." Sam looked at Trey. "Are you ready for more rides and games, Trey?"

Trey reached for Gloria's hand and vigorously nodded.

"Good. I'll meet you there in a little bit. If you leave that area, Gloria, just text me where you are. All right?"

"Sure."

As soon as Trey was gone, Sam collapsed against the wall. "Crap! That was scary!"

Nick was immediately by her side. "I'm sorry, babe. I've ridden Queen many times and seen others ride her. You must have unknowingly given her the signal to run. Doing so on her own would be very uncharacteristic.

"How about some hot chamomile tea. Or something stronger if you'd like."

Sam managed a smile. "Tea is fine. Thanks again, Nick," she whispered, flinging her arms around his neck, pressing her body against him. "I don't know what I would have done without your help earlier. I'm so glad you were there."

Nick was glad he was there, too, and that Sam was in his arms. It felt good, too good. He gently gripped her arms and meant to set her away from him. But just then she turned her face so that their lips were parallel, then pressed those soft cushions of sexy goodness against his eager lips. Whatever control he had went out the window. He placed his hands beneath her butt and lifted her up against the wall, his lips never leaving hers as he secured himself between her legs.

"Nick."

Sam's voice was light, shaky, caught up in ecstasy. He watched, mesmerized, as she reached for the hem of her top and pulled it over her head. Then to the back of her bra, snapping the clasp from the back. Everything she did was everything he'd imagined. The switch had happened so quickly he felt it almost surreal, as though he were an observer instead of a participant, needing to be prodded to play along.

"Nick, please…"

Her soft entreaty was all the encouragement he needed. He pulled a soft nipple into his mouth, unzipping his jeans while he feasted. They kissed every part of exposed flesh available, and quickly realized that was not enough. They needed more, much more. They needed all of each other.

Sam slid from the wall and reached for her pants. They quickly joined Nick's in a pile on the floor. He lifted her once again and placed her on the living room's oversize ottoman. The bedroom was too far away, would take too long to consummate a reunion more than four years in the making. Dropping down in front of her, Nick gently spread her legs apart. He slid a finger along the folds of her thong and after pushing it aside, buried his head in her heat. She squealed and squirmed but he gave no quarter. He lapped and lavished her pearl, feasted on her nectar. Her soft thighs rested on his shoulders, gripping him hard as she reached and then went over the edge. Her whimpers sent his dick rock hard. He retrieved a condom from his pants pocket, positioned his shaft where his tongue had been and deepened the dance.

"Nick, Nick," she purred, in beat with this rhythm. He thrust and plunged himself into her core, grabbed the juicy cheeks that drove him wild and ground deeply some more. Their bodies came together like two long-lost pals who'd known each other forever, who'd always loved this way. They ended up in the bedroom, where Sam performed oral feats that left Nick shaken to the bone, that made him forget about every other woman who in the throes of passion had ever called his name. When he felt Sam ready to burst again, he increased his thrusts to join her going over the edge. There was one woman on his mind, one name on his lips. He whispered it as he shuddered.

"Sam."

Eleven

Sam's orgasm had barely ended before regret set in. Not that she and Nick had sex. In retrospect, the act seemed a foregone conclusion from the time she'd stepped in his office on that first interview. An ending they both saw coming but tried to ignore. No, Sam's regret was about what had been unleashed inside her. Rekindled. Reawakened. It was the feeling she'd had the first time she saw Nick. A palpable hunger. An undeniable connection. But leading to what? Even now, as Nick stood behind her, held her, kissed her neck and nibbled her ear as the shower water washed over them, Sam felt a longing in her heart for something she feared Nick could not fulfill, or wasn't interested in fulfilling.

"We need to hurry," she whispered, stepped away from him and reaching for a loofah on one of the shelves. She quickly unwrapped it, performed her ablutions and left the bathroom. By the time Nick came out she was dressed and on her phone, texting Gloria as to her and Trey's whereabouts. She went to the kitchen and reheated the tea that had earlier been poured and forgotten, added cream and sugar, then took small sips to calm her nerves. This helped her put the tiger of desire back in its cage, regain control of her body and rid her mind of happily ever after fantasies that only came true in romance novels.

He walked straight toward her. "That was amazing, babe."

She dodged his intended embrace and put distance between them. "We need to talk about what just happened."

A smile slid onto Nick's face, as slow as molasses and Sam knew, equally sweet. "I hope you're not expecting that talk to include an apology, because I am not at all sorry about being with you. In fact, I want to do it again. Soon. And often."

Sam worked to stay focused on what needed to be said and not how good Nick looked in the white tee, low-slung black jeans and sandals that now covered the body that had so pleasured her just moments ago. Hard to do. Every movement reminded her of something he'd done. How the fingers fastening his belt buckle had played her body like an instrument, had trailed from the back of her neck to her thighs and left goose bumps in their wake. How his soft, thick lips had touched, branded, almost every inch of her body, and how his tongue had—for those few intimate seconds, or hours, who's counting—wiped away every worry about Oba, Trey's parentage, the projects and everything else. She turned away as he looked up, convinced that the desire dredged up by those too-recent memories were written all over her face.

She took a breath and began again, her back toward him as she walked to an abstract painting hung on the wall. "No regrets, it's not about that. Or the attraction," she continued, boldly turning to face not only her fears, but him as well. "Which especially after what just happened, I won't try to deny. This is about you being my boss. And me having a job to do. A physical relationship might get in the way of that."

He smiled in obvious agreement.

The grip on her mug of tea tightened. "It would definitely get in the way."

"You're probably right." His eyes never left hers while raising a bottle of water to his lips.

Both sipped in silence.

"That's it?" Sam finally asked.

Nick shrugged. "What else can there be? I don't agree with your position but your message is clear."

"I don't want this to create an awkward vibe between us."

"We're both adults. I don't foresee a problem if you don't.

Although I don't think tamping down what's flowing between us will be as easy as you think. I mean, damn. What happens when we're together, the way our bodies fit like perfect puzzle pieces, the way you mold around me like a custom-made glove..."

Damn if hearing that sexy voice and seeing that lethal tongue didn't make her want to do it again. "Nick, stop. I'm serious."

"So am I. Look, beautiful, may I suggest something?"

Not in the voice that makes my panties wet. "What?"

"Why don't we relax around what's happening, not make any rules or resist what is abundantly clear. I'm not dating anyone right now, are you?"

"No, but…"

"No buts. I get that you want to focus on business. I respect that and will be a total gentleman. I won't do anything you don't want to do. I'm just saying that if the situation arises, as it did just now, let's deal with it then, in the moment, and see what happens."

"Okay." Sam's phone buzzed. She checked it. "That's Gloria. She and Kirtu are with the kids in the Fun Zone."

"Do you want to get your face painted, too?" Nick teased.

"No, but I might accept one of the clown's animal balloons…since I feel like an ass," she finished, mumbling under her breath.

"What was that?"

"Nothing."

Sam was determined to try Nick's approach. She tried to act casual, as if it were just another day. But as they neared the crowded fairgrounds, she felt that the fact she'd just been screwed to within an inch of her life and loved every second of it was readily apparent. If so, however, Gloria didn't let on. She relaxed even more and instead of feeling paranoid with Nick beside her allowed herself to enjoy his company. He really was amazing with children. Clearly his niece adored him.

"Hi, Uncle Nick!"

"Come here, Angel." He easily lifted Christina into his arms.

Trey, feeling left out, whined to also be held in Nick's arms. "Pick me up! Pick me up, too!"

Sam prepared to admonish him, but Nick complied. He reached down, easily balancing a child in each arm. They laughed at the kids' obvious attempts to garner the most attention from a man both children clearly liked. So caught up was she in the joy of the moment that danger sidled up beside her undetected.

"Nick, or Noah?"

Sam turned to see a beautiful woman with flawless skin and long black hair peering carefully between the kids and Nick. The smile Nick put on Sam's face with his lovemaking and charming personality slid off faster than she'd slid off Queen earlier. The last person on earth that she wanted to see appeared like an apparition before her.

Joi.

Nick looked at her. "I'm sorry. Do I know you?"

"Not really." Joi smiled at him while looking every inch of amazing, and seductive. "We've met socially a couple times. A few years ago, we were at the same costume party, in fact."

She slid a quick glance at Sam. Sam stopped breathing.

"My name's Joi." Nodding toward the children Nick was placing back on the ground, she said with hand outstretched, "Which one is yours?"

Nick uncoiled back to his full height. "Nick."

Joi shook Nick's hand, then looked at Trey standing close by Nick's side and tried to shake his, too. Trey pulled it back. Sam stopped herself from stepping between them.

"Hello, little one! Is this your son, Nick?"

"No. Trey belongs to this beautiful lady, Sam Price."

Joi turned, eyes wide in feigned surprise. "Sam!"

Sam had the distinct feeling her presence was not a surprise to her former sister-in-law. She worked to keep a WTF look off her face.

"Oh my goodness, I was so focused on Nick and those cute little kids I didn't see you!"

"A woman you've known for years?" *And a child who's your nephew?* Sam so wanted to add that line, but now wasn't the time. "I find that hard to believe but…okay."

Joi leaned into Sam for a hug. It was like embracing a board. "Don't play me," Joi quietly hissed. "Or you'll get played."

Not a hint of meanness showed when she stepped back, all smiles and bright, wide eyes. Joi was a beautiful girl, Sam decided, whose performance could have easily won an Oscar.

What an actress. It was incredible that the same woman who appeared as an angel years ago could behave so much like the devil right now. Her threat answered one question. Joi may not have suggested that Oba blackmail her for money, but Sam was convinced that Joi was somehow involved. Their knowing what Nick didn't was a very real threat to Sam getting back on her feet. But she'd be damned if she let Joi think they held an advantage. When pressed, Sam could be an actor, too.

"I heard the news about your getting a job with CANN International."

"I heard you've been spreading quite a bit of news about me and you need to stop." Said as quietly as Joi's warning, and as sweetly as though honey had been poured over the words. But the glint in Sam's eyes conveyed "don't start none, won't be none."

A slight narrowing of Joi's eyes was the only hint that Sam's words had hit a mark.

"You two obviously know each other," Nick said, as tension crackled.

"We're family," Joi replied, with a fake laugh that made

Sam's skin crawl. Her mind whirled with possible motives for Joi being here. None of them were good.

Sam turned to Nick. "Not anymore. Joi is my ex-husband's sister. She's how he and I met."

"Ah, I see." Nick looked at Joi with renewed interest and an unreadable expression. Sam imagined that information caused him to look at this overly friendly interruption in a new light. "Yet you didn't recognize Trey?"

Good question, Sam thought. Would-be actress Joi didn't miss a beat.

"It's been a couple years since I've seen him. He was just a baby when a myriad of business opportunities brought me back to live full-time in the States. He's gotten so big!"

She looked pointedly at Sam. "Wonder where he gets his height? My brother is average height, as are most men on that side of the family."

"My brother's tall," Sam said before reaching for Trey's hand. "So is my dad. It's understandable you'd be confused since you never met my side of the family, and since the few interactions we had at the palace were too brief and infrequent to develop a bond."

"Since we're both back in America, maybe we can change that. You and Oba are divorced. But I'm still Trey's aunt, right?"

In light of no good answer, Sam remained mum.

Sam didn't want to leave Joi alone with Nick, but she couldn't stay and watch the Oscar-worthy performance one moment longer. There would come a moment when Sam could tell Joi just what she thought of this messy charade. But not today.

"We've got a date with a puppet or two," Sam finally said, forcing a casualness into her voice that she didn't feel.

"Hang on," Nick said. "I'll bring Christina."

"Enjoy the fair," Nick said, already turning to walk away from Joi.

"Goodbye, Joi!" Sam kept her voice light, tried to hide

how much she'd been affected by the exchange. She was only partly successful. The smile in Sam's voice did not reach her eyes.

When they neared the tent where the puppet theater was housed, Sam sent Trey in with Gloria. Nick followed suit with Christina and her au pair. Once alone, Nick's concern was immediate.

"You okay?"

"Why wouldn't I be?" Sam snapped back. It was enough that Joi had come and effectively ruined what in spite of her roiling, disjointed emotions and unplanned romp in the sack with her boss had been a pretty awesome day. Had Nick picked up on it?

"That was a pretty tense situation back there."

Yes, he had.

Sam shrugged. "Joi's known for starting trouble. I don't care much for folk like that."

"Yet she's the one who introduced you to your ex."

"I rest my case."

Nick chuckled. "I don't remember ever meeting her. Then again, I meet a lot of people so it's entirely possible that she and I traveled in the same circles. As I always say, this town is small."

"Speaking of small, I'm going in." She nodded toward the theater tent. "Are you coming?"

"No. I think I've met my kid-stuff quota for today. I was going to suggest we become kids ourselves and enjoy some of the adult rides."

"Thanks, Nick, but I'm going to have to pass. I head to South Carolina first thing tomorrow and have quite a bit to get done. After this show, I'm going to take Trey home."

"Come here." Before Sam could react, she'd been pulled into Nick's arms. "Today was amazing," he whispered, his voice wet and hot against her ear. "Thank you."

"Sure. See you later." Sam hurriedly ducked inside the tent, her body thrumming from his embrace, her mind whirling from seeing Joi and reliving conversations with Oba.

That night, she sent him a text.

I saw your sister today, which you probably know. I didn't appreciate your threats about Trey. I don't appreciate your sister's, either. Back off, Oba. Let me rebuild my life.

His response? A smiley face.

Seriously?

Sam didn't bother trying to interpret what that meant. She forced her focus from what had happened at the fairgrounds to the three homes on the Carolina islands and what she needed to accomplish next week. Hopefully her text was enough to throw off Oba or anyone else from thinking Nick was Trey's dad. Either way, she needed to tell Nick the truth. Time was running out.

Twelve

Nick had planned to fly over to the Carolinas the day after Sam arrived. But other CANN business demanded his focus the first part of the week. It wasn't until Thursday afternoon that he boarded Christian's private jet and headed to the other side of the country. He told himself it was to see in person the 3-D images and photos Sam had sent over. The truth was, he wanted to see her. Just moments from landing in Charleston, he texted Sam of his whereabouts and invited her to dinner.

Dinner?

Yes. Landing in Charleston.

Charleston, SC?

Nick smiled. A slightly confused Sam was adorable. Yes, beautiful. I have impossible-to-get reservations at a quaint spot with only ten tables. Highly recommended.

A minute passed. Then five. Ten.

Nick began to get nervous. That never happened.

Can't. She finally texted back. Contractors on the island. Problems. Call after landing.

We'll talk tomorrow. I'll be there at 8.

Nick was disappointed but of course he understood. He also realized he'd been highly presumptuous to think that someone with the type of deadlines Sam had could drop everything to skedaddle over to the mainland for a ridiculously expensive candlelight meal personally prepared by an award-winning chef. As for problems with construction, they were as common as dust. He'd worry about those tomorrow.

Knowing from Sam's photos that furniture had yet to be delivered, Nick had Anita arrange a room at a hotel, and set up one of the chefs who'd responded to their targeted ad for personal service on the islands to be at the house the next morning. He planned for Sam's day to start with a delicious, satisfying breakfast. No matter how busy the day was, she had to eat. Once those plans had been made, he forwarded them to Sam so she wouldn't wake up to a stranger knocking on her door.

"What are you doing here?" was her greeting the next day.

Not quite the warm welcome he expected but again, he understood.

"Good morning."

"That's debatable."

Sam looked haggard, as though she'd hardly slept. "Come here."

She gave him the briefest of hugs. "I know this is your baby, Nick, but there's a ton happening today. I can't believe that you'd arrive unannounced."

"It's good I did from the looks of things. Did you get any sleep last night?"

"Very little and thanks, but I've got this. I know how to call in reinforcements if needed."

"I wouldn't have hired you had I not thought you capable. I wanted to see you, okay? As Nick, not your boss."

Those words seemed to break through the wall of frustration around her. When he again invited her into his arms, she stepped in and squeezed back when he wrapped his arms around her. He kissed her cheek, eyes, forehead.

"Did the chef arrive?"

"In the kitchen."

"Hungry?"

"I could eat."

Nick looked around at the empty rooms.

"There's a railing outside on the patio where we could sit," she said.

Someone behind them cleared their throat.

"Excuse me, good morning, sir."

Nick turned to the chef in a signature white coat, his long locs neatly wrapped into a bun at the nape of his neck.

"Hi, I'm Nick."

"Gregory, sir. Nice to meet you. I've set up a bit of a beverage station in the other room. My instructions were to forgo taking personal orders and fix something amazing."

"That sounds like Anita," Nick said, smiling. "Thanks, Gregory. We'll help ourselves to the drinks and be waiting outside."

"I've taken the liberty of preparing a spot out back, sir. There was a picnic table and benches set up. I hope you don't mind."

"Not at all." Nick looked at Sam.

"It's where the construction crew eats. Let's get our drinks and head out there."

They walked into the other room where Gregory had set up a table with coffees, teas and juices.

Sam filled a tall mug with coffee. Nick poured tea. Both grabbed glasses of orange juice, then walked outside to a beautiful, slightly humid day in the Palmetto State. The dusty construction area had been transformed into an idyllic scene. The area around the table had been swept of debris. White linen covered the table where a vase of wildflowers sat in the center of the table.

"Hope you're hungry."

"A private chef, Nick. I appreciate the gesture but seriously… I would have been fine with a breakfast sandwich."

"Each vacation home comes with a staff, including a

chef. The guy fixing breakfast is on an audition of sorts for one of three positions on this island that will need to be filled."

"These magnificent homes and a private chef, too. I'm almost afraid to know the nightly rate."

"The smaller homes go for just under 10K, nightly. The price and amenities go up from there."

"Crazy that some people can spend in one night what could pay somebody else's rent for a year."

"Rich people are going to spend money, babe. Might as well be with us."

Sam held up her orange juice. "Touché."

While waiting for Gregory, they engaged in small talk about the weather, Nick's family and the kids.

"Speaking of, where is the young equestrian?"

"Back in Vegas with Gloria so that he can attend his cousin's birthday party."

"Sounds like she's working out for you."

"She's a godsend, and very good with Trey."

Once the food had been brought to the table, Nick returned to business. "I'm very pleased with the progress I see so far. Tell me about the problems you're having."

Over a superb breakfast that included crispy spiced chicken over fluffy pecan waffles, truffle-infused egg whites and mouthwatering crab cakes, Sam shared the challenge with suspending the bridge as her drawings had rendered, over a sizable koi pond. Later, they met with the contractor and with Nick's insightful suggestions, came up with a workable alternative. Sam loosened up. Nick spent the night. With Sam obviously having forgotten about them not repeating their sex romp, they christened the shower with their lovemaking, then cuddled in a twin-size futon, the home's lone piece of temporary furniture until the main shipment arrived next week. He returned to Breedlove spent and satiated, able to once again focus on work.

The day after returning back home and having put in al-

most ten hours at the office, he called his brother to hopefully shoot some hoops.

"Twin, let's ball," he said, once Noah answered.

"You're back?"

"Yeah, where were you today?"

"Working from home."

"How's Dee?"

"Better. The premature contractions stopped and there's
been no bleeding."

"Whoa, TMI, dude!"

"Hey, it's all part of bringing another being into the
world."

"I'm happy to leave that up to my brothers and be the
best Uncle Nick in the world." Noah didn't respond. "That
was a joke."

"When are you coming over?"

The seriousness in Noah's voice could not be missed.
Had he caught attitude because of Nick's joking comment?
Nick chalked it up to Noah being concerned about his wife
and the health of his child. Damaris "Dee" Glen Breedlove
helped save his brother's life once. Nick knew Noah would
do all he could to return the favor.

Nick stopped by his place, changed clothes, then continued down the road, around the bend and toward the mountains to his brother's new home. Noah and Dee had designed
it together, a combination of the styles Dee grew up seeing
in Utah and the rustic yet modern touches Noah enjoyed.
There were cows for fresh milk and chickens that provided
Dee's preferred organic eggs, a pet pig named Rosy, two
dogs, and a cat. Dee had changed his twin brother, no doubt
about that. It made him wonder what kind of changes someone special would bring into his life. An image of Sam
floated into his mind. Remembering there was no time in
his life for that kind of special, he pushed it away.

He knocked on the door. Dee answered. "He's out back,"
she said, her hands dusty with flour.

"What are you making?"

"Pies, and yes, I have one for you."

Nick gave her a thumbs-up, then jogged around to where Noah was putting up free throws on the combination basketball and tennis court located several yards beyond Dee's garden. Anyone else would see a guy loose and relaxed, casually playing a sport. But Nick knew his twin almost better than himself. Something was going on.

"What's up, bro?"

"You got it." They exchanged a fist bump. "How was the Carolinas?"

"Hot. Humid."

Noah jogged for a layup. Nick jumped up to block it. Noah faked left, rolled around and easily laid it against the board.

"How's Sam?"

Nick couldn't help smiling. "She's good."

Noah stopped bouncing the ball. "What does that mean?"

"There are a few challenges but so far we think this build can stay on schedule."

"I meant the smile."

"Oh. That."

"Are you sleeping with her?"

"Wow, kind of blunt, don't you think?"

"Well, are you? I have my reasons for asking."

"Which are?"

Noah began bouncing the ball again but made no move toward the hoop. "Really, Nick, I don't even want to respond. It's all gossip, and you know how much I hate being a part of something like that."

Nick stole the ball and rested it on his hip. "What's the rumor?"

"It's about Sam."

Nick's heartbeat increased. Was she getting back with her ex? Was there another man?

"What about Sam?"

"And Trey," Noah said.

"Spit it out, twin."

Noah sighed. "I guess that's best. There's talk going around that the dude in Nigeria, the African prince, isn't Trey's biological father."

Nick began breathing again. Was that all? Since the two were divorced that didn't seem so important; may have even been why they broke up.

"Doesn't sound like any of my business," Nick said, pausing to shoot three from the top of the key.

He headed over to retrieve the ball. Noah intercepted him and grabbed it instead.

"Word is the father lives here, in Vegas."

Nick shrugged. "I still don't see what that has to do with us. I hate gossip as much as you do. Someone obviously has too much time on their hands. Wait a minute. Where'd you hear this?"

"Lauren. She has a client who's opening a high-end boutique and travels in certain societal circles, the bougie crowd and whatnot. Said Sam's son didn't belong to the prince."

"Was the person who put this bug in her ear named Joi by any chance?"

Noah's brow creased. "Who's Joi?"

"Oba's sister. Sam's ex-sister-in-law. I met her last weekend at the carnival. Sam was with me and it was clear that there was no lost love between them."

Nick swiped the ball from Noah. "I wouldn't put too much stock into that kind of gossip, man. Come on. Twenty-one. Let's go."

"Normally, I'd say you're right. I wouldn't give those kinds of rumors the time of day. But this one is different, bro."

"Why?"

"Because of who they're claiming is Trey's father."

"Who?"

"You."

Thirteen

Sam woke up with a bad feeling, a complete paradox given she was working in what looked like a swampy paradise. She got up, made coffee and tried to shake it off. She called Gloria, texted Danni and her dad. Everyone was fine, yet the feeling persisted. She finally allowed herself to consider that the continuing angst was from the incident with Joi at the fair. The text she'd sent her ex and the reply she'd gotten. And how he'd gone radio silent since then.

What an impossible situation. It seemed that every major decision she'd made since that heavenly night she initially spent in Nick's arms had been less than smart. Not telling Nick that she was pregnant. Moving to Africa. Marrying Oba. Returning stateside to Las Vegas instead of LA. Taking the contract for CANN Isles. Not telling Nick about Trey after they began working together. Underestimating Oba's greed. Not telling Nick the moment Oba threatened to do so, then sleeping with her child's bio dad more than once. Thinking that any of this would be easy, that Nick would somehow understand her betrayal. How could she think he'd be understanding when she was finding it increasingly difficult to justify her actions? At the end of the day, Sam had to face the hard truth. There was only one person to blame for what was happening right now.

Her.

Sam's mind settled enough for her to start the workday. Admitting her role in this mess, acknowledging that what she was experiencing was something that she in large part had created, was strangely liberating. In taking responsibility Sam felt some of her power being restored. She'd felt vulnerable after the confrontation with Joi, as though someone else had the ability to call the shots on her life. That was an illusion. It wasn't true. She'd made mistakes, but it wasn't the end of the world. Most importantly, the end result of that night hadn't been all bad. It had produced that which she treasured most in life. Her son.

For the next few hours, Sam focused on the home's furnishings—double-checking that shipments were still on schedule; confirming contractor appointments and speaking with the landscaping crew. Finally, she took a long shower and rather than heating up one of the meals left by the chef, decided to take the yacht into Charleston for a proper meal.

Thirty minutes later, she was at the boat's stern, watching the Atlantic churn beneath the sleek yacht's powerful motor. People often dreamed of a rich, carefree life where having a job or not was an option. Sam had lived that life, and until now didn't realize how much she'd missed her career. She was thankful for the tight timeline, and the plethora of problems to solve it presented. Doing so gave her less time to think about her own. And just like that, the sense of foreboding came back.

She knew just the person to help lighten her mood, reached over and picked up her phone. "Hey, Danni."

"Cousin! I was just thinking about you. It's about time you called. How's it going?"

"Okay, for the most part."

"I hope you're calling to say you told Nick about Trey."

"I'm going to. Soon. How was the birthday party?"

"Loud. Scott bought Jaylen a drum set. I wanted to take those sticks and beat him with them!"

Sam laughed. "I bet Trey was happy. I miss him."

"Hmm, I see. Do you miss his father?"

"Next question."

Danielle laughed. "Where are you?"

"Off the coast of South Carolina, heading into Charleston."

"From the island?"

"Yes, the island where the homes are located. They're super secure, super private and available only by boat."

There was a slight pause, and then, "How do you do it?"

"Do what?"

"Land these dream situations in your life. First, the marriage to a prince—"

"You had a hand in that."

"And now designing island homes for a rich guy? I'm doing something wrong."

"You're doing everything right. You've got a good man, a great kid and an amazing nephew."

"Ha! I can't argue with that. Hey, speaking of my nephew, he just ran down the hall. You want to speak with him?"

"In a minute. How are you?"

"Rested. That angel named Gloria who calls herself a childcare specialist is just the type of person I need in my life. She volunteered to help with the party and a few times since then, and made me wonder how I worked and ran this household without her."

"Frankly, I don't know either. Working full-time, taking care of a family and helping with Trey? I swear there's an S on your chest."

"Ha! I'm not your superwoman," Danielle sang. "Seriously, the workers at the day care are like family and my boss is a gem. As a single mother, she's well aware of the struggle in balancing family and work."

Sam looked out over the water, rippling and glowing in the sunny afternoon. Her cousin was right. She was blessed. Even with the design problems she'd encountered and her recent divorce, all the trouble she'd left behind in Africa and the secret she kept, life was good. She was on a yacht sailing in the Atlantic, having scored a contract any designer would want, one that would boost her résumé to the point she could be picky about clients and name her price. Her son was healthy and her dad was glad she was back on his side of the world. There was no room for complaints. At least, that should have been the case. But...that feeling.

"Sam."

"Hmm?"

"You got quiet all of a sudden. What's going on?"

"I don't know. I woke up with an eerie feeling that I've had all day."

"Was it a dream about Oba?"

"No. But something happened over the weekend that I didn't tell you about." Sam told Danielle about the run-in with Joi.

"And you're just telling me now?"

"I didn't want to even think about it, much less talk about what happened."

"Sam, you need to tell Nick about Trey. Today. The last thing you want is for him to find out about it from someone other than you."

"You're right. I know. I almost did that this weekend, too, right before Joi walked up and interrupted. And something else happened that day."

"What?"

"Nick and I slept together."

Danielle sucked in a breath. "No!"

"Yes." She painted the picture of them out riding, the spooked horse, sharing the saddle with Nick, and the inevitable conclusion from such close proximity.

"It was just that one time?"

"No."

"Twice?"

Sam sighed.

"You guys are working and dating?"

"Not officially dating, no."

"Friends with benefits?"

"You might say he's now a part of my compensation package." Sam's attempt to lighten the mood was an epic fail.

"You've got Nick hanging out with a child he doesn't

know is his, and sleeping with him, too? Sam. You've got to tell that man the truth."

Sam's screen lit up. Her stomach flopped. "Well, Danni, looks like we talked him up."

"Who, Nick?"

"He's calling. I've got to take it. Look, I'll call you back."

"Tell him!" Sam heard Danni yell before disconnecting the call.

"Hey, Nick."

"Sam."

Uh-oh. Was it paranoia about her secret or was there an ominous tone in Nick's voice? It had to be her freaking out. There was no way that he knew.

"The one and only," she said with a forced cheerfulness. "If you're calling about the drawings, that'll have to wait until I get back to the island. I'm on my way into Charleston. Wish you were here to join me for dinner."

"In a way, I wish I were there, too. But I'm not sure I'd have much of an appetite."

"Why? What's the matter?"

"Earlier today I hung out with my brother, who'd heard a crazy rumor, that your ex is not Trey's father."

Sam felt nauseous and she wasn't seasick.

"Who told him that?"

"Lauren heard it last weekend, from a client she met."

Sam sighed. "That is not a rumor. Trey is not Oba's biological child."

"Whose child is it? Do I know the father?"

Sam closed her eyes, unaware of how tightly she squeezed the phone. "You don't want kids," she said, in what hopefully sounded like a teasing tone. "Why this sudden interest in Trey's dad?"

Nick paused for so long Sam thought they may have gotten disconnected. She glimpsed her phone's face. He was still on the line.

"Nick?"

"Am I Trey's father?"

There was a lump as big as the future in her throat. She swallowed past it. "Yes."

Silence.

"Nick? Hello?"

She looked at the phone again. Nick was no longer on the line. Danni's words had proven prophetic. The secret was out and pierced her like an arrow. Straight through the heart.

Fourteen

Nick didn't think it possible to feel so many different emotions at once—shock, anger, bewilderment, confusion. He was Trey's father? Impossible. He went through all of the reasons that could not have been true. All but a sliver in the back of his brain was convinced that there was no way. But that 1 percent chance kept him from sleeping. The next morning, the sun had barely announced its presence when he walked through the front doors of the estate. Helen the housekeeper greeted him. She whispered, a nod to the early hour.

"Nick, is everything okay?"

"No, Helen, it's not. I need to see my parents."

"They're sleeping."

"I figured as much. They won't be for long."

Something in his voice must have warned her against making a fuss. Instead she asked, "Can I get you something? Coffee or tea?"

A shot of whiskey, Nick thought, but shook his head. One shot wouldn't be enough. This situation called for an entire bottle.

He reached his parents' suite and tapped on the door. "Mom. Dad. It's Nick."

"Nick?"

He heard the grogginess of his mother's voice, accompanied by shuffling noises, and felt a twinge of guilt, but only for a second. There were times when even a grown man still needed parental counsel. Now was one of those times.

"Just a moment, son."

Victoria opened the door wearing a floral lavender robe

with a matching silk cap and heeled house shoes, the epitome of style even in sleepwear.

"Good morning, darling." She touched his face. "What's the matter, son?"

Nick hugged her and walked into the room, past the sitting area and into where his dad was leaning up against the headboard.

"Son?"

Victoria came in behind him and joined her husband on his side of the bed. "Nick, what's wrong? You've got me very concerned."

"You know Sam, the woman who's working with me?"

"Of course. You don't forget a woman like her."

Nick snorted. "You don't know how right that statement might be. After confronting her about a rumor, she blindsided me with the news that Trey is my son."

He watched his parents exchange a look.

"What do you have to say about that?" Victoria asked.

Nick began to pace. "I say it's impossible!"

His father, Nicholas, raised a brow. "Is it?"

Nick turned to look at him. "Yes!"

"You two have never been intimate?"

"A long time ago but—"

"How long ago, son?" Victoria asked.

Nick frowned as he did the mental calculations. Around the time Sam got pregnant, a thought he didn't share.

"He's not my kid."

Victoria moved from the bed to sit on the antique bench beyond it. "You're sure? You always used protection?"

"There's no doubt about that," Nicholas interrupted, confidently crossing his arms. "That's how I taught all my boys. To use protection every single time."

"And you did?" Victoria pushed.

Nick ran a frustrated hand through his curls. "There may have been one time…"

"Then there's only one thing to do. Have a paternity test taken and then go from there."

"Go where from there? I don't have time to be a father. I told her that these island homes are my babies right now."

"So you two have discussed this?"

"No. We talked about kids once and I let her know then as I've told every woman before her that having a child wasn't a part of my plans and still isn't…not for at least another ten years."

Nicholas eased out of bed, straightening his pin-striped designer pajamas. "Was that before or after the unprotected sex, son?"

"How old is her son?" Victoria asked.

"Four."

"Yet you're only now learning that he might be your child? Why?"

"I don't know!"

"Well, you need to find out. If the child is yours, you've lost four formative years of his life. He's missed out on being a Breedlove and we may have someone with our DNA that we don't know. All of that is reason enough for a conversation with Samantha. That girl's got some explaining to do."

The conversation moved from his parents' master suite to the breakfast nook where over coffee they talked for more than an hour. Victoria worked her mother magic. Nick left the house feeling infinitely better than when he arrived. He was angry with Sam, beyond disappointed in her actions, but because of the people who raised him, he would try to follow their advice and not judge her too harshly or prematurely. A hard ask, but he'd try.

Nick was in no shape to go to work. He called Anita and rearranged his schedule to work from home. Once there, he retreated to his home office but still couldn't work very much. His thoughts kept drifting to the possibility that he was a father. He could close his eyes and see's Trey's face, searched his memory for any sign of himself in it. He went back to the day that he met him, how he'd actually told Sam the adventurous child reminded him of himself at that age. He went over every detail of the day they went horseback riding. He replayed the showdown between Sam and Joi. Sam's behavior now made much more sense, as did Joi's comment.

Which one is yours?

She knew. Sam knew. Yet kept him in the dark.

And there was one more thing. Those anonymous calls he'd been getting from the blocked number and the person who never spoke. Did that have something to do with the secret that Sam had been keeping?

Nick spun around angrily, determined to focus on work. He fired up his laptop, gritted his teeth against the myriad of emotions and opened his email. His eyes were instantly drawn to one from Sam. Something about the build, he thought.

But it wasn't.

Nick,
I'm sorry. I wanted to tell you. I should have told you. I was afraid of your reaction. I didn't know how. Please give me the chance to explain why at the time I thought what I did was best for everyone. I'm not saying it was right. In hindsight, I realize it was a horrible decision, one not fair to you, Trey or me. Please forgive me. For everything.
Sam.

Nick didn't respond right away. He didn't trust himself to write an appropriate answer. Later that morning, his reply was succinct.

The only thing we need to talk about, besides work, is a paternity test. I'll schedule it and forward the details. N.

To say they talked that week would have been generous. While she was in the Carolinas Nick communicated through email and text. Dr. Lucas, a longtime family friend who could be trusted to operate in confidence, orchestrated the testing. It was he, not Nick, who contacted Sam, who swabbed herself and Trey in the privacy of her condo when they returned from the Carolinas. After swabbing Nick, Dr. Lucas personally delivered the tests to the lab and ordered the results be rushed.

Twenty-four hours later, all doubt was removed. Nick was a father. Trey was his child.

Fifteen

Sam had never been this nervous. Even while pregnant, while facing an uncertain future with a man she'd just met and carrying the child of another, her nerves had been less traumatized. Nick had agreed to come over to the condo so that they could speak in private. Trey was with Danielle. It was what needed to happen, and what she wanted. But that didn't stop another part of her from being scared to death.

She'd gone through her closet and changed several times. Finally, already mentally exhausted with frayed nerves, she pulled on a pair of jeans and a cropped tee. Her locs were pulled to the top of her head. She wore no makeup. She expected him. But when the doorbell rang she jumped from the couch, then paused for a deep breath. Was he angry? Hurt? Shocked? Resigned? The only way to find out which Nick was on the other side of the door was to open it.

"Hi, Nick."

"Sam."

The look on his face made her mouth dry. A combination of anger and sadness, disappointment and fear. That handsome face that was usually smiling was now almost ashen in its somberness.

She stepped back. "Please, come in."

He took a couple steps inside and stopped, his back to her.

"Let's, um, sit…at the table." Sam walked into the dining room and took a seat. Nick silently complied, barely meeting her eyes.

"Can I get you anything—"

"Let's get one thing straight. This is not a social visit. This is the opportunity you asked for, a chance to explain why almost five years later I'm finding out about someone out there with my blood in his veins."

He hadn't raised his voice, but Sam felt the restraint it had taken to not do so, could almost feel the heat on his words. Tears burned the back of her eyes. She dug fingernails into palms and dared herself to cry. She was not the victim here. She'd perpetrated a problem that now needed to be fixed.

"When getting dressed to go out that night, I had no idea how that party would change my life. Like you I was single and loving it, living life like it was golden, totally carefree. I think that's one of the reasons we gravitated to each other. We had the same energy, the same thought about living our lives.

"Discovering that I was pregnant sent me straight into shock, and panic. I'd recently ended a relationship with a guy in LA, had come here to get him out of my system. Boy, did you ever help me do that! As soon as the home test I took came back positive, I knew it was you. But I didn't know you—I mean, we'd seen each other in passing what, maybe five or six times? Then I followed up with a doctor's visit and his timeline further confirmed it."

"But you still didn't tell me, Sam."

"I couldn't."

"Why not?"

"You didn't want kids! I'd gone online to find out more about you and the first article I read was about how dedicated you were to your family's business, how you were happily single with no time for a family of your own. Then, as fate would have it, shortly after that Danni got talking with Joi and found out about Oba's dilemma."

Nick's head shot up. "What dilemma?"

"Oba's elderly grandfather was pressuring his grandsons to get married and produce heirs. Oba was determined to beat Isaac having a child."

"Isaac?"

"His brother."

Nick's frown deepened.

"I know. It's complicated, the same as Oba and his brother's relationship. They were born less than a year apart. Their grandfather cultivated a fierce competition between them and upped the ante when he said the first one to marry and provide an heir would get the throne."

"How'd you get involved?"

"In a moment of frustration, Joi shared the stress of watching her brothers' ongoing fights with Danni, and how if given a choice she thought Oba would be the better king. Danni knew how freaked out I was at the prospect of being a single mother. She told Joi I was pregnant. Joi told him about me. Danni told me about Oba and…" Sam heaved a sigh. "The next thing I knew I was an African princess."

"That is totally crazy."

"In repeating the story out loud it sounds like pure insanity, but back then, in my mind, getting married solved everything. You wanted nothing to do with children, yet here was a guy where a child was not only what he wanted, but what he needed as well. I envisioned my son growing up royal and privileged, who'd lack for nothing he wanted in life."

"Nothing except the truth."

"There is no excuse for what I did. There's no way to make it right, only to make it better. For almost five years, I've deprived my son of his birthright. I will regret that decision for the rest of my life."

"I think your ex has been calling me."

Sam's head shot up. Her eyes registered fear.

"It was just a few times and I can't be sure. It was a blocked number. They never said anything. But since it's never happened before and considering what I've learned…"

Sam sighed and ran weary fingers over her eyes. "It was probably Oba. He's been trying to blackmail me."

"What the hell?" Nick had never been a violent man but

he was glad Sam's ex wasn't anywhere close to him right now. "Why?"

"It's a long story, but don't worry. If it's him, they'll stop. Now that the secret is out he has nothing to use against me."

"Even with what you've told me, I still don't get it. How you could justify not telling me that you were pregnant? I don't know if I can ever get over that type of betrayal, the lack of trust, the anger. You watched me play with the kid, teach him how to ride a horse, and stayed silent while knowing I was interacting with my own son. That's fucked up, Sam!"

Nick stood and walked away from the table, as if just being near her was too much to handle.

Sam steepled her hands and worked to remain calm. "You're 100 percent correct. I effed up, in what may very well be the biggest mistake of my life. I don't expect you to understand something that no longer makes sense to me. I only hope that there can be some type of relationship between you and Trey and that one day…you'll forgive me."

"Of course there'll be a relationship. What kind of man do you think I am? Oh, that's right. You didn't think I was man enough to even want to know I had a child. So scratch that question. I don't give a damn what you think about me.

"I'm sure you know that if there was any possible way to pull you off the island project, I'd do it today. But given the time constraints and what has already been designed, it wouldn't be economically or logically prudent. That said, I can't be around you right now. Noah is familiar with much of what I'm doing. I'll bring him in as a go-between. All exchanges between us need to be electronic. In just over three weeks, the necessary homes will be completed. It'll be difficult, but I think I can handle the interaction for that long."

"What about Trey? I understand that you hate me right now, but I'm his mom and a necessary bridge between the two of you. Is there a way that we can at least work together to ensure as smooth as possible a transition for him, from considering Oba as his father to knowing you're his dad?"

Nick's eyes remained fixed on the window, though Sam doubted he saw anything beyond the mess she'd made.

"What do you suggest?" he finally asked.

"Maybe bring him over to the estate. He already loves going there. He really likes you, too."

Nick winced. The hole in Sam's heart tore wider.

"Maybe Christina can be a part of easing him into your family. I don't know what they think about all of this but…

"I'm so sorry, Nick." Instinctively, she took a step toward him.

"Don't." His jaw rippled with the force it took to not say more. Words Sam doubted she wanted to hear anyway.

"What about his nanny, what's her name?"

"Gloria?"

"Yes. She's friends with Christina's nanny Kirtu. I think it would be better if Trey came with her."

Ouch. "Okay."

"My family is understandably upset. They need time to absorb all of what's happened, as do I."

That night, Sam told Gloria about Nick being Trey's father, the conversation they'd had and Nick's request. The next morning Sam woke up Trey and helped him get dressed. That she wasn't going to be there for this first father-son interaction where Nick knew the truth literally hurt her heart. Still, she was grateful that Nick wanted to get to know his son. For that reason alone, she found a smile to put on for her child.

"Where are we going, Mommy?"

Sam looked at her heartbeat, melting as she always did when she heard Trey's voice. "You and Gloria are going someplace to have lots of fun."

"Where"

"Do you remember Nick, the man I work with, the one who taught you to ride the horse?"

"Yes. I'm going over there?" Trey's eyes were wide and bright with anticipation. In that moment, to her mind, he looked like Nick's chocolate-covered mini-me. "I like horses, Mommy."

"I know you do."

"I want a horse, Mommy."

"That would be fun, huh?"

Trey nodded. "I would ride it every day."

"But horses are a lot of work, Trey. They require a lot of care, to feed them and house them and give them exercise."

"I'll do it!"

"Who'll watch the horse while you're at school?"

Trey's brows scrunched together as he pondered this question. Studying his face, Sam was taken aback. Why hadn't she noticed Nick's features before on Trey's face? Was it only in the truth being revealed she could see them?

"Are you going, Mama?"

"No, Mama's been working really long hours so while you and Gloria are riding horses, I'm going to get some rest. Is that okay?"

"Okay."

Sam would have liked there to have been a little push-back, to feel that her son needed her to tag along. But Trey had always been adventuresome, with an independent streak. Just like his father.

Sam heard a tap on Trey's bedroom door before it opened slightly.

"Good morning!"

Said a little too forced and a little too brightly. Sam could only imagine how awkward this had to be for her childcare specialist.

"Good morning, Gloria." She walked closer and lowered her voice. "Are you sure you'll be okay?"

"I still think it should be you who takes him over."

"Maybe next time. Right now, it's better this way."

"Should I fix him breakfast?"

"Knowing Nick and his family, any kind of gathering will likely involve food. I'll get him a Pop-Tart to tide him over."

Sam kept up the casual chatter until Gloria and Trey left the house and she locked the door behind them. She made it all the way back to her bedroom before the tears came, and then allowed herself a good cry. Trey would get to spend time with his father, even as Sam's days were numbered. She tried to find comfort in that.

For the next three weeks, a routine was established. Gloria took Trey to the Breedloves' on weekends. During the week they traveled with Sam, who buried herself in work. The good news was that for the most part she stayed on schedule, finishing the last home mere days before the occupants were set to arrive. The more challenging news was that she'd done all of this while consumed with a myriad of feelings about Nick and Trey. Delight that they were getting to know each other. Sorrow that things between her and Nick would never be the same.

The ice had thawed somewhat. The texts and emails had graduated to a call here and there, focused strictly on work or questions about Trey. She still wasn't sure how she felt about his reaction, that he'd been less than enthused about claiming the smartest, cutest, brightest most intelligent kid on the planet as his own. But in the end, as Danielle had so aptly pointed out, it would have been less than responsible for him to react any other way. His disappointment in missing out on Trey's first four years overshadowed the joy Sam was sure that Nick also felt. Whether he knew it, acknowledged it or ever owned up to it or not, Nick was a perfect father for her son. And thanks to the contract they'd negotiated, she would be fine financially and otherwise, whether or not Nick chose to be in her son's life.

She was in Maine preparing to catch a flight back to Vegas when her phone rang. Nick.

"Hey."

"Hi, Sam. You're headed back tonight, right?"

"Yes, headed to the airport now."

"What time do you land?"

"Seven forty-five."

"We need to talk. Can you meet me for dinner?"

Could it be that Nick was finally coming around to the two of them at least being friends for their son's sake? Sam's heart leaped.

"Sure. Should I bring Trey?"

"This needs to be just the two of us."

"Okay, text me the address and I'll meet you there. And, Nick?"

"Yes?"

"Thanks."

Once home she swapped jeans for a flowy jumpsuit and headed to Breedlove. Her phone rang. Thinking it was Danielle, she clicked the Bluetooth immediately.

"Hello, Sam Price," she fairly sang, her heart lighter than it had been in ages.

"Is that you, baby?"

Hearing the accent almost made her run off the road. Before Oba had only texted. Now he was calling. The nerve of his actions caused a rage to form in the pit of Sam's gut. That with all she was going through, he'd put her through more. But what could he do now? He'd lost his power. The thought calmed her anger. She almost smiled.

"Oba, we've been through this already. It's over. We've no need to talk."

"Oh, really? Then maybe you'd like me to talk to your baby's real daddy."

"Oba Usman, I don't give a damn what you do. There's nothing you can tell Nick that he doesn't already know. I told him, all right? He knows that Trey is his son. Call again threatening blackmail or anything else and you will hear from my lawyer. Think I'm playing? Try me. Now go off and have a nice life."

Sixteen

Having grown up in a nurturing, supportive environment filled with love, Nick wasn't used to being nervous. Yet as he pulled into the parking lot of BBs, his brother's popular hamburger joint, he felt wisps of discomfort, uncertainty, even a little despair. He'd always been the master of his own destiny, in total control of his life. Yet in the span of a few pivotal weeks that had all changed. He was a father. He had a son named Trey. Life was no longer all about him and while he'd already developed true feelings for what his brother Christian called Nick's "mini-me," he didn't quite know how he felt about that. Or about Sam.

He entered the restaurant, aware of the desirous eyes from female patrons that followed him only because the hostess pointed it out. After taking a seat near the window he pulled out his phone to check messages and texts until Sam arrived about fifteen minutes later.

"Sorry I'm late," she began, with a flustered demeanor. "There was an accident and…"

He put a hand on her arm and gently squeezed it. "Relax. It's fine. This isn't an interview."

Sam blessed him with a smile that lit up those warm brown eyes. "I guess you're right. Thanks for the reminder."

She sat down and threw her purse strap over the chair back. "This is your brother's place?" she asked, looking around.

"His pride and joy, except for the ranch and the cows he raises."

"I like its no-nonsense casual atmosphere. A contrast to what I imagined it would be."

"Adam wanted a place that would feel comfortable for

everybody. Non-pretentious, as it should be when scarfing down burgers and fries. And speaking of, don't you dare say you're not hungry. I'd put these burgers up against anybody, and bet my vacation homes that they'd win."

"Wow, lofty bet."

"Confident brother."

They spoke casually until the server delivered their drinks and took their orders.

"A premium champagne would have been more appropriate, but such is not on BBs menu. This is all I have." Nick held up his frosty mug of beer. "A toast is in order."

With a slight frown, Sam held up her iced tea. "To what?"

"You. Congratulations on a job well done."

"Oh. That."

"I know the team congratulated you on managing the impossible. Noah, and my brothers. I think even my dad. I realized that no matter what was happening personally between us, not giving props where they were due made me a total jerk."

"It means a lot to hear that, Nick. It was the most difficult job I've ever tackled, and the most rewarding."

"To the only woman who could have pulled it off."

Sam lifted her tea. The glasses clinked. Each sipped from their glass as they drank in each other.

"We're having a dinner at CANN to celebrate the project's completion. I'd love for you to join me."

"As your date?"

"As one who deserves to be officially recognized."

"Are you sure? At our last physical interaction you hated me, Nick. This change, it's…welcomed, but uncomfortable."

"You're right. All I wanted was you out of my sight. Not telling me about my son was cruel and unthinkable. I thought I'd never forgive you."

Sam's head dipped. "I totally understand that, because I'll never forgive myself."

"Then I talked with Grandma Jewel, my dad's mother.

She told me that the unforgiveness in my heart wouldn't hurt you or myself as much as it would Trey. That kids are closest to spirit and could feel words that remained unspoken. My son has already been through enough. I don't want to be the cause of more pain.

"One more thing," he continued, before Sam could speak. "Since I've done the impossible and forgiven you, you might as well forgive yourself."

Nick watched as Sam's head dipped lower, and she brought a hand to her face. He was out of his chair in an instant and sitting beside her.

"Come on, none of that," he said as he reached for a napkin and blotted her tears. "This is a celebration, remember?"

Sam pulled herself together, her expression über-serious as she turned to face him. "There's only one thing left to do."

Nick's heart skipped a beat. What had he missed? "Go ahead," he said. "I'm listening."

"We've got to tell Trey that you're his real father. He doesn't know that he's your son."

For the rest of the evening conversation swung between CANN Isles and Trey, mostly. The celebratory dinner took place a couple weeks later. Sam looked delectable in a designer original. Her good looks and effervescent personality endeared her to everyone in the room. Pics of her achievements were leaked to the media. In several issues of local and national newspapers and websites, she was the focus of both the business and society pages. No one was more impressed with her than his family. As though the person she was had overridden what she'd done. When Trey asked him if his mom was joining them for Thanksgiving dinner at the estate, Nick told him he'd like nothing better. The day marked for giving thanks seemed infinitely appropriate to being the one where his son learned the truth about their relationship.

Thanksgiving at the Breedlove estate was its usual grand

affair. Nick and Sam, however, excused themselves shortly after the Christmas tree lighting, for a talk before Trey went to bed. He was excited from the day's festive activities but after Sam had given him a bath, he slid into his Black Panther pj's more than ready for sleep. Nick and Sam followed him into the massive guest room that had been renovated into a little boy's dreamland. Trey crawled onto the bed shaped like a race car. Nick sat down beside him. Sam, in the nearby chair.

Trey looked from one parent to the other. "You're both going to read me a bedtime story?"

"Not from one of your superhero books," Sam offered. "But Mama does have a story to tell."

Nick watched Sam take a deep breath as a myriad of emotions played across her face. "I know you think Prince Oba is your father, baby. But he is not your real dad."

Trey's look of confusion was understandable to both Nick and Sam. "He's not my father?"

Sam slowly shook her head. "No, baby. When I married him, you were already in my tummy."

Trey thought on this a moment and then asked his mom, "Do I have a father?"

"Absolutely," Nick interrupted, pride underscoring the word. "I'm your father, Trey. I only found out when you guys returned to America that I am your real dad."

He held his breath and watched Trey's young mind try to process adult information. "For real?"

Nick nodded.

"Like Christian is Christina's dad and Scott is Jaylen's dad?"

"Yes," Sam told him. "Exactly like that."

"Is that okay with you?" Nick asked him, unaware that he was no longer breathing.

"I love it!" Trey finally screamed, shooting like a missile into Nick's arms.

Trey's arms around his neck felt better than he could

imagine. Nick finally exhaled. Sam didn't go home that night. The love shared between them was better than bliss. The work done. No more secrets between them. The next morning, she fixed them breakfast. Then Nick and Trey went riding with Adam and Noah. Family life continued when they returned and watched a movie.

The time felt so right, so natural, that Nick did the unthinkable when just before Sam and Trey prepared to leave that Saturday, he asked her, "Would you like to live here, to move in with me? Trey loves being here. There's plenty of room."

And other reasons, which Nick had yet to admit to himself.

Sam was understandably taken aback and didn't answer immediately. Nick understood. When it came to relationships, she'd gone through a lot. Yet his emotions surprised him as he awaited her answer, and at how lonely his home felt when he was the only one there. As he continued about his routine and enjoyed the rest of the holiday weekend, he knew one thing for sure. Even though the project with Sam Price was finished, the business between them wasn't over. Not by a long shot.

Seventeen

"Hey, cousin!" The front door had barely opened before Sam pulled Danielle in for a hearty hug.

Danielle stepped back. "What was that for?"

"Can't your cousin be happy to see you?" Sam entered the home.

"You're a little too happy. Where's Trey?"

"With Nick."

Danielle stopped and turned.

"For real? Even though it's not his weekend?"

"All the cousins were over playing in the pool. He begged to stay and hang out with them. With all I have to do trying to restart my business, I couldn't say no."

They continued down the hallway. Danielle glanced back a time or two.

"Somebody's holiday must have gone very well."

"Better than I could have thought possible."

Sam entered the living room and walked over to where her young cousin sat engrossed in a game.

"Hey, Jaylen!"

"Hi, Sam." Said with eyes still glued to the screen, his hand quickly shifting the control to combat and destroy enemies far and wide.

"Jaylen, take that warfare into your room. Mommy and Sam have some grown-up talking to do."

"Wait! I've almost vanquished the leader!"

"Vanquished?" Sam asked. "Good word."

"Boy, I'm going to vanquish your behind if you don't move!"

To prove she meant business Danielle walked over, picked up her son and began blowing smoochies—loud, air-filled kisses that tickled the skin. Jaylen's laughter floated down the hallway. Sam smiled, reminded of the rough-housing that Sam witnessed between Trey and his uncles. It seemed they were experts in everything from Adam and bucking broncos to Christian and any sport. Noah's collection of robotic toys had dropped Trey's jaw. Hers, too, actually. She'd never seen her son more impressed.

"Whew!" Danielle joined Sam on the chenille-covered sofa. "I'm too old to have a six-year-old."

Sam gave her a look. "You're thirty."

"Tell that to my body." Danielle shifted with a hand to her back. "That boy is getting too big to pick up. Now my back is killing me."

"That's because you need to work out."

"I need Gloria to find a twin to come help run my household, that's what I need."

"I hear that. She's been such a blessing to me and Trey, like part of the family."

"I'm teasing. That kind of help is above my pay grade."

Danielle shifted to a more comfortable position. "Enough about our angel assistant. It's time for you to spill the tea on all that happened in Breedlove. I want the turkey tales with all of the trimmings, thank you very much."

"Wow." Sam grabbed a pillow and leaned back, too. "So much happened. Where do I begin?"

"How about the beginning?"

Sam chuckled. "Good idea. You remember how incredible their place is, right?"

"They held a frickin' carnival on the most beautiful spot in all of Nevada, land that went on forever. How could I forget?"

"The holiday decor is even more spectacular."

"That's hard to imagine."

"Hopefully you and Jaylen will get a chance to see it. There were games and live music and incredible food. The night ended with a lighting ceremony that rivaled any I've seen, officially beginning the Christmas season. But I'm getting ahead of myself. The fun started with my meeting the true Breedlove matriarch, Nick's grandmother Miss Jewel…"

Sam recounted the unparalleled Breedlove Estate experience that for the past four days had been her enchanted life.

"You know I don't get along with just anybody. I can spot a fake real quick and don't suffer them lightly. But I have to tell you, Danni, the Breedloves aren't like most bougie folk. And I've seen one or two. Can we say 'royalty'?" Sam used air quotes.

"We could but we won't."

"Agreed. Nick and his family are different. They can hold their own with the caviar crowd but are down-to-earth, too. They're the real deal. I like them. The brother's wives were open, friendly, made me feel like family."

"Sounds like a family you want to join."

"Slow your roll, chick. That's unlikely to happen. Nick is warming up to being a father. The same doesn't necessarily apply to his taking a wife."

"I know you have to act as though it's not something that matters."

"For now I'm just happy we're getting along."

"That's all? No sex?"

"Well…"

"Girl, quit playing. Don't make me have to drag words out by consonant and vowel."

"I spent the night."

Danielle squealed. "That's good, right?"

Sam shrugged.

"Nick is one fine brother. You could do far worse than him."

"Look, I'm perfectly fine being sin—"

"Really? Then perhaps you should let your face know. Now back to the story before your nose starts to grow."

Sam burst out laughing. "I hate you."

"Thanks, hon."

Sam shifted the conversation out of the bedroom and back to the variety of activities that the estate offered, and how comfortable it was hanging out with members of Nick's family she knew already while meeting others for the first time.

"The brothers all have a natural affinity for socializing, comfortable mingling with others regardless of social status. The staff was treated more like family than employees. But I thought the family gathering, especially Thanksgiving dinner, would be different somehow. Haughtier, buttoned-up. I envisioned a dining room straight out of a castle with bone china, pristine manners and a servant behind each chair."

"What? No servants?" Danielle feigned indignation.

"Yes, but only behind every other chair," Sam deadpanned. "I'm kidding." Added a beat later.

Danielle bopped her with a throw pillow.

Sam's plan for a quick visit with Danielle turned into a chat-athon lasting all afternoon. After speaking with Nick, Jaylen joined Trey in Breedlove so that Sam and Danielle could take a rare spin on the Strip. Vegas residents seldom ventured to the areas that made their state famous, but Danielle felt lucky and Sam wanted to shop. When they returned to the estate that evening, the holiday theme was on full display. Danielle was as blown away as Sam thought she'd be. It was the perfect ending to her four-day weekend, and probably Sam's last bit of downtime before Christmas. There was work to do. Decisions to make. After a particularly wonderful evening involving the three of them, Nick had invited her and Trey to move in with him. Tempting offer. But he'd focused on Trey, not her or their relationship. She'd be the first to define herself as a modern woman, one leery of vows with a failed marriage under her belt. Still, she loved the security of commitment and knew few successes topped that of a good marriage. Seeing Scott and Danielle together was proof of that. Then there was her old-school grandmother's most popular saying that after being with Nick sometimes played in her head.

Doesn't make sense for a man to buy a cow when he gets the milk for free.

On their way home from Nick's after his offer, those words had played on a loop in her head. By the time she'd pulled into her garage, she'd made a decision. Sam and Trey would continue to call the condo home. Grandma, 1. Modern woman, 0.

On Monday, Sam rose early. She'd created a to-do list the night before and was ready to tackle each project. She showered and dressed as if she were headed to an office. Sometimes a suit produced better results than yoga pants and a tee. Five minutes after sitting down with a mug of peppermint tea, her phone rang.

"Sam Price."

"Good morning."

"Hi Nick." *Breathe.* "What's going on?"

"Thinking about you. Thought I'd call."

"You're not working today?"

"Not for another hour."

"Oh."

Sam fell quiet, conflicted, as she'd been off and on all weekend. No doubt she was very attracted to Nick and loved being with him. Maybe a little too much for a casual affair. She'd played it off when Danielle teased her, but the deeper she'd examined her feelings about Nick and the more honest she'd been about the probability that they'd deepen further the longer they dated, the more she realized that continuing the casual affair might not be a good idea.

"Are you working? Did I interrupt something?"

Yes. You interrupted the lie I've been telling myself.

"Yes, I am working. There's only three short weeks until the world shuts down for Christmas. I have a lot to do before now and next year."

"Okay, cool. No worries. We can talk later today."

"Goodbye." Sam hung up and turned back to the to-do list on her computer. She tried to focus but her mind kept returning to her unresolved feelings about Nick. Getting up from the couch, she set down her tablet and walked to the window, her life over the past four-plus years playing like a video across a mental screen. The party. The pregnancy. Oba. Africa. CANN. Trey. The actions that had shaped her past. Her vision for the future. What did she want it to look like?

Determined to complete at least some of the tasks on her list, Sam picked up her phone and called Danielle.

"Hey, Sam!"

"Hey, cousin. Do you think the day care would mind watching Trey this afternoon? Gloria isn't here. I need to focus and right now home is too distracting."

"Probably not, but I can call and find out."

"Jaylen's there?"

"Yep. Scott will pick him up on the way home. He can get Trey, too, if you're not done with what you're working on by then. You can pick him up here later."

"Perfect. Let me know."

"Okay."

Minutes later, Danielle texted that the day care would watch him, but at the full-day rate even though it was almost one o'clock. Sam would have gladly paid them double. She was out of the house in less than thirty minutes and another half hour after that had dropped off Trey and was seated in a local library's private room with her tablet on and cell phone off.

The change of scenery helped but didn't squelch the thoughts completely. She managed to check off a few items and make the most time-sensitive calls. But three hours later, thoughts of Nick and their situation were still all-consuming. Her shoulders were tense with stress. Rotating her neck to try to remove the kinks, she remembered a conversation with Adam's wife Ryan, who co-owned a spa and suggested she should come for a visit. Maybe a little pampering was just what she needed to ease her body as well as her mind. After making an appointment online, Sam called Danielle to have Scott pick up Trey. She left the library and soon after arrived at the Integrative Healing Group, located in a nondescript mall about fifteen minutes from the Strip. The place didn't look like much from the outside, but one step inside the red door that marked Ryan's business and Sam was transformed.

A soothing shade of blue covered the waiting room walls, with a backlit fountain as the room's showpiece. The water flowed into the vase of a tall, vibrant plant. More plants were set in floor urns and on tabletops. Notes from the instrumental music—something spiritual, earthy and from the East—seemed to wrap themselves around her, while the scent of lavender added to the paradise-like atmosphere. Sam looked around for the button that would announce her arrival and pushed it, as the confirmation email had instructed. It wasn't long before she heard the sound of bells, these tinkling as the door to the inner rooms opened and Ryan appeared.

"Sam, hi." Ryan stepped forward and offered a quick embrace. "I was so excited to see your name come up on our scheduler and actually moved a client over to another specialist so that I could personally attend you."

"Thank you, Ryan." Out of the three Breedlove sisters-in-love, Sam had most connected with Ryan, who never seemed to judge her after learning of Trey. She was effortlessly attractive yet genuine and kind. Her heartfelt gesture made Sam like her even more.

"I didn't know what to expect when I pulled up outside, but your place is truly beautiful."

"Yeah, the outside is pretty deceiving. But we put our heart and soul into the designing that went on inside, wanting to effect a certain mood and vibration that would immediately put the client at ease."

"You designed this?"

Ryan nodded. "My and my partner Brooklyn's souls are in every room."

They entered a massage room. Here the shade of blue was darker, contrasted against a stark white ceiling flecked with gold. Abstract paintings, angel statues and renderings of spiritual masters brought in an ethereal effect. "Ryan, I love everything about what I've seen so far. You guys did an amazing job."

"Oh my gosh, Sam, I appreciate your saying that. Nick brags that you're the best designer money can buy, so coming from you that's high praise."

So much for getting away from thinking about Nick. Then again, she'd made an appointment at the business of one of his family members. What did she expect?

As soon as Sam was ready and the massage began, so too did the questions.

"You're really tense, Sam. Working a lot of hours?"

Sam nodded. "Now that my contract with CANN is over I'm focused on rebuilding my company, Priceless Designs."

"That can be stressful."

"Yes."

"Because of Adam, I know that CANN's business is booming right now. I'm surprised Nick didn't have you stay on for other builds."

"It was discussed early on but a contract worked best. The last few years have been a whirlwind. I need time to regroup, focus on Trey and decide how best to move forward."

"I don't know much about what happened, but divorce is never easy."

"No."

"Nick seems to care a lot about you."

"Sorry, Ryan, I know he's your brother, but I'd rather not discuss Nick right now."

Ryan graciously changed the subject without missing a beat before ending conversation all together to focus on her work. She was skilled and thorough. When finished, Sam's body was as limp as a noodle. Ryan gave a short tour and explained other services. Sam scheduled another appointment for the works—facial, body wrap and float tank session—the latter of which she'd heard of but never tried. When they reached the outer door, Sam turned and hugged Ryan.

"Thanks for inviting me to your spa. I feel so much better and can't wait to come back."

"I can't wait for your visit, which doesn't have to be limited to the spa, by the way. If you're ever in need of some girl time or want to bring Trey and hang out at the ranch, you're always welcome. Just give me a call. The business card you picked up has my cell number."

"Okay. Thanks again."

They stepped outside.

"Sam?"

She turned around.

"I know it's not my business and you don't want to talk but if I may offer a bit of advice about Breedlove men?" Ryan waited and when Sam didn't speak or turn to leave, continued. "They are fierce companions who love as hard as they work. If you grab their attention, even fleeting, it's pretty amazing. If you're lucky enough to capture their heart, though, don't release it. You won't find a better man."

For the rest of the night, Sam's feelings remained scattered. She woke up to them cemented behind the strength of her truth. The desire at the core of her heart that until now she'd dared not think about, let alone speak. She was precariously close to falling in love with Nick and wanting more than the man was willing to give. She wanted a real relationship. She wanted love. Commitment. A forever man. Happily ever after was sometimes hard to come by, but it was possible. She believed she deserved to have the life that she wanted. And that true love was worth the wait.

Showering and preparing breakfast, Sam felt more grounded and sure of herself than since leaving Africa.

The insecurities that had dogged her since the divorce were replaced by feelings of a woman who remembered who she really was—worthy enough for a man to want to put his name behind hers. It might be a while before she was ready to jump back into the dating waters. There was still baggage from the marriage of convenience left to unpack. But one thing was for sure. Whenever she was ready and open to look, she'd be highly unlikely to find him while rolling around in Nick's bed.

Later that day, after crossing off 75 percent of what was on her schedule, she didn't wait for Nick to call her. She called him. She needed to set things straight before losing her nerve or, after seeing that hard, toned body again, her will.

He answered quickly, his voice low and sexy. "I was just thinking about you. Again."

"I've been thinking about you, too, all day off and on."

"All good thoughts, I hope."

"It probably depends on how you look at it. Either way, I've come to a decision."

"Uh-oh. This sounds serious."

"I think we should cut out the intimacy between us and focus on co-parenting Trey."

"Okay." The word had only two syllables but the way Nick dragged it out made it seem to have more. "May I ask why you feel that way?"

Sam sighed. "I'm still figuring that all out myself. What I do know, what I recently discovered or acknowledged about myself, is that I'm past the whole casual dating thing. While Oba's and my marriage didn't work out and I'm not looking to blindly jump into another, I am looking for more than someone just to spend time with."

"Such as?"

"Feeling connected more than physically. Feeling that I'm not alone in the world, that someone has my back and will be there for me. I don't want to use the word *claim*, that sounds so draconian, but there's a part of being a woman that wants to be wanted, needed, loved, who wants to be valued enough by someone willing to acknowledge that she's enough for him, that she's all he wants."

"That sounds like the marriage thing you're not wanting to jump back into."

"Mine was mostly a marriage in name only, and I said blindly jump."

"Y'all didn't have sex?"

"We had sex. We never made love."

"And that's what you want. Love, not sex."

"Yes. That's what I want."

As she talked, revelations continued to pour into Sam's soul. Fear diminished. She was emboldened to stand in her truth. She wanted a real father for Trey and real love for herself. To have both was possible. She now knew that for sure. If she couldn't get the love she wanted from the father of her child, she'd get it somewhere else.

Eighteen

Nick tossed a stack of papers on his desk and punched the office intercom button with more force than necessary.

"Yes, Mr. Breedlove?"

He didn't answer her because he'd jumped out of his chair and stormed out of his office.

"What in the hell is this?" he yelled before reaching his destination. He tossed the report on Anita's desk. Files, pens and sticky pads went flying. "The revisions I requested are not on that doc."

"Oh no, Mr. Breedlove!" Anita hurriedly straightened the messy report papers, then scrambled to retrieve the items off the floor. "I absolutely made the changes and must have forwarded the uncorrected document."

"Find it. Send it," Nick growled, punching the air with a finger for emphasis. "Now!" Instead of waiting for an answer he marched back into his office and but for the hydraulics would have slammed the door. He continued to the window, his brow creased in a perfect bad-boy scowl as he shoved his hands in his pockets and tried to calm down. He wasn't angry about the report. He was upset at the restrictions Sam had placed on their relationship. Wait, there wasn't a relationship. That was the problem.

The intercom sounded. "Mr. Breedlove, I just emailed the corrected version. I thought I'd deleted the first one after it was revised. My apologies for—"

"None needed, Anita." He walked over and plopped into his chair, then spun around to face the phone. "I'm the one who needs to apologize."

"It's okay, Nick. There's a lot going on."

She had no idea. Then again, Nick suspected she'd had

an inkling. Victoria called it Mother Wit. Plus, Anita had been with CANN for over twenty years, back in the days when Nick and Noah played Nerf ball in the halls and stole candy from the vending machines. It's the main reason he corrected her when she first called him by his surname.

"Call me Nick," he'd said.

She refused, wanting to give him the respect due an executive and, if his hunch was correct, boost the confidence of a twenty-two-year-old who was wet behind the ears. But when a bit of chiding or support was needed, she reverted to being the mother she was, with sons and daughters almost Nick's age.

"That's no excuse," he said after the long pause.

"Well, I know you're busy and want those letters to sign before end of day. So I'll get back to work. But if there's anything else you need or ways I can help relieve any stress, just let me know. Okay, kiddo?"

Nick smiled. "Yes, ma'am." He reached over to disconnect the call. "Hey, Anita. Got a question."

"Yes, Mr. Breedlove?"

"So we're back to that, are we?"

She chuckled. "Absolutely. Sir."

"Cut that out."

"What's your question?"

"I'm seeking your opinion as a woman, not my assistant."

"I think I can handle that."

"Is it true that no matter how independent a woman acts, she secretly wants companionship and...you know...to get married?"

"Are we speaking...generally?"

"Yes."

"Then generally speaking, yes, I believe that's true. Much has changed, with the women's movement, the rise of feminism and such, and some women are able to remain single and be happy. But I personally believe that deep inside most women, most people in fact, want to love and be loved, to have a partner in life. You're still young, Nick, and driven. But one day I believe that you, too, will grow tired of dating, and want something more substantial, more grounding in your life. Until then, have fun!"

"Good advice. Thanks, Anita."

"Anytime."

Nick went back to work. He perused the report Anita had corrected. Went to the meeting he'd mentioned to Sam. The hardest work he did all day was trying to forget about her and the decision she'd made. His fingers itched to tap her name on his phone, but he didn't. Until now he hadn't realized the easy flow they'd fallen into of talking almost every day. Mostly about Trey, sometimes with design or architectural questions. He'd grown used to regularly hearing her voice, and missed it. Then on Thursday night, as he left the office early to prepare for one of his mother's many social functions, his phone rang. Sam. Coming to her senses about her sex ban, he hoped. He'd had his share of women but when it came to his child's mother, he had to admit that their connection was different from those others. Special. At another level. He was a passionate brother. She was the first to match him stroke for stroke.

"Breedlove."

"Nick, it's Sam."

"I know. What's up?"

"It's about Trey."

So the call wasn't about sex, or him. He ignored a pang of disappointment.

"He's okay, right?"

"He's fine."

"Then what is it?"

"Is it possible that he can stay with you this weekend? Gloria is off for the holidays. As soon as my lease is up, I'm moving back to LA. I want to fly over there tomorrow, do some house hunting, speak with a few potential clients, stuff like that."

Nick's bad week just got worse.

"What's wrong with Vegas?"

There was a slight pause before Sam answered. "Nothing. However, the bulk of clients requesting my assistance are in metro LA. It makes sense for that to be my home base."

"What about Trey?"

"What about him?"

"Will he be staying here, on the estate?"

"Most definitely not."

"It's not definite at all, babe. I don't want my son growing up amid smog, gang violence, police misconduct, the celebrity culture. He needs to be here in Breedlove, where he can run, play, breathe fresh air and be a worry-free kid."

"He's my son, Nick. There's no way I'm going to be separated from him."

"Me, either."

"There's got to be a way we can come to a mutual agreement that will allow me to grow my business and for us to continue to co-parent Trey. You've got the plane, and money is no object. You can visit on the weekends and spend time together, just like now. There's tons of father-son adventures that you can have there."

"That wouldn't work."

"Why not?"

Because that would leave little to no time to work on us. The thought startled Nick. The truth unnerved him. Did he really want an "us" with Sam? The past couple months had been amazing. What about six months from now? A year? Five? He'd had his pick of women since the age of sixteen. Variety had always been the spice of his dating life. All of his brothers were married and seemed happy. Nick thought he was fine living single. He enjoyed the bachelor life.

"Because I don't want to be a long-distance dad. I won't let you take him out of state."

"You won't let me? You can't stop me. You may be his

biological father but that's where it ends. Your name is not on his birth certificate. You have no legal rights."

"That can be changed."

"Where is this coming from? You've never seemed concerned about it before."

"You never before suggested moving Trey out of town!"

"You have all of the resources in the world and can see him whenever you want!"

"How about I set up an account to cover your flight expenses so that you can come here and see our son. Whenever, as you said."

"If you start a joint custody battle, believe me, you'll lose. There's no way a judge would grant that to a man who's known his son for less than six months."

"Whose fault is that?"

"Doesn't matter. The court will rule in the child's best interest."

"And you think that's away from an estate with over a thousand acres, with trees to climb and lakes to fish in? You think the judge will look unkindly upon an extended family that is successful in business and pillars of the community in a town that bears the child's grandfather's name? Don't bet on how a judge will handle this, Sam. Or on how hard I'll fight."

He heard a sigh and could imagine her pacing, running a frustrated hand through those gorgeous locs as she often did.

"Look, Nick. I don't want to argue. So far, you've shown yourself to be an amazing dad. I don't want to take away from Trey the opportunity for you to be a big part of his life. I also need to rebuild my business in a city that will provide an almost unlimited amount of potential clients. We should be able to make a decision that will work for all of us."

"There's an unlimited amount of work for you at CANN. You should come back to work here."

"I think that given the circumstances it's best that we keep our lives separate, except for Trey."

"I'm fine with that." Not. "As long as you remain here, where I can see my son as often as I like, and where he can grow up as part of our clan."

"You're being unreasonable, Nick. Are you using this as a way to get back at me for not having sex with you?"

"Do I look like a brother who can't get sex?" He instantly regretted the words and hurried on in an effort to clean them up. "This isn't about us. It's about Trey. The best place for a young, growing boy like him is in Breedlove, Nevada. I'll understand it if you decide to relocate. But Trey stays here."

Sam hung up without saying goodbye. She was pissed, no doubt. Nick didn't blame her. He'd be upset, too. But he meant every word he said. So much so that he reached for his phone, tapped the face and then a number. "Hey, Chris. Quick question."

"Shoot."

"Didn't Barry's divorce involve a custody battle?" Barry Hammel was an up-and-coming architect CANN had snagged from a competing firm.

"A straight-out war, brother. The wife used the poor kids as pawns. Brainwashed them into thinking Barry didn't love them. Insinuated that there'd been sexual abuse. It was ugly. But he won in the end."

"He got the kids?"

"Joint custody, and a ruling that without his knowledge and permission, she could not take the kids out of state."

"Do you know his attorney's name?"

"No, but I can get it. Why?"

"Sam's thinking about moving to LA. But Trey's not going anywhere."

Nick exited the highway as he ended the call, feeling sure about what he planned to do. He couldn't control what had happened in Trey's life before finding out he was the boy's father. But he'd have a hand in everything that took place from here. That was for damn sure.

Nineteen

An hour later and Sam was still so hot from the conversation with Nick that she probably could have flown over there on her own steam, with Trey tucked under an arm. He was beside her in the passenger seat gabbing away, excited to see his father. And the horses. And birds. For that reason, she played nice. From the answer to the text she sent, Nick wasn't calm either. His response to the fact she was on her way over? One letter. K. She reached the estate and waved at the guard who opened the gate for her to drive through. She'd been impressed with these lands since her first arrival. Nick's words wafted like rings of smoke in her ears.

It's about Trey.

It surely was, which was why Nick shouldn't have a problem flying to California. A child belonged with his mother, and this mother was about to be in LA.

The best place for a young, growing boy is in Breedlove, Nevada.

She slowed around a curve and took in the landscape. Breathtaking, with lush green grass, sparkling lakes, animals dotting the countryside and majestic mountains beyond. Straight out of a storybook. Did she have the right to deprive Trey of growing up here? Maybe not, but she couldn't imagine not having a daily presence in his life. Was it right to request it of Nick?

I'll understand it if you decide to relocate. But Trey stays here.

The obvious solution was for her to accept Noah's offer and stay in Las Vegas. But could she survive regular contact with a man she wanted for the long term but would most likely never have?

She pulled into Nick's driveway. Memories assailed her. The Thanksgiving holiday. His master suite. The night they'd spent under the stars making love. Sam jerked the door open. There was no time for a trip down memory lane. She had a plane to catch. Trey got out of the car and ran to the door. Sam had hoped Nick would be outside. Easy handoff with little talk. He wasn't. She caught up with Trey and grabbed his hand as they mounted the twenty-plus steps to Nick's front door. The landscaping made for mind-blowing curb appeal, with its majestic waterfalls and towering trees that hid the five-thousand-square-foot man cave that Nick called home. A thought assailed her that was so unnerving she almost tripped.

Trey loves it here.

The door opened just as they reached the last step. Security system cameras, Sam surmised. He was at his home and could do what he wanted, but did he have to be shirtless, showing off the abs she loved to tickle with her fingernails? His hair was damp as though just out of the shower. He clutched a red towel hanging from his neck. He looked tempting. Devilish. Perfect for all sorts of sins. More images assailed her. She hadn't shared the details of that night with anyone, but she'd never look at a shower stall or marble bench the same.

Nick crouched to look Trey in the eye. "Hey, buddy. You ready to have fun?"

"Are we riding the horses again?"

"If you want."

"With Christina and Jaylen?"

"Sure."

"Yes!" Trey pushed past him and ran into the house.

"Trey!" Sam stepped around Nick. "Are you going to leave without giving me a hug?"

Trey spun around and trudged back toward Sam. "I forgot." The hug was brief and noncommittal. "Daddy, can I play video games?"

Nick nodded.

"Bye, Mama!"

They watched Trey race down the hall. Nick turned to her. "Hey."

"Hey."

The air pulsated with words neither dared say. Nick kept his feelings behind a hooded gaze.

"You coming in?"

Sam shook her head. "I need to get to the airport."

"Still going to LA?" He leaned on the doorjamb, cocked a brow, looked like a centerfold.

"Yep." Sam pulled the carry-on holding Trey's clothing and toys toward Nick. He reached for the handle. Their hands touched. Something akin to an electrical shock ran up her arm. It took everything within her not to jerk away. She played it cool, stepped back and headed down the stairs. She took a couple, then turned. "I'll be back Sunday night. Will text you on the way from the airport."

A short nod was his only response before stepping back into the house and closing the door. An uncomfortable feeling swirled in Sam's gut. She reached her car and hesitated before starting the engine and driving away. One of the clients she was scheduled to meet the next day interrupted her thoughts. By the time she arrived at the airport, the exchange with Nick had been forgotten. She boarded the plane and lost herself in 3-D designs.

Forty-five minutes later, the plane descended over the massive metropolis known as the City of Angels. Sam looked out at the imagery of the place she'd called home since the age of five, when her family left their Tennessee roots and chased her mother's acting dreams to Hollywood. It was a place she'd found a little scary but immediately exciting. Her family had settled in the San Fernando Valley. Sam flourished there. Her dad Marcus preferred country living. She'd always loved the city. Yet as the plane touched down and taxied on the runway, she felt strangely disconnected.

After securing a rental, she plugged into Bluetooth and tapped a number on her screen.

"Hey, Dad!"

"Hey there, babe. How you are you doing?"

"Good. But I'd be doing even better if you say you're not busy tonight and agree to meet me for dinner."

"You're here in LA?"

"Yep."

"For good?"

"Maybe. I'm meeting with two new clients and have an appointment with a Realtor."

"Is Trey with you?"

"No. He's with his dad."

"The prince is over here, in the States?"

The feeling of discomfort Sam had shaken during the plane ride returned and rumbled in the pit of her gut. Moving back to California wasn't the only thing she needed to share with her dad.

Marcus spoke into the silence. "It's a shame that child barely knows his grandfather."

"We need to change that. I'll bring him with me next time, promise. Where do you want to meet?"

"Hmm, there's a Mediterranean spot that opened up not far from here. I've been meaning to try it out."

"Text me the address. I'll meet you there."

Sam pulled into the parking lot of a restaurant anchoring a small strip mall. She spotted her dad's pickup and parked beside it. Inside, she saw Marcus right away.

"Hi, Daddy."

He stood to greet her. She melted into his embrace and was surprised to find herself fighting tears.

"You all right, baby girl?" Marcus asked after the hug.

Sam sat in the chair Marcus pulled out for her. "Life's a little crazy, but overall I'm good."

The first few minutes were spent perusing the menu while talking about family and mutual acquaintances. After they'd placed their orders and received their drinks, Sam felt her father's eyes boring into her.

"Why are you staring? Has it been so long you'd forgotten what I looked like?"

"Damn near." He shook his head. "Hard to keep up with that fast lane you're living in. I still don't know what happened with you and the prince."

"Just didn't work out, Dad."

"Was he violent? Did he hit you?"

"No."

"Was he a good father?"

"A great deal of his time was spent on royal duties. I don't doubt that he loves Trey, but he wasn't hands-on."

"I never understood why you married him in the first place. If you ask me, everything happened too fast. At least your mom got to see you wed."

Sam nodded. That her mom got to see her walk down the aisle was the best that could have happened.

"You came back from Africa, had barely unpacked your bags before moving to Nevada and now you're coming back here? Sam, what's going on?"

It was a dicey question. As far as her parents knew, Sam and Oba had met, fallen in love and enjoyed a whirlwind romance before her "unexpected" pregnancy led to a grandiose albeit hasty wedding. It was time to tell her dad about Nick.

"You remember why I moved to Las Vegas, to work on a specific project?"

"With the casino hotels."

"Specifically CANN International. It's owned by the Breedlove family. I worked on the project with one of the sons, a guy named Nick, whom I'd briefly dated in the past."

"Oh, Lord. Don't tell me y'all got into it and you lost a good job."

"No, the contract for what I worked on is over. But not me and Nick."

"You just got out of a marriage, honey. Now, I'm not one to tell you what to do but you might want to let your heart heal."

"Nick is Trey's father. He's my son's biological dad."

"Something tells me that for this story I might need something stronger than that cola I ordered." Marcus flagged down a server. "Miss!"

Sam gave her father the condensed version of what happened. Even with her father's questions, she wrapped up the story before the entrées arrived.

"What about getting more work down there, close to his father? It can't be healthy moving Trey around so much."

"There's more work here. Nick can visit often. It's a short flight. Plus, we'd be closer to you. Kids are fairly resilient. Trey seems to adapt easily. I think he'll be fine and you said it yourself, he needs to know his grandpa."

"He needs to know his daddy, too. The one he just met."

Sam thought her father would be thrilled about her move back to LA. Instead, having dinner with him brought up questions she'd thought resolved. When she boarded the plane Sunday night, however, her decision to move back to Los Angeles and reclaim her life held firm.

Sam arrived back in Vegas to a text from Nick to pick up Trey after Monday's preschool. She quickly unpacked her luggage and placed an order with her favorite Chinese restaurant for delivery an hour later. She turned on the water to fill the jetted tub, then walked back into the bedroom to undress. The zipper of her jeans was only halfway down when her doorbell rang. Sam looked at the clock and frowned. Surely that wasn't the delivery guy already. She'd just placed the order.

After rezipping her pants, she strode to the door and looked out the peephole. The man on the other side looked like a delivery guy. She opened the door.

"Yes?"

"Sam Price?"

"That's me. But I just placed my order five minutes ago."

The man reached into what she now realized was a pouch containing several types of mail. He pulled out a large manila envelope and held it out.

She took it. "What's this?"

"Those are papers that required a personal delivery. You've been served."

The man hurriedly turned and began walking away.

"Wait, who are you? What?"

"Have a nice evening, Ms. Price!" he yelled over his shoulder.

Puzzled, Sam watched the man until he'd reached the end of the short hallway that led to her unit and turned the corner. She eased back inside her house, closed and locked the door. She surveyed the envelope the man had delivered, then walked over to her desk, pulled the mail opener from a cup holding pens, markers and other office items, and slit it open. Inside was a stapled document of several pages. She didn't have to go past the first one for her world to tilt. The bold, black letters at the top stole the joy from the weekend—the new client, housing prospects, reconnecting with old friends, starting life anew again.

Nick had petitioned the court for primary custody of her son. What would she do now?

Twenty

Nick walked into work Monday morning carrying a bag of guilt. He could only imagine how Sam had reacted when she got served papers from him seeking primary custody of Trey. He wasn't sorry for filing them. He had every right to be a part of Trey's life, to share an equal role in raising and shaping his young, spongelike mind. He hadn't wanted to do it. His mother had suggested doing so from the time she learned she had another grandchild. He hadn't. There was no need. The arrangements he and Sam had agreed to worked for both of them. The less involvement the judicial system had in his life, the better. The conversation on Friday changed everything. Trey's living in California was not an option. Going from one home to another in the same town was hard enough. He would not subject Trey to commuting between states.

He'd barely fired up the Keurig in his office when Anita beeped in. "Mr. Breedlove, someone is here to see you."

Nick sighed. "Send her in."

He didn't have to ask who. Today there was only one person who would arrive at his office first thing unannounced. Sam. She swirled into his office, a look of anger mixed with determination on her face, and threw the order at him.

"You have some kind of nerve."

"I had to do it."

"You did not have to do this. We could have worked something out!"

"We tried that on Friday. You want to move to California. I want to keep Trey here. It's an impasse I didn't see us getting past without third-party intervention."

"You will not get my child, Nick Breedlove. I will do whatever it takes to keep him with me."

"There's no place you can run to with him that I won't find."

"I'll fight you tooth and nail, and I'll win. You didn't even know Trey six months ago. Do you really think there's a judge in any state in America who would assign a virtual stranger as the custodial parent?"

"Any judge would once they heard the details of how I was purposely kept out of being a part of my child's life. And for the record, I'm no stranger to Trey. I'm his father!"

"I never should have told you."

"You should have told me from day one."

"We've already been down that road. You know why I didn't."

"I know what you told me. It doesn't change the fact that it was wrong to outright lie to both me and Trey, presenting another man as the father of the child you claim to love so much."

Sam's gasp should have been a warning that Nick was going too far. But the horse was already out of the barn and running at a full-speed gallop.

"If that's true, prove it. Stop making it so difficult for me to be a part of his life. Stop thinking only of yourself and think of what's best for him."

"How dare you!"

"The best place for him is here, in Breedlove. If you want to continue having equal access to him I suggest you rethink your relocation plans."

"I hate you right now."

"You'll get over it. Or not." Nick strolled over to where the cup of coffee that was now lukewarm still sat in its holder. He felt Sam's eyes boring into his back and considering her state of mind right now, thought he'd be better off not turning said back.

He walked to his desk. "You're the one making this difficult. Not me. I offered a solution. You weren't interested."

"Moving into your home so that we could play family? So that you could have the life of an adult while still acting like a kid who'd not yet put his toys away? How was our living together supposed to look, Nick? How would the whole revolving-door dating situation work out? And once I found happiness, which I am ready to do, where would he and I hang out? Oh, but wait. Your home is pretty roomy. Or we could expand it. Each have our own wing to do our own thing."

"Ha! I wish you would try to bring another man into my house."

"I'd do so the minute you brought in another woman."

The intercom sounded. "Excuse me, Mr. Breedlove?"

"Yes, Anita. My nine o'clock meeting. I haven't forgotten."

"Just checking. Thank you."

Nick reached for a folder on his desk, opened it as he leaned back in his chair. "This conversation isn't going anywhere. Neither is Trey. You need to decide what's more important. Your career or your son. It's as simple as that."

Sam said nothing for several seconds, just stared, eyes narrowed, hands clutched into fists. She took a deep breath, walked calmly over to where Nick sat, and slapped him squarely across the face. Then with head high and back straight, she walked out of the room.

Nick watched her exit, slowly rubbing the area she'd smacked. "You're forgetting something," he said as she reached the door.

She paused, then continued out. Nick's eyes returned to the court papers she'd left behind. If someone tried to take his child he'd have them taken out. Given that consideration, that all she'd given him was one slap in the face, he'd gotten off easy.

Nick finished the nine o'clock meeting. He returned to his office, packed his briefcase and stopped by Anita's desk.

"I'm going to be out for a while. If anything urgent happens, hit me up. Tell everyone else I'll return their calls tomorrow."

"Will do. Are you all right, Nick? When that woman left she seemed extremely angry."

"Her name is Sam. She's Trey's mom."

"Oh."

"We're having a bit of a disagreement. But I'm okay. Hold down the fort."

Nick got into his Bentley Azure convertible, popped the top and sped down the highway. He was headed to the one person he could depend on in times like this. Someone whose advice was always spot-on, who gave it to him straight no chaser and suffered no fools.

Victoria Breedlove.

When he pulled into the circular driveway, he saw his father Nicholas just back from walking Ace, the newest family member. The long-haired Komondor with locs like Bob Marley, only blond, was a bit too friendly for Nick's taste and sure enough, the moment he saw him came bounding over, tail wagging, tongue hanging, ready for love.

"Hey, son."

Nick sidestepped the dog. "Hi, Dad."

"What brings you by in the middle of a workday?"

"Needed to talk with Mom real quick. Is she here?"

"No, son. She and Lauren left early this morning for an impromptu shopping trip."

"When will she back?"

"Day after tomorrow. They're shopping on the Champs-Élysées."

Victoria would choose this crucial time in his life for a Parisian jaunt. Exasperated, he let out a short huff.

"Something I can help you with, Nick?"

"I was hoping for a woman's perspective, but I guess you'll do."

"Ha! Come in. Let's have a cigar."

They walked through the spotless mansion and entered Nicholas's office. The stately room, with its high ceiling, dark woods and a lingering scent of premium tobacco, had a calming effect. Nick felt his shoulders relax as he walked over and took a seat in one of two high-backed chairs that had been imported from France and were purported to have once been in the royal palace. He watched Nicholas pull down a box from the shelf, almost reverently, his eyes sparkling as he sat and opened the lid.

"New brand?"

"More than a brand, son. This is a happening."

Nick wasn't that into cigars but even he was impressed with the story his father told while carefully preparing the cigar to be lit. Learning about pre-banned Cuban and Dominican leaf-wrapped tobacco that had been soaked in the most expensive cognac created, and that only one hundred boxes of the exclusive brand were sold each year, made Nick eager to taste it. Once he did, he was even more impressed. People didn't spend five hundred a pop without blinking for one cigar for no reason.

The next few minutes were consumed in the ritual of cigar smoking, of enjoying the first puffs of the exclusive smoke in the silence it commanded. Nick knew his dad took his cigars seriously and waited for him to break the silence.

He blew out a puff and smiled at Nick. "Now, for sure, I've lived."

"It's amazing," Nick agreed.

"Okay, son, tell me why you're here."

"It's about Sam."

"I figured as much."

"And Trey."

A slight frown marred Nicholas's handsome face, an

older, slightly more rugged version of Nick's. "What about my grandson?"

"Sam plans to move to LA and take him with her."

A slightly raised brow was Nicholas's only reaction. "What do you have to say about that?"

"I said hell no. Trey belongs in Breedlove. I tried to tell Sam that but she wouldn't listen. So I hired a lawyer. She got served papers last night. I'm going for primary custody."

Nicholas nodded. "Good for you." He tapped the cigar against a tray before placing it there. "What is your question for me?"

"Sam flew into my office first thing this morning, angrier than I've ever seen her."

"Can you blame her?"

"No. She was so upset that she slapped me."

"Is that all? Had I done something like that to Victoria I imagine she'd have come after me with something that held bullets."

"Mom wouldn't let anyone take us from her, which is why I feel bad for where Sam and I are now. The attorney and I discussed joint custody first. But that would involve an immense amount of travel for Trey, a disruptive school schedule, that every-other-holiday mess that would be painful as hell. I couldn't bear to put him through that and I will not live without being a part of his life. I didn't see any other way around it."

"You did what you had to do, son. I would have done the same."

"Seriously?"

"Without a doubt."

Nicholas's words were comforting and should have made Nick feel better than he did. He left the estate and headed to Adam's and a horse ride to further clear his head. He believed that filing for custody of Trey was the right thing to do. Then why did it feel so wrong?

Twenty-One

Sam stayed pissed for three days. She canceled a couple appointments. Didn't take calls. Except for texts to Danielle and her dad, calls from potential clients, and Trey of course, she didn't speak with anyone. The situation between her and Nick was too personal. She imagined that those close to her would be on her side, just as she assumed Nick's family had affirmed his position. In this instance, she'd seek her own counsel. After what felt like thousands of hours of thought, she made a decision and placed a call.

"Breedlove."

"Hi, it's me."

"Sam, if this is about Trey, I've been advised not to speak with you. Communication has to go through my lawyer."

"I've decided to stay." Silence. "Nick, did you hear me? I'm not moving to California. I'm staying here."

"What made you change your mind?"

"Trey. Not anything he said, but the decision became clear when I focused on him. I'd never deny Trey the chance of knowing and being close with his father. You were right. Breedlove is the best place for him to grow up. I'm not sure there are any affordable options for me out there, but it's worth finding out."

"I wish you wouldn't do that."

"What, move to Breedlove?"

"No, spend unnecessary money. I know you don't want to live with me, but there are guest homes available on the estate."

"I appreciate that, Nick, but that would be too close for my comfort. I care about you," she continued, voicing a truth she hadn't planned to share. "Not just as Trey's father, but as someone for whom I have a deep attraction. But you've made it clear that there's no chance for a real relationship. So I need to put myself in the position to attract the love I want. It's the most beautiful place I've ever set eyes on, but your family estate is not that place."

"I can understand that."

A major declaration and that's all he could say? Sam wasn't sure he understood at all. In fact, she'd place a CANN casino bet that he hadn't a clue she'd fallen in love with him.

"What are you doing later? Perhaps we can get together over dinner and discuss how to do what's in Trey's best interest from here on out."

"I can do that."

"What about seven? I'll book one of the private rooms and—"

"I'd rather we meet in a neutral location."

"Fair enough," Nick replied without hesitation. "You choose the spot."

"I'll text it."

"See you then."

After making arrangements to drop off Trey at Danielle's house, she texted Nick the address to her favorite Indian restaurant, walked into her closet and began the search for the perfect negotiation-wear. There was no mistaking the mission. This would be a negotiation. Sam needed to convince Nick to withdraw the papers requesting primary custody of Trey. She'd also like to increase the amount of time Trey and Nick had together; to work out something more regular than every other weekend and "whenever he was available or felt like it" they'd established just after Nick learned he was a dad. She wanted them to come to a place where if not being friends, they could at least be friendly. Sam didn't want Trey to grow up with them fighting, with him in the middle feeling that he had to choose. Sam wanted a lot.

She aimed to dress for success in this meeting with Nick. It was an interview of sorts, the most important one to date in her life. Jeans were out, as was a casual maxi or anything too sexy. Nick would perceive that as a ploy for favor or worse, a mixed signal of what she wanted. Her bed became littered with unacceptable choices. Her hand finally touched the perfect item—a grape-colored knee-length number that complemented her curves without squeezing too tightly. She pulled her locs into a loose topknot and left a few tendrils to hang around her face and neck. Swarovski crystal earrings and necklace were her only jewelry pieces. They matched the blinged-out slingbacks she chose to finish off the look. Makeup was minimal but the grape-colored matte MAC made her lips pop. A spritz of cologne and she was ready for her close-up.

There was little traffic. Sam arrived at the restaurant with ten minutes to spare. She parked, went inside and sat at the bar. Maybe a glass of chilled chardonnay would help calm her nerves.

A young bartender with a shock of red hair ambled over, slowly wiping the bar as he neared. "What can I get for you, pretty lady?"

"A glass of white wine, please."

The bartender rattled off a list of options. Sam settled on one and ordered the drink. Seconds later the door to the establishment opened again and all Sam could think was that a god had strolled in. Nick, looking incredible. Literally, good enough to eat. He wore black. Black suit, black shirt beneath it, black shoes. His face was clean-shaven, his hair newly cut. A diamond stud sparkled in one ear. Sam didn't even bemoan her body's reaction. The way her nipples pebbled and her inner walls clenched. For a woman not to react to a brother that fine she'd have to be blind. Or dead.

He approached her with a leisurely stroll and a hint of wariness in his eyes. "Good evening."

Sam gave a cool nod warmed by a soft smile. "Nick. How are you?"

"I'm okay." She felt him relax. "You look nice."

"Thank you." He looked better than nice, greater than amazing and finer than wine. Sam kept that opinion to herself.

The waiter returned. "Your chardonnay, ma'am." He looked at Nick. "What can I get for you, sir?"

"I'll order from the table." Then to Sam. "Shall we?"

The server led them to a corner booth of a spacious dining room. The stark linen, dark carpet and dim lighting made for a romantic ambiance. The smell of Nick's cologne that wafted past Sam's nose as she walked beside him made her work to remember that this was basically a business meeting. Definitely not a date. She wished it were. After they'd ordered and the server had gone, Sam spoke up.

"I'd like to start this conversation off with an apology. I can't remember ever being as angry as I was that day in your office but it doesn't excuse my behavior. I should not have slapped you. I'm sorry."

"I think both of us could have said or done things differently. I accept your apology and offer mine as well. There has never been any doubt in my mind that Trey comes first in your life. For me to suggest otherwise may have warranted a slap. And for the record, woman, you pack a mean palm."

"I've never hit anyone in my life. Losing my temper like that was not cool. The suggestion that I would put work before Trey cut deeply. But hearing that caused me to take a step back as well. It made me become unflinchingly honest with myself and the real reasons behind my decision to move back to LA."

"Something besides it being a bigger, better market with more potential for work?" Nick reached for his water glass.

"Yes." Sam's chin lifted a bit as she said, "I was relocating to get away from you."

Nick almost spewed out his drink. "Whoa!"

"Too honest for you?" Sam shrugged. "It's all I've got. I figure being as honest as possible is the only way to move forward, the only way we can develop an authentic relationship where we get along. Again, for Trey's sake."

"How was I responsible for you wanting to move?"

Sam gave him a look. "You have no idea?"

Were men really that stupid?

"You want to get married but… I'm not ready for that."

"I know. That's the problem. It's difficult for me to be around you and not…want to be with you. Yet it's hurtful to be with you intimately and know that's all it is."

"That's all it was the night we met. We were practically strangers."

"Which is why it was easy. My heart wasn't involved."

Nick eased back against the booth, sipped his water. No response. Sam figured it was just as well. Since he wanted to continue to sow his opulent oats, what was there to say? She decided it was time to stop talking about the "we" that wasn't and focus on why they were there.

"About Trey…"

He leaned forward, steepled his hands, engaged again. "Yes."

"I'd like you to withdraw your case for primary custody."

"Done."

Sam didn't try to hide her surprise. "Really? That simply? What's the catch?"

"No catch. I'll no longer seek primary custody. However…"

"Ah, here we go."

"Wait. Hear me out. I'm not a fan of the judicial system involving themselves in family matters unless absolutely necessary. We're intelligent people who both love Trey and want the best for him. I think we should be able to work out a mutually agreeable joint custody arrangement, one that will be drawn up by my attorney—"

"So much for no judicial involvement."

"This is legal involvement, an officially written position on what we both decide is best for Trey. It holds us accountable and in the case of another major disagreement would prevent either party from doing something crazy."

"Oh, so you're calling me crazy?" The twinkle in Sam's eye let Nick know she was teasing. The atmosphere lightened, a little.

"Not at all, though you did marry a prince you barely knew and move to the other side of the world. It's not a stretch to believe you could change your identity and appearance and go on the run with my kid."

Sam put a finger to her chin. "Hmm. Ideas."

"Woman, don't you dare."

"I wouldn't."

"There's not a place on earth you could hide with Trey. I can't imagine him not being in my life."

"Me either. Drawing up a legal document is reasonable, I guess. That way neither could change our mind and go off on a tangent."

"There's one more thing."

"What?"

"I want my name on Trey's birth certificate."

"Done, and we can change his last name."

"Really? That simply?"

"Stop mocking me."

"Hard to do. You're so pretty with a chagrined face."

"A chagrined face? Is that supposed to be a compliment? You'd better be glad your looks get you women because your flirt game needs work!"

Dinner was served. Nick and Sam fell back into the easy camaraderie that marked their being together when not fighting like cats and dogs. Over the next ninety minutes they worked out a schedule that suited them both. Because he was often busy weekdays, Sam agreed for Nick to have Trey every weekend, with wiggle room for special events or celebrations when Sam would want Trey with her. During the week, with advance notice, he could stop by and visit Trey, or take him out for dinner or to the estate. Nick understood how important it was for Trey to bond with Sam's father, and would give up a weekend or two if Sam was scheduled to be in LA. They discussed a few more particulars such as schooling, doctor appointments and male bonding during haircuts.

"One last thing."

Sam's fork stopped in midair. "You said that about the birth certificate."

"Okay, this is the last of the last thing." He paused to finish his bite. "I want you to move to Breedlove."

"If things were different it would be a dream come true. The place is like paradise. But we've already discussed this, Nick. I don't want to live on the estate."

"I know. You've made that painfully clear. So I called up a buddy of mine and asked about properties around town. Turns out there's a three-bed, two-bath place near the town center that just became available. It's small, less than two thousand square feet, and is a bit unfinished. I told him you were a designer and not to worry about that. It might be better that there's work to be done. You can put your own stamp on it."

"What's the asking price?"

"Don't worry about it. I'm buying it for Trey. I'm doing what I wasn't able to for the first four years of his life—be financially responsible. Take care of him."

It was a position Sam couldn't argue.

"So how does that work? The house would be in his name?"

"He's not old enough to own it legally until he's eighteen. I've established a trust for him. If you both like it and want to move, the home will be bought in his name through the trust."

"Good to know I get some say in it," Sam teased.

"Of course. He sent me a picture of the outside. Would you like to see it?"

"Sure."

Nick tapped his screen, scrolled a bit and then handed his phone to Sam. The home was nothing like the simple abode she imagined. On the outside at least it was stunning, a contemporary Craftsman, with what looked to be sweeping city and mountain views, and large windows across two-story ceilings that she imagined let in lots of natural light.

"If you'd like I can give you his number. You two could take it from there, let me know what you think."

Sam nodded. "Okay. This doesn't mean that for sure I'll move there but it's worth checking out."

Dinner ended. Nick and Sam went their separate ways. Her mind reeled with the implications of Nick buying the home where she and Trey would reside. She didn't know how she felt about that but damn if it didn't feel good hanging out with him again.

Twenty-Two

Nick bopped up the stairs and tapped a tune on his twin's doorbell before opening the door and walking inside.

"Yo, No!"

He continued past the impressive foyer and down the hall in Noah's new home. "Noah!"

Noah's expecting wife Damaris rounded the corner. "Wow, you're up early."

"A lot to do. Where's Noah?"

"Swimming."

Since facing health challenges the year before, Noah had taken to daily swims to keep his body toned and his back muscles limber. He and Damaris had built a stunning home near the estate's mountain range and included an indoor pool with a retracting roof for an outdoor feel in the summer months. It was a stunning construction, a clever mix of the English Tudor style popular in Damaris's home state of Utah and the clean, simplistic yet ultramodern look common in the Scandinavian country of Denmark, where Noah and Damaris traveled several times a year.

Nick bent his face to Damaris's stomach. "Hello, nephew!" He held the greeting as an echo.

Damaris laughed. "You mean niece."

"You'll have a son, trust me. Ask my mom," Nick threw over his shoulder as he proceeded toward the home's north wing that along with the pool contained a full-size exercise room, sauna and game room. "It's the Breedlove way."

He reached the pool. It was empty. "Twin!"

Noah came out of the shower, wiping off with a fluffy white towel. "It must have worked." He pulled on a pair of long shorts.

"What?"

Noah's lips eased into a smile. "Yeah, it worked. Sam's moving into the house."

"I'm pretty sure of it. Larry called last night. She made an appointment for a walk-through first thing today."

"I think you're on the hook, twin."

Nick turned to Noah. "What do you mean?"

"You know what. I think Sam has caught a big fish. You look like a man in love."

"I'm a father who wants a secure life for his son."

"And the son's mother. Don't even try to lie. That smile is too big for one little boy, even one with your DNA."

Nick didn't answer. The twin thing. When one of their hearts beat the other could feel it. No doubt Noah could feel the seeds of love for Sam that had been steadily growing in Nick's heart since before he even realized.

Noah began walking toward the main part of the house. Nick fell into step beside him.

"You're feeling pretty good about yourself, aren't you? By the way, you're welcome."

Nick gave Noah a playful punch. "I'll give credit where it's due. Sam would have never accepted a home I purchased for her outright.

"Going from the Trey angle worked perfectly. What mother would deny their son a beautiful place to live?"

"Not a smart one."

"Sam's very smart." Nick winked.

"Beautiful, too."

"Man, don't remind me. She showed up last night with a dress that hugged her body the way I wanted to do. Locs caressing her neck. Skin showing, eyes glowing. Damn!"

They reached the kitchen. Damaris had prepared a smoothie and handed it to Noah.

"Thank you, baby." Noah gave his wife a quick kiss.

"You want one, Nick?"

"No, I'm good."

"We'll be in the office, baby."

"Remember, love, the doula comes at ten. Will you join us?"

"Yes, Dee. I'll be there to learn all I need to know about helping bring my son into the world."

Damaris chuckled as she shook her head. "You two."

The men continued down the hall into Noah's office.

"You not going to work today?"

Noah shook his head. "Working from home, bro. That's the good thing about Utah being virtual. I can monitor everything from the central control center."

Noah referred to a layout in the next room that gave him the ability to see everything happening in CANN's Mountain Valley, Utah location, where Noah had done the impossible and brought gambling to the state.

"All right then, man. I'd better let you get to it." Nick walked over and gave his twin a shoulder bump and fist tap.

"You heading to the office, or over to your lady's new home in Breedlove?"

"She's not my lady."

"Not yet, but from the look in your eye when you talk about her…she will be."

Nick didn't answer his brother, but long after he'd left the house, slid into his fancy ride and headed toward the Strip, what Noah said stayed on his mind. Did he want Sam to be his lady under the terms she presented? Truth of the matter was he hadn't been with another woman since he and Sam reconnected. But he was only twenty-seven. Was he ready to commit to being a one-woman man for the rest of his life?

Once in the office his mind was quickly pulled elsewhere. A private island in the Seychelles that Christian and Nick had their eyes on for over a year had just come on the market. It was one of less than half a dozen large enough to hold the type of opulent casino hotel they wanted to construct, one that included individual tiki-type houses that would sit directly over the water. Both knew they had to act fast to secure the deal.

Anita buzzed him. "Boss, Silver State Bank is on line one."

"Thanks, Anita." Nick tapped the line. "Breedlove."

"Nick, good morning. It's Harold. How are you doing?"

"Any day is good that starts out with a call from the bank president."

The two men conversed about the hundreds of millions needed for the Seychelles project, and how they would go about positioning funds that would be used by a variety of parties across continents. They scheduled a meeting among all necessary players for later that week. Afterward, the chat turned more social. Updates on family, plans to play golf. Nick's phone pinged with a text from Larry. He wrapped up the call.

"Harold, I have to run. Nice talking to you, buddy. See you soon." He hung up the landline and returned the call to the real estate agent from his cell. "Larry, talk to me."

"Sold!"

"Ha! She liked it, huh?"

"Are you kidding? She loved it."

Nick stood and walked to the window. The smile on his face could have replaced the sun. Having worked with Sam on the CANN Isles projects, he'd gained valuable insight into her tastes and design aesthetics. He knew she'd love the high ceilings, the myriad of windows and the open layout. Everything installed was high-end, yet there was enough left unfinished for Sam to stamp it with her signature style. He couldn't wait to see what she did with the place. Not that he felt she'd invite him over. But he'd have to go there to pick up Trey. The child that he never thought he wanted was becoming ever more intertwined in his life, and either directly or indirectly leading him toward a certain destiny. And though he wasn't quite ready to admit it, even to himself, Sam's stock was rising, too.

Later that night, as he was thinking about her, Sam called.

"Are you sure you didn't have anything to do with selecting that house?" she asked.

"Why would you think that?"

"The backyard is a boy's paradise."

"I heard there was a rock-climbing wall," was Nick's noncommittal answer. "I think Larry also mentioned that it was open concept as well."

"We… Trey loves the house."

"Great. I'll put in an offer tomorrow."

The home had already been purchased but Nick had to follow the charade all the way through.

"I'm still grappling with the fact that you're buying the house."

"I understand. But it's an investment for Trey. When he becomes an adult he'll have a place to stay, or an investment opportunity. If the market continues to move in a favorable direction and the city expands outward, the price of that home could double or triple in the coming years."

"It's an amazing gift for him, Nick. Having a home and with it financial stability at such a young age. Thank you."

"You're welcome."

Nick got the impression she wanted to say more. But she didn't.

"Like I said, I'll get with Larry tomorrow to put in an offer. When is the lease up on your condo?"

"Month after next."

"Will that be enough time for you to get the home ready?"

"I think so, if I can get the right help."

"CANN has a healthy Rolodex of contacts—electrical, flooring, installation, landscaping. We have established accounts within all of construction. I'll give you a card to get whatever you need."

Again. Silence.

"For Trey."

"Yeah, okay."

"I'll be speaking with my attorney later this week, to have him draw up the papers we discussed."

"You mean that you demanded?"

"Demanded is a rather harsh way of putting it, don't you think?"

"Do I have a choice in whether or not to participate?" Nick didn't have a comeback. "As I thought. I believe demand is perfect."

"Sam…"

"It's okay. I'm sorry. It's been a long day."

"Do you want to talk about it?"

"No."

"Listen, I don't want the legalities of my involvement in Trey's life to become a problem between us."

"It won't. I understand why you're doing what you're doing."

"But you don't agree with it."

"I wish it wasn't necessary but considering the circumstances and not knowing what tomorrow will bring, I guess it is."

Nick stretched out on the couch, feeling a strange yet definite comfort having Sam's voice in his ear.

"The document will only outline what we previously discussed. I want you to feel comfortable with what you're signing. So I'll have a draft version sent over to you before we lock in the wording. If you find a problem, let me know. We'll work it out. The attorney drafting this is Coleman Hughes. I can send his number as well, so you can ask any questions you have directly."

"I appreciate that."

"See how easy life is when we get along?"

"Bye, Nick."

Said sternly yet softly, in a way that made Nick feel all warm and sticky inside.

"Bye, Sam."

Nick watched a bit of television before retiring to bed. He lay awake for a long time, thinking about his dating life, trying to recall the women who'd most affected his life. There'd been more than a few but for the life of him Sam's was the only face that came to mind.

Twenty-Three

Sam's professional life was in chaos but thanks to Nick, the personal side was easy breezy. Diving into Trey's home's renovation brought the joy she felt these days. As for her son, she'd never seen Trey so happy. Every afternoon after preschool when they went to the home, he was out of his seat almost before the wheels stopped turning. The backyard was already his unspoken domain. The construction team had surprised both of them with a customized wood-and-steel fort-styled playground with holes for play shoot-outs and an enclosure to take cover. There was a slide and swings and beyond those, a sandbox. Behind it was a mini-trampoline. Sam was sure that Trey could live out there until he was a teenager and except for meals and bathroom breaks be perfectly fine.

"Sam!"

Danielle's voice bounced throughout the largely empty rooms.

"In the bedroom!"

"Which one?" Danielle said, with a laugh.

"Master."

Danielle stepped into Sam's favorite space. "Ohmygoodness! Look at your chandelier and ceiling fan combo. Just like you wanted. Where did you find it?"

"What I envisioned wasn't out there. I had it designed."

"Looks like it cost a fortune. Are the blades glass?"

"It's the next level up from PC, polycarbonate plastic. It's lighter and more durable than glass."

"I love the shape, like a sexy octopus."

"Now that you mention it, there is a resemblance."

"The way the crystals sparkle and play off the shiny

stainless steel is just stunning. It's like magic. Every time I come over there's something beautiful and new."

Sam slid her hands into her jeans back pockets and looked around. "I have to admit, it's all coming together nicely."

"Nicely is an understatement. Sam, this place is amazing. It's perfect for you and Trey. Does it have a dimmer?" Sam nodded. "For those oh-so-romantic nights."

"With who, the hero from my latest Reese Ryan?"

"No." Danielle laughed at Sam's recent fixation with romance novels and her new favorite author. "Your baby daddy. I don't know when you're going to stop acting like a virgin and holding this all-or-nothing position. You love him."

"I never said that."

"Don't have to." Danielle spread her arms to take in the room. "Obviously he feels some kind of way about you. He's not just buying any woman a house like this."

"This house belongs to Trey."

"Son might own it but the mama runs it. Come on, Sam. Stop splitting hairs with the fact. Nick bought this place for you. He may not be ready for a relationship on your terms but love is a verb. The verbiage here is pretty awesome. Keep being stubborn and somebody else might snatch up that beautiful black king. Take a chance with your heart and let life flow!"

Sam kept the chain around her heart firmly in place by ignoring everything Danielle said. Easy for her to think life clear cut. She and Scott had dated off and on for years before tying the knot. Danielle had no idea what it was like to have your mind blown and body scorched by a lover like Nick, to be in the company of someone brilliant and witty and sexy and strong, and know that at any moment it could be over. That someone he felt was more beautiful or exciting could come along and take away his breath.

After the Thanksgiving holiday, when she didn't hear

from him for a week and then the talk, when he made his preference for the single life abundantly clear, Sam tried to cut Nick from her heart. The longer she went without him, the deeper her feelings grew. It felt that if she ever again allowed herself a taste of him without promise, it would be like gambling with air.

Later that evening back at the condo, Sam was in the middle of a rare act—cooking. Trey had requested tacos, the one dish she'd mastered. He preferred hers to those from a drive-through. The day Trey shared this observation Sam had felt like a Michelin chef.

"Alexa, play nineties hip-hop."

Though Sam hadn't been alive when these songs were released, Sam's father Marcus was a die-hard nineties hip-hop head. It was the soundtrack of her life through high school and beyond, along with today's popular pop, neo-soul and a little R&B. While bobbing her head to the beat, Sam poured oil into a stainless-steel skillet. She crumbled up a couple pounds of ground beef, added it to the oil, then began chopping onions and peppers to add to the mix. She'd just reached for a jar of diced garlic when the doorbell rang. No one ever came to her house uninvited. Who in the heck could it be?

She quickly grabbed a towel and wiped her hands as she walked to the door. *Nick? What's he doing here? And what's he brought with him?* She opened the door and verbalized those thoughts directly.

"There is an explanation. Can I come in?"

"Sure. You probably texted me but I was in the kitchen and didn't have my phone with me."

"No, I didn't, but I couldn't help it. I got so excited about what I brought over that I headed out of the door without thinking to call."

"What could be that impor—"

"Daddy!" Trey bounded out of his bedroom and into the

arm that Nick had free. He placed down the large box he carried and scooped up his son. "What'd you bring me?"

"Who said what I have is for you?"

"It's mine, Daddy!" Trey said, laughing. "You never bring Mommy anything."

"Trey, Nick brings you goodies because you're his son."

"So? You're my mom!"

Sam locked eyes with Nick. "Kids."

"Gotta love them." Nick pulled the bag open. "Actually, son, this is for your mom."

"Really?" Nick had thought to bring a gift for her? Sam's heart fluttered.

"Well…in a way."

Nick reached inside the large bag and pulled out an equally sizable box.

"What is it, Dad?"

Nick's eyes warmed as he looked at Trey's cherubic up-turned face, his expression one of wonder and awe.

"Something pretty amazing."

All eyes were on the box as Nick pulled a cutter from his slacks pocket and cut the box top. He tossed protective bubble wrap to the floor, then lifted out a silver-colored head and torso with a childlike face.

Sam squinted her eyes. "Is that an r-o-b-o-t?"

Trey gasped. "It's a robot!"

Her eyes widened. Had his spelling capabilities grown that much?

"R. O. B. O. T!"

Yes, they had.

"The Academy is one of the best preschools in the nation," Nick said. "I thought you knew."

He pulled the bottom portion of the machine out of the box and now connected several wires before attaching the two parts together.

"Is it a robot, Dad?"

"Yes, but more specifically this…" He pulled a remote

from the box and tapped a button. Lights began to flicker. The eyes of the robot lit up a bright blue.

"It's Ven." He tapped another button. "Ven, say hello to Trey."

There was a short pause before the robot turned to where Trey stood wide-eyed. "Hello, Trey."

The voice was not the electronic, robotic monotone Sam expected, but that of a boy who sounded about Trey's age.

If possible, Trey would have jumped out of his skin. "Mom! He said my name! He talks! He said my name!" He took a step to approach him, then stopped, a bit unsure.

"It's okay, Trey. Ven is very friendly. In fact, in Danish, *ven* means friend."

"Can I touch him?"

"Sure, come on over." Trey walked up to the machine that stood slightly higher than the taller-than-average four-year-old. "Hold out your hand and say hey." Nick sniffed the air. "Is something burning?"

"Oh, shoot! The meat." Sam ran from the room.

Nick hollered after her. "Did I interrupt dinner?"

Trey tugged Nick's hand. "Dad, we were talking to Ven!"

"Hang on, son." Nick walked into the kitchen in time to see Sam scraping the contents of a skillet into the sink.

"What's that?"

"Before the doorbell, it was ground beef. Now it's burnt garbage." Sam flicked the garbage disposal switch. "Dang it! The one dinner Trey likes that I know how to fix and I mess it up."

"What were you making?"

"Tacos."

"It's my fault. I'm sorry."

"Daddy!"

Sam looked over the bar counter at Trey's impatient face. "It's okay. You'd better finish assembling Trey's gift."

Nick pulled out his phone and sent a quick text. "Okay,"

he said, walking back to where Trey stood next to the robot with remote in hand.

He nodded toward the robot but spoke to Trey. "Talk to him."

"What do I say?"

"What do you normally say when you meet someone new?"

"Nice to meet you?"

"Okay. Try that."

Trey looked at Ven. "Nice to meet you."

The robotic arm began to move. Trey gasped, then giggled with delight as the arm slowly raised until the rubberized steel hand was perpendicular to his waist. The mouth moved rhythmically. "Nice to meet you."

"Wow!" Trey threw his arms around Nick's legs. "Thank you, Daddy!"

Sam looked at Nick, as impressed as her son. "Where on earth did you get this?"

"Denmark. It's the next frontier of Breedlove Bionics."

"When did the company get into bionics?"

"They didn't. Noah and I did." He shared how similar technology had helped Noah through a health crisis. The twins had been so impressed that they started their own bionics company and hired personnel to design cutting-edge products.

"Last year, when the world changed and America found millions of children home from school and largely isolated, the group began toying with the idea of robots to replace the schoolmates they could no longer interact with physically. Video games are great, but nothing beats one-on-one interaction."

"I'd say. It's almost human."

"The wonders of AI."

"Daddy, can Ven and I go play?"

"No, honey. We need to run out and get you something to eat. Or I can have something—" The doorbell rang. Sam looked at Nick. "Delivered."

He began walking toward the door. "Mind if I get that?"

Sam simply crossed her arms. Nick opened the door, had a brief conversation with whoever was on the other side of it and returned with a large bag of something smelling delicious.

"What's that, Daddy?"

"Tacos." He winked at Sam. "Your favorite."

"Yippee! Mama, can Daddy stay for dinner?"

Two pairs of identical eyes fixed on Sam. There was only one right answer, yet it took several seconds to push it through her lips.

"Sure."

Trey grabbed Nick's hand and began pulling him toward the dining table. "Let's eat." He reached his seat and turned. "Ven!"

"Coming!" The robot rolled across the hardwood floor. It stopped beside Trey.

"Sit down!"

The robot did, except there was no chair. It toppled over. Everyone laughed.

"It's a prototype," Nick offered. "Needs more work."

"If you pull out the food, I'll grab dishes and pour drinks."

"You got it."

Sam entered the kitchen feelings all sorts of ways. The scene was too comfortable, too homey, too much of what she wanted but knew could never be. She gritted her teeth, ready to pull and lock emotional bars around her heart. Then she heard Danielle.

Take a chance with your heart and let life flow.

Might as well, Sam decided. Life was heaven whenever he was around and close to hell without him. Right then she determined to stop living in the future and enjoy what happened now. An image of what could happen flashed into her mind and caused her walls to constrict. Nick had brought Trey a playmate. She was in love. Maybe it was time to let Nick be her boy toy again.

Twenty-Four

Something shifted after the night filled with tacos, laughter and Ven. Nick and Sam settled into a comfortable co-parenting flow, centered on their shared love and adoration for Trey. They began spending more time together, the three of them, at least once a week. The two who'd started out as lovers now began getting to know each other and becoming friends. Sam invited Nick to check out the ongoing new home renovation. Nick invited Sam out for horseback riding. Sam invited him to the condo for tacos she'd cooked. That night, Nick helped her stack the dishwasher before settling on the couch to watch an animated feature. Trey fell asleep before the movie ended. Nick and Sam watched it until the end. Afterward it felt totally natural to carry Trey into his room and tuck him into bed and when he turned, having Sam leaned casually against the wall watching them was the perfect portrait.

He'd almost kissed her that night.

That was a month ago and since then, his desire to do so had only deepened, along with his feelings for her. Watching Sam with Trey made his heart sing. She was an incredible mom. She was an intelligent, business-savvy, beautiful woman. She was the best interior designer in the game. And she wanted him. He could feel it, could see it in her eyes. There was only one thing in the way of their reconnecting on a deeper, more intimate level. Her terms.

Tonight, Sam had invited him to what she'd termed a "small gathering" in her new home. She and Trey had moved in the week before. He'd been in the Seychelles finalizing the island purchase and couldn't wait to get home. Tonight, he'd have two things to celebrate with Sam. His new is-

land. Her new home. The invitation had listed dress as business casual. It had been an unusually cold winter. As Nick
walked into his dressing room, he was definitely feeling the
fresh newness of spring. He walked past rows of signature
black and stopped at a group of clothing recently sent over
by A-list fashion designer Ace Montgomery, items tailored
for him from his spring collection. His hands caressed the
expensive fabric as he checked out each piece, bypassing a
baby blue suit of finely spun wool and a deep gold number
that gave a nod to the seventies leisure suit. He paused at
a pair of ivory-colored slightly baggy trousers, a sophisticated mix of sporty elegance with a fitted waist, flared pant
leg and 18-karat-gold threads running throughout. Since it
was still a bit cool in the evenings, a light gold turtleneck
was the perfect complement to the slacks. Nick finished
the look with his new favorite timepiece—appropriately
called the Billionaire—and his signature three-carat diamond stud. A splash of cologne, a cigar to enjoy later and
he was out the door. On the way over, he ruminated on his
decision for a housewarming present. To think what he'd
chosen was a good idea may prove to have been presump-
tive. Time would tell.

Pulling up curbside, Nick couldn't help but feel proud of
Sam's handiwork. He'd purchased the house but she'd made
it a home. The landscaping was impeccable, lush and com-
manding without being showy. Carefully placed outdoor
lighting highlighted the slate siding, the redbrick walkway
and the front door's stained glass. He tried the knob. The
door opened. Softly playing neo-soul greeted him amid a
din of cheery-sounding voices. He glimpsed himself as he
passed a mirror in the foyer and noted how the five-foot
floral arrangement anchored the hall just as he thought it
would.

He reached the living room and stopped to look around.
The first person he recognized was Sam's cousin Danielle,
who spotted him at the same time, waved and walked over.

"Hey, Nick!" They exchanged a light hug. "Well, don't you look like a breath of spring!"

"Thanks, Danielle."

"Call me Danni. The other is only used if I'm in trouble or in court."

Nick chuckled. "Got it."

As they briefly exchanged chitchat his eyes scanned the room. He wasn't surprised to see faces he didn't recognize. Noah was there with Adam and Ryan, along with Larry and his girlfriend. Their eyes met, followed by a head nod as Larry held up a drink in greeting. His perusal continued beyond the L-shaped living room into the dining room, where Sam, looking like the queen that she was, sat chatting animatedly with a handsome older man.

"That's her father," Danielle offered, having followed his eyes.

"Really? He came down from LA, huh. Nice."

"Sam was very excited to show this place off." Danielle leaned in. "She may never tell you but she has never treasured anything more than she does this home. She always corrects me when I say her house—" she used air quotes "—by telling me that you bought it for Trey. That may be true legally. But a part of me says you bought it for the both of them. Am I right?"

Nick missed the last of what Danielle was saying and didn't hear her question at all. In the middle of it, Sam had looked up and seen him. Her eyes widened slightly. She said something to her father, who looked over, before rising to come toward him. She looked like an ebony goddess, draped in an ivory jumpsuit that made Nick jealous because it hugged her body the way his arms longed to do. The simple elegance of the one-piece, one-shoulder design was complemented by gold jewelry. As she grew closer, he noticed thin strands of gold beading wrapped around an errant loc. No adjective was strong or accurate enough to describe the perfection before him. His body reacted on its own. Arms reached out and pulled her into a light yet firm embrace.

"You look incredible," Nick murmured huskily into Sam's ear before releasing her. "I see you got the ivory dress code memo."

Sam smiled. Nick's penis pulsated. If his hormones continued raging, this was going to be a long night.

Sam appreciated Nick's hug and teasing comment. It gave her time to catch her breath, gather her composure and recover from seeing the man she had fallen head over heels in love with walk into the room and outshine everyone present.

She couldn't deny it now if she tried. Not after seeing this six-foot-two-inch bundle of *GQ*-sexy stroll confidently into the room. She. Was. In. Love. With a capital *L*.

"You look good, too. I can't believe you're not wearing black!"

"It's springtime, according to the calendar at least. Thought I'd switch it up a little bit. It seems that great minds think alike."

"Indeed."

Danielle loudly cleared her throat. "Um, clearly I've been dismissed."

"My apologies, Danni," Nick began, a hand to his chest.

"Save it. I'm just teasing." Danielle reached into her purse. "You guys belong on a magazine cover. Let me take your picture. By the fireplace." She adjusted her screen. "All right, here we go."

All eyes turned and conversation stilled as Nick and Sam struck a pose.

"Give me a couple more."

They offered another angle, then Nick surprised Sam by twirling her around and dipping her down.

Danielle squealed. "Perfect!"

The room broke out in applause. Sam was completely embarrassed. But damn, that man smelled good.

Nick looked around. "The place looks incredible, babe. Perfect for entertaining."

"It's exactly what I wanted. There's not one thing I would change. Come with me. There're a few people I want you to meet, starting with my dad. And while he's probably not as...curious...as your mother, there may be more than one question from him that you won't want to, nor are obligated to answer."

"Thanks for the warning."

"Ha! Anytime."

Sam was surprised at how nervous she was for her dad to meet Nick, and how much she wanted him to be impressed by the man walking confidently beside her.

"Dad, I'd like you to meet my former business partner and Trey's dad, Nick. Nick, this is my dad, Marcus Price."

"A pleasure to meet you, sir."

Sam watched her father measuring Nick up. "Likewise."

"Considering we just met I might be speaking prematurely," Nick said. "But would you by any chance like a good cigar?"

"Why? Do you have one?"

Nick nodded. "Have you heard of the Cubano Rare?"

Marcus looked from Nick to his daughter and back. "You have one of those?"

Sam couldn't guarantee it but was pretty sure she heard reverence in her dad's voice.

"In my car. It'll blow your mind."

Marcus slapped Nick on the back and gleamed at Sam. "I like this guy already."

Sam's smile reflected how happy and relieved she was that Nick and her dad seemed like they'd get along. Because the truth of the matter was not only was she in love with her child's father, but she really liked him, too. The next time the opportunity presented itself, she intended to let him know how much.

Twenty-Five

A month after Sam's housewarming, she was on a CANN private plane headed to the Bahamas. Nick was beside her, but the trip wasn't about work. It was about their burgeoning ongoing attraction. And what they were going to do about it.

During the flight over they kept the conversation light, mostly about Trey, now truly a Breedlove, having had Nick's name added to the birth certificate and his last name officially changed. They talked about the home on a small island not far from Nassau that because of legal and other logistics had only recently been completed, and even flirted a bit. The plane's landing was smooth and once outside, they were welcomed with hugs from the balmy Bahamian wind. After a short helicopter ride from the capitol of Nassau to CANN Isle-Bahamas—the home that would be their private paradise for the next several days—the couple were minutes from their final destination. With everything about Sam having driven him wild for the past few hours, Nick couldn't get there soon enough. He and Sam hadn't yet moved out of the friendship zone back into that of lovers, but he hoped this trip would change that.

They reached the home that in luxury and originality rivaled the New York villa that was Sam's first assignment. They were met by the house staff, conferred with the chef, and went to change for an agreed-upon swim before dinner. Nick went to one of two matching master suites. He donned swim trunks, grabbed a towel and slipped into a pair of sandals. Stepping into a living room shared between the two suites, he encountered a sight that stopped him in his tracks. Sam's juicy booty, a work of perfection that was just right for squeezing, swayed rhythmically from side to side as she walked toward a patio on the other side of the room. She wore a gold-colored wrap over a bikini bottom almost powerless to fully encase her lusciousness. Its luster made her ebony skin appear all the more radiant, wrapped in a way that highlighted curves deadlier than those found in Tail of the Dragon, one of the most scenic roads in Tennessee. He'd gripped the handlebars of a rented Harley while navigating its 318 curves in eleven miles, but it didn't compare to the ride he experienced whenever he journeyed to paradise with Sam in his arms.

Sam turned, her brow arching when she discovered Nick in the room, watching her. "You coming?"

Nick's long strides quickly ate up the distance between them. "I'll come later," he whispered once beside her.

"One-track mind."

He grabbed her hand and squeezed it. "The best kind."

The two accepted refreshing adult drinks from Colin, their thoughtful chef, then made their way to a stretch of soft, white sand, miles away from eyes that might be attempted to pry. After a brief splash in the water, they settled into a sturdy hammock erected under a tree by the shore.

"Hold my drink, please?" Sam handed her drink to Nick and then shifted her body to remove the wrap and settle into a comfortable position beside him. "There, that's better."

"If we're to keep this relationship platonic, I don't know about that."

He handed Sam back her drink.

"To us and a lifetime of adventures with our son."

"Eighteen years, anyway." Sam lifted her glass to clink it against the one Nick held.

"What, after Trey graduates from high school you're running away?"

"One never knows what the future holds."

Nick took a long sip of his beverage and pondered Sam's comment. He had plans for this vacation, felt fairly sure of how they'd go. But Sam was right. In life, nothing was guaranteed.

"How's your drink?"

"Delicious. I can't believe that here where they have the best rum in the world, you chose to drink beer."

Nick shrugged. "Obviously Colin got the memo. He knows what I like." He placed his arms more securely around Sam's shoulders. "When I find something I like, I usually stick with it."

"Hmm."

Sam said nothing more but the way she moved her butt so that it brushed his manhood made Nick believe his double entendre had been received.

"I like your stick."

"Now who's bringing it up?" He lifted his head to look her in the eye.

"Must be the rum."

"Hmm." His hands began a lazy journey up and down Sam's thigh. Goose bumps sprang up almost immediately, as did his python. He kissed her temple, shoulder, cheek. "I'm glad we did this."

"Me, too. So much has happened."

"I know."

They slipped into a companionable silence. Nick placed his foot in the sand to push the hammock into a gentle rocking.

"Did you ever think we'd get here?"

"I didn't even know there was a here here," he replied. "If someone had told me a year ago that I had a son and was about to be…"

"About to be what?"

"…in a serious relationship, I would have thought them way off. I thought life was perfect. Business going great. All the girls I wanted. I didn't know my life was empty until you came back into it. And brought Trey."

"Life is crazy."

"Right."

"Want to know something?"

"Hmm."

"I almost didn't go to that party."

"What party?"

"The costume party where we met. I'm not big on those types of functions."

"Then who do I owe the million dollars to for talking you into coming? Danni?"

"It was Danni, but I'd say you owe her at least two million."

"Naw, probably more like five or ten."

Sam shifted, turned up her face. "Kiss me."

He did. Leisurely. Lovingly. Sam gave as good as she got, even outlined his mouth with her tongue when they finished the sultry exchange.

"Damn."

"Uh-huh," Sam murmured, again grazing his dick with her behind in the way that he loved.

"Okay, baby, after that and on second thought, I'll just give your cousin a blank check."

They finished their drinks and swam in the ocean. The sun began to set, splashing vibrant colors along the sand and cooling the air. They went inside.

"The next time over, we'll have to bring Trey."

"He'd love that."

"Know what I'd love?"

"Another beer?"

"Another kiss." Nick pulled Sam to the couch and plundered her mouth. She had other plans, shimmied out from beneath him and turned her body so that her mouth faced his crotch. Without fanfare or permission she slid her tongue down the length of his penis, while softly fondling the family jewels. Nick had always appreciated a take-charge woman, especially one whose treasure hovered just beneath his nose. He placed a hand on each cheek, brought her heat to his mouth and slid his tongue between the fleshy folds.

Yum.

They took their time. Sam lavished Nick's dick from base to tip, using her fingers and tongue to make his slack member steel. Nick nibbled her pearl, sampled her star, feasted on her dewy kitty until she fairly meowed. Until the dew became a fountain of ecstasy, and she screamed his name. Nick could have easily joined her in going over the edge.

But this dance wasn't over. It was just getting started. He led them into the bedroom.

He removed their clothes. They lay down, flesh against flesh from head to toe. He eased his hand between her thighs, slid his fingers into her sweet spot and began to play. They kissed, the essence of love on their tongues—swirling, dancing, flicking across the cavernous warmth until he reached such depth of passion Nick thought he might drown.

"Who does this belong to?" His breath was hot, branding, as he whispered into her ear.

"Me."

"After all that good loving?" Nick said. "Wrong answer."

Sam chuckled, her hand lazily running over six-pack abs. "Oh, really?"

Nick slid off the bed. "Get on your knees."

Sam traced a finger along his jaw. "What if I don't want to?"

Nick smiled. "Oh, you'll want to."

She chuckled and rose to her knees as instructed.

"Turn around."

She complied, her round, plump booty in the air and fully exposed. Just right and ripe for…plucking.

With a hand on each hip he eased her body to the edge of the mattress. The king-size four-poster was the perfect height for the takeover he had in mind. He watched Sam wiggle her backside. Impatient. Anticipating. But Nick wasn't in a hurry. They had all night.

Nick reached over for the glass of water on the nightstand. He took a drink, held a cube in his mouth, then quietly dropped to his knees. Instead of the warm, hard shaft she was expecting, a cold sword of delectation slid into her womanly folds.

A harsh intake of breath followed. Goose bumps appeared. She pulled her body away. But not far enough. With Nick's hands still securely on her hips, he held her body in place and continued his relentless assault. Sam swirled her hips against his tongue. He bathed every inch of intimate areas, kissed and massaged her smooth, dark skin. After she'd cried out for the second time he stood, placed his dick at her core, then slowly, oh…so…slowly, eased himself inside her. His manhood pulsed with pleasure at her tightness, even after having a kid. He pulled out to the tip, then slid in again. In. Out. Thrust. Sway. He went at this pace for as long as he could, then settled into a rhythm he could have danced to all night. On the bed. Against the wall. Out on their private balcony, where the breeze was as hot as the sex. Back in the room on a chaise, he covered her and entered her completely.

"Whose is this?" His voice was harsh, labored, as his body rumbled. He scorched her insides with passion, pressed himself deeply into her core. Over and over he loved her. Their bodies shone with the evidence of the hearty endeavor.

"Who. Does. This. Belong to?" A thrust punctuated each word that was growled.

He felt her body grip him, heard the familiar sounds that began at the base of her throat, felt her grinding faster against him.

"Ah! Oh my God!" Sam screamed with pleasure.

Nick quickened the pace, joined her in cascading over the edge. Spent, satiated, they crawled into bed.

Sam kissed him lightly, snuggling her backside against him. "You," she whispered, and fell asleep.

The deep sleep lasted just a few hours. Awakened by the

hazy Bahamian sun, Nick stretched amid a yawn. He rolled over slowly so as not to awaken the sleeping beauty. Perched on an elbow, he took in her serene expression. It shouldn't make someone this happy watching somebody else sleep. A few minutes is all he lasted until he kissed her. Softly, just at the edge of her eye.

Her lids fluttered before her eyes opened fully. The look in her deep brown orbs was mesmerizing as her lips slowly morphed into a smile.

"Good morning, beautiful."

"Good morning. I can't believe you're awake already."

He nodded toward the open balcony door. "The sun."

Sam perched on her elbow and looked over her shoulder. "This view is to die for, truly paradise."

She threw her arm over Nick's body, resting her hand on his shoulder. "I think I kinda love you."

Nick kissed the top of her head. "Really?"

Sam fixed him with a look. "And?"

"You aiiight."

She reached behind her for a pillow to smack him. "Just all right?"

"Okay. Better than all right."

Sam turned her body to face him directly, adopting her sexiest tone. "How much better?"

Nick licked his lips. "Damn. A lot more. So much so that…wait a minute. I can show you better than I can tell you."

He bounded out of bed.

"Nick, where are you going?"

"Be right back!" There was the sound of rumbling before Nick spoke again. "Okay, now close your eyes."

"Why?"

"Must you always engage that beautiful brain? Just do it, woman!"

"Okay."

Nick peeked around the corner before walking back over to the bed. "Okay, hold out your hands."

"Why? Okay, never mind." Sam lifted her hands. The sheet floated away from her body. Her nipples pebbled against the early-morning breeze. Nick almost forgot what he was about to do. Change both of their lives. After which, there would be plenty of time for lovemaking.

Still, he kissed the exposed nipples before covering her up.

"You're making it hard to keep my eyes closed."

"Yeah, you're making me hard, too. You've made me a lot of things. An executive with rental properties sold out worldwide. A father to the most adorable boy on the planet. A man who's ready to stop playing around and make a real commitment."

Sam's eyes flew open.

"What did I tell you?"

"I can't keep them closed when you're talking like this! What are you saying?"

Nick reached for her hand, began stroking her finger. "I'm saying that I love you, and that I'm in love with you."

He brought the hand from behind his back and slipped a ring on her finger.

Sam was shocked speechless, her eyes tearing up as she gazed into his.

"I'm saying, Samantha Price, that I can't imagine spending my life without you and Trey, and maybe a few brothers and sisters for him to play with."

"Nick…"

"I'm asking if you'll do me the honor of becoming my wife. And that the only acceptable answer is yes."

Sam's eyes sparkled. She remembered. It's the same thing he'd said when she got offered the job.

"Are you sure that's the only acceptable answer?"

"Unless or until I hear it, we're not leaving this island."

"Well, in that case…yes, Nick Breedlove. I'd love nothing better than to become your wife."

"Good answer."

Without another word he reached over, slid the sheet away from her body and began covering it with soft, wet kisses. There were no more secrets, big or little. Tonight, there was only love…

* * * * *

COMING SOON!

We really hope you enjoyed reading this book.
If you're looking for more romance, be sure to
head to the shops when new books are
available on

Thursday 13th May

To see which titles are coming soon, please visit
millsandboon.co.uk/nextmonth

LET'S TALK
Romance

For exclusive extracts, competitions
and special offers, find us online:

Get in touch on 01413 063232

For all the latest titles coming soon, visit
millsandboon.co.uk/nextmonth

MILLS & BOON

THE HEART OF ROMANCE

A ROMANCE FOR EVERY READER

MODERN

Prepare to be swept off your feet by sophisticated, sexy and seductive heroes, in some of the world's most glamourous and romantic locations, where power and passion collide.

HISTORICAL

Escape with historical heroes from time gone by. Whether your passion is for wicked Regency Rakes, muscled Vikings or rugged Highlanders, awaken the romance of the past.

MEDICAL

Set your pulse racing with dedicated, delectable doctors in the high-pressure world of medicine, where emotions run high and passion, comfort and love are the best medicine.

True Love

Celebrate true love with tender stories of heartfelt romance, from the rush of falling in love to the joy a new baby can bring, and a focus on the emotional heart of a relationship.

Desire

Indulge in secrets and scandal, intense drama and plenty of sizzling hot action with powerful and passionate heroes who have it all: wealth, status, good looks…everything but the right woman.

HEROES

Experience all the excitement of a gripping thriller, with an intense romance at its heart. Resourceful, true-to-life women and strong, fearless men face danger and desire - a killer combination!

To see which titles are coming soon, please visit

millsandboon.co.uk/nextmonth

JOIN US ON SOCIAL MEDIA!

Stay up to date with our latest releases, author news and gossip, special offers and discounts, and all the behind-the-scenes action from Mills & Boon...

 millsandboon

 millsandboonuk

 millsandboon

It might just be true love...

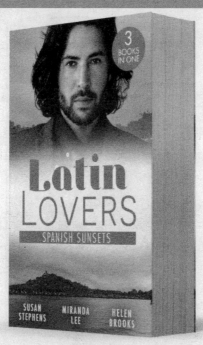

OUT NOW!

Playing games

Available at
millsandboon.co.uk

MILLS & BOON